A Home On Carroll Avenue

by

Jean Jegel

Published by Emery Press at Kindle Direct Publishing

ISBN: 978-1-953003-04-1

Discover other titles by Jean Jegel at jeanjegel.com

Cover by Dave Simmons

Dedication

To dear and lifelong friends

Chapter One

San Francisco, 1875

"Look at me, Harvey. I'm trying to tell you the nanny quit, again. It's Dee. There is something wrong with that child."

"Don't be ridiculous. She's a baby. How could she possibly do anything to drive nannies from our employ? Even the boys and all their pranks never managed that."

"She's six and just because she has you wrapped around her little finger doesn't mean other people aren't disturbed by her behavior."

"I won't have this, Georgia. She's a precious child. Find some way to deal with her. Your father is coming by for dessert and brandy. I need to prepare. We're going to discuss the new contracts. I haven't time to appease your hysteria."

"Very well. If you won't listen to me, I'll talk to Daddy when he comes."

"Really, Georgia? Aren't you rather old to complain to Daddy? That may have worked when we were newly married, but your father understands I control this household."

"Do you seriously believe Daddy will continue to employ you if I leave? Where would you be then, Harvey?"

Fifteen years of matrimony served to harden Georgia. Sick to death of men controlling her life, she ejected Harvey from her bedroom not long after Dee's birth for that exact reason. Their marriage was something taken out for show much like the sterling silver tea service. But this was important. Something must be done about Dee. She noticed Harvey's sanctimonious grin had vanished. His auspicious wedding to an heiress ended his life of poverty. She knew he had no desire to revisit that existence.

"Don't do anything you'll regret," Harvey warned, but Georgia knew it to be a hollow threat.

"I want to send her to boarding school. Somewhere she'll be watched closely. Somewhere she'll be disciplined appropriately." When there was no response, Georgia turned and marched out the library door, slamming it behind her.

After climbing the winding staircase, she walked down the hall toward the nursery and paused outside. Normally, she would give a knock before entering. Instead, she charged through the door.

Dee sat on her bed, neither startled nor afraid. Her lips were pressed tightly together in a thin line, never smiling nor frowning. She stared at her mother as if she were some servant come to fetch the chamber pot.

"Why are you wearing that dress? I told you to take it off hours ago."

Dee refused to comment on her mother's ridiculous request. She was fond of the plain black dress; it was her favorite. Mourning clothes suited her. The fact she wore it to the neighbor boy's funeral only served to endear the garment to its young owner.

"What smells?" Georgia crossed the room to open the window then walked toward the bed. "What is that smell, Dee? Answer me. It smells like burnt hair. Did you burn your hair?" Georgia took hold of her daughter's shoulders and turned her from side to side. Every brunette hair was perfectly placed, as always. It seemed unnatural for any child to appear so prim and proper. Georgia heaved an exasperated sigh, knowing Dee would never mar her own appearance.

Georgia gasped when another idea entered her head. She released Dee to peek under the dresser, then the bed. "Where is your kitten, Dee?" Georgia gripped her daughter's chin and forced Dee to look into her eyes. She appeared as menacing as an angry adult could possibly look. "Answer me, now!"

Unintimidated, Dee stared right back. "He may have swished his tail in the candle flame. He's not very bright." Her clever comment caused Dee's eyes to sparkle.

"Where is the kitten? *Where is he*?"

Chapter Two

Los Angeles, 1890

"I'm back," yelled Noah Chandler as he burst through the kitchen door. At least he found consolation for his condensed ride on Checkers. He grabbed a lemon tart off the table and took a bite before Margarita used her wooden spoon to smack his hand.

"That is your dessert, Mr. Noah," she yelled as he quickly exited.

It was a good thing Margarita was such a fine cook because the woman had absolutely no sense of decorum. He really shouldn't put up with her.

Still working on the tart, he noticed his mother conversing in the parlor. Noah assumed he missed the new companion's arrival. Then he got a better look at the guest.

"Deidre? What are you doing here, dearest? And greetings to you, Mother." Noah stuffed the last bite of tart in his mouth.

"I came to see you, silly." When Noah approached, intending to give his fiancé a warm greeting, Deidre raised her hand before he could touch her. "Not in those clothes. No, you don't." She gave him a smirk. "You've been riding. Why don't you get cleaned up? Then we can plan my visit. Cousin Theodora invited me for a few weeks and I thought it would give us an opportunity to discuss the wedding." She shooed Noah away. "Go on. Your mother and I will visit while you change."

Lula Chandler watched her son's expression evolve from affable fiancé to belligerent opponent. She doubted Deidre perceived the change. Noah was never one to willingly take direction from the female sex. She was not surprised when he turned toward the liquor cart.

Her son was a handsome man, a fact he didn't hesitate to use to his advantage. Clean-shaven to show off the cleft in his square chin, Noah had dark brown hair, always perfectly trimmed. His light grey eyes sparkled beneath heavy black lashes. Blessed with a tall, athletic frame and broad shoulders, Noah also possessed a rich, deep voice tailor-made for his chosen profession.

In his most lawyerly tone, Noah replied, "I believe I'll indulge in a brandy before I clean up." He poured the amber liquid into a glass and took a seat beside his betrothed, placing a dirty boot atop his knee near her dress. "I take it your companion has yet to arrive, Mother."

"What companion?" Deidre asked.

"My health is not all it might be," admitted Lula. "When Noah's partner, Jack, hired a companion for his aged aunt to good result, Noah suggested we do the same. It offended me when Jack asserted his aunt enjoyed having someone to boss around, as if I would enjoy a similar pursuit. I refused to be a party to such nonsense. Nonetheless, Noah ordered Mr. Nelson from his office to place an ad for a companion."

"That idiot was duped into believing he would save money by placing the ad nationally. He paid four times what he would have for a local ad." Noah remained bitter over the blunder. "Applications flooded in from every corner of the United States."

"One of the applicants captured my interest," explained Lula.

"Yes, one who needed transport across the entire continent. One we couldn't even interview."

"Don't exaggerate, Noah." Lula knew full well the ticket wasn't expensive. In order to promote travel to the West Coast, Santa Fe Railroad rates to Los Angeles had been drastically lowered. "You're being a poor host."

Noah glanced at his fiancé who held her handkerchief to her nose. "This will interest you, Mother. My opponent today proved to be none other than Mr. Tinley. You remember him? He tried to pull the same stunt in court he attempted last time."

"One would think the man might learn his lesson," Lula replied as her future daughter-in-law fumed. "Perhaps you should explain to Deidre."

"Of course. You see, dearest, many practicing attorneys are not well-educated and read the law in lieu of school. After all, only ten percent of the population are high school graduates.

"Mr. Tinley attempted to endear himself to the jury by highlighting his affinity for 'plain folks.' He disparaged me as an outsider—a big city attorney with a fancy education—not a man of the people. It's a tactic I've handled on previous occasions and one I use to my advantage. Let me demonstrate." Noah stood and dramatically placed his right hand over his heart.

"Gentlemen of the jury, my able opponent describes himself as one of you, a common man, uneducated, unintelligent. Mind you, I'm not disparaging his ability in any way. Why, Abraham Lincoln read the law and never stepped foot in a university. I had the opportunity to attend law school and as a result, practiced law at an early age. I will even share the fact I've been quite successful. I won't speak down to you or alter my methods because I think you're too stupid to understand. Unlike my adversary, I respect your intelligence."

Although he never expected to impress Deidre, Noah waited for a response. His desire to irritate was partially satisfied as Deidre gave a weak cough.

"You must excuse me, Noah, but you are so dusty and dirty, I believe I'm getting a headache. Won't you be a dear and do as I ask?"

Noah shrugged his shoulders and ambled from the room. Why did it seem he had no control over his own household? Obviously, there were too many women underfoot. He much preferred his office where he was valued and respected.

As she slapped her handkerchief on the spot where Noah had been seated, Deidre turned and gave a sneer to her soon-to-be mother-in-law. "I hate this dirty city," she commented. "Now, where were we? Oh, yes, the guest list."

* * *

Slightly perplexed at the scene before her, April Stringham prepared to exit the trolley at the corner of Temple and Edgewater. Opulent homes seemed to grow from a gently sloping hill without a tree in sight. The district was called Angelino Heights. She rechecked her directions and stepped onto the sidewalk.

After walking three blocks past newly built homes separated by picket fences, she turned down Carroll Avenue and stopped in front of a beautiful Queen Anne-style house detailed in dark green, yellow and white. Could she really be about to take up residence in this grand home? For the first time since her journey began, April felt a rush of apprehension. There could be no turning back. Nervously fingering her mother's cameo necklace, April walked up the steps and crossed the wrap-around porch. She set her valise down, firmly gripped the knocker and tapped several times. No one answered.

Considering her options, April flinched when at last, the door opened. An elderly lady stood on the other side.

"I didn't mean to frighten you. Evidently no one else heard your knock. You must be Miss Stringham."

"Yes. Are you Mrs. Chandler?"

"I am. Come in. Let me see if I can find someone to take your bag."

"It's not necessary." April collected her valise and placed it inside the door.

"You look rather stunned, dear. Are you all right?"

"This is such a lovely home and I never expected you to answer the door."

"Well, it's not my normal duty here."

"I mean, I thought you were an invalid."

"I see. No, I don't appear to be."

April laughed. "I'm sorry. I didn't mean to be rude." She offered her hand, patting the back of Mrs. Chandler's hand as she shook it. "It's so nice to meet you."

"It's nice to meet you, as well." Mrs. Chandler had an odd feeling as if her son's house suddenly came to life. "Allow me to give you a tour before I let you settle in."

April stared wide-eyed at the elegant furnishings. She stood in a lovely entryway where a finely crafted wooden staircase turned to the next floor. A beautifully carved table occupied the center of the space. Two identical stained-glass windows provided light from the landing and above a fainting couch tucked beneath the stairway. Mrs. Chandler directed April to the parlor.

"The parlor and sitting room are open to each other through this large curved doorway." April gazed out the window beside the fireplace. Mrs. Chandler stopped to see what drew the new employee's interest. "Oh, there's my son, Mr. Chandler, and his fiancé outside."

"What a handsome pair." April noted the tall gentleman and a diminutive, brunette, young woman in the garden. They were dressed in the height of fashion. April eyed the woman's hourglass shape, contorted by what must be a tightly-laced corset. "They look like a couple from a fairytale," she noted as she turned to continue her tour.

"They are hardly that," Mrs. Chandler candidly remarked.

April noted the sarcasm in Mrs. Chandler's reply and looked at her curiously.

"I'm sorry, my comment was improper. They are a visually stunning couple, I agree. Unfortunately, my son is the next thing to an imbecile." Lula Chandler had a sudden urge to unburden herself. "Why don't we sit down and have a chat. I think the tea is still warm. Help yourself."

April poured a cup for each of them and settled against the chair she was offered.

"My son's law firm, Broadmore and Chandler, began to flourish about three years ago. He asked me to travel to California and furnish his new house in a manner that would reflect his success. I've been here ever since.

"As you noted, my son is a good-looking man. Quite naturally, the ladies take notice. California voted down an amendment for women's suffrage in 1878. Noah figures it's only a matter of time until women populate juries. Once that happens, he alleges he might never lose a case again. I know it does sound rather vain, but Noah has never been particularly modest."

Lula took a sip of tea and studied her new companion who seemed completely enthralled by her diatribe. This served to encourage Lula's recitation.

"I've always had a soft spot for my boy. I'm especially proud of the pro bono cases he takes. They don't contribute to the success of the law firm or the balance in his bank account, but they demonstrate he is much more than a cold opportunist." Lula squirmed in her seat. "I only say that because his engagement paints him in a conniving light. I've said too much, but let me add, I know what's best for Noah. Unfortunately, grown men are reluctant to admit anyone might know better than they. I also need to tell you, my plan is to return home to New York in June should Noah continue his current, absurd course toward matrimony. I'll be certain to keep you abreast of my plans."

April soon found herself returned to her tour.

Beautiful furniture graced every room. Oriental carpets, luxurious window dressings and the finest porcelain, silver, crystal and china provided a rich and genteel setting.

As they proceeded through the dining room, April paused to view a painting.

Mrs. Chandler admitted, "I have no use at all for the art my son collects. It's the one flaw in his otherwise impeccable abode. Noah is an enthusiast of the impressionists and has acquired many American artists including Childe Hassam and Mary Cassatt—a woman! A complete waste of finances."

They continued to the kitchen.

"We have the most modern conveniences. This is our ample ice box and the latest in gas stoves."

April was duly impressed.

"We sometimes take breakfast in the solarium and here is the bathroom." April tried her best to appear cosmopolitan as she peered into the small room, which contained a modern water closet and claw foot tub.

"This is handy, right near the stove so water can be heated for the bath." Mrs. Chandler led the way to the front staircase, pausing to explain one last feature. "You can see on the chandelier, some of the glass shades point down, some up. The downward facing shades have light bulbs. Since electricity is so unreliable, we also have gas lamps, which face upward." Mrs. Chandler gave a quick lesson on how to turn the lights on and off. "Your room is up two flights in the tower. You won't have any trouble finding it. It's the only room up there. Take as much time as you need to settle in."

* * *

"How is it the lovely Deidre did not join us for dinner?"

"Her cousin expected her to spend the evening there," Noah replied as he finished his soup.

"Why weren't you invited?"

"Are you trying to get rid of me, Mother? Were you anxious to play with your new toy?"

"You are impertinent. This was your idea, not mine. And she doesn't start until tomorrow. She's settling in."

"Did you want me to talk to Miss Stringham, explain her duties?"

"I've done that. She will join me for breakfast and luncheon, but our dinners will remain family only."

"As usual, you have my household well in order. Whatever will I do once you return to New York?"

"Your new wife will manage your household, as she should. But it likely won't be here, will it?"

"It's true, Deidre much prefers life in San Francisco."

"What will happen to your firm?"

"We could open a second office up north or Deidre and I could simply reside in different cities."

"That's right, the object of your affection has always been the heiress, not the woman."

"You know that's not true, Mother."

"I know no such thing."

"Father never made any secret of the fact he married you to advance his career. Why blame me for following suit? Deidre is a railroad heiress, but her money never interested me. Her family will undoubtedly throw a lot of work my way, my true goal."

"So, you achieve your goal. What does your new

wife get out of this?"

"Me. I intend to be a devoted and honorable husband."

"You will give up horses and poker? How about that ridiculous baseball you're always going off to play?"

"Certainly not. Why should I give up any of my interests? I don't expect Deidre to give up her social activities, whatever it is she does."

"You've been engaged three times since I came here. Why should I believe this engagement will turn out any differently than the other two?"

"Because I've traded up about as far as I can go. This wedding will happen in June as scheduled. Mark my words."

"And then I can return to New York."

"Did you explain your plans to your toy?"

"As a matter of fact, I did."

"How did she respond?"

"She seems a bright enough girl. June is eight months away. I'm certain she'll have some plan in place by then. She assumed she would be caring for an invalid. Jobs of that sort don't last forever. Maybe I'll be dead by June anyway."

"You'll never die, Mother. You're much too ornery. God doesn't want to put up with you any longer than He must." Noah sat back in his chair and finished his wine. Perhaps the companion made a difference already. His mother seemed unusually animated.

* * *

In her wildest dreams, April never imagined having a bedroom so grand. Dormer windows were located on all four sides of the room. A simple wooden dresser, dressing table and stool, bed, wardrobe and small tufted chair and ottoman decorated the space. Several rag rugs covered the wooden floor. It appeared to April no one used the room before. Everything seemed new. There was more than adequate space for a sewing machine once she saved up enough wages.

As she lay between crisp white sheets in the darkness, April succumbed to a moment of reflection. Was it only a week since she left home?

She had turned to fix the image of the farm in her memory. A few trees sported fall foliage. The autumn sun cast a golden light. Having never been more than ten miles from home, April knew she was on the adventure of her life.

She'd been surprised at Mr. Farmer's greeting when his buggy approached.

"I thought you could use a ride," he offered.

"You shouldn't have gone out of your way. I can walk."

"No, you have your valise. Climb up. It's no trouble."

Mr. Farmer did not conform to April's ideas of bankers—notions gleaned from books. Fiction was her one true passion. The bankers in books were cold, callous men who cared only for profit. April came to appreciate Mr. Farmer's incredible kindness.

As her mother's health steadily failed, April took on more responsibility. Mr. Farmer was always there to offer help, both financial and practical. If not for his support, she knew they would have lost their home.

When it became apparent her mother's health would soon fail completely, April perused classified ads in the newspaper. Initially discouraged, she finally found what appeared to be an ideal opportunity. A gentleman in California advertised for a companion to his elderly mother. What could be a more perfect occupation for April? She wrote an enthusiastic and cheerful reply. When Mr. Chandler wrote back, he included money for her travel expenses to Los Angeles and expected her within the month.

Once her mother passed, Mr. Farmer had no choice but to recover as much of the bank's investment as possible. The funeral and subsequent auction of the farm, house and all its contents went off without a hitch. April held her head high and remained calm throughout.

She packed all her worldly possessions in a valise—a few clothes, several favored books, her collection of periodical articles and her mother's prized cameo necklace. Then, there was the $500 bond she found amongst her mother's things, an incredible surprise. It served as a safeguard on her current undertaking. Her bond was sewn into the hem of her pink-striped, high-collared, long-sleeved church dress.

April rode in silence until Mr. Farmer nudged her arm and reached in his coat pocket. "I have something here for you." He handed April an envelope.

Peering inside, she found the envelope contained money. April thumbed through the bills. "What is this?"

"There was a little left once the estate settled. I wanted to catch you today so you could take it along. It's not much, but I thought it might come in handy."

"Thank you, it will. This is such a surprise. I was certain the bank would take a loss."

"Once the clerk went over the numbers, the overage became obvious."

Mr. Farmer seemed more awkward than usual as he bid her farewell. It seemed almost as if he wished to hug her, a completely inappropriate gesture.

April quickly thanked Mr. Farmer and shook his hand before hopping off the buggy.

"No problem at all. I wish you luck. Oh, and here's my card. I'd appreciate if you'd let me know when you're settled. If more funds are owed, I may need to forward them. There is a bit of outstanding paperwork."

"I'll be sure to send a letter as soon as I'm settled. Thank you again for your help. I don't know what we would have done without you all these years. I wish I could repay you."

Smiling warmly, April turned toward the station. For the first time in her life, she was free.

* * *

For her first day of work, April chose her new brown skirt and a simple white blouse. She admired her accommodations one last time before heading downstairs. Patting her bun, April felt ready to take on the world.

Breakfast was served at eight. April arrived early to find Mrs. Chandler seated at the dining table.

"Good morning," April offered in a cheery voice that reflected her mood.

"Good morning, Miss Stringham. Did you sleep well?"

"I did. The bed is comfortable. The room is delightful. Thank you so much."

"Help yourself to breakfast. Margarita has Mondays off so we enjoy Mrs. Fitzpatrick's cooking today. She and her husband live over the carriage house. Mr. Fitzpatrick tends the garden and occasionally helps out in the house, especially when we entertain. Mrs. Fitzpatrick is our housekeeper and maid. I'll introduce you later."

"What did you have in mind for today?"

"What do you mean?"

"What activities have you planned? What do you expect of me?"

"On Mondays, I plan the menu for the week so Margarita can order groceries tomorrow morning."

"And then what?"

"I'm not as fit as I used to be. Lately, I haven't been well enough to take an interest in much of anything." Mrs. Chandler attempted to gauge her new companion's reaction. "Did you have something in mind?"

"Not especially. But Los Angeles is such a vibrant and interesting place. It seems a shame to stay in all day."

"You must have been tied to home during your mother's illness?"

"Oh, most certainly. But I had cooking and cleaning and laundry to do. I started caring for Mother when I was 12. I had to give up my schoolwork then."

"How unfortunate."

"No, not really. Such is a child's duty to their parent. I felt entirely fortunate—at least I always had a roof over my head and food to eat."

"Your application stated you're 29 now?"

"That's correct."

"Seventeen years is certainly a long time to languish in ill health."

"I suppose so."

"If you could do anything you liked today, what

would it be?"

April did not hesitate to answer. "It's a beautiful day, like yesterday. So warm and sunny. When I arrived, I shopped and toured the city. There's every kind of store here, wonderful merchandise, so much to see and do. But if I could do anything I liked, I would definitely go to the public library. It's over on Broadway. I plan to go there at my first opportunity."

"Goodness, I've been here for three years and you know more than I do."

"But you must travel around the city?"

"Merchants made it easy for me to shop. They brought seller's samples, fabric swatches, even catalog items to the hotel where we stayed. I'm afraid I became something of a hermit. I haven't been out in months, aside from Sunday church service. I haven't been into the city—goodness, it's probably been two years. What did you see when you arrived?"

"I imagine when I stepped off the train in Los Angeles, I appeared quite the bumpkin. The Arcade Station is as elegant and modern as can be. Have you seen it?"

Mrs. Chandler shook her head.

"It reminds me of massive, wooden Victorian train stations I've seen in pictures of Europe. The arched rail shed has skylights and soars 90 feet above the platform.

"There were lavish gardens flanking the depot and a huge fan palm growing outside the entrance where I boarded an electric trolley. Since I imagined Los Angeles to be a wild frontier town, I was surprised to find multi-story buildings of a cosmopolitan city. Construction sites abound. Los Angeles seems a beacon of civility at the end of the earth.

"A fellow passenger recommended the Westminster Hotel for fine lodging. I planned to pamper myself before beginning my job.

"I assumed my workday dresses and braided hair would serve well enough in a rugged western town. My brief hotel stay ensured time for shopping. Suddenly, I needed to convince a clerk I belonged in an exclusive hotel.

"I'm not exaggerating when I tell you the desk clerk's demeanor fairly dripped with condescension. But I put a friendly smile on my face and explained my appearance was due to recent travel. I agreed to pay cash in advance and asked if the clerk could arrange delivery of my letter to Mr. Chandler, confirming my arrival. His name had the desired effect."

April appeared proud of her accomplishment. Mrs. Chandler nodded approval.

"After a good night's sleep, I headed for Wineburgh's, located in the 300 block of South Spring Street. The ad I saved promised a large assortment, cordial treatment and the latest in fall clothing, which proved accurate. Have you been there?"

"I have, when I first arrived. Their selection also impressed me."

"A young clerk named Hattie helped me select skirts, blouses and a tweed jacket. She tried to pressure me into buying a corset, which she claimed to be the proper way to show off a trim waist, but I wasn't having any of that. I've read all about the unhealthful aspects of corsets propounded in the recently published *Wife and Mother, or Information for Every Woman*.

"Hats were another issue. I'm not fond of trendy large and elaborately decorated hats, although I tried a few on for fun. I settled on the small-brimmed rust-colored hat I wore yesterday and a practical broad-brimmed straw hat. I bought a pair of black high-button shoes and brown slippers. I never bought ready-made clothes before so I felt quite affluent as Hattie catered to my every shopping need and arranged delivery to the hotel.

"I couldn't resist a stroll through the yardage department on my way to the cash register. Silk was on sale for 39 cents a yard, an almost irresistible bargain. The Singer Improved Family Sewing Machine I noted in the Sears-Roebuck catalog sells for $50 at Wineburgh's, hardly a bargain. Oh! I've talked too much, haven't I?"

Miss Stringham's enthusiasm was contagious. "No, your adventure is fascinating. But I'm not sure I understand your desire to visit the library above all else."

"I love to read. My preference is the fiction novel, but I'm not averse to virtually any other form of the written word. Even reference books hold a certain charm. It was normally taboo to remove those volumes from my local library, but the librarian overlooked the rules for her most loyal patron. Concord has a rich history, home to many literary giants. I visited the Concord Free Public Library every week. I've read through entire volumes of the Encyclopedia Britannica."

Mrs. Chandler shook her head, trying to think of a way to accommodate her delightful companion's wishes. "I can't walk far."

"I saw a wicker wheelchair on the porch when I arrived. Is it yours?"

"I've used it on occasion, but it's too difficult for you to push. The wheels tend to get stuck in the dirt.

It's not bad on the sidewalks, but we wouldn't get far—only around the block."

"I'm a very sturdy girl, Mrs. Chandler. And I am entirely determined. I think we should take an airing once your menus are complete."

Chapter Three

April displayed a huge grin as she pushed the wheelchair toward Carroll Avenue. The day was a complete delight. She penned a letter to Mr. Farmer while Mrs. Chandler worked on her menus. After lunch, the ladies headed for the library.

Realizing the wheelchair would be difficult to take on the trolley, Mrs. Chandler was at the ready with a solution. Handing her young accomplice a quarter, she suggested an ample tip for the conductor might suffice. Predictably, the conductor appeared more than eager to help once April awarded him the hefty tip.

Impressed by the library and its shelves of books, Mrs. Chandler abandoned her wheelchair to prowl. She eventually settled on *The Gentle Art of Making Enemies* by the famous painter James McNeil Whistler. The scandalous book supposedly documented Whistler's grievances against acquaintances and friends. April chose a murder mystery, *The Firm of Girdlestone* by Arthur Conan Doyle. Excited by the prospect of reading after dinner, she fairly floated on air. Her mood was contagious. Mrs. Chandler could not recall the last time she felt so alive.

"Miss Stringham, I have a question."

"Certainly."

"When your mother grew ill, didn't neighbors help? Family, church members?"

"My father's family lived in Ohio. I'm not certain if Mother had any family left. Ladies from church volunteered, at least in the beginning."

"Did they tire of providing aid over all those years?"

"Not in the way you might imagine. You see, my mother was extremely particular. She liked things done a certain way. The ladies who came to help eventually—gave up I guess would be a good way to put it."

Mrs. Chandler thought on this for several minutes. No wonder the girl was happy to be out in the sunshine. Mrs. Chandler decided she provided more than a job. This was an escape, albeit a tardy one, for her companion.

"You're not too tired to push the wheelchair, are you?"

"Oh, no. I'm having too fine a time to be tired! We won't get back much before dinner. Maybe I'll have the opportunity to meet Mr. Chandler tonight."

"He may not be home. My son has an active social life and his fiancé is in town."

"She's a beautiful woman. He's a lucky man."

Mrs. Chandler could not quell the snort of derision that escaped of its own accord. Surprised at her own reaction and embarrassed over her diatribe the day Miss Stringham arrived, she straightened her clothing in an attempt to regain her dignity. "Why don't we take dinner in the backyard together tonight?

I know it's your free time so if you'd prefer not to, I understand."

"No. I'd be delighted to join you."

And so, the ladies began a tradition of taking their meals in the garden while Mr. Chandler entertained his fiancé.

April was startled one night when a chicken ran from a flower bed she admired. Slightly embarrassed, she returned to the supper table, laughing. "It's not as if I've never seen a chicken before. Does it belong to you?"

"No, they wander over from a neighbor's backyard. It looks like you've become a city girl already!"

"Chickens are good for a garden. I guess you're reaping the benefits. Even though your plants are new, they're doing well."

"Speaking of plants, I'd like to get some bulbs for the garden. I originally thought Mr. Fitzpatrick could choose, but it might be fun for us to pick what we want."

"Sounds like an adventure for tomorrow," noted April. "Do you know where we might go?"

"The Germain Fruit Company on South Main Street has a fine selection of bulbs or that's what their ad claims."

The prospective wonders in Mrs. Chandler's bag of bulbs did nothing to calm her ruffled feathers the next afternoon.

"That man was so incredibly rude. Someone should box his ears."

"It's not important. I managed to push the wheelchair through the doorway. Don't you think the purple irises will look wonderful with the daffodils?

Are you disappointed they talked you out of tulips?"

"That man walked right through the door you opened as if you'd been put on earth to be his servant. Surely, he could see my wheelchair. No one has any common courtesy these days.

"It's unfortunate—the natural tendencies men have: lust, avarice, control, violence. Such untidy inclinations. They are such imbeciles. Take the 100 Years War. Can you even imagine—100 years of war? It's not as if those men could pick up the newspaper and learn of the latest injustice. They couldn't even read for heaven's sake. Generations of men blindly left their families and their livelihood to die on a battlefield because some other man told them it seemed a good idea.

"Then there was the recent War Between the States. Thousands upon thousands of men engaged in mortal combat, brother against brother, father against son. Since time began, men have gone to war. Women, being the resourceful creatures we are, have always gotten along quite well without them, although we are loath to admit it. After all, the poor dears need all the confidence we can give them, rather like insecure children who need constant reassurance and instruction. I should have given that man a piece of my mind. I assure you, he would never hesitate to open a door for a lady again."

"My father went to war. He returned an invalid. I was a baby when he left so I had no recollection of the strong, handsome man of my mother's memories. She nursed him for years until his war injuries took their final toll. No sooner was he in his grave than she took to her own sick bed."

"I'm so sorry. But this only proves my point."

April had become accustomed to Mrs. Chandler's frequent and amusing outbursts.

As their adventures continued, Mrs. Chandler realized she didn't need to do much walking. Miss Stringham quickly learned the trolley routes. Seating was available at or near most of their destinations. The wheelchair was abandoned.

April never tired of her view from the trolley window. The streets of Los Angeles were unpaved. Electrical wires serviced buildings and trolleys alike, although there were still streets where horses pulled trolleys. Wagons and buggies filled the roads. A vast array of businesses lined the streets: boarding houses, cigar stores, hotels, liquor and wine dealers, livery stables and milliners. April took a special interest in the bicycles and tricycles displayed at Gibson & Alexander and made a point to peer inside the window each time they went by. She'd come to a modern and surprising place and had not experienced a single pang of regret.

It became apparent the two ladies were well-suited and enjoyed each other's company. April's delight in daily activities stimulated the older woman's enthusiasm. Mrs. Chandler happily introduced her companion to a new and entertaining life. She understood her own life was considerably enhanced. Formalities were suspended as they became simply April and Lula.

Mr. Chandler came in late each evening and left before breakfast. He had yet to make the acquaintance of his new employee.

Although April's position in the household seemed socially awkward, she managed to fit in remarkably well. She lived in the house but was not a member of the family. She was paid help yet could not be categorized as Margarita and the Fitzpatricks who spent their days working for the family without social interaction. April's positive attitude pulled her through this discomfiture.

She helped herself in the kitchen and praised Margarita's cooking. The woman prized April's compliments and gratitude.

April did not hesitate to assist the Fitzpatricks at every opportunity. She cheerfully pulled weeds in the garden and gave Mrs. Fitzpatrick a hand with cleaning and serving duties.

April enjoyed cleaning her own room. After all, she spent her life keeping house. The other employees relaxed once they understood the new resident made no extra work and alleviated theirs.

The ladies' daily excursions were limited to window shopping and exploration, although they occasionally indulged in a bakery item or ice cream if they were out late in the afternoon. But that was about to change.

After the women enjoyed breakfast, April thumbed through the newspaper. "This has been the most amazing experience!" April confessed as she took a sip of tea. "It's almost as if I'm living someone else's life instead of my own."

"I'm glad you think so," Lula replied. "I have to admit, this is the best I've felt in a long while. I enjoy your company and our excursions."

"Listen to this," April jabbed the paper. "It says Harry Lacy is playing in *Still Alarm*. It's a love story. There's a real fire engine and horses. How could that possibly be true?"

"Where is it playing?"

"The Illinois Hall. It's on Broadway, about four blocks from the library."

"How much are the tickets?"

"75, 50 and 25 cents."

"Would you be willing to accompany me to the theater?" Lula took delight at the awed expression on April's face.

"Oh, I can't possibly. I shouldn't spend my wages on a ticket until I save money."

"It would be my treat. I couldn't go without you. What will you wear?"

Almost too excited to answer, April finally replied, "I have my tweed jacket. I can wear a skirt and my best blouse. I purchased a lace one."

"That won't suffice. When we take the trolley, we'll buy something appropriate for the theater—a new dress and a proper hat. And we need to pick up the tickets from the box office. There! We have an agenda for today."

* * *

Lula Chandler closely observed the dress fitting. She already considered her young protégé more a project than an employee. April did not possess a fashionably curvaceous figure. While not masculine by any means, she had a trim appearance—no doubt the result of a life spent walking and working. The gauzy, high-collared teal gown accentuated her femininity. Lace appliques crossed the shoulders and drew attention to a gathered bodice. Mutton sleeves ended at the elbow. Twenty buttons fastened each lower sleeve to the wrist. The simple skirt flowed from a V-shaped waistline. A short train was attached. Lace gloves and a waist-length velvet cape completed the ensemble. Then, of course, came the hat.

"How tall are you, April?" inquired the benefactress of the shopping excursion.

"Five feet, eight inches," April admitted, somewhat shyly.

"Goodness, I didn't think you were that tall." The dressmaker needed to apply a facing on the skirt hem to lengthen the gown.

"I'm as tall or taller than most men."

Slightly shorter than the average woman at five feet, two inches, Lula usually looked up at people. She realized after accounting for shoes, a proper hair style and hat, April would approach six feet in height.

The girl looked quite stunning. She would draw eyes in social settings for her stylish ensemble and for her height. Although April balked at the hat she now modeled, Lula thought it complimented the dress to perfection. The large brim sported a black and white striped satin bow and velvet floral arrangement. But the frippery she wore did not compare to the absolutely radiant expression on April's face. The girl was enchanting. Overwhelmed at the beautiful clothing, she looked about to burst.

"I never dreamed of wearing anything so magnificent," April beamed. "You must let me pay you back."

"Nonsense. It's my pleasure. I look forward to our outing tomorrow night." Lula assessed April's face. She was not a striking beauty but had a lovely complexion. Her skin glowed with good health. Her deep blue eyes sparkled, reflecting not only joy but intelligence. She would make someone a good wife. Lula determined to find her a husband, despite her age. Being an old maid was not as serious a problem as it was on the East Coast. Women in the West were greatly outnumbered. Besides, in the grand scheme of things, was 29 really so old?

"There is one problem, though." April pulled on her thick braid. "My hair is too heavy to put up. It doesn't lend itself to current fashion. Despite new clothes, my hair will give me away as the prim old maid I am. I don't think I can do your hat justice. Then again, if that's the biggest problem in my life, I'm an extremely fortunate woman."

"I am entirely confident I can help. There's a knack to dressing hair, you understand."

But as Lula practiced putting April's light brown hair up, she quickly lost confidence in her ability to arrange such thick tresses. No matter how secure each hairstyle appeared, within five minutes it tilted precariously on one side of April's head or the other.

"It's one thing to arrange my hair," admitted April, "It's quite another to keep it in place. A few stray wisps are not unusual. I believe it makes a hairstyle more natural and feminine. But when the entire coiffure collapses onto your dinner plate, it's a hard thing to overcome. You can't exactly smile and pretend you planned the whole debacle."

"Has that ever happened?" laughed Lula. She could see from the grimace on April's face, it had indeed. "I have one more idea. Bend over and let your hair fall frontward."

Before too long, Lula French-braided April's hair from the nape of the neck to the top of her head. Securing the braid, she then pinned the ends into a loose bun. Having placed most of the weight of her hair in the braid, it looked as if the rest might stay in place.

"There. Why don't you see if this works? If I put my mind to it, I might have a few other ideas, but this should do nicely for now."

April eyed her reflection in the mirror. She looked quite the lady, but her reverie was interrupted at a loud crash from downstairs. Voices were raised. Lula and April glanced at each other and headed straight for the kitchen in time to see Margarita toss what looked to be dinner into the trash bin and stomp out the door.

A red-faced Deidre stared in amazement as the door slammed shut.

"What's going on here? When did you arrive, dear?" Lula inquired of her future daughter-in-law.

"Noah sent me to see to dinner. He's entertaining an important client from Texas."

"I didn't hear you knock. I had no idea you were here."

Deidre lifted her chin in defiance. April thought the gesture rather rude in light of the fact the woman addressed her elder.

"I let myself in. I will be mistress of this house shortly. I didn't see a purpose in knocking. This cook of yours is completely unsatisfactory. When I pointed out her meal plan for tonight did not meet my standards, she threw her bowl across the room. I fired her."

"She seems to have heard you," noted Lula. "Her food is in the trash bin and on the floor. Even if dinner was unsatisfactory, now there is none. Were you planning on cooking?"

"Me? Certainly not."

"What is your plan for entertaining Noah's client, then?"

Gathering what little dignity she could muster,

Deidre replied. "I'm not feeling well. Please tell Noah I won't be able to hostess his dinner this evening." At this, the young woman made a hasty retreat.

Lula and April turned to stare at each other, then burst into laughter.

"What will you do without Margarita?" inquired April.

"Oh, she quits all the time, almost every week. She becomes offended and tromps off, I think because she wants to spend time at home. She always returns the next day. It does sound as if she truly took offense this time. The main difficulty is, what will we do about dinner? I haven't cooked in probably 25 years." If she were being honest, Lula would admit she had never cooked in her life. "Do you think you could manage?"

"What happened to Mrs. Fitzpatrick? Besides, there's nothing to cook."

"You don't know Mrs. Fitzpatrick well. The woman is a bundle of nerves. She wouldn't be able to handle this situation."

As a rooster crowed, the two women peered out the window. Grinning slyly, April turned to her employer. One of the neighbor's chickens would not be returning home.

* * *

Upon arrival, Noah struggled to hide his anger over the menu and Deidre's sudden illness. By the time he dabbed his napkin to his lips, the evening had clearly proceeded to great success.

Deidre was his ace in the hole. Mr. Devlin would have found her enchanting. But the Texan appeared enamored by the southern-style dinner. Delicious crispy fried chicken, mashed potatoes with gravy, and succotash were impeccably prepared. The hot apple pie and vanilla ice cream made a perfect dessert. Margarita really outdid herself. She never prepared a meal even remotely similar to the one they enjoyed tonight. Despite her absence, perhaps Deidre was a better household manager than Noah imagined.

"Devlin, would you join me for after-dinner brandy and a cigar? I'm certain my mother would excuse us."

"Sounds like a fine plan, Chandler. But I'd like to thank the cook before we adjourn. It's something of a tradition in my home and I'm much reminded of home this evening."

"Mr. Fitzpatrick, would you mind asking Margarita to join us?" Noah was puzzled by the look of astonishment he received in reply to this request.

"I'll fetch Margarita." The gentlemen rose as Lula proceeded to the kitchen.

If Mr. Devlin paid attention to his host, he would have recognized something was amiss. Noah gawked as a strange woman emerged from the kitchen door. Before he could utter a word, his mother took charge of the conversation.

"This is our Margarita," Lula beamed, her arm wrapped around the stranger's waist.

As Mr. Devlin lavished praise on the cook, Noah's amazement turned to suspicion. He observed this new version of Margarita closely. The tall, slender woman seemed sweet and well-spoken as she graciously accepted Mr. Devlin's compliments. Dressed in a pink-and-white striped dress and starched white apron, her hair fashioned into a prim bun at the back of her neck, she could not have appeared more different than the real Margarita. Unwilling to jeopardize the goodwill dinner engendered, Noah recovered sufficiently to move the conversation along.

"Yes, thank you, *Margarita*. Job well done." Turning to his client he added. "I'll be sure to thank my fiancé. The dinner plan was hers. Unfortunately, she couldn't join us this evening."

"Please express my thanks as well," added Mr. Devlin.

As the gentlemen adjourned to the parlor, Noah bent down to hiss in his mother's ear, "I can't wait to hear your explanation."

Lula turned to her accomplice once the men were out of range. "Sorry you didn't get all the credit. That little snot Deidre only caused problems; she certainly didn't solve any. I'll be certain my son understands your contribution once his guest departs."

"Don't worry about it." But one thing April despised was a person who took credit for another's work. She had no doubt, whatever Lula told her son, he would believe his fiancé if she claimed the dinner plan had been hers.

* * *

Once April finished the dishes, she heard Mr. Chandler and Lula arguing in the parlor. Although the words were indistinct, the tone and volume were easily understood. She untied her apron and quietly made her way up the back staircase.

"What I'm trying to tell you is your fiancé was the root of the entire problem tonight. Miss Stringham saved the day. You owe her gratitude, not Deidre."

"What I think, Mother, is you're unwilling to accept the fact Deidre is about to usurp your power in the household."

"Don't be absurd. I never planned to stay here once you married. My sole intention was to help you set up housekeeping. If you didn't commence your series of engagements, I would have gone home long ago. I changed my plans to attend your wedding. Perhaps I should leave now."

"Perhaps you should." But Noah desired his mother's attendance at the wedding. The elderly woman might not endure another trip to California in June if she went home now. "I'm sorry. I misspoke. I've been busy meeting Deidre's social obligations and trying to keep up at work. It would make things a lot easier if you tried to get along."

"Fine. I'll ask her for tea next week."

"Thank you." But a sense of foreboding overtook Noah at the thought the two women, unsupervised, might wreak havoc on his life.

* * *

Lula and April exited the Illinois Hall arm-in-arm as April gushed about the play.

"Weren't you thrilled? I can't believe what I've seen. I'm simply amazed. Thank you so much for this evening. I'll never forget it."

"What was your favorite part?"

"Oh, definitely the horses, Bucephalus and Pegasus. To think they were able to pull a fire wagon onto the stage. I thought the dog was incredible, too. How do they get a dog to perform so well?"

"Have you never been to a circus or a fair?"

"Not that I recall."

"Harry Lacy is a Broadway actor. I've seen him in plays before. I'm surprised actors of his renown are willing to come all the way to Los Angeles to perform.

But this city is growing like wildfire. I'm sorry Noah took the carriage tonight."

"Oh, the trolley is fine by me. How are you doing?"

"Never better," admitted Mrs. Chandler.

Neither woman noticed the tall, observant man across the street. Noah exited the restaurant for a breath of fresh air. Deidre, her young friends and cousin were intolerably irritating. It appeared his mother and her protégé were having quite a fine time. Noah took a deep breath. He would have to make a point of meeting this woman who so enchanted his mother.

* * *

As Noah helped Lula into the carriage after church, he made an effort to return to her good graces. He had tired of uncomfortable silence.

"Did Miss Stringham wish to join us today? I didn't think to ask."

"It's a little late since church is over," Lula sarcastically replied. "Besides, it's her day off. I wouldn't wish her to feel obliged."

"What can I do to make things up to you?" Noah graciously offered. "I'll be busy with Deidre this week, however."

"She's coming for tea on Wednesday."

"Thank you for inviting her. She explained her role in the fiasco on Friday."

"I'm sure she did."

"You two have quite different versions of that afternoon."

"No doubt." If her son could not see the truth in front of his face, she would not help him. Often, allowing children to make their own mistakes proved more effective than pointing errors out as they occurred.

"I saw you last night. Why didn't you tell me you were going downtown?"

"Are you spying on me now?"

Noah snorted in derision. "Hardly. I happened to be across the street and noticed you exiting the theater. How risqué of you. Public conveyance at night?"

"I don't think it's any of your business."

"Fair enough. I could have arranged your transportation, had you bothered to tell me."

"But you needed to haul the lovely Deidre to her destination, didn't you?"

"Why do you find it necessary to be so snide? The girl will be your daughter soon."

"Girl. That's the problem. She's much too young for you." Lula comprehended how quickly she abandoned her plan to allow her son his own errors. As he prattled on in an effort to ingratiate himself, an idea took root in Lula's mind. An undeniably brilliant idea.

* * *

"Mrs. Fitzpatrick informs me dinner will be ready shortly," Lula announced as she took a seat in the parlor and picked up her book. Her son sat at the writing desk, reviewing bills. "I better warn you. You'll be getting an invoice from Wineburgh's."

"My, you are making the rounds lately. A shopping excursion?"

"Yes, for Miss Stringham."

A scowl met her comment as Noah turned to obtain more information. "Why? I spent enough money on that woman just getting her here."

"Nonetheless, I wished to go to the theater and she didn't have proper attire." Lula knew when her son caught sight of the bill, there would be further unpleasant discussion. She might as well prepare the way.

"She's a paid companion. She couldn't attend in her workaday clothes?"

"Not with me. No, she couldn't."

"I'll tell you what I think. Miss Stringham is playing you like a fiddle. She's taking advantage. I will not be liable for any further purchases on her behalf, do you understand?"

"You owe her far more than the price of a dress. Whether you choose to believe it or not, she's the one who saved your dinner. How much will you make from Mr. Devlin's business? He seemed quite pleased when he departed. I imagine he won't hesitate to use your services. The price of a dress hardly seems an issue."

"When did you buy the dress? Before the dinner, I would imagine."

"That doesn't make it any less owing on your part."

"Your inference I owe her anything is becoming tedious. She's a servant in this household. She should be grateful for her salary and the home we provide. I don't want to hear any more about her. I don't want you spending another dime on her. I believed at first she might prove useful, but I'm sorry I ever hired her."

Lula looked toward the doorway to find an ashen-faced April who evidently had come in from out of doors. Noting his mother's expression, Noah also looked toward the entrance.

"I'm so sorry," April commented. "I didn't mean

to interrupt." The sound of hurried footsteps on the stairs proved a precursor to another uncomfortably quiet evening.

Chapter Four

Once she reached the attic, April took a deep breath and gathered her composure. No matter how much Lula liked her, Mr. Chandler employed her. His dissatisfaction seemed obvious.

Her journey to California came to mind. Quickly adapting to life on the train, April chose to sleep in her seat rather than splurge on a sleeper car. Meals were taken in the dining car or quickly obtained at a Harvey House Restaurant, which catered to passengers during brief stops along the route.

She managed to purchase a Los Angeles newspaper at one stop. The *Los Angeles Herald* proved a fountain of information. April was first intrigued by a tragic tale of drowning. A man and woman were swimming in the ocean at Long Beach when strong currents carried them out to sea. The man drowned trying to save his companion who was later rescued by another gentleman. The victim's wife, having recovered from recent illness, watched the tragedy unfold from her seat in a buggy on the beach. The poor woman suffered a setback and recovery seemed unlikely.

April became enthralled by another article titled

"A Profitable Occupation for Girls and One That They Enjoy." The informative commentary included the interview of an attractive young woman who relished her job as a bill collector. She found businessmen were almost always willing to settle their accounts on the spot. Collecting from women proved only slightly more difficult. The ladies tended to keep her waiting and weren't as cordial. Even so, she rarely needed to go on a collection more than twice. The interviewee also offered practical tips on how to collect bills. April found the article extremely enlightening and contemplated the idea women were less constrained by convention in the West. Using tiny scissors kept in her reticule, she carefully clipped the article for her collection, feeling it didn't hurt to have a few career ideas in case her new job did not pan out.

Since her arrival, April snipped articles from the *Herald* almost daily. Sorting through her stash, she pulled out the one about bill collecting. She found a few help wanted ads and made a stack on her nightstand. Boarding house advertisements made a second pile. Having not been fired yet, she had time to find another position.

As April picked up the articles, she uncovered a book. A closet fan of the dime novel, she understood the source of her ideas about the Wild West was laughable. She fully expected to step off the train to find saloons full of drunken cowboys, wild Indians riding bareback through the streets, miners toting pickaxes, and shootouts occurring on every street corner. Towns she saw from the train appeared as she imagined Los Angeles must be, although she only managed a distant view of life from her window.

There was an idea. Always believing she could

imagine more entertaining dime novels than she read, perhaps she would try her hand at writing. April certainly lived in the proper locale to add authenticity to her tales and had ample free time each evening to explore this possibility. April even found an ad for a publisher looking for fresh material. There would be no Black Bart in her novel, but she grinned at the idea of a villain based on Mr. Chandler.

* * *

April and Lula enjoyed their breakfast until they were startled by the flamboyant entrance of the man of the house.

"Good morning," Noah's voice boomed across the table. "I thought I might join you for breakfast today." Noting congenial banter ceased upon his entrance, Noah wondered when he became such an ogre. Women were likely not worth the trouble, but he decided yet again to smooth things over. He was a lawyer after all and could be charming if he wished to be. At this, the recently returned actual Margarita poked her head through the kitchen door.

"I get you a plate, Mr. Noah."

There was another expenditure. Margarita's reemployment hinged on her assertion she deserved yet another raise.

"Miss Stringham, I must apologize. I've been busy since you joined our household and haven't had the opportunity to properly make your acquaintance." Noah offered his hand to provide a sturdy handshake. "Nice to meet you. I understand you've successfully entertained my mother since your arrival. I thank you for your efforts and for the excellent meal you provided last Friday."

"How lovely, Noah. Now please refrain from ruining our breakfast," commented Lula.

"But, how would I?"

"By talking." At this, Lula handed her son the newspaper and directed her attention to April. "I thought today, we might return to Wineburgh's if you wouldn't mind accompanying me."

April noticed her employer's glare over the top of the newspaper.

"We can take the trolley," April offered.

"Excellent. I'm considering purchasing a household item."

"What exactly might we be needing?" inquired Mr. Chandler.

"You never questioned any expenditure I previously felt necessary. Is there some reason why you would doubt my judgment now?"

Mr. Chandler first glanced April's way before carefully replying, "Certainly not. As always, whatever you feel we need. Although I did assume the house was in order. I'm a bit surprised we're wanting anything further."

Lula gave her son a condescending smirk. "It's become apparent I overlooked an important purchase. I intend to correct my error today."

Noah became lost in his own thoughts as the two women conversed. His trial would begin at the end of the week. He much enjoyed this aspect of his profession but never relished the exhaustive preparation. Juggling his work responsibilities with Deidre's extensive social calendar proved difficult. He desired a diversion, something physical. His baseball team, the Boyle Heights Browns, disbanded until spring. Perhaps he might be able to fit in a ride on

Checkers if he finished early today.

* * *

April's eyebrows furrowed. "I don't think you should do this."

"Why ever not?" inquired Lula. "I thought this was exactly what you had in mind."

"That's the thing. *I* had it in mind. It was never my intention for you to buy a sewing machine, much less something marked up this much."

"But the more I thought about it, the more I feel it's a necessity. We can do our own mending this way. The machine will pay for itself in no time."

"Perhaps if you were running a Chinese laundry, it might prove profitable."

Lula laughed. "I have the feeling you're attempting to keep me out of trouble."

"Yes, I suppose I am."

Lula linked her arm through her companion's and wandered toward the counter. "I need to explain a few things to you. My son never questioned any purchase I made while I furnished his house. He never intended it as a home. To him it's a showcase, an extension of his office, something he very much desired but felt inadequate to complete properly on his own. I spent lavishly and I believe I managed to make a real home and a proper venue for Noah to entertain clients."

"It is lovely."

"My point is, Noah wanted the house; he never questioned what I spent. Since he has what he wants, his bank account is suddenly subject to careful scrutiny. Trust me, if he can afford what I spent, he can afford an over-priced sewing machine. Let's look at fabric after we order the machine."

"It's just—I wish to keep my position."

Lula smiled and patting April's hand, encouraged, "Don't worry, my dear. I have my own funds. Noah won't be booting you out of the house, you have my word. Tell me something."

"About what?

"Why did you never marry?"

"School friends drifted away over time. To be honest, the only boy who ever showed any interest was William from the neighboring farm. He seemed pleasant enough, but I never encouraged him. He was dull beyond belief. My life had a single focus—the care of my mother. Eventually, he gave up."

"Well, that's simply another instance of the idiocy of males," Lula surmised.

* * *

Sneering as his silver tooth sparkled in the lamplight, Charlie Boatman ignored the girl crouched on the floor at his feet.

"Please, sir, I beg you. My father is not well. I'm sorry I'm late. I can scrub the floor in no time. You don't even have to pay me. A bowl of gruel is all I require. Please, sir, please."

"Get out," Charlie mocked.

Sobbing, Little May rose to her feet and dragged her weary body toward the batwing saloon doors. As she reached the portal, Charlie Boatman pushed her with the heel of his shiny black boot. Little May, struggling to keep her balance, soon sprawled in the street. At least there was snow to cushion her fall.

April tapped her pencil on her lips as she considered the next sentence. Realizing Lula was at tea for a considerable amount of time, April decided to see if she could help.

Slowing her pace at the bottom of the staircase, she entered the parlor where Lula and her future daughter-in-law conversed.

"Can I get you anything?" April inquired.

"Would you mind bringing another plate of Margarita's cookies?" inquired Lula. "This one seems to be empty." The older woman frowned as she nodded at her young guest. "Why don't you join us when you return?" she added enthusiastically.

"If you wouldn't mind, I'd love a cup of tea. I'll be right back."

"Your friendship with servants is rather alarming, Mother Chandler," commented Deidre. "And as a matter of fact, I *do* mind."

"That is rather too bad. This is still my home and I can invite whomever I like to tea." Lula smiled condescendingly. The meeting had not gone well. Lula grew weary of pretense.

As April set the plate of cookies on the side table, Lula requested, "Would you mind pouring out another cup of tea, Deidre?"

Although her reply was proper enough, "Certainly," Deidre appeared immensely unhappy at the request. She quickly poured the tea and handed the cup to April without looking in her direction. She scooted her chair toward Lula in an attempt to distance April from their conversation.

"Mother Chandler, my parents are eager to meet you and naturally wish to become better acquainted with Noah. I believe they plan to invite you to San Francisco for the holidays. I hope you'll consider their request carefully. Coming to grips with my impending marriage has taken my mother some time. She always loved her cats more than me. It's the reason she sent me to boarding school."

A number of interesting responses flitted through Lula's thoughts, none of them polite.

"Travel is somewhat difficult for me, but I'll keep an eye out for the invitation."

"It would be to your advantage," the younger woman commented.

April thought the response wholly inappropriate, almost a threat.

Deidre continued, "I have a problem and hoped you might help. I want something special for Noah's Christmas gift. Perhaps you have suggestions. I wish to consider his preferences as far as presents are concerned. Did your family have opulent celebrations? Would an expensive gift be appropriate or considered only an obligation to be returned in kind?"

How like the girl to couch gift-giving in a monetary framework. She actually seemed eager to force an obligation on her betrothed. "When the children were small, I enjoyed splurging on toys and games, but our gifts have never been what I would call opulent," Lula replied.

"But you don't feel a lavish gift would be unwelcome?"

Understanding her ideas would not be appreciated, April decided to join the conversation regardless.

"I always thought a gift should remind the recipient of the giver, for instance, something your future husband would use every day and remember you. He is a natty dresser. Some exquisite handkerchiefs would make a lovely gift. He would think of you each time he placed one in his pocket, over his heart."

Deidre's obvious displeasure was reflected in the tone of her next comment. "It's not the caliber of gift I had in mind. I'll simply have to find something on my own."

The stilted conversation continued for a brief time before Deidre glanced at the clock and quickly rose from her chair. "Goodness, I'm late for my dress fitting. Noah is taking me to a concert at the Chautauqua this weekend. Thank you, Mother Chandler. This has been lovely."

Ignoring April, Deidre kissed Lula on the cheek and made a hasty exit. As Lula closed the front door, she and April dissolved into laughter.

"That child is such a fool, pretending to be a great lady when she's barely grown. I'm sorry, April, I shouldn't have asked you to join us, but I lost my patience. Your presence managed to keep me in check." Heaving a rather heavy sigh, Lula admitted, "I'm concerned about Noah."

April, surprised at the comment, inquired, "Why?" Lula and Mr. Chandler shared a feisty relationship from what April observed.

As the ladies took their seats and poured more tea, Lula continued, "I don't want him to throw his life away and I'm quite certain it's exactly what he's doing."

"But they make such a fine-looking couple. For all her immaturity, Deidre seems devoted to your son."

"You could be confusing devotion with competition. Noah was engaged twice before. I believe little Miss Deidre simply wishes to succeed where others failed. A distant cousin of hers named Martha was Noah's last betrothed. I even believe the girl is so desperate to capture my son, she would stop at nothing to assure the marriage contract will be fulfilled, if you get my meaning."

Rather shocked, April continued, "Why would she marry simply to best her cousin?"

"Oh, Noah certainly has his charms. I'm not denying that. But he has misguided ideas about marriage. It's quite odd the way a boy accepts some of his father's plans but adamantly rejects others.

"You see, I had six children, three boys and three girls. Eve is my eldest, then there were two boys. One died as an infant and one at birth. Then Noah came along and the two younger girls, Anna and Sarah. Anna and Noah were inseparable. She died in childbirth, my, it's been ten years now.

"Since Noah was the only surviving male child, my husband focused a great deal of attention on him, not necessarily for the good. Marshall probably meant well, but he pressured Noah from an early age. Noah had to be the best at whatever he did and was groomed to take on the role of head of household and head of the family law firm. In many ways, he lived up to exactly what his father wished him to be. He always excelled in physical and academic competition. He obtained his law degree and it appeared to me he would fulfil all of Marshall's expectations.

"Noah is his father's son, ever eager to give his clients an advantage, even if the advantage is merely aesthetic. A well-groomed and fashionably dressed defendant never fails to portray innocence. My husband always went for the jugular in court. Noah's forms of persuasion can be more subtle but equally dramatic.

"Unexpectedly, he rejected the idea of staying in New York and following in his father's footsteps. His plan proved unappealing to my husband. Marshall and Noah argued bitterly before Noah departed, unable to resist the allure of the West. My husband passed away within the year. They never saw each other again."

"I'm so sorry."

"Such is life. For some reason I cannot comprehend, Noah has again taken his father's ideas to heart. You see, my husband pursued me for my family's financial advantage. He never made a secret about the benefits he felt he achieved from our union."

"Did you love him?" April didn't intend to blurt out her query. "I'm sorry, it's none of my business."

"That's the thing, I did love him and I know he loved me. I never understood why Marshall felt it necessary to encourage Noah in this manner. Noah has reached an age where he desires a wife and family. He has 'traded up' as he puts it, to greatest business advantage. Deidre is a railroad heiress, or rather her mother is. Her family will, no doubt, be of tremendous benefit to Noah's law firm. But this girl is completely inappropriate as his wife. I have argued and tried to make Noah understand, but there doesn't seem to be much I can do about this disastrous marriage."

Seeing Mrs. Chandler's distress, April changed the subject in an effort to salvage the remainder of the afternoon. "Why don't we stop by and visit Mrs. Barnes tomorrow?"

Lula failed to make many friends in Los Angeles, but she did occasionally visit a few ladies from church. She met Mrs. Barnes when she stayed at the St. Angelo Hotel on Bunker Hill before Noah's house finished.

"It's a fine idea. April, have you ever been to the beach?"

"No. I've never actually seen the ocean, although the train went through Boston."

"Did you know the Pacific Ocean is only a short distance from here? Do you think you could determine how we might make our way on the train to Redondo Beach?" Lula could not help but grin at the overjoyed expression on April's face. What a delight she was, so different in every way from Deidre.

* * *

"Noah, you understand how much I hate the beach, don't you? We need to get out of the wind and sea spray immediately. It's ruining my hair and can't be good for my new dress."

Appreciation of the fantastic setting proved difficult while Deidre pouted and whined. Nonetheless, Noah attempted to enjoy the sound of the waves and the fresh air as they walked from the Chautauqua Amphitheater toward the station. He was intrigued by the various beachfront amusements and regretted their visit would end with the concert. Ignoring Deidre, Noah strolled slowly down the boardwalk, lit by gas lamps. Steam engine train service only recently connected to Redondo Beach.

The new Hotel Redondo loomed over the seaside. Noah would gladly have indulged his desire to take a look at the interior. During a recent business trip, he stayed at the Redondo's sister hotel in San Diego, the Hotel Del Coronado.

Redondo was the main port for Los Angeles. Sport fishing was allegedly unsurpassed. The largest salt water plunge in the world was here. On the pier, games and rides competed for space with a thriving shipping trade. Lost in his reverie, Noah stopped abruptly, having caught sight of a most unexpected couple making their way from the pier.

"What is it?" Deidre complained. Frantic to get out of the salt air, she craned her neck to determine what halted Noah in his tracks.

"Why Mother, fancy meeting you here," Noah commented. Arm-in-arm, delighted expressions graced the features of his mother and the younger, sun-burned woman who paused at his greeting. He would have to admit, the pair seemed surprised at his presence. Leave it to his mother to be having the better time. "What exactly are you up to?"

"We decided to take the train to Redondo. We've had a marvelous time. First, we picnicked at the shore. We spent hours collecting moonstones and gems. They're piled on the beach. It's quite a magnificent sight. We visited the carnation gardens and dined at the hotel. We even tried our hand at a few games, even though I know better. But look! April won this small stuffed cat. She's quite a good aim."

"Or simply lucky," added Miss Stringham.

"What are you two doing here?" inquired Lula of her son, but he was not the one who replied.

"Why Mother Chandler, you know very well. I mentioned the concert when I joined you for tea earlier this week."

"That's right. You certainly did. I didn't remember the Chautauqua Amphitheater was here."

Noah could tell his mother was lying. He imagined Deidre knew as well. Miss Stringham, however, appeared to be completely taken in. Although he believed the woman to be the root of his current problems with his mother, she always appeared an innocent. Perhaps his mother was becoming senile. She never behaved inappropriately as long as he could remember. Or perhaps Miss Stringham was far more cunning than she seemed.

"It's getting late. Why don't you ladies join us on the ride back to Los Angeles?"

"I don't believe we're quite ready yet, Son. We were contemplating ice cream sodas."

"I insist. It wouldn't be proper for you to stay out any later unchaperoned." In fact, he thought his mother's recent escapades wholly improper.

Noting the large bunch of carnations poking from a picnic basket on Miss Stringham's arm, Noah grabbed the handle, expecting the flower-filled basket to be light. Instead, he nearly dropped the heavy object, surprised the handles did not give way.

"What the hell is in here?"

"Please, Noah, there are ladies present. They will think you were poorly brought up if you continue in this vein," noted his mother. "The moonstones and gemstones are inside."

"The two of you must have cleaned off the entire beach," Noah complained.

"Oh, those belong to Mrs. Chandler," April noted. "Mine are here." She pulled her precious stones out of her pocket, having been more discerning than her elder.

Frowning severely, Noah escorted the ladies to the train as Deidre continued her tirade. He suddenly dreaded the 90-minute ride back to the city.

* * *

Lula clasped April's arm and headed into the theater.

Although Lula was older than most in the crowd, she felt far younger than her years. Her companion's enthusiasm had an invigorating effect.

"I did once see a magic lantern show at church," April spoke quickly in her excitement. "The Bible stories fairly leapt off the wall they used for a screen. The congregation joined in hymns as the words appeared beneath pictures. I felt it awe-inspiring, but some parishioners thought the entire display too theatrical and not properly solemn for church."

"I don't believe this Halloween program will be solemn in any way. But then, it's not meant to be." Lula thought the more risqué magic lantern shows she'd seen in New York would likely shock her young companion. Perhaps the Halloween program would even prove too intense.

Once the show started, Lula couldn't tell which she enjoyed more, the program or April's reactions. As always, the audience provided sound effects. Lula stopped watching the show completely when the image of a snoring man appeared. She knew what came next. As April made her own snoring sounds, a large rat appeared near the man's face. April nearly jumped out of her seat and gripped Lula's arm when the man snored so loudly, he swallowed the rat whole. She then dissolved into wild laughter, so intent on the screen, she didn't notice Lula's delighted observation.

There were goblins, ghouls and ghosts aplenty; giant bugs crawled into Victorian beds. Ghoulish songs played in the background during a recital of *The Raven*. "The Parade of Goblins" served as a finale. *The Worms Crawl In, The Worms Crawl Out* accompanied animated monster slides.

The ladies went for chocolate milk shakes, the

latest craze, before taking the trolley home. An excited April chattered on about the performance.

"This was much more dramatic than the program at church. Did you notice how the point of view shifts? The dissolving images, close-ups and fade-ins were quite artistic."

Lula replied, "Mr. Beale is extremely good at his craft. It's why his programs continue to entertain. I believe we should make it a point to attend shows highlighting faraway places and historic sites. Some recreate great literature and history. The newer programs use actual photographs."

April became more enthusiastic at each of Lula's suggestions. Lula could not recall the last time she felt so alive, an odd result considering the macabre drama of the evening. The ladies agreed to incorporate magic lantern programs into their activities whenever possible.

Chapter Five

A crestfallen Little May stared into the icy cold, grey eyes of Charlie Boatman. The few coins in her hand were all that separated her from complete poverty. She clutched them as tightly as possible, determined to return home with the ever-dwindling profits from her eggs.

"Where do you think you're going?" growled Charlie.

"Home, sir."

"What have you got there?"

"Nothing, nothing," Little May nervously replied.

Grabbing her arm, Charlie snarled, "I think that is something." He pried Little May's fingers apart.

"It's only my egg money. Please, sir, it's all I have to feed me and Pa."

"Your Pa owes me money."

Little May stared up at the tall man, afraid to move. Charlie snatched the coins from Little May's hand and pushed her toward the wall. Sliding to the floor, Little May resolved not to show weakness in front of her tormentor. But as soon as he walked around the corner, spurs jangling, she dissolved into tears. Whatever would she do now?

Pleased by the progress on her story, April considered her life since Mr. Chandler and Lula left to spend Christmas in San Francisco. The household was tranquil and frankly unproductive. Margarita rarely made an appearance. The Fitzpatricks continued to maintain the garden and house although winter and the absent Chandlers made for little work. April had ample time to write. Working up the gumption to submit her work to the publisher seemed her only stumbling block.

She gleefully purchased a ticket to the *Victorian Christmas Show*, a magic lantern production. The program featured magnificent hand-painted slides of *The Night Before Christmas* and *A Christmas Carol*. She joined in singing the illustrated carols. *Joy to the World* was her favorite. April thoroughly enjoyed the extravaganza. As she left the theater, April felt bewildered; her first Christmas away from home having caused no melancholy.

Was she an unfeeling woman? What kind of person could bury her mother and leave her lifelong home yet never experience a single regret? Hard as she tried now, April could not think of a single reason to return.

There were those in Concord who pitied her. She understood why people felt badly for her. That didn't make her any more accepting of their curious stares and false smiles. By their judgment, she'd been dealt a cruel hand. April never thought much about her lot in life. She was too busy trying to keep up.

Now, she had a new life—her own life, of her own making. If her job ended in June as it appeared would be the case, she could find another. As much as she enjoyed Lula's company, the thought of returning to the East Coast was not appealing.

The incredible California winter proved fascinating. Most days were quite mild, a few were even hot. It rained only occasionally and never for long. Out of habit, April expected it would turn cold and snow any day, but Christmas was as green as could be.

She made modest gifts for her fellow employees and even prepared a tin of homemade fudge for Mr. Chandler. April still needed to bind the quilt she made for Lula. The Chandlers were set to return shortly after New Year's. Since they were away, decorations seemed unnecessary although April set up a small tree in the kitchen. She cooked Christmas dinner for the Fitzpatricks. The household seemed to be on vacation.

Since her arrival, April had been intrigued by the modern conveniences in the Chandler home. Her appreciation continued to grow since she had free range of the house and no agenda. Never wanting to inconvenience others, she hastily used the claw foot bathtub. Now she lingered in the tub each night, reading and soaking to her heart's content. She delightedly cooked on the gas stove. The ice box kept everything fresh. Electric and gas lighting meant April could read or write anywhere in the house, even all night if she chose. She couldn't believe she was earning a living while doing exactly as she pleased.

By all rights, she should have been in San Francisco performing her duties. The fact she would be left behind became obvious one evening as she descended the stairs to retrieve a book from the kitchen. Lula and Mr. Chandler were arguing in the parlor.

"If you won't pay her train fare, I will," argued Lula.

"Deidre's father provided the tickets. He didn't send one for your companion and I think it best she stays here."

"I want her to come. She cheers me."

"No. She upsets Deidre and is a bad influence on you."

"Then I will stay. I'm not feeling well."

"If you think I would leave you to your own devices when you have behaved so outrageously, you must be out of your mind."

Feeling guilty for eavesdropping, April scampered up the stairs to her room. She didn't hear how the argument ended but knew the result well enough. A dour Lula accompanied her son to San Francisco.

Although she went to church every Sunday and knew Lula's few friends, April hadn't made friends of her own. Her long-held routine of church attendance remained intact. She acquired the habit of sneaking into the back pew as the service began then left before the closing hymn in order to avoid the pitiful stares she so detested. Church now seemed the perfect venue to make acquaintances, but women of April's age appeared to be married. She failed to identify a single spinster to befriend.

Longing to add authentic detail to her story, April fervently desired to travel past the city limits of Los Angeles. Knowing there were authors who wrote about the West having never set foot across the Mississippi, she wished to be less disingenuous. When she brought up her longing to explore, Lula explained it simply wasn't safe for women traveling alone, even by train.

April initially discounted the comment. She felt completely safe on the train and thought Lula might be exaggerating. But when Lula noted even Mr. Chandler carried a gun in the countryside, April's bravado dimmed.

So, it seemed a bit of a shock to learn her link to the Wild West might be living above the carriage house. On December 30, the headlines of the *Herald* were riveting. As April sat across the kitchen table from Mr. Fitzpatrick, she could not help but read aloud.

"Listen to this! The headlines are 'Indian Treachery.' There has been a massacre, Mr. Fitzpatrick, near Wounded Knee, South Dakota." April read bits and pieces of the article, which ended, "These Indians who had no guns rushed on the soldiers with tomahawk in one hand and scalping knife in the other. Oh, it was a demoniac, a hellishly horrible rush."

Although Mr. Fitzpatrick was unable to quell his curiosity, he finally shushed April and added, "Don't let Mrs. Fitzpatrick see the article about the Indians."

Before April could make an inquiry, Mrs. Fitzpatrick appeared in the kitchen doorway. "Indians? What Indians?" she almost screamed.

"Not your Indians," Mr. Fitzpatrick quickly assured, but it was too late. His wife pulled her apron up to her mouth and ran from the kitchen, hastily retreating to her home.

"Now, that's done it," Mr. Fitzpatrick proclaimed as he threw his napkin on the table and departed in kind.

April absently picked at the remainder of her breakfast while dramatic scenarios developed in her imagination. Had Mrs. Fitzpatrick been the victim of a vicious Indian attack? Had she been taken hostage? Had she lived amongst the red man? Perhaps the answer to her prayers worked right beside her all this while. But how could she possibly address this issue?

Perhaps Mrs. Fitzpatrick was treated roughly or possibly violated. She might never be able to assuage April's curiosity. April wished her attempt at journalism to have historical significance even if the plot was sensational and dramatic. The focus of her research abruptly settled mere yards from the back door.

After April spent the afternoon reading through her story—being as neutral as possible—she declared this first effort ready for submission. She would do her best to find ways to add authenticity to her next tale.

Having dropped off the manuscript on Wednesday, New Year's Eve, April headed for home, realizing her work would likely never see the light of day much less provide any financial return. April stopped at Germain's as a reward for her initial journalistic effort and her bravery at actually submitting it. A small heliotrope for the attic windowsill comprised her modest purchase.

The clerk assured, although it was late for starting sweet peas, they would do fine if planted right away. If April never previously comprehended California's different climate, it hit home now. It would have been much too early to plant her favorite flower in the Northeast.

Having acquired some fine gauge wire on one of her shopping expeditions, April wove lengths of wire on the diagonal, then attached gemstones from Redondo Beach at each intersection. This hung in the west-facing dormer window where she intended to place today's purchase. Her attic bedroom remained her refuge although she spent considerable time on the lower floor in recent weeks.

The Chandlers would soon return. An eager April wanted to know all about Lula's trip. She hoped Mr. Chandler's time would be occupied by wedding plans and work. Perhaps she would start on the next volume of her novel in the meantime should her first effort prove fruitful.

* * *

Since Mrs. Fitzpatrick failed to emerge from her apartment over the carriage house, cooking and household chores fell to Mrs. Chandler's companion. Mr. Fitzpatrick enjoyed April's cooking. He did not hesitate to convey his gratitude.

"Did Mrs. Fitzpatrick enjoy her breakfast tray?"

"She did. I imagine Margarita will make an appearance today and things will return to normal. I believe my wife is up to some dusting and cleaning. Thank you again for your help."

"So, Mrs. Fitzpatrick is feeling fit?" Seeking solid information, April didn't want to signal her curiosity.

"She seems to be doing well. Her little holiday did a world of good. Our home over the carriage house is her sanctuary."

"Her reaction to the story about Wounded Knee seemed quite extreme," April fished for information, any information.

"Oh, Wounded Knee didn't particularly upset her, aside from the natural distress anyone would feel about the story. It was the mention of Indians."

"I see. Your wife had an unfortunate experience with Indians, I take it." Trying to appear nonchalant,

April busied herself at the stove, fearing Mr. Fitzpatrick would think her overly nosy and end the conversation.

Mr. Fitzpatrick chuckled. "Not our kind of Indians, no."

"What other kind of Indians are there?" April didn't intend to blurt out the question and was relieved when Mr. Fitzpatrick continued talking.

"The kind Columbus searched for. India Indians." Mr. Fitzpatrick peered over his coffee cup to find his cooking benefactress sporting a befuddled expression. "My father-in-law was a career military man in the English Army, stationed in India. Charlotte's mother died when she was 19 and he sent for her. As you can tell, my wife has a delicate constitution. She found life in India too rugged. She detested the bugs, the oppressive humidity, the poverty and sickness. She became quite severely ill. That's when I showed up to rescue her. I had a stint in the military and was sent to India. I couldn't wait to see the world so I bought passage once my time was up. Charlotte married me for the price of a ticket.

"Once we set foot in California, I couldn't budge her. She liked the dry climate and sunny days. You wouldn't believe how much Los Angeles has changed since we arrived. They pull down and build up at an astonishing rate here. People started coming in droves once the railroad came through. We found a refuge working for Mr. Chandler. Hopefully, he'll keep this house once he marries. I'm concerned about our positions. I know God will provide and I haven't brought this to my wife's attention." Mr. Fitzpatrick looked up from his meal to warn, "I believe we all should be concerned."

April nodded. Despite uncertainty over future employment, she felt devastated her source of information dried up. She needed some other way to provide authentic detail to her writing.

As Mr. Fitzpatrick predicted, Margarita appeared that afternoon. The Chandlers returned from their journey before dinner. April noted a stony silence between Lula and her son. Since both retired early, she had to wait for morning to satisfy her curiosity about their trip.

* * *

April bounded down the stairs and took her place at the breakfast table bright and early, surprised to find Lula already seated. No sooner did April lay her napkin in her lap than Mr. Chandler passed outside the dining room door tersely declaring, "I'm going for a ride," before making a hasty departure.

"What happened?" a curious April inquired, taking a close look at Lula who appeared quite haggard.

"I sent Mr. Fitzpatrick to order a horse from the stable. I need to do some errands today."

"You didn't want to take the trolley?" April understood Mr. Chandler's horse, Checkers, was for his entertainment and not trained to pull a carriage. On Sunday mornings or any other day Lula wished to use the carriage, the livery stable delivered a horse and driver and billed Mr. Chandler accordingly.

"Not today. My morning is full of boring business matters. There's no reason for you to come. I intend to catch up on my rest this afternoon. So you, my dear, have the day off." Although Lula focused on her errands, she displayed a warm smile after reciting her agenda.

April attempted to contain her glee at this turn of events. After having been free to do as she liked over past weeks, she hesitated to request time off. A missive arrived late yesterday afternoon from one Mr. Lynch who read her story and wished to meet. For better or worse, April would soon discover the fate of her writing venture.

And so, the two women, each with a secret, each with an agenda, set off in separate directions.

* * *

Mr. Lynch seemed a rather coarse individual. The man offered April a chair across his desk but did not stand as a gentleman would when she entered his office. She sat in silence, waiting to begin their meeting. Mr. Lynch stared at the last page of her text, restlessly tapping the end of his pencil on the desk. She wondered if he bothered to read the story before he summoned her.

April guessed the man to be about 50. Bald except for a band of short graying hair above his neck, he puffed furiously on a pipe. Smoke filled his office. April noted icy blue eyes squinting over thick spectacles when Mr. Lynch finally remembered he had a visitor. She believed his sharp glare was meant to intimidate. April glared right back.

"Who wrote this story?" he began.

"My father is A. Stringham." This was an honest enough statement even if it didn't answer the question.

"*You* wrote this, didn't you?"

Lifting her chin in defiance, April replied, "What makes you think so?"

Lynch liked the spunk of this girl. He relaxed into

his chair to observe her more closely. "You're an old maid?"

"I hardly think that is any of your business, Mr. Lynch."

"It is my business. I want to know who I'm getting involved with here."

This seemed an encouraging comment. April decided to cooperate. "I am unmarried, yes."

"And you wrote this?"

"I did."

"Why did you try to lie about it?"

"Because you will pay me less than you would were I a man."

"That is entirely true." Lynch was intrigued. "Are you currently employed?"

"I am."

"And your father approves of your using his name to sell your piece?"

"My father is much too dead to care."

Lynch tried his best not to smile. "I take it from the length of this story, you intend it as a dime novel?"

"Correct. It's almost 25,000 words, a 100-page book—exactly what your advertisement requested."

"It did." Surprised the woman could be at all knowledgeable about what she submitted, Lynch continued, "But I want your story for something else. You've heard of *The North American Review*?"

April couldn't hide her enthusiasm. "I have indeed. It's quite prestigious."

"Well, that's not mine. I'm interested in developing a magazine uniquely western along those lines."

"What is the name of your periodical?"

"You've heard of *Atlantic Monthly*?"

"Of course."

"Well, that's not mine either. What I want to do is publish your story in segments. It lends itself to a serial format. I hope women will clamor to read each installment and sales of my weekly magazine will hit the roof. I'll pay you $10 for your first story."

Knowing the going rate for dime novelists was well above his offer but thrilled to become a real authoress, April countered, "I'll let you have it for 25."

"Your demand is outrageous. You're an unknown. This is a risk on my part." Lynch stared at his adversary who gave him a critical look. "I tell you what. I'll give you $20 but not a cent more. You can submit your next story and we'll negotiate further then."

April considered the fact she made $3 a week plus room and board. If she continued writing at the same rate, she could add substantially to her savings before June. Wanting as many options as possible when she lost her position, April rose and offered her hand. "You have a deal, Mr. Lynch. But you didn't tell me the name of your magazine."

"*Pacific Weekly*."

"I don't think I've heard of it."

"That's because we're about to launch the premier issue. You're getting in on the ground floor, little lady. I do believe you need a pen name. Stringham is much too unusual and I prefer our readers think you are a man."

"Fine, I'll be known as S. Armstrong. Will that do?"

April harbored doubts about Mr. Lynch and his premier edition, but she was $20 richer. She had nothing to lose.

* * *

No sooner did April walk through the front door than she turned to answer it. She found a well-dressed, tall, slender, blond man. He seemed shocked to see her.

"Oh, you must be Mrs. Chandler's companion. I expected someone more advanced in age." Jack believed the words "old maid" did not do justice to the lovely woman who answered the door.

"You have me at a disadvantage, sir."

"Sorry, I'm Jack Broadmore, Noah's partner. Is he in? He was supposed to be at work a few hours ago."

"I only recently arrived myself. I'd have to find out." But April's quest became unnecessary as another man bounded onto the porch.

"Is Mrs. Chandler here?" he inquired, so breathless he could hardly speak.

"I believe so. I can see," April offered.

"Please tell her Checkers returned to the stable rider-less. Mr. Chandler is missing. We're about to mount a search."

"I'll come along," offered the dapper Mr. Broadmore.

The two men hurried on their way, leaving April to explain the unfortunate news to Lula Chandler.

* * *

"I'm certain everything will be all right," offered April as she sat across the dinner table from her friend.

"I'm sure you're right, my dear." Lula only picked at her supper. "Noah is an excellent horseman, there's really no need for concern. He might have been far from the city. It's a long walk back."

April didn't know what more she could say to

-68-

ease the strain.

Lula initiated a dialogue, as if she thought aloud. "I love Noah. I know it must not look as if I do. He is actually my dearest child. He and Anna were such sweet children. My other daughters are a bit, how would I say, prickly. They've always been difficult girls. They are their husbands' problems now."

She looked directly at April. "Our recent trip was most unsatisfactory. We did nothing but fight from the time we left Los Angeles. I don't believe there's anything I can do to dissuade Noah from this marriage. It's a difficult thing for a mother to watch her favorite child throw his life away. Noah is well-suited to Deidre's family. He seems quite in his element. But Deidre is not suitable to be his wife and I will never change my opinion of that arrogant, rude, childish girl. Dee, as her family calls her, is spoiled and sullen. She'll make Noah miserable. I've never been so sure of anything in my life. I normally don't form such strong opinions, but my impressions solidify more each time we meet."

Lula laid her fork on her plate, unwilling to continue her meal. "On our way back to Los Angeles, I told Noah I planned to disinherit him. I didn't know any other way to sufficiently demonstrate my displeasure at his present course."

"What did he say?" April could not hide her curiosity.

"He pretended it didn't matter. It's not as if my money is important to him, although he seemed to take issue. He stands to make his own fortune from business Deidre's family will provide. It was the shame of disinheritance that undoubtedly caused his headlong flight out of here this morning." Tears glistened in Lula's eyes. "I went today to alter my will and do some banking before I changed my mind. What if he's been injured or worse? This is my fault."

"Nonsense. Whatever happened is hardly your fault. If Mr. Chandler fell off his horse, it was his own doing. And if the horse simply ran off, you're worrying for nothing."

Lula looked across the table, knowing full well she would have continued home on the train if not for April. The girl depended on her job in the Chandler household. Lula played her last card as far as her son was concerned. She doubted anything further could be accomplished by staying in Los Angeles.

"Thank you for your help. I'm tired. I'm going to lie down. Promise me you'll come for me whenever there's news?"

"I will," April confirmed then retreated to her attic to pass the time.

* * *

Little May listened intently at the window.

"I won't marry you, Mr. Boatman."

"Call me Charlie. We're about to be wed."

"My heart belongs to another."

Boatman sneered. "I assure you, Delia, I intend to have you as my wife. If you fail to appear at the courthouse tomorrow morning, you'll be visiting the graveyard by the end of day. Your precious Albert won't survive to see the sunset."

Little May moved to the side of the cabin as the evil Charlie Boatman exited. However could she rescue her sister from a fate worse than death?

April flinched at the sound of men's voices in the

stairwell. Mr. Chandler's angry diatribe was completely audible.

"Why the hell would you knock on the door? I live here."

"Calm down, Noah."

As the men made their way toward the front bedroom, another knock sounded at the door.

"It's probably Bill and the doctor. Go get him, Jon. I'll grab your knee, Noah. Lay back on the bed."

April could hear Mr. Chandler groan loudly as she walked down the stairs and rapped on Lula's door. "He's here," she whispered as the door opened.

April put her arm around Lula's waist as the women proceeded to Mr. Chandler's bedroom.

"What has happened?" Lula inquired from the doorway.

Mr. Broadmore replied. "A snake spooked Checkers and he reared and fell. Noah didn't manage to get out of the way. His leg is broken. We already sent for the doctor."

April craned her neck to get a better view. Two men stood beside a large four-poster bed in the well-appointed room, the most spacious April ever saw, not that she had much experience to draw upon. Although curious, she avoided exploration of the second-floor rooms when she had the chance. The walls were richly paneled below the chair rail. Opulent draperies covered windows on three walls. Ornately carved furniture decorated the room, including a heavy roll-top desk. Magnificent oriental carpets covered dark wooden floors. April could not help but admire Lula's taste. This room was every bit as grand as the parlor downstairs.

Her attention returned to the bed, where

Mr. Chandler groaned as the men repositioned him. April could see Mr. Chandler's leg made an unnatural turn above his boot. The two women moved through the doorway to allow the doctor to pass.

After tipping his hat to the ladies, the doctor approached the bed. "What have you gone and done to this leg, Noah? You sure as hell can't play catcher like this." The doctor opened his bag and withdrew a vial and syringe. "I'm going to make you comfortable then we'll set this leg so you'll be ready to play again come spring."

"Miss," the doctor looked toward April. "Do you think you could get the gardener to bring a bucket of sand?"

"I know where it is," offered April.

By the time she returned, Mr. Chandler's leg hung off the end of the bed. His boot had been cut off and a cloth sling tied to his foot. The doctor poured sand into the sling. The weight of the sand pulled Mr. Chandler's leg straight. As he applied a splint, the doctor explained, "I gave Noah a shot of morphine. He should sleep through the night. I'll be back in the morning."

Lula looked extremely pale. "Will my son recover?"

"I can't say for sure. Bones are tricky. If this is a clean break and he follows my instructions, once the bone heals, he will walk normally. From what I can tell, we should be hopeful."

"And if the break isn't clean?"

"He may have a limp. He could be a cripple. Only time will tell. We'll all say a prayer for him tonight. He's the best catcher the Boyle Heights Browns ever had."

April gave a curious glance toward Lula. Neither

woman knew what a catcher was, but they would say their prayers just the same.

Chapter Six

The joy April experienced since arriving in Los Angeles quickly dissolved. Lula declared the household could adequately provide the care her son required. After all, only his leg was out of commission. April had ample experience caring for the infirm. No nurse need be hired. Mr. Fitzpatrick could assist with the more discreet daily necessaries. Lula proclaimed men much better equipped for debility than women. April did not initially understand that comment but quickly caught on.

Mr. Chandler was ordered to stay abed for three weeks. Although his pain remained mild as long as he was still, he grew restless and irritable after three minutes.

His mother warned, "You will never go riding or baseballing if you fail to follow your friend's advice. He seemed anxious to have you return to former activities." Mr. Chandler, pouting childishly, crossed his arms and followed doctor's orders.

Lula abruptly had all manner of important engagements. Her advice and participation were curiously indispensable to any number of church activities. Her friend, Pearl Barnes, needed assistance due to serious health issues. Lula had important business in the city. April was left behind to do her part for the household. In other words, she became the reluctant nursemaid to the short-tempered Mr. Chandler.

It was not as if respect for women and employers slowly dissolved as days wore on. April remembered the first day clearly.

"Miss Stringham, I need help. Put that tray down and come over here," Mr. Chandler imperiously commanded. "I have tidied up, but I can't reach my left foot. You can use the washrag in the basin." Noah could see his new nursemaid did not understand his order. "What seems to be the problem? You've never seen a man's naked foot before?"

Indignant at his tone and command, April retorted, "As a matter of fact, I have not."

"Well, I can assure you, a foot is a foot." At this, Noah pulled the sheet from his left leg. "Be careful now," he warned.

Not having much choice in the matter, April rung out the cloth to wash the foot in question. Noah relaxed, enjoying the most sensual experience he had in some time. He relished the way Miss Stringham gently washed his foot, even delicately separating and washing between his toes. He laid his head back on the pillow and closed his eyes.

As she lightly toweled his foot dry, Noah did not wish to appear too appreciative and barked, "Is my foot so different than yours?"

"Other than the fact it is immense, no. However do they find a cowhide large enough to make your boots?" April shot back.

Piqued by her comment, Noah decided arguing

about the size of his feet, which he knew to be entirely normal, would not gain him any advantage. "Now you have not only seen, but touched a man's foot. I suppose I offended your feminine sensibilities." This did not draw a comment. "I know you're an old maid, but even you must have had some suitor through all these years. Are you telling me you never saw him naked?"

"Mr. Chandler! I am a Christian woman. How dare you imply such a thing!"

"Then there never was a suitor. What a tragedy."

"I did have a suitor."

"Truly? Who?" Noah seriously doubted this prudish, naïve woman could ever have been around men.

"William."

"What happened to William? Why did you not become Mrs. William like a proper girl?"

"That is none of your business." April turned toward the basin of dirty water. "Since you have no trouble finding naïve dolts who agree to marry you at the drop of a hat, you wouldn't understand. Not every woman is anxious to bind herself to some arrogant idiot in marriage."

"So, this William did not meet your standards?"

"No, Mr. Chandler. He was a polite and chivalrous man. It's you who appears to be the arrogant idiot." Before Mr. Chandler could respond, April ducked into the hallway.

And this was only the opening salvo.

Mr. Broadmore appeared at the front door after lunch that first day. He deposited a sizeable stack of law books and paperwork in Mr. Chandler's bedroom proclaiming, "If we have to fill in for you, the least you can do is office work. I brought everything you need; I even lugged a typewriter over here. It's in the carriage."

This news intrigued April, who followed the affable Mr. Broadmore out to his carriage. "Can I see?"

"Certainly." Jack removed a piece of canvas to reveal the latest in typewriter technology. "It's a Remington. It has the popular QWERTY keyboard and the new shift key." Jack pointed out the feature on the typewriter. "The shift key greatly reduced the number of keys necessary to operate a machine while also reducing the cost. Each strike bar now has the ability to type two different characters."

"What is QWERTY?"

"It's the way the keys are scientifically arranged." Jack pointed to the top row of letter keys. "It's all about comfort in typing. Anyone can type at amazing speeds once they memorize the location of the keys. The keys strike the underside of the paper, so you can't see what you're doing as you go but you quickly get a feel for accuracy."

April held the door as Mr. Broadmore carried the typewriter into the house. This new technology could prove useful to her own writing. April considered volunteering to help with Mr. Chandler's work. That would certainly make for a better day than washing his feet.

* * *

"Men are not at their best when they're ill. We must take this into consideration."

April wondered who exactly the "we" was in Lula's statement. Lula avoided her son's sickbed with a diligence April never imagined possible. After placing the first forkful of lunch in her mouth, April frowned when Mr. Chandler's bell rang out. She tended to ignore his incessant yelling, claiming him insufficiently noisy to summon her from the far corners of the house. Now whenever some whim overcame him, Mr. Chandler clanged his most precious possession, the dinner bell Mr. Fitzpatrick provided.

"You be still here and have your lunch. I'll go see what the problem is," offered Lula, quite uncharacteristically.

April contemplated the weeks since Mr. Chandler ruined her life. He did not hesitate to bait her into argument at every opportunity. No matter how she resisted his taunts, he always managed to rouse her temper.

The typewriter rested on the roll-top desk where April willingly typed Mr. Chandler's dictation. Due to her inexperience, she was slow and rarely kept up. Someone constantly yelling and complaining what a dullard you were made learning difficult. Then again, Mr. Chandler had no idea her "practice" was actually time spent writing for *Pacific Weekly*.

April replayed this morning's argument as she took a sip of tea.

"Slow down. How do you spell ad litem?"

"A-D space L-I-T-E-M. Are you dense? I spelled it for you the other day.

"No, you did not."

Distracted by her question, Noah asked, "Are you telling me your mother was dying for 17 years? How can that possibly be? I can't imagine a doctor coming by to explain she might not live through the day, or the week, much less the year."

"The doctor didn't come by every day. He never explained how long my mother might live." A determined April attempted to elude yet another fight.

"Of course, he didn't. I believe your mother took advantage of you. She used you all those years."

"She certainly did not. She was infirm." Again, the calm reply.

"Tell me her diagnosis."

"I don't know. I was a child when she became ill. She never explained the nature of her malady."

"Let me try to understand. You kept the house. You did the cooking. You managed the money. You cared for the chickens and shopped and budgeted and planned while your mother lay abed and let you wait on her for 17 years. And it never occurred to you she was using you, not once in all that time?"

"Well, she died, didn't she? *Something* killed her." April yelled. "You're hardly one to criticize a parent-child bond. I cannot imagine an unhappier relationship than the one between you and your mother. She's even gone so far as to disinherit you." April knew she struck a blow, no matter how inappropriate her comment. Her statement was met with silence as Mr. Chandler seethed. Realizing he might fire her at any moment, she changed the paper in the typewriter to "practice."

Little May stared at the drunken Charlie Boatman, passed out on the poker table in a puddle of his own spittle. The saloon was closed. All the patrons left for home. A solution to all her problems floated through May's thoughts. She could take the gun out of Charlie's holster and put a bullet through his temple. It seemed a merciful way to die. He would never know what happened. She could take the knife from behind the bar and slit his throat. Claiming self-defense, she could grab the andiron from the fireplace and bash his head. Somehow, she felt most satisfied by this last, gory alternative.

Oh no. It occurred to April in her reverie, May couldn't slit his throat if he passed out on the poker table. She would have to edit her paragraph.

Lula offered a smile as she returned to the dining room.

"There, problem resolved."

"Have I been fired?"

"Certainly not. Why would you think such a thing? Noah is testy now, but the doctor comes tomorrow. Three weeks is up. Can you believe how quickly the time flew by?"

April could, indeed, imagine.

"He'll have a new regimen. Hopefully he'll be mobile and things will return to normal."

April could only hope.

* * *

April assumed Mr. Chandler would be thrilled at the prospect of getting out of bed. This did not appear to be the case after Mr. Fitzpatrick helped him dress. The scowl on his face was impossible to ignore. Mrs. Chandler's elegant wicker wheelchair would soon get a workout.

"I imagine you'll want to sit at your desk and do your own typing today." April did not welcome this aspect of the recovery. She enjoyed typing. Rough drafts on the typewriter were accomplished efficiently and she believed her speed would only increase.

"Would you like me to fetch Mr. Fitzpatrick to help you into the wheelchair?"

"I don't believe that's necessary. Since you are descended from Amazons, I'm certain you can manage on your own. Actually, if you'll support my leg, I can transfer myself to the wheelchair. Would you mind terribly putting my socks on first? It's rather chilly today."

Despite his obviously ugly mood, Mr. Chandler attempted a polite smile. April quickly pulled on the socks and supported the splint as he slid into the wheelchair parked beside the bed.

"I think perhaps you should be afraid of me, under the circumstances," April toyed.

"Why?"

"Herodotus carefully documented how the Amazons were taken captive but quickly murdered their captors. Then they so enchanted the Scythians, the men foreswore their country in order to marry."

"Yes, but you forget, when the Scythians schemed to tame the Amazons by impregnating them, the women were eager to oblige. You may be tall, but your similarity to Amazons ends there. Perhaps it was a poor analogy on my part." Noah scrutinized his caregiver who pursed her lips and took her place behind the wheelchair. She wasn't ignorant, he'd give her that.

"Stop at the dresser." April obediently did as commanded. Mr. Chandler opened the top drawer to remove a handkerchief and place it in his pocket.

April could not help but notice the beautifully embroidered linen fabric and absently touched its twin in the drawer before she slid it shut. "You have excellent taste."

"Thank you. I do. But Deidre purchased those as part of her Christmas gift to me. I'll have to tell her how much I appreciate them next time I see her."

April frowned. The little witch took her suggestion after all.

Unaccustomed to allowing anyone control, Noah felt uncomfortable when Miss Stringham wheeled him toward the desk. He did not attempt to curb his impatient criticism as she rounded the bed.

"Be careful! Mind the bedpost! You don't need to go so fast!" he yelled. To no one's surprise, April turned the broken leg into the side of the desk.

"Damn it. I told you to be careful. If my leg weren't already broken it sure as hell would be now."

"I'm sorry, Mr. Chandler," she apologized, but then felt an all too familiar flare of anger. She barely touched his leg against the desk. "But what do you expect when you're constantly yelling. I'm only trying to help. Things would be a lot better if you'd keep your mouth *shut*!" At this, April stalked out of the room. If that man wanted anything else this morning, he could crawl on his hands and knees and get it himself.

When April reluctantly returned to clear away the luncheon tray, Mr. Chandler uncharacteristically thanked her. Then he explained, "I'll finish my work shortly and Jack won't return until tomorrow. I believe I'd enjoy a game of cribbage. Do you play?"

"No, I've never played cribbage."

"Excellent. I'm an extremely good teacher. You'll learn in no time."

April anticipated an afternoon to herself since Mr. Chandler achieved some mobility. She hadn't had a day off in three weeks. Her disappointment at this turn of events was clearly evident. This only caused

Mr. Chandler to smirk in his most imperious manner.

"Cribbage derives from an English game by the name of Noddy. It's the oldest card game known to man."

April could only imagine what other tidbits of information would soon be thrown her way. If Mr. Chandler commenced her instruction in the Dark Ages, it might take decades for him to teach the game. The man did love to hear himself talk.

* * *

Lula stopped in her tracks at the delightful sound of April's giggle coming from her son's bedroom. Turning her ear toward the door she barely made out words.

"I believe I reached the end of the cribbage board before you, Mr. Chandler. Let's see, what could this mean exactly? Oh, I remember! It means *I won*."

Noah sounded quite cross. "It's inevitable you would win sooner or later, Miss Stringham. This is the third day we've played and you have an excellent instructor. Besides, I let you win."

"You certainly did not."

"Fine, I'll play to my optimum ability and we'll see who wins next time."

"Yes, you play to your optimum ability and I'll certainly be playing to mine," April threatened.

Noah was not amused when his pupil won again.

* * *

April grabbed the cribbage board on her way to Mr. Chandler's desk. "Are you ready for our match?" she inquired.

"No. As a matter of fact, I have another diversion

planned for today. I want to go downstairs."

"Amazon that I am," she replied, "I cannot manage to control the wheelchair on the staircase."

"I don't expect you to. I believe I can lower myself to a seated position and descend the stairs on my ass." He could tell Miss Stringham did not appreciate his vulgarity. "Then all you have to do is guide the empty wheelchair down the stairs. I would like to spend the afternoon in the parlor playing chess. Do you play?"

"No."

"Well, you're about to learn." Content in the knowledge it would take a long time for Miss Stringham to get the best of him at chess, Noah wheeled the chair toward the staircase. The first of many matches would soon commence.

Before dinner, another activity was added to the daily itinerary. Sick of the view from his bed, Noah contentedly perused his newspaper in the parlor. He glanced up to observe Miss Stringham, immersed in her reading, wander through the front door. He stifled a laugh as she almost ran into the wall.

"What book have you got your nose in?" Noah demanded.

"Oh, it's called *A Study in Scarlet*. It features a character named Sherlock Holmes. It's not a new work, but I've never read it before. It is entirely engrossing."

"Read to me."

"But I'm half-way finished."

"You can catch me up as you go along."

"I certainly cannot. That's no way to read a book. I'll start at the beginning."

"You will not."

At this, April deliberately turned to Chapter One, sat cross-legged on the floor, and started to read.

The next few days were consumed by chess and Sherlock Holmes. When the doctor returned, he proclaimed Mr. Chandler sufficiently healed to begin using crutches. In a matter of days, he would likely return to work.

* * *

Noah sat across the table in the backyard observing his chess protégé on the unusually warm winter day. He appreciated April's keen mind. She was articulate and knowledgeable about any subject he introduced. He came to anticipate their time together. He enjoyed her enthusiastic and dramatic reading of Mr. Doyle's literature. He valued her competitive nature, although he expected to be the winner in any of their contests. They abandoned cribbage entirely for this very reason.

Absorbed in his thoughts, Noah abruptly noticed his error. "Enough of this for today." He started placing chess pieces in their box.

"Wait. Haven't I won?"

"No, I can still move my king. It's a lovely day. I think we should enjoy the garden a bit before we go in for supper."

"But you're stuck in the corner."

"I can move between those two squares. You can't prohibit me from moving no matter what you do."

April examined Mr. Chandler's expression carefully. He seemed in a hurry to pack up the game. She grabbed his king and walked backward from the table, hiding the chess piece behind her back. "I won. Admit it."

Noah rose from his seat and held out his hand. "I need to put that piece away. Hand it here."

"I will not. You must admit defeat."

Noah shook his head. "I could still move my king."

"I have you trapped. Checkmate!" she gleefully announced.

At this, Noah grabbed his crutches and moved toward her. The open seam of his pants leg caused the fabric below his knee to flap in the breeze.

"I won't give it to you." April backed further away. "Admit defeat."

Once he cornered her, Noah dropped his crutches and balancing on his good leg, reached around her back. Grabbing April for support, Noah never imagined how pleasurable it felt to hold her in his arms. He could barely see over the top of her head, although she wore shoes and he stood on stockinged foot. Pulling her close against his chest, he could not discern any passion in her eyes, only playfulness.

"What exactly is going on here?"

Noah calmly reached around Miss Stringham's shoulder. "Deidre, my dearest. I seem to have gotten myself into something of a pickle. Would you help Miss Stringham get me back to my chair?"

Although Deidre's expression conveyed her doubts, she complied.

Clutching tightly to the black king, April noted Mr. Chandler leaned heavily on her and only draped his arm over the shoulders of his dainty and delicate fiancé. Amazons were evidently good for something.

"Have you finally come to nurse me back to health, my beloved?" Noah inquired of his intended.

"Don't be ridiculous. You have servants for that."

* * *

The future Mrs. Noah Chandler hit the house on Carroll Avenue like a disastrous storm. Disappointed her fiancé was unable to leave his home much less take her to the theater or dancing, Deidre quickly arranged an endless stream of entertaining. This put a tremendous strain on the household that continued even as Noah returned to work.

A curious April noticed odd behavior in the betrothed couple. Mr. Chandler played the part of fiancé well indeed—he certainly had enough practice. But April understood this to be merely a role he played. She considered him a vain man, realizing he never hesitated to use his looks to his advantage. Deidre's young and flighty friends fairly swooned whenever Mr. Chandler looked their way.

He seemed more a trophy than a love interest to Deidre. But April recognized Deidre was nothing more than a business advantage to Mr. Chandler. The two seemed well matched in that regard, or so April supposed. Their relationship appeared devoid of love, passion, or even attraction.

April felt intense sympathy for Lula. No wonder the woman was at her wit's end trying to convince her son this marriage seemed doomed to fail—at least in a traditional sense. But who was April to judge? Perhaps a marriage based on mutual advantage might be as likely to succeed as any other. At least this pair knew what each expected of the other, even if their motives appeared shallow.

One afternoon, April overheard Deidre's snide response to her cousin Theodora's question as the girls and several friends enjoyed tea in the garden.

"Noah must be declining if he's breaking bones.

Aren't you worried about marrying a man so much older?"

"Noah is well past his prime. I have no illusions. It simply makes him all the easier to control."

April believed the man cut a fine figure and appeared quite fit. Mr. Chandler seemed agile enough during his disability and powerfully built when he tried to retrieve his chess piece from behind her back.

Deidre's friend continued, "You will soon lose your fine hourglass figure from childbearing. Less competition for the rest of us."

Deidre snorted in derision. "That remains to be seen."

Thankfully, the Chandler family problems were not April's. Work and his future wife kept Mr. Chandler constantly occupied. Free once more, April fled the house with Lula every day. The ladies made their rounds, visiting, participating in church activities and shopping. Although Lula remained distraught, she managed to hide her anxiety.

During one of their excursions, a delighted April accepted a free premier copy of *Pacific Weekly* from a boy on the sidewalk. She quickly glanced inside to locate the first installment of her story—*The Life of Little May*. Pressing the magazine against her bosom, she said a prayer of thanks. Mr. Lynch would not make money by giving his magazine away. She hoped he knew what he was doing.

Hiding her enthusiasm proved difficult. Once they got home, Lula proclaimed herself worn out from the day's activities. April immediately retreated to the attic where she could enjoy her accomplishment.

Another lavish dinner had been scheduled for the evening. April planned to take early supper in her room, a habit she commenced once Deidre embarked on her round of entertaining. April entered the kitchen to find Margarita loudly complaining in Spanish as she stood at the stove.

Mrs. Fitzpatrick gingerly crossed the room to inquire, "Could you help me?"

April didn't hesitate to respond to the rarely social Mrs. Fitzpatrick. "Certainly. What can I do?"

"The hem has come out of my apron."

"So it has. I can sew it up on the machine in no time. Do you know how to use a sewing machine?"

Mrs. Fitzpatrick shook her head.

"Would you like to learn?"

A sweet smile lit Mrs. Fitzpatrick's face as she nodded. The women retreated to the attic carrying the apron and April's supper.

As thanks for her sewing lesson and the mending, Mrs. Fitzpatrick invited April for late night dessert in the suite above the carriage house.

When April knocked on the door that evening, she imagined she might be the first guest who ever stepped foot inside. It was no wonder Mrs. Fitzpatrick enjoyed her home. The enchanting suite contained treasures from the far reaches of the world. White lace curtains covered windows. Everything appeared immaculate. April could imagine herself there, reading, cooking, writing and sewing without need to ever emerge.

"Oh, this is lovely, Mrs. Fitzpatrick! You have a beautiful home." The older woman beamed in response.

"I wanted to show you this tablecloth. It belonged to my mother. Do you think we could repair it on the machine?"

"I'm certain we could." This proved the beginning

of a quiet friendship. Several times a week after the dinner dishes were done, April was invited for one of Mrs. Fitzpatrick's fantastic though tiny desserts. Occasionally, the women climbed the stairs to the attic to sew.

April never observed a married couple before. The quiet, shy and sensitive Mrs. Fitzpatrick was also a dedicated wife who took great care of her household. Mr. Fitzpatrick appeared incredibly gentle and loving toward his wife. Their true relationship seemed less obvious when the two worked together in the main house. In fact, Mrs. Fitzpatrick could not have been less evident in the household had she been a ghost. She somehow managed to do her daily chores in unoccupied rooms. April knew the woman appeared especially nervous while cleaning Mr. Chandler's room during his confinement. April also understood her unpleasant exchanges with Mr. Chandler must have upset her new friend. The woman had a delicate spirit.

Chapter Seven

April occupied one of her favorite spots—the swing on the front porch. Awed by mild weather, she couldn't help but doubt Mr. Fitzpatrick who asserted rain might be over for the year. She took one last deep breath of fresh evening air before making her way into the house. Mrs. Fitzpatrick's delicious strawberry shortcake was still on her mind as she headed for the staircase.

"Miss Stringham?"

April jerked her head toward the parlor, surprised to find Mr. Chandler.

"I'm sorry, did I bother you? I thought you retired once your fiancé and her entourage left for the evening."

"They are quite tedious. I thought I'd enjoy a brandy before I went upstairs."

"If your future wife is already tedious, what will happen after you marry?"

"I imagine things will be remarkably as they are now. We have our own interests, Deidre and I. She'll grow up in time."

"But you'll be an old man by then."

Noah ignored her barb. "We never finished our

book. I believe there were two chapters left."

"I'll get it for you. I planned to return it tomorrow. I can renew it if you like."

"You finished it then?"

"I did. It's right here on the entry table. I didn't want to forget to take it along in the morning." April grabbed the book and walked toward Mr. Chandler.

"Would you mind? I enjoy your reading. I know it will be repetitious for you, though."

"No trouble." April plopped down cross-legged on the floor in her accustomed spot. She made quick work of the remainder of the tale and looked up at Mr. Chandler to see if he enjoyed the conclusion.

"There's a newer story about Mr. Holmes called *The Sign of the Four*. I hoped to find it tomorrow. It was published in *Lipponcott's Monthly* last year."

"I might be able to help you." Mr. Chandler approached the paneling on the far side of the room. Releasing a latch hidden beneath the chair rail, he slid the panel to the side to reveal a large bookcase. "I take *Lipponcott's*. Let me see, it looks as if I have all the issues from last year. You're welcome to find Mr. Doyle's story. If you wouldn't mind, could you mark the articles? I'd like to read them. You're welcome to anything in the bookcase. The latch is right here."

"That's quite ingenious."

"My mother considers books to be terrible dust catchers. The sliding panels were her idea."

"I'm always impressed by Mrs. Chandler."

"She seems equally impressed with you. She's not all you think."

"I really don't care to hear—"

"My mother seems happy to take you under her

wing. I believe you're the daughter she always wanted. I'm her favorite child and she disinherited me. You can imagine what she thinks of my sisters. You might stand to profit by her discontent. Maybe she'll leave you her fortune."

"Mr. Chandler!"

"Come, come. You wouldn't be the first person to ingratiate themselves for personal gain. You won't be the last."

"Just because you would marry for money or business—or whatever it is you're doing—doesn't mean I would stoop so low. How dare you cast me in such an ugly light? And how dare you malign your own mother in such a way? You should be grateful to her!"

"Why?"

"You've led a privileged life. You live in a big house, had a grand education and every advantage possible. My entire Concord home would fit in your bedroom. Yet you are cruel and unfeeling."

"Hold on, hold on. You should understand, my mother is not normally so, well, motherly. She comes from wealth. She felt childrearing to be a burden. We were all foisted off on nannies. If Deidre and I have children, I wouldn't hesitate to repeat my mother's practices. And someone has to inherit her money, why not you?"

Stunned at the course the conversation had taken, April didn't know how to respond.

"I actually stopped you for a reason. Our discussion has veered completely from the question I wished to ask. I know you put in a lot of extra time when I broke my leg. As you can see, I've finally parted ways with my splint. I only have to rely on my elegant cane for another couple of weeks. I'm as good as new, as a matter of fact. I wanted to assure you there will be a bonus in your pay envelope this week—my thanks for all your care. I also wanted to know if I could do anything to show my appreciation."

April considered her request for only a moment. What would it hurt to ask? "I want to go in a saloon. Would you take me?"

"Miss Stringham, I had you pegged as a teetotaler. I should have asked you to join me in a brandy."

"I do not imbibe spirits, Mr. Chandler. I've read a great deal about the West. I want to experience as much as I can while I'm here. I can't go in a saloon by myself."

Noah rubbed his chin as he considered the request. "Do you ride?"

"Horses?"

"Yes, Miss Stringham. What else would you ride? An African elephant?"

April pursed her lips but then answered, "Not that I recall. I do remember a horse when I was small. I don't believe I ever went riding. But in light of your recent accident, perhaps I should be asking if you ride?"

Noah chuckled. The woman had wit and spunk even if she could be entirely difficult. "Let me see what I can do. Deidre and her cousin had a tiff. The future Mrs. Chandler will head back to San Francisco shortly. I'll have more time once she leaves. In fact, we might resume our chess matches before long. I seem to be missing my black king. I can't imagine where it could be."

"You know perfectly well where it is. I'm holding it hostage. I'm waiting for you to concede the game I won. You remember, the one where I beat you. Outside. In the backyard. When you *lost*."

"Be careful, Miss Stringham, or I'll be leaving you in a saloon."

* * *

Between his broken leg and Deidre's visit to Los Angeles, Noah successfully avoided his mother in recent weeks. He knew she attempted to avoid him since their trip to San Francisco. Now the two sat across the dining table, a wall of silence between them.

"Perhaps we should have Miss Stringham join us for dinner. She's a lively conversationalist." Noah's suggestion was met by an icy glare. "Your companion will not be available on Saturday."

"Why?"

At least Noah managed to break his mother's silence. "I'm taking her riding. We'll be gone most of the day."

"Does she know about this?"

"Our excursion is actually at her behest."

Realizing April longed to explore outside the city, Lula couldn't believe she agreed to accompany Noah. She understood better than anyone how abysmally Noah behaved in April's presence. "I had no idea she was a horsewoman."

"You are correct. She's not. Miss Stringham expressed her desire to see the countryside and experience the West before our household disbands so I will accommodate her. I assumed you invited her to join you on the East Coast after the wedding. Have you decided against offering her a job?"

"I'll take her if she's willing to go. I hoped she would make a match before June."

"Playing matchmaker? How unlike you."

"Oh, I haven't made any inroads as far as finding her a beau. She doesn't seem to need my help."

"What makes you think so?"

"She receives regular correspondence from Concord. I couldn't help but notice the return address. A Mr. Farmer writes regularly. Then there's correspondence from some Mr. Lynch here in Los Angeles. I can't imagine why someone so nearby would bother to write. I assume they must be love letters."

Noah was taken aback at the flare of jealousy he experienced. He quickly hid his reaction but not in time to avoid his mother's notice.

"Perhaps you could help outfit Miss Stringham for her ride. Whatever you think best. I'll take care of the bill. Buy something practical. There will be no side saddle."

* * *

Despite her anxious expression, Miss Stringham outwardly appeared quite the horsewoman. On initial observation, the charcoal divided skirt and simple gray calico blouse did not appear expensive. Noah scrutinized April as she donned an exquisitely tailored tweed coat and large-brimmed straw hat. The band of the hat matched her skirt. She pulled on a pair of black kid gloves. Noah noticed her boots were also new. His mother certainly spared no expense. No surprise there.

They might easily have taken the carriage, but Noah took delight in placing the ever-confident Miss Stringham in an uncomfortable position. He grinned as he gave her a boost into the saddle. A nervous and unsettled April clutched the saddle horn as if it would save her from the precipice of hell.

"The horse will know if you're nervous or frightened."

"I'm not frightened," fibbed April. "It's only this is so very high."

Raising his eyebrows, Noah nodded agreeably, then slid a rifle into the scabbard on his saddle. He mounted Checkers in one fluid motion. The muscles in his broken leg weren't completely recovered. The ride today would undoubtedly be as tiring for him as it would be trying for his fellow traveler.

April noticed a pistol on Mr. Chandler's belt when he climbed on his horse. "You're awfully well-armed. Are we going on a ride or to war?"

"It pays to be careful when you leave the city."

"Do you know how to use a gun?"

"It would be foolish of me to wear one if I didn't. That might invite difficulties. Didn't anyone wear a gun in Massachusetts?"

"No one I knew." But April would admit she didn't know many men.

Noah gave Checkers a kick. The gentle mare he selected for Miss Stringham followed his lead.

"What's my horse's name?"

Noah had no idea. "Rosie."

"What a sweet name." April patted the side of the horse's neck.

"How far was your farm from the city?"

"First of all, Concord is not really a city. It's a pretty small, boring town. As Louisa May Alcott noted, 'Poor dull Concord. Nothing colorful has come through here since the redcoats.' She was correct in her assertion. We were about five miles out."

"How did you get there if you didn't have a

horse?"

"Oh, I walked."

No wonder Miss Stringham seemed so fit. "Here," he said disgustedly. "The goal is not to bump up and down like a jackrabbit in love. Let your hips sway with the movement of the horse, back and forth."

His comment drew a glare, but Miss Stringham took direction well.

The strain of spending the day in the company of the rude Mr. Chandler in unfamiliar activities made a dent in April's normally cheery outlook. Her next words fell unbidden from her lips. "You would never make such an outrageous comment to your precious Deidre."

"You are entirely correct." Miss Stringham stared at him, inviting further explanation. Noah shrugged. "She's my betrothed," as if this explained everything.

"That is rather disingenuous of you. She assumes you are a gentleman. What will happen when the truth becomes evident?"

Noah laughed. "I suppose it will be too late by then. So, you are of the opinion I'm not a gentleman." Observing Miss Stringham's continuing discomfort in the saddle, he decided to divert her attention. "Sit up straight and pay attention."

"To what?"

"We are set on an intriguing course."

"Are there Indians?"

"No, no, no. This location is steeped in lore. We're headed for a pass—formerly an Indian trail, later known as El Portozuelo, which means The Little Doorway. Eventually, it became part of The King's Highway. You've heard of it, haven't you?"

April nodded.

"Our story begins in 1864, not so long ago. The French ensconced Archduke Maximilian of Austria and his wife, Carlota, as emperor and empress of Mexico. Mexico's resistance to this move was led by Benito Juarez. Juarez amassed a treasure of gold and gems with an estimated value in excess of $200,000.

"Four of his agents took the fortune to San Francisco to buy arms for the rebels. Along the way, one of the men died a mysterious death. The other three assumed he died at the hand of French secret agents. Once they arrived in San Francisco, they found the entire city crawling with French spies so they headed for the hills, quite literally, and buried the treasure in six bundles."

"We're not riding all the way to San Francisco, are we?"

Noah frowned and continued his tale, "A wanderer named Diego Moreno observed the men burying their treasure and when they departed, he dug it up and headed for his home in Mexico. When the three remaining Juarez agents returned to retrieve the treasure, they accused each other of theft. Two of the men murdered each other. The last of the four agents later died in a bar in Tombstone, Arizona. So the first four men who carried the treasure all died.

"Our wanderer, Diego, stopped in a tavern in an area called Cactus Patch in the very pass where we're headed. That night, he dreamed he died after taking the treasure into Los Angeles. The dream seemed so vivid, he decided to bury the treasure under an ash tree before he reached the pueblo.

"Once he arrived in Los Angeles, Diego visited his friend Jesus Martinez. Diego explained how he found the treasure and described where he buried it.

No sooner were the words out of his mouth than he suffered violent convulsions and dropped dead. His dream had become reality. After they buried Diego, Jesus and his stepson, Jose Correa, departed to find the treasure. When they located the tree Diego described, Jesus collapsed and died of heart failure. Believing the treasure to be cursed, young Jose ran off." Noah paused to observe his companion. Intent on his story, she seemed more relaxed.

"About five years ago, a Basque shepherd who grazed his sheep nearby discovered a parcel of gold and jewels dug up by his dog. Elated at his good fortune, he left the site not realizing five parcels remained. The shepherd displayed his new-found wealth in a nearby tavern. He decided to use his treasure to return home to Spain. Legend has it, he stood at the rail of the ship as it approached the dock, stumbled into the sea and drowned, pulled down by the weight of the fortune sewn into his clothing."

"What happened to Jose Correa?"

"He's a lawman in Los Angeles. So far, he's the only person to be near the treasure who survived."

April considered the dramatic tale as she rode along in silence. "What are those?" She pointed toward strap-leaved plants growing in tidy rows.

"It's a pineapple orchard. They grow well here. This farmer also grows alligator pears—have you ever had one?"

"I've never even heard of them."

"If we have time on the way home, we might stop and buy a few. I enjoy them with lime, salt and pepper for breakfast. You eat them like a grapefruit after you remove the large seed. They also make a good salad with hardboiled eggs and dressing."

As the adventurers began a gentle ascent into the hills, the farmland gave way to orange groves.

"Our destination is just ahead, the summit of Cahuenga Pass. Cahuenga is the Spanish name for the Tongva village of Kawengna, which means place of the mountain."

April had never seen this side of Mr. Chandler. He eagerly shared his knowledge of Los Angeles, its abundant blessings and history. Soon, they were in a canyon, a chaparral wilderness. A stand of eucalyptus rose in the distance. Their destination was the hotel hidden in the trees, the Cahuenga Tavern.

"I probably should explain; we could have visited a saloon in Los Angeles."

"Why are you telling me this now?"

"A woman in a saloon is not the taboo you read about in novels. In big cities, many saloons have a side door for ladies. Women are welcome to enter alone, with friends or even male escorts. They drink or carry out alcoholic beverages. Sometimes saloons host social events and dances. Saloons offer free lunches working women enjoy much the same as their male counterparts. We'll have a drink and free lunch today. You're not one of those temperance women, are you?"

"I don't know much about that issue. I haven't formed an opinion."

"I believe your desire is to see the main saloon, which is normally a male-only environment. I imagine your vision of saloons is walking through batwing doors, bellying up to a bar beside malodorous card sharps? The Cahuenga Tavern doesn't have a ladies' door. It's so far removed from the city, there's no need for discretion. They cater to travelers here, men and women."

"What about ladies of the evening?"

"I hate to disappoint you further, but I have never been in a saloon where prostitutes offered their charms. One would have to visit the worst slums to find a dive of that sort and I won't take you there."

"Oh, I'm not disappointed. Thank you."

"For what?"

"You've been thoughtful about our journey today. I appreciate your consideration."

The pair rode up to a large wooden structure. Noah tied the horses. April swung her leg over the horse and was surprised when Mr. Chandler grabbed her waist and set her on the ground. Unsteady at the sudden drop in elevation, she clutched his sleeve.

"What's wrong?"

"I got used to being so high up, now I feel extremely short." Noah laughed and offered his arm.

"My, aren't we acting the gentleman all of a sudden."

"You're right, acting. We're in public now. You'll be seeing the best side of me, at least until we head for home. I'm a businessman after all. It never hurts to sell yourself whenever you have the opportunity."

Miss Stringham tightly grasped his arm, arousing Noah's curiosity. Suddenly unsure of herself, she was, after all, the one who asked to come. He noted her look of amazement as they entered the swinging doors.

April took in every detail of the dark saloon. The large eucalyptus trees provided natural shade and the wood-paneled room had few windows. She noted an elegantly carved mahogany bar, much as she imagined. Mr. Chandler walked up to the bar, made a friendly greeting to the bartender and ordered two beers, mentioning they intended to partake of the lunch at the far end of the sleek bar top.

After he set the beers on a nearby table, he directed his travel companion to the buffet. "Do you know what this is?"

"Spanish food. Margarita has been teaching me how to cook it. That's frijoles, tamales; these are enchiladas, my favorite. I don't know how to make tamales yet."

"You like our California cuisine, then I take it?"

"Very much."

Once seated, Miss Stringham winced when she sipped her beer. "Something wrong?" Noah sampled his beer to find nothing amiss. "Tastes fine to me."

"It smells appealing, but it doesn't taste good."

"Here, give me yours." April slid her beer across the table. Mr. Chandler revisited the bar and returned carrying a small glassful of red liquid. "Try this."

"This is quite tasty," April approved.

Lunch was consumed without commentary. Miss Stringham downed her fruity, sweet red wine. When Noah offered to buy another, she agreed. It quickly became obvious the woman was unaccustomed to alcohol as she giggled.

Amused, Noah inquired, "Something about this is funny to you?"

"I can't quite believe I'm here. I longed for a taste of the Wild West before it's gone and here I am, actually sitting in a saloon in the middle of nowhere. Men are playing poker. As often as I imagined what this might be like, it's incredible I am experiencing this right here, right now! This is truly the heart of the West."

As agreeable as Noah determined to be, he took issue with Miss Stringham's strange ideas. "First of all, we're not exactly in the middle of nowhere. Second, the only person who believes this is the heart of the West would be a drunkard."

April finished off the last of her wine. Silly moments earlier, she became belligerent. "I am *not* a drunkard."

"I didn't say you were."

"You certainly did. I heard you."

"No, Miss Stringham. I believe churches are the foundation of society in the West. Saloons, general stores and hotels may pop up first, but it never takes long for churches to come. Women and church are the civilizing forces in the world. Churches unite people, serve the needy and the community. Churches provide proper societal interaction. And it's a good thing because 20 years ago, Los Angeles was a violent place. You've seen how many churches populate the streets of the city. I'd be hard-pressed to tell you if there are more saloons or churches. Surely you were engaged in charitable church functions in Massachusetts?"

He could see by her expression the answer was no. Perhaps Miss Stringham had been on the receiving end of the church's good works, given her past. He might be treading in dangerous waters. A change of subject seemed wise.

"If you've finished lunch and had your fill of the sights and sounds of the saloon, we should begin our journey home. It takes a while at our slow pace."

"Why? How fast do you normally make the trip?"

"At a trot, 30 minutes. But I don't believe you're quite up to that."

"You're the one who fell off his horse last time out as I recall." April saw muscles play across Mr. Chandler's cheeks as he clenched his teeth.

Whatever truce developed this morning had clearly gone by the wayside over lunch.

Noah rose and held Miss Stringham's chair. He took her arm and escorted her to the door as she craned her neck to observe two men playing checkers near a window. He could not comprehend what fascinated her. She seemed bright enough, surely well-read. He almost pulled her through the swinging doors as she turned one last time to cement the vision of the saloon in her memory.

After riding for about 30 minutes, Noah noticed Miss Stringham failed to keep up. This seemed odd since rented horses were always eager to return to the stable. He stopped and waited, then noticed Miss Stringham looked rather green. Before he could comment, she attempted to dismount but landed on her fanny in the dirt. Noah watched her leap to her feet and run off the side of the trail, where she dropped to her hands and knees behind a sagebrush and vomited loudly.

His mother would be furious if she could manage to be angrier at him than she already was. He took her friend away for a single morning and got her drunk. Every muscle in Miss Stringham's body would undoubtedly ache from the ride if it didn't from her clumsy dismount. To think, his intentions were honorable when he planned this outing.

Noah dismounted and ambled toward the sagebrush. "Are you done?"

"Go away."

"I wouldn't linger over there were I you. This is rattlesnake country."

At this, Miss Stringham attempted to leap to her feet, but her knee caught in her skirt and she fell backward. Giving up, she dropped her head onto her knees. "Just leave. I don't want to ride; it makes me seasick."

"Now there's an interesting analogy. The lawyer in me needs to ask if you've ever been on a boat."

"I'll walk back."

Noah pursed his lips to keep from smiling. "It wouldn't be chivalrous of me to leave you out here alone. Those riding boots are not particularly good for a stroll."

"I'll take them off. I can find my way back. I have a good sense of direction."

"What about the rattlesnakes? What about highwaymen? An unarmed and virtuous woman could find herself in dire straits, although you might be able to argue any marauder to death. You do have that in your favor. But then there's bears and mountain lions. Maybe you should give Rosie here another try. I have a feeling the seasickness might abate since you and your lunch parted ways."

Noah went to his saddle and poured water from his canteen on his handkerchief. He walked back to Miss Stringham as a rattler sounded its warning.

April sprang to her feet and grabbed Noah's arm. "What's that?"

"I already explained. It's a rattler letting you know where he is. He's not close. He wants us to keep our distance." Noah placed the wet handkerchief on his companion's neck and offered her a drink. "Have a sip."

Taking April's arm, Noah guided her back to the road. He retrieved her hat from the dirt where she fell. Taking the reins of both horses, he commenced the journey home.

"We'll walk a ways and then we'll try the horses again. Do you approve?" Noah almost laughed as he looked into the sorrowful face of Miss Stringham. Her hair toppled to the side of her head. Her clothes were dusty and her face remained a faint shade of green. Dirt smudged her cheek and chin. She avoided his attention, too embarrassed to engage in her normally witty repartee. It was a long and quiet trip to Los Angeles.

Chapter Eight

April slowly wandered home. She never would have believed her 30th birthday could cause such dismay. To be honest, the thought of it bothered her ever since her trip to the Cahuenga Tavern. She felt incredibly old for several days after her adventure. Her muscles ached. Her head hurt. She could barely sit and her feet were full of blisters. She never wanted to see another glass of wine much less drink one.

Why would turning 30 bother her? It was just another birthday although it might mark the end of her youth. She didn't want to consider the eventuality of spinsterhood, dying alone and unloved on some not-so-distant day. Even Mr. Farmer's incredibly thoughtful birthday greeting failed to cheer.

Evidently, Lula noticed her companion's ill humor and gave her the afternoon off. April visited her favorite haunts—the library and Germain's. A lovely but small potted palm nestled in her market basket beside an assortment of short stories. But nothing she did served to lighten her mood. Instead of taking the trolley, April imagined the next chapter of Little May's life as she walked.

Two old miners played their daily game of checkers in the shade of the porch at Charlie Boatman's saloon. Little May had only enough time to finish polishing the elegant mahogany bar before the afternoon crowd arrived. Although she should have finished this morning, she was sick. Her fever raged even now.

Making her way across the dark room, May hoped to avoid Charlie's notice. She might be lucky enough to finish before the man could complain. But she was short on luck this day.

"Yer' late," Charlie sneered.

"I'm sorry Mr. Boatman, I've been ill." May's eyes fairly glazed over as she tried to focus. "I'll finish up right away, truly." She polished the wood as if she could overcome time itself.

Charlie walked over and spat on the floor near her skirt. "You better do a good job. And scrub those spittoons before you go home."

"Yes sir," replied Little May, but she nearly swooned as she bent over her work.

"Look out!"

April stopped in her tracks and turned to see a man on a bicycle headed right for her. Squinting her eyes tightly shut, she braced for impact. He managed to stop short of knocking her down.

"What has gotten into you, Miss Stringham?"

April opened her eyes. "I'm sorry, Mr. Chandler. I wasn't paying attention."

"You certainly weren't. A person could get themselves killed walking across the street without looking. Murdering you would not be a good way to break in my bicycle."

"What a grand bicycle," April was impressed. She made a point to keep abreast of the latest display in the Gibson & Alexander window. "Where did you get it?"

"It's a wedding gift. I think I could recite the bawdy joke my friend attached.

"'There once was a fellow named Wussy,

Who married for only some p—'"

"That's quite enough Mr. Chandler."

"Would you like a ride?" offered Noah. "We might manage to keep you off the street temporarily. You would cease to be a danger to yourself and others, if only for a while."

"How exactly could I ride?"

"Climb right up here, on the bar in front. I'll take you home. Hold your skirt tight so it doesn't get caught in the spokes."

April fumbled with her skirt and became mortified when Mr. Chandler dismounted, squatted in front of her and pushed his hand between her shoes. Grabbing the back of her skirt, he pulled it through to the front and handing it to April, grinned at her horrified expression.

"Hold onto this," he commanded.

Holding her basket in one hand and her skirt in the other, April managed to slide onto the bar of the bicycle once Mr. Chandler remounted. Her heart raced as he put his arms around her and grasped the handles.

"You better hold on," he advised.

Pulling the back of her skirt higher, she managed to lock her legs securely around the fabric. She slid her arm through the basket handle and gripped the bars in front of Mr. Chandler's hands.

"Do you know what you're doing?" she asked nervously.

"Oh, Miss Stringham, you should understand by now, I always know what I'm doing," Noah boasted. With a quick push of his feet, they were off.

Although April found her new mode of transportation incredibly thrilling, glares from a few pedestrians clarified her inappropriate situation. Mr. Chandler, evidently uninterested in displaying his businesslike public persona, simply reached up and tipped his hat to the disapproving citizens of Los Angeles.

"Did the future Mrs. Chandler also receive a bicycle?"

Noah laughed at the thought. "This was more of a joke than a gift. I cannot imagine the spoiled and fashionable Deidre on a bicycle, can you? Her corset is so tight, she can't even walk up a flight of stairs without turning blue. I meant to ask about your lack of corset. Isn't that considered rather scandalous? I think it puts you on the verge of naked."

"It certainly does not," April replied solemnly although she was having a wonderful time. "I adhere to the advice of Dr. Chavasse who believes corsets damage the internal organs and are the true cause of vapors from which so many women suffer. And how would you know whether or not I wear a corset?"

"I noticed when I helped you down from your horse at the tavern. You can imagine my initial shock," he teased, but April took him seriously. "To think I'm riding on a bicycle beside a nearly nude woman. What will people say?"

"I agree this appears quite scandalous. Perhaps we should stop and I'll walk the rest of the way home."

"And here I was thinking we might ride right on by Carroll Avenue so I could show you one of the local sites." Noah noticed his passenger breathed rather heavily. She seemed to relax and leaned against his chest. Since he received no reply, Noah continued down the dirt road, passing his turn.

"This is the Woolen Mill Ditch. Let's stop here a minute. You must miss all the lush vegetation from your home."

April looked around, much enjoying the lavish display of wildflowers. "I can't say I've missed home. I've relished the adventure of coming west."

April was dazzled by the sight of water as Mr. Chandler slowed to a stop. She hopped off the bicycle to allow her driver to dismount. "I assume the Woolen Mill Ditch goes to a woolen mill?" she inquired.

"So it does. It flows from a nearby reservoir. It seems the city may turn the area into a park." Mr. Chandler offered his arm and escorted Miss Stringham along the bank. "I'm sorry I have no blanket to offer, but would you like to sit and enjoy the locale before we head home?"

"I would." April was surprised when Mr. Chandler removed his coat and laid it on the dirt near the water. She demurely took a seat as he plopped down beside her, then laid back, staring at the blue sky and puffy white clouds. "I have to thank you. This has turned into a fine day."

"Why, were things not going well?"

"I was a bit melancholy today, but I enjoyed the bicycle ride and it is beautiful here."

"Although we aren't far from home, I suggest you refrain from coming alone," Noah warned.

"Why, are there Indians?"

"Miss Stringham, I assure you there are no bands

Jean Jegel

of wild Indians roaming anywhere near here. The Indians who lived in this area were remarkably peaceful. It's simply not wise for a woman alone to wander about. Some mountain man could claim you for his own and you'd be gone without a trace. My mother would never forgive me. We're already on poor terms."

"We haven't been seeing much of you at home."

"I've tried to avoid confrontation. Perhaps once the wedding is over and the world doesn't end, my mother will discontinue hostilities. I don't expect congenial exchanges for now."

"I never imagined a pleasant home life held much interest for you. I'm surprised it's your goal."

"Well, you do seem to bring out the worst in me. Perhaps we got off on the wrong foot. Mother insisted you were the one she wished to hire, despite the fact there were local applicants. Your train fare became a sticking point. I do believe she made the correct decision, however. I must admit, you've been good for my mother. Are you planning on going to New York in June?"

"I haven't decided. I have interests here in Los Angeles now."

"Suitors?" Noah was curious.

"Suitors? Where did you get that idea?"

"From my mother. She assured me men were writing you from as far away as Massachusetts. She assumed they were suitors."

"Oh, I see. I wouldn't exactly describe them as suitors. I never had expectations of marriage."

"I thought every girl's dream hinged on matrimony. However did you escape childhood bereft of ambitions of weddings and babies?"

"Work kept me busy. My dreams evolved from stories I read about faraway places, adventures, and travel."

"Those dreams seem somehow less likely for you than one of marriage. You never owned a doll?"

"How do you know of such things? I did have a rag doll when I was small."

"I have three sisters. I know something of little girl's dreams and habits. What was your doll's name?"

Uncomfortable at the turn of conversation, April responded, "Ethel."

"Such an ordinary name. I would have thought her name would reflect your wandering spirit. Something like Jasmine or Sophia seems more likely."

April needed to change the topic. It seemed too personal. "Did your sisters rope you into playing daddy to their dolls?"

"They did, on occasion. Actually, my older sister never had much use for us. We didn't have much use for our youngest sister."

"Who is 'we'?"

"My sister Anna and I. She was only a year younger. We were inseparable. She would play soldiers or pirates with me and I played house with her. She married a dear friend of mine. He actually asked me for her hand before he asked my father." Noah looked into Miss Stringham's face. "She died in childbirth. I miss her."

"I'm sorry." April noted the soft expression on Mr. Chandler's face harden.

"Such is the way of the world."

"Are you planning a large family?"

"I don't care one way or another," Noah replied coldly. He changed the subject abruptly. "The flowers here are probably unfamiliar to you. Let me see if I can identify a few."

The pair engaged in light conversation for some time before Noah declared, "We should head back soon or we'll be late for supper."

"Are you planning on joining us this evening?"

"Why not?" Noah pushed himself off the ground. As April moved to get up, Mr. Chandler took an unfortunate step and tripped over her foot. Falling backward, he ended sitting in the ditch.

Dumbfounded, April laughed. "I'm so sorry," she managed as she rose to her feet. "Here, let me help you." She offered her hand.

"I'm tempted to pull you in here," Mr. Chandler admitted as he took her hand. But as he stood, he grasped Miss Stringham's arms and applied a hesitant kiss. Shocked at his own behavior, he pushed her away. "I'm sorry, I'm sorry."

April looked at him with a dreamy and perplexed expression. He could not resist and pulled her tight against him to apply a lingering and passionate kiss. He abruptly broke away and held her at arm's length.

"That was entirely inappropriate. Please forgive me, Miss Stringham. I promise, it won't happen again." She said nothing. "I think we should go back now."

Noah found the ride to Carroll Avenue uncomfortable, aside from his wet trousers. As an employer, his actions were reprehensible. But Miss Stringham sported the most irresistible and innocent expression. He enjoyed the sound of her laughter. Her hair smelled of lavender. If she told his mother how he behaved, he would never hear the end of it. He felt about six years old. Noah would not have understood the grin on Miss Stringham's face had he been able to see it.

April received a birthday present she could never have envisioned. She might be an old maid, but she'd been properly and thoroughly kissed. This day provided an event she would treasure forever—yet another experience she could draw upon in her writing.

* * *

Lula's frustration appeared evident. Her attempts to dissuade Noah from marriage to Deidre only resulted in hostility. She even managed to find him the perfect wife. To her disgust, he could not see it.

Surprised when Noah made an awkward appearance at dinner, she was reminded of days long gone when he guiltily hid some childhood crime.

Quiet in an attempt to keep the peace, Lula felt relief when April broke the silence.

"Thank you, Mr. Chandler, for letting me ride on your bicycle. I enjoyed the truly exhilarating experience."

Seemingly relieved of some burden, Noah replied, "It was my pleasure."

The two young people then commenced an uncharacteristically civil discussion. Certain Noah behaved improperly and was guilty as could be, Lula nonetheless delighted in their cordial conversation.

* * *

As the beautiful spring days flew by, Noah made a habit of joining the ladies for meals whenever possible, even occasionally appearing for lunch. Although his mother remained aloof, they did not come to verbal blows. He speculated she finally accepted the eventuality of his coming nuptials.

"My, you're looking beautiful this morning," Noah gushed as he applied a kiss to his mother's forehead.

"What do you want, Noah?"

"Can't I compliment my charming mother without ill intent? Is Miss Stringham late this morning?"

"She had a caller and won't be joining us."

"Is that a common occurrence?" wondered Noah.

"No. But Mr. Nelson from your office has been dropping by. I believe he became attracted to April while playing delivery boy when you broke your leg. He turned up bright and early to take April out for breakfast." Lula surveyed her son closely, intent on his reaction. She was not disappointed as the darkest scowl she ever saw settled on his features. Quickly realizing it might be wise to encourage her son's jealousy, she continued, "Perhaps a spring romance is upon us. I do believe April is quite marriageable, despite her age."

"She's too old for Mr. Nelson," pouted Noah.

"Actually, they're the same age. It's almost fortuitous, don't you think? What could be more romantic? She crossed the entire country only to find true love."

"Aren't you getting a bit ahead of yourself?"

"Probably not. It may have taken him a while to call on her, but I witnessed Mr. Nelson's besotted expression first hand. A man in love is hard to miss. Unfortunately, I've never seen that expression on your face. I wish I had."

"You know perfectly well, my ambitions for marriage are not romantic. Do we really need to retrace our differences yet again?"

Noah scarfed down his breakfast and departed for

work. Lula unexpectedly felt sorry for Mr. Nelson who would undoubtedly bear the brunt of Noah's rage. He wouldn't even understand why.

In order to better observe April's return, Lula took up a position on the front porch. Although she appeared to be absorbed in her cup of tea, she closely watched Mr. Nelson shake April's hand at the front gate and with a light step, head back to the trolley stop. He was likely already late for work, a fact his employer would not hesitate to use against him.

April plopped down on the elaborately woven wicker rocker across from Lula.

"Did you have a lovely breakfast, my dear?"

"I enjoyed myself."

April certainly did not have the look of a woman in love. "Will you be going out again?"

"I didn't mean to upset your morning. I'm sorry if I did."

"No, no. I haven't planned a thing for today. And you're back so early. Mr. Nelson seems a polite man."

"I suppose so."

"You're not interested in him?"

"I don't believe I'm particularly interested in having a beau, but I don't want to hurt his feelings."

Lula could not have hoped for a more perfect response. No need for April to fall in love with the wrong man. "Well, perhaps you should see him a few more times so you can be sure."

"I don't know—"

"Trust me. It won't hurt to give the boy a chance." Lula hoped her plan would not backfire.

* * *

Lula found herself anticipating mealtimes. If April

joined them, she and Noah carried on delightful conversations about books, the news, events in Los Angeles, even Noah's work. If she was absent, Noah ate quickly and hastily departed. Although curious about goings on at work, Lula didn't want to appear overly interested in Mr. Nelson. But even she was surprised at the turn of conversation one Friday evening.

"Miss Stringham, it occurs to me you might enjoy accompanying me on an adventure."

"Does it involve horses?" April's trepidation seemed obvious.

Noah laughed. "I believe you have it in you to become a true horsewoman, Miss Stringham. You certainly have the wardrobe for it. However, I think it wise to take equestrian endeavors more slowly. This adventure has to do with gold." He obviously piqued her interest. "Did you know the first gold strike in California was not at Sutter's Mill as most believe?"

"I didn't know that."

"About 40 miles north, there's a small town named Newhall. Gold was discovered in Placerita Canyon six years before the gold rush in Northern California. The appealing thing about it is, we can take the train. Since you're used to walking, we could easily walk to Placerita Canyon and try our hand at panning. I'll have Margarita pack a picnic for us. I know you're interested in experiencing all California has to offer. I thought you might enjoy this excursion."

"Do you know how to pan for gold?"

"I've panned in Placerita Canyon before as well as the Sierras. It will be a tiring day. I don't want you to think gold is simply lying on the ground for the taking. Panning is hard work. But I don't believe you ever shied away from arduous endeavors, or am I mistaken?"

Lula thought her son quite clever. He literally threw down a gauntlet. Even if April's curiosity had not already gotten the better of her, the girl would not back down now.

"You've presented an almost irresistible opportunity, Mr. Chandler."

"Good. We'll make a day of it."

* * *

Noah played the part of history buff on the train, explaining the wonders of the San Fernando Tunnel that connected Los Angeles to all points north.

"The tunnel took one-and-a-half years to complete by mostly Chinese laborers. They worked from both ends and when they met in the middle, they were only half an inch out of line. It's truly incredible when you consider the tunnel is almost 7,000 feet long. There were frequent cave-ins due to water and oil in the rocks above."

About halfway through the dark tunnel, April inquired, "This is completely safe?"

Noah chuckled. "It's been in operation for 15 years. I think we'll make it through all right. How's your romance with Mr. Nelson going?"

"I don't believe I would qualify our weekly breakfast as a romance."

"How would you qualify them?" Noah did his best to sound nonchalant.

"I believe Mr. Nelson and I are developing something of a friendship. If this is a romance, it will be the slowest in history. He shows no sign of asking me for anything but breakfast."

Noah observed Mr. Nelson's euphoric mood after his breakfast outings. Miss Stringham may not equate their relationship as a romance, but Noah was certain Mr. Nelson did.

April felt much a frontierswoman as she exited the train in Newhall, the first stop after the tunnel. She dressed in a workday skirt and blouse she brought from Concord and wore an old straw hat. Her thick hair fell in a long braid down her back. April carried a large picnic basket full of food.

Mr. Chandler's appearance stimulated her romantic notions. He wore an old plaid shirt, vest and a pair of Levi's riveted pants. He carried his gun in the belt around his waist and sported a black Stetson. A rucksack filled with tools and a canteen suspended from a strap over his shoulder promoted his image of the cowboy April imagined in her fantasies. Mr. Chandler bore no resemblance to a successful Los Angeles attorney.

"We'll walk as far up the canyon as you like," offered Noah as they started out. "We can pan most anywhere, but given the sunny morning, I suggest we find some shade. The Oak of the Golden Dream is about two miles from here."

"What is the Oak of the Golden Dream?"

"As the story goes, one Francisco Lopez fell asleep under the tree and dreamed of gold. When he awoke, he pulled some wild onions from the ground and found gold dust in the roots."

"Well, I suppose we should go as far as the tree. Your tales certainly tend to devolve around dreams."

"A less romantic version is Senor Lopez was no ignorant vaquero. He actually studied mineralogy at the University of Mexico which makes it unlikely his discovery was accidental. I much prefer the first legend."

"Personally, I've never had a clairvoyant dream in my life. I doubt I would follow up on it if I did."

"Perhaps those from more primitive cultures take their dreams seriously. Maybe they're simply more in tune with nature. We'll have more luck if we go further up the canyon."

"Why did you tell the man at the train station I was your sister?" April wondered aloud.

"I attempted to guard your reputation. Most people would not approve our unsupervised adventure today, no matter how innocent."

"My, I never imagined I had a reputation to protect. Isn't that something only the rich care about—the appearance of virtue?"

"I always thought old maids were particularly fond of their virtue," Noah could not seem to refrain from teasing Miss Stringham. Noting her frown, he knuckled her arm as they walked. "I'm kidding, Miss Stringham."

Although she gave him a dirty look, it seemed Miss Stringham desired a successful outing more than she cared to bicker. "Perhaps you should explain how to pan for gold so we won't waste time once we find a spot. How do we find a spot?"

"A bend in the flow of water is always a good place to look. If you can find rocks near the bend, gold tends to settle behind a large object on its course down the creek. I'll show you how to fill your pan and what to look for."

"I think I can tell if I've found gold."

"You'll be surprised how many things look like gold that aren't."

Chapter Nine

April was clearly disappointed in Placerita Creek, which she quickly renamed Placerita Trickle. Although the creek supported a bit more vegetation than seemed evident in Newhall, it was hardly an oasis. They began their hike amidst dry brush and the occasional live oak. As the canyon narrowed, Noah pointed out ferns, white alder and maple trees, sages and wild flowers. April remained unimpressed.

Noah's fellow prospector quickly abandoned decorum, apparently so intent on striking it rich, she no longer abided by rules of convention. First, she discarded her shoes and stockings in order to wade in the shallow creek. Next, she applied her new-found knowledge of managing skirts only instead of holding the hem, she pulled it high and firmly tucked it into her waistband. Her lacy knickers peeked from beneath the improvised pants. Taken with her shapely legs, Noah refocused his panning efforts to better observe Miss Stringham's curvaceous limbs.

He imagined the woman bore the look of avarice countless men before her displayed. Noah shoveled the first panful of rocks and sand for her. He showed her how to swirl the pan in the water and inspect the bottom for gold. She became excited over a single golden flake clinging to the side of her pan and doubted his explanation when Noah purported her find was too shiny and too light to be gold. She could only boast of being the proud owner of a fleck of fool's gold. Distrustful, April pushed the fleck into the small jar of water she carried in her pocket. He laughed when the fleck refused to sink to the bottom.

Next, he explained how gold dust might be extracted from the black sand remaining in the bottom of the pan. The black particles could be blown away once dry. Heavier gold would remain.

Having quickly been dismissed after his brief introductory lecture, Noah recognized his pupil needed to discover some nugget of gold, however small, or she might never be willing to return home. He found one tiny nugget and was intent to deposit it in her pan, thus avoiding disappointment. But that occurred before his attention focused on her legs. He became further distracted by the growling of his stomach.

"I think we should eat. We can pan a bit after lunch, but then we need to head back down the canyon." He could tell from her expression, Miss Stringham thought him daft.

"We've only just begun."

"It's well past lunch." Noah extracted his pocket watch and held it up, although it was too far away for his cohort to make an accurate appraisal. "It's 2 o'clock already."

April trudged through the water to have a better look, not trusting him to provide an honest time. "Oh, you're right. We can spread the picnic blanket up there." Noah looked to the side of the creek. They were in a narrow area, boxed in by a hill on one side and a three-foot embankment on the other.

The prospectors enjoyed the fine lunch Margarita prepared. The highlight was lemonade, which April thoughtfully deposited in the creek to keep cold. Due to the fresh air and invigorating exercise or possibly the late hour, both were ravenous and made quick work of the meal. Miss Stringham did not dress for luncheon. Leaving her shoes and stockings near the creek and keeping her skirt tucked into her waistband, she sat cross-legged on the blanket, much to Noah's delight.

"Miss Stringham, I have a question. You once mentioned you didn't have a horse on your farm and I've been trying to understand how that could be possible. What on earth did you grow? How could you farm without a single horse?"

"When I was small, we had hired men who worked the farm and I know we had a horse then. Once my father passed, our banker, Mr. Farmer, leased out our land to neighbors. Management of the farm seemed beyond my mother's abilities. Evidently, she took a mortgage and the leases paid the mortgage—at least most of the time. I'm certain the bank took a loss. I did little more than break even after the auction. The farm was all around. But none of it really belonged to us. I only kept chickens."

"You never considered staying on and farming yourself? You seem an industrious sort. You might have prospered."

"The bank wanted their money. Staying was never an option. Are you still sorry you brought me here?"

Noah smiled awkwardly. Miss Stringham put him on the spot. "You've successfully entertained my mother—perhaps not in any traditional way—certainly not the way I envisioned. But the answer to your question is no. I'm pleased at the way things turned out. You should consider going to New York with Mother."

"To inherit her money? Are you back to that, then?"

"Perhaps. But she loves you like a daughter. She could provide a rich life."

"How do you know I don't already have a rich life?" April teased.

"Oh, Miss Stringham, you sound quite intriguing. If I didn't know better, I'd think you have some exciting secret life."

The beautiful spring day grew more than a bit warm. The sound of water trickling over rocks in the creek had a relaxing effect. Noah wanted nothing so much as to lie in the shade of a nearby oak and have a nap. He even entertained locking Miss Stringham in his embrace while doing so. But it became apparent the woman had other ideas as she left the picnic blanket to stare down the embankment toward the creek. She undoubtedly assumed fortune must be at her fingertips.

April turned around, intending to repack the picnic basket when she spotted a rattlesnake slithering from behind a boulder. It curled and shook its rattle not two feet from where April stood. Before she could utter a word, a shot rang out. Mr. Chandler quickly drew his revolver and shot the snake as it lunged toward April. Startled, she jumped back, falling off the edge of the embankment into a bush.

"Miss Stringham!" Mr. Chandler yelled as he jumped off the embankment to her side. He knelt beside her and grabbed her shoulders. "Are you all right? Did he get you?" He too quickly released her shoulders and April fell back into the bush. Examining her feet and legs carefully, Noah found no marks, other than scratches from twigs. "Talk to me! Did you feel anything?" Alarmed at her silence, he again grabbed her shoulders.

"I think I'm all right," admitted April. "The snake didn't bite me and the bush broke my fall."

"Oh, thank God, thank God." Noah took her in his arms and hugged her tightly. "I have gone years without seeing a single rattler, I don't know why they're plaguing me now."

April rather thought the snake plagued her. She had to admit it felt incredibly good to be in Mr. Chandler's protective embrace. She was actually disappointed when he let go and helped her up.

Feeling terribly shaken, April appeared reluctant to commence the trip home. "Maybe we could rest for a while."

"How thoughtless of me. It would be pleasant to rest under the oak where we ate lunch." Miss Stringham appeared unsteady and apparently needed a chance to gather her wits. If he managed to indulge his naptime fantasy, what could be the harm in that?

* * *

Noah was startled awake by the caw of a crow. When he urged Miss Stringham to lie on the picnic blanket beside him, he offered his shoulder for her pillow. He quickly fell asleep. But now, Miss Stringham was nowhere in sight.

He came to his feet, certain of her location. Walking toward the embankment, he looked upstream to find her crouched in the middle of the creek intent upon her new obsession. Noah walked along the embankment where it descended to a wider part of the canyon.

"I see you're ready to leave," he suggested.

A sheepish grin met his comment. "I thought I'd try a new spot before we left. I didn't want to wake you. I think I found a few nuggets! Nothing big, mind you, but they look like gold to me." Noah hated to quash her enthusiasm, but it was getting late and he had no desire to spend a night in the canyon.

Before he could roust Miss Stringham from her pursuit, two men on horseback approached. Reflexively moving his hand over his gun, Noah realized he left it near the picnic blanket while he napped. He gazed at Miss Stringham as she released her skirt from its waistband, allowing the hem to fall in the creek.

"Howdy there, ma'am," began one of the riders. "We thought you might have a few vittles to share."

Noah answered as the men dismounted. "Sorry, boys. We ate our lunch some time ago, there's nothing left. We were just leaving." He didn't like the way the men eyed Miss Stringham. He was stupid to have left his gun behind. Noah approached the horses.

Noticing the tall cowboy appeared unarmed, the two men weren't inclined to ride off empty-handed.

"Well, seems to me you likely have some change you could loan us. We been out of work for some while. We need to eat." The shorter, stockier of the two could not take his eyes off April as she emerged from the creek. It appeared money was not his only goal. The two men dismounted and approached Noah.

"It seems to me ya'll wouldn't bring a lady out here without funds."

Noah reached in his vest pocket and withdrew two

silver dollars. He threw them in the dirt at the men's feet. "That's all I have."

"Naw, that can't be right." The plump man lunged at Noah. Noah landed a punch on the side of the man's face and braced for the second man's assault. The three exchanged blows. Although younger and taller, Noah was at a decided disadvantage. The skinny vagrant finally managed to pin his arms as the plump one landed blows to Noah's face and gut. After kicking the plump man who fell backwards, Noah struggled to free his arms.

"*Stop*!" came Miss Stringham's commanding voice. Noah looked in terror as Miss Stringham stood on the embankment and pointed his gun toward them. Knowing she could not shoot, he felt an unlikely kinship with his attackers. He was more willing to face them than Miss Stringham's wayward gun. The last thing he needed was to be shot by his mother's companion in the middle of nowhere. As he encouraged her to lower the gun, the plump man raised his hands in the air.

"Now, little lady, don't do anything rash." All three men could see an unsteady Miss Stringham needed both hands to hold the gun. She visibly shook from both fear and the weight of the revolver. The barrel of the gun swayed in a circular motion. "Why don't you put that down so we can be on our way?"

Before the man could utter another word, April cocked the gun and pulled the trigger. Noah stared at the plump man, who danced away from a bullet at his feet.

"All right, all right," he yelled. "Don't shoot, we're leaving. Come on, Johnny, let's leave these two to their business."

Noah dropped to his knees as the skinny stranger released him then scrambled to mount his horse. The pair were out of range in moments.

April hurried toward Mr. Chandler. "Are you all right?"

"I've been better. You made quite a shot. How did you manage?"

Deadly serious, April admitted. "What are you talking about? I missed. I tried to shoot him through the heart."

Noah burst into laughter, holding tight to his stomach. "Oh, shit, that hurts."

* * *

After removing the gun from her custody, Noah gladly submitted to Miss Stringham's ministrations as he sat against a tree trunk. April retrieved the silver dollars from the dirt and replaced them in his vest pocket, then used her handkerchief, moistened by water from the creek, to cleanse his face and cuts. But when she went to unbutton his shirt, Noah grabbed her hand. "What are you doing?"

"I need to take a look. You could have a broken rib."

"I assure you, I don't have a broken rib."

"How do you know?"

"I was young and reckless once. I got in my share of fights. I learned long ago to tighten my gut to take a blow. I may be sore, but nothing is broken."

April thought this unlikely. A person could have internal injuries from the kind of abuse Mr. Chandler had taken.

"Nonetheless, I would like to examine you."

It occurred to Noah, he wouldn't mind at all if

Miss Stringham took a look. In fact, he wouldn't mind showing her everything if he could find a way to do it. What was the matter with him? His ideas were entirely inappropriate. "Suit yourself."

April appeared much more competent than she felt. She'd never seen a man's bare chest in her life. The most of Mr. Chandler she'd seen was his feet. Nonetheless, she pulled his shirt aside and carefully ran her fingers along his ribs. He did not flinch at her examination. Two bruises were beginning to show on his abdomen, although April felt too distracted to focus on the bruises. Mr. Chandler's torso displayed prominent muscles. Aware of his gaze, April tried her best not to stare. "I believe you're correct. Nothing seems to be broken," she admitted as she buttoned his shirt. "Do you think you can walk?"

"Certainly," Noah declared, but it soon became evident he was in pain. He leaned heavily on April as they walked up the embankment toward the spot where the picnic basket sat.

"I don't think we can walk all the way back to the road. We only have an hour or so of daylight and you can't walk fast." April refrained from admitting her doubts about supporting Mr. Chandler's weight for any distance.

"Is there food left in the basket?" Noah inquired.

"Some bread and jam. I believe there's an apple and a few cookies."

"That's plenty. We can eat the snake." Noah wanted to laugh again at Miss Stringham's appalled expression, but he knew it would hurt. "Trust me, you can eat snake. It tastes like chicken. Did you see the lean-to about a mile downstream from here?"

"I can't say I noticed."

"I think we can go that far. Can you build a fire?"

"Yes." April folded the picnic blanket and placed it in the basket. "But I don't think I can abide any more snakes or rats or critters, four-legged or two-legged. If we utilize this structure, it better be vacant." She would have to go down to the creek to get her shoes and stockings and gather the tools. Patting the pocket where she stowed her gold, April prepared to depart.

* * *

They ate bread, jam and rattlesnake for dinner, deciding to keep the cookies and apple for breakfast. Mr. Chandler was correct. The meat did taste like chicken. He spared April the preparation, skinning the snake and cutting the meat into chunks. She cooked in one of the gold mining pans using wild onions she found for flavoring. April couldn't resist an inspection of the roots, which unfortunately showed no trace of gold.

She volunteered to stay awake in case the two men returned and promised to awaken Mr. Chandler at any strange sound. The lean-to turned out to be a mess, undoubtedly full of vermin. April sat against the outside wall staring at flames from the fire she built.

Mr. Chandler's head rested in her lap. He fell instantly to sleep. She could not help but wonder at the man's ability to sleep in the dirt. Having never slept anywhere but a bed and her seat on the train to California made staying awake less of a challenge. April hoped by morning the meal and rest would revive Mr. Chandler sufficiently. She didn't relish the idea of going for help alone in light of their unfortunate recent experiences.

April acquired a wealth of first-hand knowledge

to apply to her writing and contemplated ways to implement newfound information. Try as she might, she was having difficulty developing her plot. Ever since Mr. Chandler kissed her, she seemed unable to write about the malicious Charlie Boatman. Previously, April only needed to recall Mr. Chandler's multitudinous shortcomings and Charlie exploded across the pages of her story with incredible cruelty and sinister intent.

Perhaps she would concentrate on the two villains who attacked Mr. Chandler. Her storyline could use something fresh.

* * *

Noah collapsed into his seat on the train. Today seemed endless. The walk out of the canyon was uncomfortable though not impossible. He tried his best not to be a burden and thankfully felt somewhat refreshed after sleep. Miss Stringham proved a real trooper. He never believed she would stay awake and keep guard the entire night, but she evidently had not slept. She carried the knapsack full of tools and the picnic basket and served as a crutch during their walk. Dirty, tired and hungry, she found abundance in their situation Noah could not see. Though not exactly cheery, she seemed more agreeable than he imagined a woman would be after their harrowing experience.

"Aren't you tired?"

"Yes. But I plan to sleep on the train. A bath will feel wonderful. When you're done, of course," April added as an afterthought. She was the employee after all.

"No, Miss Stringham. You surely deserve a soak in the bathtub when we arrive home. You can take your time—luxuriate in peace for as long as your heart desires. You earned it. If not for your crack shot, who knows what might have befallen us," Noah charitably remarked. "By the way, you never showed me your gold."

April's face lit up at the thought of gold in her pocket. She retrieved the small jar and held it up for Mr. Chandler's inspection.

"Why, I do believe you have the genuine article there, Miss Stringham. I see one the size of a pea and two smaller nuggets. Am I missing anything?"

"No," April beamed. "It's all I found. But that one is quite large, don't you think? How much is it worth?"

Noah did not believe the nuggets had much value but didn't wish to disappoint. "I don't know. Do you want me to take them to the assay office and redeem them for coin?"

"No, no. I want to keep them. Gold always holds its value. Maybe someday I could find more and have a whole ounce." She yawned and laid her head against the seat back.

Soon Miss Stringham fell soundly asleep. The ride to Los Angeles was not long, but Noah surmised a nap would help alleviate her fatigue. He didn't mind at all when her head came to rest against his shoulder. After all, Miss Stringham was alone in the world. He relished his protective inclinations until an unpleasant scenario occurred to him. What would this adventure have been if Deidre was his companion?

* * *

"I know you've been up to no good."

Noah stared at his mother over his cup of coffee.

"What makes you think so? Did Miss Stringham

regale you with some outrageous story about our trip?"

"She gave me exactly the same story you did. You tripped and fell and couldn't walk out of the canyon last night, which I know to be a lie. You may be a good liar but April is not. I want to know what went on. April isn't a worldly woman. She's naïve and sweet and if you've taken advantage of her—"

"Don't be ridiculous. I'm engaged to be married. I have never in my life met such an exasperating woman as Miss Stringham. You needn't worry, her virtue is entirely intact."

"You were much too solicitous when you got home, commanding her to bathe and take her dinner in bed, even ordering me to find bath salts for her. Something is amiss."

"I've never known you to be so melodramatic. She simply doesn't want you to worry any more than I do. Our adventure held a few more risks than I anticipated but nothing serious. I was simply grateful for her help. Now if you don't mind, I believe I'll retire as well." Noah rose from the table and kissed his mother on the forehead. "Besides, you're already mad enough at me. If I damaged your protégé in some way, I know I'd never hear the end of it. Good night, Mother."

Lula went upstairs and attempted to pressure April into providing a more thorough account of her gold panning experience, to no avail. April proudly produced her tiny jar of nuggets, proof of her adventure. Contemplating her misgivings, Lula finally retired to her own bedchamber.

* * *

"What the hell is this, Miss Stringham?"

"Please, Mr. Lynch, language."

Mr. Lynch pursed his lips for a moment and started over, without much improvement. "Who the hell are these men, Tex and Johnny? We have a lucrative collaboration here. Why are you changing course?"

"I'm happy you feel our collaboration is lucrative because this manuscript will cost you $150."

Mr. Lynch appeared to be on the verge of some apoplectic fit. "That's twice what I paid you last time and even $75 was an absurd amount."

"Nonetheless, $150 is the going rate for 25,000 words. My work sells your magazine. This is my third submission. I will be paid accordingly."

"I don't know where you get these outlandish ideas, Miss Stringham. I certainly am not going to pay you $150 and I expect you to change the ending."

"First of all, if we can't agree on a price, I'm prepared to offer my work to the *Times* and the *Herald.* It will go to the highest bidder. Someone else will publish Little May's adventures and on a daily, not weekly basis. Secondly, if I am to keep my work fresh, I need some artistic license. Sticking to a tired plot will eventually bore my readers. You need to have some faith in my ability, Mr. Lynch," although April was the last person to have faith in her own abilities. She bit her lip and waited to see if her bluff would work.

Mr. Lynch resorted to yelling. "You are the most exasperating woman I have ever met and I'm including my wife in that evaluation. You are arrogant and cold and entirely selfish."

"There's no need to get personal, Mr. Lynch. I'm simply a businesswoman. I find it difficult to believe you treat your male authors so contemptuously." She rose to leave the office.

"Well, be sure to pick up your draft for $150 on the way out!" he yelled. He looked through the frosted glass as Miss Stringham waited for her money at the front desk. He smiled. The woman had some gumption. And she brought unimagined notoriety to his new publication.

* * *

"I believe I'm all packed," Lula breathed a sigh of relief as she entered the parlor. "After living here all these years, I've acquired too much baggage."

Noah glanced up from his law book. "I'll take you to the station in the carriage."

"I still believe this arrangement is entirely improper. April should not be alone in the house with you."

"I'm not going to rent a room when I can sleep in my own bed. And you're the one who told her she could stay. It certainly wasn't my doing. I'm not going to rent her a hotel room, either. She won't even be an employee once you leave."

"This is still not proper."

"She's an old maid, Mother. I don't believe she's concerned about her reputation. Miss Stringham has to be gone before Deidre takes up residence, whenever that might be."

"I imagined you'd want her to stay and keep an eye on things. I think you should pay her."

"She has free room and board, which should suffice. My affairs are no longer your concern. Go to San Francisco and enjoy your daughters and grandchildren before the wedding."

"When are you coming?"

"I have a trial on Monday. It shouldn't take more than a day. I plan to come on Wednesday."

"Only three days before the wedding?"

"I thought you ladies had matters well in hand? I'm only supposed to show up. That's the main function of the groom."

"You are certainly not an eager groom."

"Don't start on this again. Why don't we part on good terms? I'm certain you'll settle back into your life in New York after the wedding and the next time we meet, you'll see how happily married I am."

"You will never be happily married. You will be a successful lawyer but never happily married."

"I am a successful lawyer. I'll soon be a rich lawyer with a lucrative practice. I'm intelligent enough to know what will make me happy. Are you ready to go?"

"I want to wait until April gets back so I can say a proper goodbye."

Noah could see his mother tearing up. "She's only a servant, Mother. You should never have become so attached to her."

"She has been the joy of my life for nearly a year, which is more than I can say for any of my own children."

Noah ignored the remark. The sooner he loaded his mother on the train, the better.

Chapter Ten

Once Lula left for San Francisco, a heady feeling of freedom washed over April. She was completely independent, a working woman with a good income and free lodging. April could not stop smiling. The captain of her own life would be living alone in a grand house once Mr. Chandler departed. She had money in the bank and Mr. Lynch bought her stories as fast as she could write, although she decided to slow down in an attempt to improve the quality of her work. She didn't need to maintain the pace of writing three dime-novel-sized books every six months. As April made plans to investigate the price of a typewriter, she grabbed a pencil and started to write.

Charlie Boatman, having lost his saloon in a poker game to the evil Tex and Johnny, sat in a corner of the barroom nursing his whiskey. Little May almost felt sorry for the man.

Charlie might have been cruel, but May's life took a definite turn for the worse once Tex and Johnny controlled the saloon. The men loaded work on her. She often stayed at the saloon 20 hours a day, scrubbing, cooking, cleaning and serving drinks. She seldom bothered to go home, falling asleep on a pile of burlap bags in the storeroom behind the saloon.

No longer a girl, May became alarmed at the way the two men eyed her when they thought she wasn't looking. Determined to protect her honor, she carried her father's Derringer in her apron pocket.

A knock on the front door interrupted April's work. She answered to find a Western Union delivery boy holding a telegram from San Francisco addressed to Mr. Chandler. Fearing something dire might have occurred, April thought it best to take the missive directly to her former employer who left to play baseball this beautiful Saturday afternoon.

Knowing only that the game was located in nearby Boyle Heights, April grabbed her reticule and hat and hurried to the corner of Spring and First Streets where the newly built Boyle Heights line branched off. April observed the hustle and bustle once she climbed aboard. This was the business center of the city where cable cars came and went every few minutes. A fellow passenger helpfully provided directions to the baseball game.

Clutching the telegram in her hand, April advanced toward a field where men sported short-sleeved shirts with the name Boyle Heights Browns emblazoned across the front. They wore short pants, a wide belt and some unusual small shoe unfamiliar to April. Every Browns player had a brown, billed cap.

She spied Mr. Chandler squatted behind a man holding a shaped stick. A wire cage evidently was meant to protect his face. Not wanting to interrupt the game, April carefully placed the telegram in her bag and took a seat on a bench beside a young woman.

"Will there be a pause in the playing?" April inquired.

"Between innings. The man coming up to bat is my husband," the girl gushed.

April had no idea who the girl's husband could be. She readjusted her straw hat, deciding to wait and see if she could determine when the so-called inning ended.

Noah Chandler was focused on his pitcher. Wild Bill gained fame for his spitball, a pitch so unpredictable few batters could make contact. Difficult to hit, the pitch was almost impossible to catch. Bill determinedly coated the white ball with tobacco spittle until it resembled the color of a football.

Having caught sight of Miss Stringham seated near the opposing team's bench, Noah redirected his attention. As he rose from his crouch, Bill let go his pitch, which clonked Noah in the side of the head.

Noah came to, spread-eagled on top of home plate. He looked up into the worried eyes of Miss Stringham. His head lay in her lap. Her hands gently cradled the sides of his face. Her anxious expression reminded him of the night they spent at the lean-to. Hers was the only face that expressed concern for him in years. As he gazed into her eyes, he spoke from his heart. "Marry me, April."

Two of his teammates sniggered in the background. His fellow Boyle Heights Browns were gathered around.

"What did he say?" asked Wild Bill.

"He asked her to marry him! You got a bad hit in the head, there Boatman, you better back off and take it easy," replied the second baseman.

April looked up at Jack Broadmore, the only

familiar face in the crowd besides the man named Bill who helped find Mr. Chandler the day he fell off his horse. "Why do they call him Boatman?" she asked.

Jack failed to note her alarm and offered, "Oh, there's that silly story in the *Pacific Weekly*. All the girls are reading it. Somebody noticed the name reflected Noah's. Noah—Boatman; Charlie—Chandler. Charlie in the story supposedly looks like him. He's been getting razzed about it ever since." In a louder voice he added, "Look here, Noah, you need to get your wits about you. Don't go marrying anybody on the spur of the moment here. You're getting married next Saturday in San Francisco, remember?"

"Don't listen to them," urged Noah, his eyes riveted on April's face. "I've never done anything so right in my life. Marry me right now, today. Will you marry me?"

"All right, Mr. Chandler."

"I think it best you start calling me Noah."

* * *

Judge Warner at first believed the two attorneys were playing some sort of prank. Looking ragged, the law firm of Broadmore and Chandler remained on the porch since the maid refused them entry. Mr. Chandler tightly clutched a tall, slender woman. All three were dusty and dirty. The woman sported a smudge on her nose. The "gentlemen" had obviously been playing baseball.

"What's going on here?" the Judge demanded. These two were a handful, always pushing the limits of the court's patience, occasionally theatrical beyond the Judge's tolerance.

"I know this seems an unusual request, but I

would like you to marry us. Jack is my best man. Can we come in?" Noah asked hopefully.

After determining the man was serious in his request, Judge Warner invited the trio into his home. His wife improvised a hasty bouquet of hortensias from her garden and tearfully witnessed the brief ceremony in the Judge's library. She had always been emotional at weddings.

Noah Chandler slid the paper band off a cigar on the Judge's desk to use as a ceremonial wedding ring. Moments later, a jubilant Mr. and Mrs. Chandler walked down the sidewalk, arms wrapped tightly around each other. Completely dumbfounded, Jack Broadmore stood on the Judge's front porch shaking his head from side to side.

"What is this about?" asked the Judge. "This marriage is binding. Your partner understands he is really and truly married?"

"Oh, it's exactly what he wanted, Sir. At least for today. You see, he got hit in the head by a baseball. It evidently made him fall in love. He was supposed to be married next week."

"So they simply moved the wedding date forward a week?"

"No. That's to another woman."

Judge Warner laughed. "Well, he seems like a man in love. I'm not so sure about the lady. I'm afraid it won't matter what he decides he wants tomorrow. The man is married now."

* * *

"What have I done?" whispered April to herself. She listened to the relaxing sound of waves crashing on the beach. The bracing scent of sea air from the open window filled the room. The sky lightened with the dawn.

After their hasty wedding ceremony, Mr. Chand—Noah took her to the station where they boarded a train to Redondo Beach. They sat in silence. Noah could not seem to take his eyes off her. He appeared truly smitten; even she could see it, as plain as the nose on her face. Perhaps she'd seen this look on other occasions since their gold panning adventure.

Assuring repayment, Noah had asked his teammates to empty their pockets. Although the banks were closed on Saturday, he wanted to give his bride a proper honeymoon. He took a suite at the Hotel Redondo before accompanying April on a shopping excursion. They purchased clothes for an elegant dinner at the hotel and more to use at the beach. Noah was determined to enjoy all Redondo Beach could offer: the flower gardens, the shore, the pier. He even purchased swimming wear so they could go in the ocean. They stopped by a jewelry store where he purchased a beautiful wedding band. A deep green emerald had moonstones mounted all around. This purchase was billed to his law firm. Noah placed the ring on April's finger as the newlyweds stood on the beach at sunset.

In retrospect, Saturday seemed like some sort of fairy tale. April glanced toward the dresser where her beautiful nightgown—wrapped in delicate tissue and rose petals—remained in its box. It was the loveliest garment she'd ever seen.

She could barely make out the features of her sleeping husband on the pillow next to hers. April's ideas about what happened in a marriage bed had not exactly come to fruition last night. She'd seen animals and birds. After all, she lived on a farm. April assumed coupling between a man and a woman would be a discreet encounter, under the covers and under cover of darkness. A person could tolerate any indignity for 30 seconds or so. She had not been prepared for the activities of last evening.

Noah was gentle and loving. But the things he did! With his hands, with his lips. Simply thinking about it made her face hot. She found the whole experience to be, well, stimulating. Even exciting.

All her life she heard preachers warn against the sin of lust. She never imagined what they were talking about. Now she knew. She lusted after her husband. Certain the entire night was completely sinful, April bit her lip.

There were other aspects of her hasty marriage that were only now beginning to sink in. She recently attained true freedom yet threw it away without a single thought. Why had she behaved so impetuously? If she could only manage to cross the room and put on her nightgown, perhaps she could think more clearly.

"Penny for your thoughts."

April flinched, so lost in contemplation she didn't notice Noah's eyes were open.

"Are we experiencing doubts with the dawn?" he continued, noting her serious frown. "I believe I heard somewhere that honesty is an important element in a marriage. Perhaps we should start out on the right foot."

"I was considering the fact I've given up all my freedom," April admitted. She could see her response displeased her new husband as his smile vanished. But then he laughed.

"I believe countless men have awoken the day

after their wedding considering that exact thought."

"But it doesn't bother you?"

"No, I've been prepared for marriage for some time. I don't believe I ever thought my freedom would be much impacted, but I may be mistaken. I planned to marry for business, not for love. Perhaps we should assure each other at least some of our freedom will remain intact. We are not, after all, joined at the *hip*." Noah gave his bride a wicked grin.

"You can rest assured, I do not intend to comport myself as the all-knowing, all-powerful head of household. You obviously would not tolerate such behavior, in any case." But having said that, he became serious. "I do love you April, have no doubt. You know me better than anyone in my adult life and yet, you've put up with me, even cared about me. I believe you love me, but this might be beyond your understanding at this juncture. I intend to win you over in any case. I will be at my most charming, most caring, most fascinating self in order to obtain your declarations of love at the earliest possible moment. We are well-matched and I look forward to an entertaining and exciting life together. I don't have a single regret and I doubt I ever will."

"How's your head? Does it hurt?" April pulled the sheet close around her body and leaned over to touch the side of her husband's head. "There's still a knot."

"I have to admit, my head does hurt. But my mind has been preoccupied. I haven't really noticed." At this, he pulled the sheet from between them to feel her skin against his own and beamed at April's wide-eyed reaction.

"I need to talk to you," April stated as Noah kissed her forehead, then her cheeks. "I'm not certain our behavior is, well, completely moral. I have concerns." Her breathing became labored. Her feelings of lust returned with little provocation.

"Hmm, I know men married for years who have never seen their wife's naked body."

April wondered how a woman might manage to have a husband like that.

"Something tells me you would find such an arrangement, how should I say, less liberating than last night's activities?" As he kissed her neck, feeling little resistance, he continued, "Mrs. Chandler, you are a God-fearing woman or am I mistaken?"

"No, you are correct."

"So, I assume you've read all those biblical commands about submitting to your husband?"

"Well, yes but—"

"There you go. That's exactly what's occurring." But Noah became too engrossed in kissing his wife to continue the conversation and she was much too filled with lust to argue.

* * *

Ravenously hungry, Mr. and Mrs. Chandler sat opposite each other at their table in the restaurant of the Hotel Redondo.

"What happens now?" inquired April after scarfing down her over-easy eggs, sausage and toast in a most unladylike manner.

"Well, I thought we would stroll on the beach and collect a few gems as souvenirs of our stay. I hoped to swim this afternoon, if you approve. I thought perhaps a nap might be in order before dinner." April could not help but notice her husband's innuendo as he raised his eyebrows in a suggestive manner. "We can stay until

Tuesday. Jack agreed to take my trial appearance tomorrow."

"It's not what I meant. What happens about Deidre?"

"I don't want you to worry. I'll take care of it. Let's relax and enjoy our days here." Noah observed his bride's expression as it turned to one of alarm.

"Oh, my goodness! The telegram. I never gave it to you." April opened her reticule and dug through the contents then handed Noah his missive. "It's the reason I came to the baseball game."

"Well, if we're lucky, this is from Deidre and she's eloped with some old beau." Noah opened the envelope. "We're evidently not that lucky. This is from my mother. She left her favorite shawl in the downstairs closet and wants me to bring it.

"We haven't spent much time talking, have we? It's not as if we planned our future. So, we need to address first things first. Do you swim?"

"No. Isn't swimming in the ocean dangerous?"

"What makes you think so?"

"I read an article in the *Herald* on my way here. It gave a tragic account of a sickly wife who watched, horrified, as her husband drowned in Long Beach. Where is Long Beach?"

"South of here. I'm a strong swimmer and I'll teach you. In the meantime, we can have fun in the waves. We won't go out far."

Doubtfully, April replied, "You're not willing to discuss any matter further in the future?"

"Well, unless you'd like to plan our nap in more detail." Noah delightedly gazed at April as she squirmed in her seat and looked about to confirm no one overheard his comment.

The honeymoon progressed in much the way Noah anticipated. He escorted his bride for walks on the beach, swimming, delicious meals and entertaining naps. They attended a concert at the Chautauqua Amphitheater on Sunday afternoon and played games on the pier Monday evening. Before they checked out of the hotel on Tuesday, the Chandlers visited the flower gardens where April filled a large basket with carnations, a flower sure to survive the June heat on the trip home. She carefully placed her wedding flowers in a box, planning to preserve them, and scolded Noah when he attempted to discard the cigar band he substituted for a wedding ring at their ceremony.

"Don't throw that out!"

"Why? You have a real ring now. I know you remember. I caught you admiring it with alarming frequency."

"It's my first wedding ring, the official one. I want to keep it always." She lovingly placed it in the box beside her bouquet.

As the couple boarded the train for home, April's anxiety became obvious. Their honeymoon seemed idyllic, the best days of her entire life—incredible beyond her imagining. She had no doubt a rougher road lay ahead.

"Look at me," Noah commanded, seeing her distress. April looked into his eyes.

He put his arm around her shoulders and reassured, "Everything will be fine. I have to go to San Francisco though. I need to tell Deidre about this in person. I owe her that much."

"I'll go along."

"No. I won't subject you to Deidre's spite. You,

my darling bride, will stay home, organize our household and take up your wifely duties. I'm planning on being back on Wednesday night, Thursday morning at the latest. We'll make all our life plans then."

"Noah, how old are you?" April considered the fact she knew little about her husband.

"Thirty-four."

"Your mother was right. You're much too old for Deidre."

"But just right for you?"

April only smirked in response.

* * *

Anxious to share her news with the Fitzpatricks, April instead met her first obstacle as the new Mrs. Chandler. Jack proved indispensable the day of their wedding, first offering to fill in at Noah's trial, then agreeing to inform the Fitzpatricks Miss Stringham was safe, sound and married, and would not return to the house on Carroll Avenue for several days. April could only imagine how shocking this information would have been but was taken aback when she received a cold and official greeting as the new lady of the house.

Noah, noticing his wife's expression when Mr. and Mrs. Fitzpatrick formally met them at the front door, decided to leave her to it and made a hasty retreat. He didn't care how or if April continued her friendship. This would be her domain and she had to sort it out.

As Noah escaped upstairs, April quickly decided on a course of action. Linking arms with both Fitzpatricks, she pulled them toward the kitchen.

"I think we should have a chat," she began, noting

their awkward reaction to her friendly gesture.

"Yes, ma'am," replied Mr. Fitzpatrick.

"No, there's no ma'am here. I'm April, I always have been; I always will be. I may be the lady of the house now, but your friendship is dear to me."

"But it's not proper," a clearly distressed Mrs. Fitzpatrick chimed in.

"Perhaps not, but I'm not a terribly proper person. Sit down at the table and I'll make some tea." She almost laughed at the appalled expressions that greeted her when she turned from the stove.

"This may not be a conventional way to move forward, but we're all adults and I believe we can work together to keep this house. I'm certain Mr. Chandler wishes your relationship to continue as it always has. I think we can be friends and co-workers and maintain a modicum of formality when Mr. Chandler entertains."

Mr. Fitzpatrick explained, "I must tell you, Margarita is gone, for good I think this time. She doubted Mr. Chandler would return with his wife, his other wife. She took a job at a restaurant where she used to work."

"Well, I don't think we'll have a problem there. I actually miss cooking. What say we split Margarita's ample paycheck? I'll have Mr. Chandler add half to your weekly pay and the other half can go toward household funds. I'll be responsible for cooking our meals and you can be responsible for yours. I'd appreciate if you will take charge of the kitchen clean-up, Mrs. Fitzpatrick. We can economize and I'll have my chance in the kitchen." From the moment she mentioned raised wages, April had them hooked.

"Now let me tell you all about the wedding and our trip to Redondo Beach," she continued excitedly.

By the end of the hour they shared tea, cookies and conversation. The household appeared to be on track and April received an invitation for Wednesday night dessert at the Fitzpatricks'.

* * *

Having no desire to spend even one night away, Noah doubted his business could be concluded as quickly as he hoped. After reluctantly packing a satchel for his brief trip to San Francisco, he decided it should be safe to find out about dinner.

Noah's stomach growled as the smell of supper wafted up the stairwell. He gathered the stack of mail that accumulated in his absence and took a seat at the dining table.

"Mr. Chandler, you need to come this way," April crooked her finger as she stuck her head through the kitchen door. "You're having dinner with the cook this evening."

Frowning, Noah picked up the mail and headed for the kitchen.

"Have a seat."

Finding his wife standing at the stove, her apron in place, Noah did as he was told.

"Has a mutiny occurred? Everyone has left our employ?"

"Margarita quit while we were gone. I don't think she believed you would return to Los Angeles to set up housekeeping. Maybe she didn't relish the idea of Deidre as mistress of the house. Who knows? They had an unfortunate history. I divided her wages in half—you need to add half to the Fitzpatricks' weekly pay."

"And I'm going to add the other half to yours?"

he teased.

"No, I'm saving you the other half. I have a desire to cook for my new husband. We're going to be considerably less formal for meals—unless there are guests. Are you offended by eating at the kitchen table?"

"I have to admit, I can't recall the last time I took a meal in the kitchen. Perhaps I never have. If dinner tastes as good as it smells, I believe I can tolerate this turn of events. But I may insist we hire a cook in time. After all, I expect my wife's attention when I'm home."

"Do you now?" April set his plate of food on the table.

"What the hell is this mess?" Noah complained.

"It's roast beef hash from leftovers I found in the ice box. I didn't exactly have time to plan or shop for dinner tonight. Taste it before you grumble."

Noah reluctantly put a forkful of food in his mouth. His expression changed immediately. He scarfed down his wife's concoction. "Is there more?"

"Well, I need some too, but I think there should be seconds. The Fitzpatricks prepared their own dinner."

"Why, are you planning on having them join us at the kitchen table for a communal meal every evening?" Noah's displeasure at this possibility was obvious.

"Shame on you for being such a snob. You've married an ordinary woman. You'll have to come to grips with that. But no, they won't be joining us for meals." April left her plate at the table next to Noah's, then sat in his lap. "Sorry to distance you from your dinner, but I want to assure you, my meals can be enormously entertaining." Placing her hands on his face, April kissed him soundly and then used her own fork to feed him a bite of hash. Noah was suddenly unsure which delight he wished to enjoy first, his dinner or his bride.

* * *

The first streaks of dawn lit the sky as Noah grabbed his satchel and took one last look at his sleeping wife. He deliberately removed the ribbon that bound her braid last night. April's hair spread across her pillow and off the side of the bed. Realizing she must be what people termed a late bloomer, Noah determined to keep her glorious image in mind during his trip.

Although April expressed her desire to send him off this morning, Noah knew she was tired and decided it best to let her sleep. Quickly descending the stairs, he scribbled a note and left it on the entry table, then headed out the door. He needed time to plan a way to break the news to Deidre. She didn't love him any more than he loved her, but this would be a blow to her ego. He would try to see her first, before his mother. At least she would be happy. The fact Deidre's parents invited his mother to stay at their home complicated matters.

Noah was tired, having been a busy groom. Precipitously remembering he cleared his calendar for the next month to accommodate his wedding and honeymoon, Noah's thoughts turned to summer days with April. Perhaps his conversation with Deidre didn't require a plan.

* * *

April gasped for air as she awoke from her dream. She looked about at the strange surroundings, finally realizing she was in Mr. Chandler's bed. No, this was her bedroom now. Tears spilled down her cheeks. She felt chilled to the bone. Her nightmare seemed so real. April struggled to recall the specifics of her vision, but only a sense of darkness and foreboding came to mind. Noah was in trouble, terrible trouble. And he was far from home.

* * *

"Hello, Mother," Noah kissed Lula on the forehead after being shown into Deidre's family parlor.

"How did your trial go?" Lula inquired.

"We can talk about that later. Have you been spending time with Eve, Sarah and their families?"

"Yes. We're to have dinner together at their hotel in an hour. Are you available to join us?"

"Evidently. Deidre made herself scarce. I tried to track her down but she apparently wished to convey the message my appearance is unimportant. At any rate, I need to talk to you. Can we leave for the hotel now?"

"Certainly. Did you remember to bring my shawl?"

"It's right here." Noah fished the shawl out of his satchel and placed it on his mother's shoulders.

"Something has happened."

"Not now, Mother, wait until we get outside," hissed Noah.

* * *

"I tell you, something is wrong. When April didn't come down for breakfast, I took a tray up. She was gone from Mr. Chandler's room. I finally found her in the attic, writing away. She seemed nervous when I set the breakfast tray beside her. She'd been crying, I'm certain of it," declared Mrs. Fitzpatrick.

"You remember what it's like to be a new bride, don't you, my sweet? She's simply full of emotion."

"She certainly appeared to be our solid, sturdy, dear April yesterday. I don't know if Mr. Chandler is the husband for our April."

"Let's don't get carried away. Maybe there's a good explanation. We'll keep an eye on her for now."

Chapter Eleven

"Delia, I have never been so frightened in my life,"
explained Little May. "It was a moonless night. I
couldn't see a thing in the shed, but when I awoke
someone lurked in the near corner. My heart pounded
as I reached under the tarp and curled my fingers
around the screw driver. Before I could gather my wits
about me, the man stood over me. I struck at his leg.
He screeched and left the shed. I couldn't go back to
sleep for fear he would return. What am I to do, Delia?
We need the money from my work."

"Charlie Boatman?"

"No, it must have been someone else. Charlie
always reeks of cigar smoke and alcohol. It wasn't
him. Look for a man who limps. If I stabbed him
deeply, he must have a wicked wound."

April dropped her pencil on the paper and rested
her forehead in her hands. Unable to shake the
unpleasant nightmare, she retreated to the attic to
write. When Mrs. Fitzpatrick brought breakfast, April
ate then selected a book for a long soak in the bathtub.
Determined to take her mind off dark thoughts, she
tried in vain to find a chore. Mrs. Fitzpatrick kept an

immaculate house so April headed for the kitchen and baked most of the morning.

In the afternoon, she took a trip to Wineburgh's and ordered a typewriter to keep in the attic where she could type manuscripts while Noah was at work. During her shopping excursion, April remembered Mr. Nelson did not show up for breakfast. Naturally, he would have heard news of her marriage. Feeling somewhat guilty, April journeyed to Noah's law office to make peace with Mr. Nelson.

Impressed by the sophisticated décor at the law firm of Broadmore and Chandler, April imagined Lula must have furnished the office but remembered the firm was established years prior. As she approached an assistant manning the front desk, she could not help but admire her husband's excellent taste. The paneled walls, lush draperies and heavy mahogany furniture gave the feel of a wealthy gentleman's library.

"Can I help you?" a warm smile accompanied the receptionist's friendly greeting.

"I'm here to see Mr. Nelson, but I don't have an appointment."

"Let me check to be certain Mr. Nelson is free. Won't you have a seat? Who shall I say is waiting?"

"Mrs. Chandler."

"Oh, my." April could see she caught the man off guard. "Mrs. Chandler, I'll be right back!" He hurried away.

An obviously downcast Mr. Nelson appeared in the hallway seconds later.

"Hello, Mr. Nelson. I wondered if I might bother you for a moment?"

"Certainly, right this way." Mr. Nelson led his guest down the L-shaped hall to the end. His office was obviously not intended for client meetings. Stacks of paperwork and law books rose precariously from every flat surface and served to entomb him behind his desk. The walls were painted white; the furniture quite ordinary. This made April curious about her husband's office. Mr. Nelson offered a wooden chair and moved a stack of paperwork so he could observe his caller from a seat behind the desk.

"What can I do for you today, Mrs. Chandler?"

"I knew when you didn't come for breakfast this morning, you must have heard about my sudden marriage. I felt I owed you an explanation."

"You certainly don't need to explain."

"This is rather awkward. I enjoyed our recent breakfasts together. And you were right not to come this morning. It wouldn't have been proper. I wanted to thank you for your consideration and our delightful meals. I'm sure Mr. Broadmore relayed the specifics of my impetuous marriage. I won't bore you further. Naturally, my new responsibilities at home keep me busy. I simply wanted to thank you for your gracious friendship. I'm certain you'll quickly find another breakfast companion much more interesting than I have been." April hoped the man would feel appreciated. She didn't know what else to say.

April evidently hit the right note. Mr. Nelson smiled, if not warmly, offered congratulations on her marriage and abruptly rose to escort her down the hall. April turned to shake his hand as Jack emerged from an office near the reception area.

"April! So happy to see you. Might I have a word?"

"Surely." April entered a large office, decorated every bit as opulently as she imagined. "Your office is quite handsome."

"Thank you. Noah always had a vision for our business. Naturally, we couldn't afford this initially. Have a seat."

April sat in one of a pair of lushly upholstered red damask chairs trimmed in gold braid. For a moment, she felt intimidated by the lavish office but no less impressed.

"When Mr. Marcus told me you were here, I wanted to take the opportunity to apologize." Jack took a seat behind his desk and leaned back in the modern, leather-upholstered piece, locking his fingers behind his head.

"Apologize for what?"

"I may have given you a wrong impression. At the baseball game, it must have seemed that I tried to talk Noah out of marrying you. Actually, I think he made a wise choice. But I understood he might be causing himself something of a, shall we say, predicament. I take it he's in San Francisco?"

"Yes, he left early this morning."

"You haven't heard from him?"

"Not so far. I believe he'll return as quickly as possible. I doubt he plans to send word."

Jack smiled, but it lacked sincerity. "I'm sure everything will work out. Noah and I have been chums since law school. We concocted our plan to start a firm in Los Angeles as we competed for lady friends. Unfortunately, we had similar tastes in women and our goals were often identical. Noah's ideas about women changed once we came here. We never competed again. I can't tell you how happy I am he finally came to his senses. Throughout his string of engagements, I tried to convince Noah we were talented and ambitious and doing well on our own. I didn't want him to marry for occupational opportunity. I'm proud of what we've achieved. No one anticipated how quickly Los Angeles would grow." Jack leaned forward and sincerely continued. "I want you to know, I support your marriage in every way. If there's anything I can do to help, please feel free to ask."

"You did so much already. You certainly came to our aid last Saturday. I need to thank you."

Jack laughed. "I'm afraid I thoroughly enjoy recounting that day's events at every opportunity."

The pair conversed for a few minutes before April rose, explaining, "I don't want to keep you from your work."

Jack escorted her through the reception area. April noted two well-dressed gentlemen waiting for appointments. "Thank you again."

April offered her hand, but Jack instead gave her a kiss on the cheek, whispering, "We're almost related. Business partners are closer than family. Welcome to the firm!"

Remembering she forgot to eat lunch, April made dinner for herself and the Fitzpatricks. She forced a smile and joined them for dessert. Although she hoped Noah could finish his unpleasant chore and return home by evening, it seemed improbable. April stayed up most of the night writing. Happy to occupy her own bed in the attic, she knelt and prayed for God to protect her husband and bring him back safely, tomorrow if possible.

* * *

Noah waited at the intimate corner table in the restaurant at the Palace Hotel where he spent the night after visiting family. Deidre was characteristically tardy. She left a message in answer to his gallant attempts to locate her, indicating she would meet him for breakfast. Admittedly, this was not an ideal location, but she gave Noah little choice.

Sipping his coffee, he glanced through the newspaper as he waited. A grin crossed Noah's face when he recalled his mother's delighted reaction to his impetuous marriage. His sisters were shocked.

He hardly recognized his nieces and nephews and repeatedly called them by the wrong name. Many years passed since he'd seen the older ones and he'd never laid eyes on the younger.

Suddenly unable to do wrong, Noah became the focus of his mother's radiant smile throughout. It seemed his marriage placed him firmly in the position of favored child once again.

When he alluded to possible unpleasantness once Deidre informed her family the wedding was off, Lula cryptically responded, "I'll take care of that, dear. Never mind about it."

Noah offered to take her to Los Angeles so she could see April and offer congratulations. Lula quickly declined, referencing some drama when she shared a home as a new bride. She remained adamant her daughter-in-law needed time to adjust without interference.

Lost in his reverie, Noah didn't notice Deidre's grand entrance.

"Ah-hum," she uttered, sarcastically.

"Ah, you finally made it," Noah rose from the table to seat his fiancé.

"What, no kiss for the bride?"

Noah leaned over and kissed her cheek.

Deidre picked up her menu and studied the breakfast entrees carefully, although she rarely ate more than a spoonful of any meal.

"Before you order, there's something I need to discuss."

"How like you, my dear. Tardy for our wedding and now eager to have a discussion. You could have waited to show up on Friday before the rehearsal. Or perhaps made a breathless appearance at the actual ceremony, frazzled and disheveled but having completed all your work."

"Why ever didn't I think of that? You should have suggested it sooner." But Noah did not come to trade barbs. "I need to talk to you about the wedding." Although he'd broken two prior engagements, they were well before the wedding, one before a date had been set. This was undoubtedly a more precarious situation.

Deidre finally noticed her fiancé's serious demeanor. Something seemed amiss. Perhaps her worst fear was about to come true. "If you think you're getting out of this ceremony, mister, you have another thing coming," she teased. Deidre covered Noah's hand with hers. "If you're nervous, we could still elope," she offered.

"There isn't going to be an elopement or a wedding." Expecting devastation, Noah was temporarily stunned when Deidre attacked.

"Listen here, I trusted you would honor this commitment. What do you expect me to do now? What am I supposed to tell people? How do I save face? You're not going to do this to me, Noah, you simply are not. Get used to the idea we will be married on Saturday."

"I couldn't marry you if I wanted to."

"Why?"

"Because I am married."

"What is this about? Who have you married?" Deidre never expected this. She understood from past performance, Noah might try to back out. But she knew he would not be able to find a bride more beneficial to his law practice. Once they got close to the wedding date, she believed he had no choice but to marry her. An insightful Deidre continued, "It's the woman in your house isn't it? The one I caught you embracing. She's nothing but an old maid."

"She's a married woman. I believe that makes you more of an old maid than her," Noah calmly replied.

Deidre scowled, "Did you knock her up? Believe me, Noah, marriage to your mother's servant did not prove you to be a gentleman. It only shows how stupid you are to let her trick you into this."

"My wife came to me as chaste as the driven snow, which is more than you would be able to say had we married. Don't look so appalled, Deidre. I'm not the fool you take me to be."

She grasped at straws, "Your marriage could be annulled. My father knows judges. They could take care of it immediately. Our wedding can still take place on Saturday."

Noah clenched his teeth. Anger would only add fuel to the fire. "You can tell people anything you like. Feel free to blame me completely. I don't care what you say, but there will be no annulment and no wedding. I'm married because I wish to be." How could he have wanted to tie himself to this selfish, calculating bitch?

"You mark my words, Noah Chandler, I will see

you ruined!" Ugly red blotches covered Deidre's face; her eyes almost bulged from her head. "*Do you hear me*?" she screamed as she rose from her chair and slapped Noah's face.

"Everyone in the restaurant can hear you. I'm sorry, Deidre. It's not as if I loved you and I know you certainly do not love me. Why would you want to throw your life away in this manner? Eventually, I hope you'll see this is for the best. I wish you a wonderful future, loved by someone who will cherish and appreciate you. But I believe we're done here."

"You are *not* done here. I'm not finished with you! Sit down! *Sit down*!"

Noah headed for the door of the restaurant. At least this was over. His lips curved into a smile as the memory of his sleeping wife came to mind.

* * *

April lay in her attic bedroom staring at the moonlight covering the end of her bed. Thursday seemed endless. She went to Germain's and spent an outrageous amount of money on flowers and pots for the front porch. Having often seen cozy summer porches in Concord, she hoped to make an area resembling a greenhouse. She saw no reason a porch in California couldn't be maintained year-round. After purchasing fabric for pillows and standing wicker window boxes, she discovered, for a hefty fee, stores would deliver immediately. Her frantic activity produced an inviting area. But all her exertion did not serve to tire her sufficiently to fall asleep and failed to keep unpleasant thoughts from her mind.

Problems plagued her. Made anxious by her dream, April doubted she could relax before Noah's return. Another more concrete and concerning problem came to mind. As familiar as she and Noah became after their gold panning trip, conversations over meals revolved around irrelevant topics. She never shared her writing pursuits, not even with Lula. How could she explain to her husband? She didn't want to give up her lucrative career. Most husbands would never allow their wives to work. April felt certain Noah would not approve. And then there was the uncomfortable fact Noah's friends were able to see his similarities to Charlie Boatman. Noah listed honesty as an important aspect of a good marriage. This presented quite a quandary.

As April was about to drift off to sleep, she heard the front door open. Bounding out of bed, April flew down the stairs and found her husband standing in the entry.

"Noah!" she breathed an audible sigh of relief and ran into his arms.

"What a welcome! I'll have to remember to leave on occasion if this is the greeting I get." But his wife clung to him ferociously. "What's wrong?"

"I had a terrible dream. I'm so glad you're home. I want you to know, we can move away. We can start our life together somewhere else. We don't have to stay here."

"Why would we? My work is here. We have a lovely home." Noah was incredulous.

"We might be better off somewhere else!"

"All of this from a bad dream? I thought you were unaffected by dreams."

"I thought so, but this was a dreadful dream, something awful happened, but I can't remember what."

"I don't think prescient dreams count if you can't remember them," Noah teased. "Perhaps we should go to bed and discuss this further—in more detail—while I kiss you."

April breathed a sigh of relief. Noah was home and safe. "Will you come up to the attic and sleep there, just for tonight?"

"I believe we could strike some kind of deal. Let me see, what would I like in return?" Noah put his arm around his wife's waist and directed her toward the stairs.

"How did things go with Deidre?"

"Not well, but that's behind us now. My mother was thrilled to hear you are her new daughter-in-law. What happened to the porch?"

"I had a lot of nervous energy while you were gone. Noah?'

"Yes."

"I think I love you."

"I think you do too."

* * *

Intent on enjoying the front porch, April sipped a cup of tea as she mulled over the morning's conversation. Noah seemed ecstatic to be home. They slept in her small bed, which April admitted did not accommodate her husband's tall frame or more than one person. She would not ask him to sleep there again, even though it felt more like home to her than did his bedroom. Eager to escape the confines of the attic, Noah urged his wife to come downstairs once the sun came up.

"I have a considerable amount of time off work. I feel guilty. I may go into the office next week to see if I'm needed."

April felt perplexed at his comment. "How is this different? You planned a honeymoon, but now you need to work?"

"I needed to settle Deidre somewhere so I took extra time. We are settled here. I feel guilty because I *was* at work when Deidre and I were together." The realization he had been stupid brought a perplexed expression to Noah's face.

April never wished to be a jealous wife. But if Noah planned time away from work to be with his wife, and she was his wife, then April deserved his attention as much as the difficult Deidre.

Noah continued, "We can plan the next few days together, stay at home or have an adventure—whatever you like. I have something of a serious nature to discuss."

"About Deidre?"

"No. Deidre is the past. The future belongs to us. Although we've been honeymooning and there is a possibility you are with child, it is my sincere wish we remain childless. I doubt you ever considered the eventuality of motherhood since you never planned to marry. I hope this isn't a disappointment to you. I am quite adamant. I'll take responsibility for implementing the necessary procedures since this is my decision. There are condoms made of vulcanized rubber I will use to prevent procreation. Catholic men have several methods they utilize to fairly effective result that I also plan to use."

Every Catholic family April ever heard of was loaded with children. She wondered how effective Noah's methods would prove to be. Mrs. Fitzpatrick was Catholic, but she had a delicate constitution.

Noah's proposal caused April to mull over prior

readings. Dr. Chavasse strongly advised women over 30 against childbirth as their bodies were no longer flexible at such an advanced age. Also, Advocates for Voluntary Motherhood disapproved of contraception since procreation was the only reason to engage in intercourse. April understood Noah would never consider abstinence. She also recognized, much to her dismay, she didn't wish to practice abstinence either.

"I never considered motherhood, but I don't understand. You once told me you didn't care how many children you and Deidre might have. I have to ask again, why is this different?"

"It's because Deidre did not matter to me and you do. Very much."

April could tell from Noah's expression, he wouldn't be offering further explanation. She decided this might be as good a time as any to make her own request. "I have something to explain, as well. I enjoy writing and have sold some stories since coming to Los Angeles. I hope you won't object to my hobby. While you were gone, I used money I earned to buy a typewriter. We discussed the need for freedom in our marriage and this is important to me."

"Well, we are in agreement all around then. Will you let me read your stories?"

"They are personal, I suppose much like art is to a painter. It's different when strangers read. But I'll let you read them when I feel comfortable." April felt relieved. She'd been honest, at least honest enough.

* * *

The newlyweds toured the city by trolley, horse and carriage. Noah took his bride to The Clock Tower Courthouse.

"This is where we used to try cases. It became crowded, so they built the Red Sandstone Courthouse. It's the first building in Los Angeles County constructed strictly for use as a courthouse. It's magnificent and represents how the county is growing. Broadway used to be called Fort Street. It's one of the few streets paved with asphaltum, but it's only a matter of time before all the streets are paved."

Noah headed to the Pico House.

"This was the premier hotel west of the Mississippi when I came to Los Angeles. Jack and I stayed there for a while upon our arrival. The old gentleman sitting in front is Don Pio Pico—the ex-governor. There are nearly 80 rooms and a grand staircase. Originally, a fountain and an aviary of exotic birds decorated the interior courtyard. The city moved south and this area is in decline."

April noticed the strange sights and smells of Chinatown beyond the hotel. She became enthralled by a Chinese wedding parade making its way down the street. This area seemed to be flourishing. They explored streets where Noah pointed out a Chinese opera theater, a newspaper office and the elaborate decoration on a temple.

He next turned her attention to the trunk of a dead tree. The smell of a nearby brewery was almost overwhelming.

"Here's a point of interest that won't be around much longer. This huge sycamore has been a landmark for many years, revered by local Indians. Unfortunately, it failed to adjust to life in the city. This spring, it didn't sprout any leaves. I'm sure they'll cut it up for firewood eventually. The Indians called it El Aliso and its branches once spread nearly 200 feet here by the Los Angeles River. The city virtually sprang up around it.

"I told you before the native Indians were peaceful—they've been nearly wiped out by the Spanish, Mexicans and Americans who settled here. The few survivors were absorbed by the Missions, where they even lost their name. Although they are often referred to as Gabrieleños after the San Gabriel Mission, they were the Tongva—boat-builders who used wood planks, tule reed and tar to craft vessels for fishing and traveling. They lived in huge huts housing up to 50 people and were governed under a monarchical system. The chief acted as supreme ruler who settled all disputes. The guilty were fined in the form of food or animal skins. Robbery and murder were extremely rare. They were rational, thoughtful people. If a man cheated with another man's wife, the other man simply took the first man's wife in reparation."

April grimaced at Noah's story, compassionate for the poor woman who was forced to trade husbands.

"They were artistic, creating sand paintings and performing music using flutes and rattles and were expert basket weavers. They worshiped one god called the Supreme Being and believed in a heaven where he received the souls of all who died. The Tongva didn't believe in the concept of evil spirits as many other natives did. Some experts consider their religion a form of Christianity. They left their mark on this land. Their trade routes have been used by all the colonizing cultures that followed."

"How do you know so much about Los Angeles?"

"I wanted to make this my home so I started collecting information when I arrived. It's not as if our law firm did much business in the beginning. There was plenty of time for research then."

The Chandlers spent time in the city center, a busy place at night. Roads were well-lit by over 200 street lamps. Pedestrians thronged sidewalks.

Noah felt certain horseback riding was an activity they could share. When he planned to take April for a ride, she asked him to rent the horse from their trip to the Cahuenga Pass. Since "Rosie" had been a manufactured name, Noah hoped he could identify the gentle mare by sight.

In a much more gracious manner than on their first ride, Noah offered suggestions to improve his wife's riding acumen. He doubted she was seated upon the original Rosie, but the horse's appearance managed to pass muster. He thought April fit enough to be a fine horsewoman. If she came to enjoy riding, he would purchase a second horse.

While traveling along the banks of the Los Angeles River, Noah explained although a man could easily jump across the narrow waterway, it regularly overflowed its banks to flood nearby homes and businesses. This drew laughter from his wife.

"You are surely not serious? I can't even comprehend why this is called a river."

"I am. The rains weren't heavy last winter but runoff from nearby mountains flows through here to the sea. The river becomes quite treacherous."

During Noah's absence from work, the pair had plenty of time for "naps" and April continued to impress her husband with her culinary skills.

Chapter Twelve

Impatient to be on their way, Noah supervised packing the picnic basket. Life seemed simpler when he commanded Margarita to fulfil his alimentary desires. He believed April's duties took too much of her attention. "Leave the dishes. Mrs. Fitzpatrick will do them."

"All right," April shot back as she untied her apron. "I found an ant on the floor. I don't want to encourage them." Noah nearly dragged her from the kitchen. "Why are you in such a hurry?"

"It's a glorious day. I don't think it will be too hot. I want to get outside."

"Where are we going?"

"On the trolley."

April didn't think this much of an answer. Noah's touch continued to excite her. After lacing her arm through his as they took a seat on the trolley, all irritation vanished.

"We're on our way to the west side," Noah explained. As they traveled down Figueroa Street, he pointed out the newly completed Stimson House. "This is the costliest house built in Los Angeles to date." The impressive three-and-a-half-story home exactly matched April's idea of a medieval castle. "The building cost exceeded $150,000; can you believe it?"

April knew her husband would gladly live in a huge home like the Stimson House. She had no such aspirations. The house on Carroll Avenue was as grand a home as she desired.

She tried to identify the lush greenery in the yards of homes they passed. Large date and fan palms, magnolias and orange trees were in abundance. Every home sported a park-like lawn of brilliant green. Roses, jasmine and heliotrope covered porches, trellises and carriage houses. She noted calla lilies, morning glories and flame-red geraniums basking in the summer sunshine.

Their destination on this Saturday morning proved to be Westlake Park. "The lake is man-made," Noah explained. "This and Eastlake Park near our house were the primary water reservoirs for the city until recently. This has become a vacation destination with luxury hotels sprouting up all around. I know the trees aren't large yet, but you can imagine how this will look once they grow."

"This is where we'll have our picnic?"

"Yes, and after lunch, we'll rent a boat. A band is scheduled to play later so we can stay to enjoy the music."

* * *

As the newlyweds rode the trolley home, Noah put his arm around his wife and whispered in her ear, "Happy anniversary!"

"What are you talking about?"

"Our one-week anniversary. It's exactly a week since I got clonked in the head by the baseball that changed my life."

"So, the baseball gets all the credit?"

Noah chuckled. "Actually, the baseball had nothing to do with it."

"How can you say so?"

"Because when I saw your concerned expression, I knew yours was the face I wanted to see every day. You were the one who cared for me. I wanted to spend my life caring for you."

"Noah, I want to thank you."

"For what?"

"For today, for every day since we married."

"I hate to admit it, but in the grand scheme of things this is a modest honeymoon. I'd like to plan something more extravagant for our first anniversary."

"No, you don't understand. I lived my life working, cooking, cleaning and watching my mother die a bit each day. Before I came to California, the highlight of my life was a trip to the library. Each day we're together seems like a lifetime of adventure to me." Tears gathered in her eyes. Noah never saw her come close to crying no matter how harsh he'd been.

"Don't cry, my darling." Noah pulled her into his embrace, not caring if it was proper or not. "I love you and we're going to have a wonderful life together. We're only getting started."

"I love you, Noah," April whispered in his ear.

* * *

When April inquired if she could make a few feminine additions to her husband's masculine bedroom, he didn't object.

"This is your house now, April. You don't need permission."

"But it's your room. It is a beautiful room. It simply doesn't feel like my room."

Noah thoughtfully nodded his head. "Do as you like. I might not be overjoyed if you paint the entire thing some sickening shade of pink. Red might not be the best color either. We wouldn't want strangers to think they wandered down a street of red-lit brothels." This comment clearly shocked his wife. "My mother's taste is all over this house, but it's your home now. It's only natural you would want to make your own mark. The bedroom seems an excellent place to start. Feel free to change whatever you like."

"I think your mother has exquisite taste. I don't plan to change anything else. What if you don't like what I do?"

"We can have a discussion if I'm appalled. Compromise is an asset in any marriage."

April made what she considered bold choices. After purchasing a dressing table, bench and mirror, she chose a wallpaper to apply above the chair rail on the single windowless wall. Large sprays of flowers in muted shades were scattered atop cross-hatched, narrow green stripes over a cream-hued background. April implemented her changes in a single day. Her only remaining chore was arranging personal items on the dressing tabletop.

Rolling up leftover paper, April thought it a good idea to save her scraps. They could come in handy in case of future damage. She made her way out the back door and entered the dim carriage house. Passing a work bench, she spied storage shelves lining the back of the barn-like structure. A large stash of clay pots was stacked in the corner. April could make good use of those. She decided to ask Mr. Fitzpatrick if he had any plan for them but then quickly reconsidered. She was the lady of the house. "The pots belong to me," she confirmed aloud, in the most imperious manner she could muster.

After walking around the carriage, April found folded tarps on the shelf and grabbed one, intent on wrapping the wallpaper securely. Making quick work of the chore, her curiosity became aroused by a tarp-wrapped object propped against the side of the bottom shelf. She pulled a corner of the tarp away to find several pieces of impressionist art secured in plywood casings. The frames were difficult to see, but the canvases were easily admired.

April inspected a beautiful picnic scene then pushed it aside to view a picture of a colorful garden. The last two paintings proved rather stunning. She found a nude, a woman sitting in front of a mirror. Only her knees were covered by a lacy piece of fabric, probably a slip. The last was a charming picture of a young mother holding a baby on her lap. While April was unsurprised by the nude, she found the tender expression between the mother and child entirely perplexing. Knowing Lula did not care for her son's art collection, she realized Noah must have purchased these. The mother and child did not fit Noah's taste, being unlike anything else in the house. The subject matter seemed too idealistic and touching.

Instantly attracted to the piece, April decided it would be charming on the wall beside her dressing table. She slid the plywood frame off the shelf and took the picture to the bedroom. Even though Noah told her these were her possessions, she felt hesitant about hanging the picture before asking permission. She placed it on the floor beside the dressing table to see what her husband thought of her choice.

Noah anticipated his wife's embrace and happy greeting when he returned from work each day. He was not disappointed as she flew into his arms.

"My, what a greeting!" He bent to apply a lingering kiss before releasing his bride.

"I have something to show you!" April fairly danced up the stairs, pulling Noah along. "Close your eyes!"

Noah complied, imagining April intended to display the feminine touches she applied to the bedroom. Hoping to appear tactful, he braced himself mentally.

She pulled him through the door and positioned him to see the wallpaper. "All right, you can look."

Noah opened his eyes to be impressed by April's taste. The paper was feminine yet subdued enough to please him. "I like it!" he stated sincerely. "Who did you hire to put it up?"

"I did it."

"You? You didn't have to."

"Oh, I wanted to. I've always dreamed of flowery wallpaper in my bedroom. Noah, this truly seems like our room now. Let me show you what else I did." She grabbed his hand to give him a tour. "I added a few belongings to the top of the bureau." Pulling Noah toward her new dressing table, April inquired, "Do you like it?"

"I do," stated Noah, but then he stopped short.

"What's wrong?"

"Where did you get that?" Noah's gaze locked on the painting.

"I found it in the carriage house when I put the extra wallpaper away. I figured it must be yours. Don't you think it would look good here? I like your art and especially this—"

"No. We'll put it away. You can choose one of the others."

"I like this one best. What's wrong with it?"

"I don't want it my bedroom," nor in the house Noah thought to himself but then attempted to lighten his comments. "You could choose the nude, I always liked her. My mother would not hesitate to hang a huge renaissance painting of naked Greek gods and goddesses cavorting in a field but considers modern nudes to be pornographic. That's why she's in the carriage house."

April could not help but wonder why the mother and child were in the carriage house but felt further inquiry unwise.

* * *

After worrying endlessly over her appearance, April finally was ready to depart. One of Broadmore and Chandler's most important clients sent an invitation to their dinner party. April would make her first public appearance as Mrs. Chandler and she did not want to disappoint.

A slightly bemused Noah reflected on the fact California was a land of vast opportunities. The newly rich rubbed elbows with older money, which frankly wasn't all that old. The way his wife behaved, one would think she was about to dine with royalty.

He was duly impressed once they arrived at the Potters' lovely home on Hill Street. Had he not witnessed her insecurity and indecision, Noah would never have believed the lovely, confident woman who took his arm could be the same one who left the house on Carroll Avenue.

Perhaps more quiet than normal, April certainly appeared at ease. As dessert plates were served, Noah whispered in her ear, "How are you doing?" He was taken aback at her reply.

"I don't really know," April glanced across the table and answered under her breath, "I've never been to a dinner party in my life and I don't know what I'm doing."

Feeling the fool, Noah should have known this would be a taxing experience for his wife. He felt protective as the young and newly wed Mrs. Potter took aim. She appeared to be at least 25 years her husband's junior.

"Mr. Chandler, I've heard such interesting things about you. Weren't you recently engaged to my friend Theodora's cousin, Deidre? I must admit, I expected Deidre this evening."

Noah smiled politely, but before he could explain, Mrs. Potter directed a comment toward April.

"You, Mrs. Chandler—where are you from?"

"I'm from Concord, Massachusetts."

"The cream of Concord society come to visit our rustic little pueblo?"

"No, I wouldn't say that."

"I heard a silly rumor you were a servant in Mr. Chandler's household. Surely, that can't possibly be true?"

April noticed a vein stand out in Noah's temple, so she placed her hand over his arm to halt his reply and enthusiastically responded, "Isn't it grand when gossip proves authentic? Or at least part of it. I did come to Los Angeles to work for Noah's mother. I'm afraid my social standing in Massachusetts was, well, virtually nonexistent. I lived on a farm and cared for my ailing mother in recent years. But this is what we all love about America, isn't it? Everyone can better themselves and we are rewarded and accepted for our efforts. It's a land of vast opportunity. Now I have a wonderful husband and a life I never dreamed possible." When she looked adoringly toward Noah, April managed to win over the entire table, but for Mrs. Potter.

As the French say, "A chacun sa tribu. J'ai trouvé que les gens cultivés ne communique qu'en francais." Mrs. Potter took a sip of wine and glared condescendingly over her glass at April.

"I'm sorry, what did you say?" April felt the muscles in Noah's arm tense.

"Oh, you wouldn't speak French, would you? Never mind. It's not important."

Realizing what an awkward position Noah was in, needing to defend her while not offending his client, April quickly responded.

"You're correct," April smiled brilliantly at her hostess. "I managed my whole life without speaking a word of French. And I'm always certain to be polite whenever I speak English. Noah, dearest, would you mind coming outside for a moment? It's rather close in here and I could use a breath of air."

Noah placed his napkin on the table and rose to accompany his wife. He caught a smirk the elderly Mr. Potter quickly hid behind his hand. "Please excuse us."

April grinned as Jack, who sat across the table, tipped his glass as if to toast her. Once the pair walked onto the balcony outside the dining room, a duly impressed Noah offered congratulations. "You were brilliant. You cleverly put our hostess to shame. I doubt her husband will make any comment. Personally, I'd like to hit her."

"Now, now, counselor, we don't want *you* to end up in jail tonight. Do you know what she said?"

"Uncharacteristically, I will admit I was less than brilliant in my college French class, but if memory serves, the first part was a saying that goes 'to each, his tribe.' Then she said speaking French is cultured, something like that. How did you manage?"

"What do you mean?"

"How did you handle that snippy bitch? You freely admitted this is all strange to you."

"I simply pretended to be a worldly heroine from a book I read once."

"I want you to know how happy I am, April."

"About dinner?"

"No. With you, with our life. We've been married a month already; I can hardly believe it."

Although the light was dim on the balcony, April noticed a sudden furrow in her husband's brow. "Is something wrong?"

"It's only, April, you didn't have your monthly time. You can't be—there isn't a baby is there?"

"I can't talk to you about this. How do you even know about such things?"

The look of incredulity on Noah's face would have made April laugh if she wasn't so embarrassed. He gripped her arms and looked into her eyes. She turned away to avoid his stare.

"April, look at me. Is there a baby?"

"No."

Her response did not relieve Noah's anxiety. "You need to explain this. How can you be certain?

Isn't that a sure sign? Look at me."

"I've never been—regular. Sometimes it's two months, sometimes it can be six." April never felt so humiliated in her life. She knew her cheeks had turned crimson. Noah succeeded in embarrassing her where Mrs. Potter failed.

She looked away again when Noah firmly embraced her and proclaimed, "All right. I'll adjust my methods accordingly so I can protect you."

Considering his reaction odd, April would soon find herself replaying the conversation in her mind.

* * *

After touring the opulent gardens of the most expensive neighborhoods in Los Angeles, April was determined to have her own prize-worthy front yard. She believed she might be on the right track while admiring her porch from the sidewalk. The sun beat down on April's head. She abandoned her hat due to high winds. Her long, braided hair fell down her back.

Mrs. Pratt, the next-door neighbor who lived with her son, his wife and their three school-age children, occasionally drew April into conversation. April waved and walked toward their shared picket fence when Mrs. Pratt whooped a hello from her front porch.

Always friendly, Mrs. Pratt often introduced April to other neighbors. Although everyone seemed cordial, she never identified a single woman near in age whom she might befriend. Women of 30ish appeared rather matronly, usually had several children and seemed overcome by household duties and obligations.

"I must say, I'm envious of the way you decorated your porch," Mrs. Pratt observed. "If my daughter-in-law weren't expecting soon, I'd have her come out and make suggestions about ours. You wouldn't mind, would you?"

"Certainly not," beamed April. "They say imitation is the sincerest form of flattery. I'm trying to decide where I might add more plants in the front yard. I like the lush tropical look of the finer gardens in the city."

"Dear me, that's my daughter-in-law calling. She's so uncomfortable now, poor dear. I'm having a tea for her after the baby comes—would you like to join us?"

"I would."

"Wonderful. It was good to see you. I wish you luck on your garden!"

April turned to see Noah arrive home from work. He usually bounded down the sidewalk, happy to sweep her into his arms. Today, he walked sedately, a frown of concentration on his face. He appeared startled when he almost ran into her.

"Did I scare you?" April teased.

"We need to talk." Noah placed his arm around her shoulder and guided April up the front stairs.

"We could sit here on the porch and have lemonade," April thoughtfully placed a pitcher of lemonade, ice and two glasses on the small wicker table near the swing.

"No. We need to go inside. We'll have lemonade later."

Noah placed his hat and briefcase on the entryway table and tossed his coat on a chair. Grabbing April's arm, he offered a seat near the bay window in the parlor. He took a chair across from her.

"I need to explain something. An article came out in the *Times*. It's not true. I want you to understand.

It's quite libelous, but since they don't name names, there's not much I can do about it. There's no doubt I'm the focus of the article."

April would always remember the way the late afternoon sunlight illuminated crystals dangling from the lampshade. Their fairy lights danced about the room. Her husband's dire expression would soon haunt her dreams. She could feel sweat beading on her arms in the heat. April had the eerie feeling she'd lived this moment before. It was the instant when everything began to go wrong.

* * *

Word of Noah Chandler's immoral behavior spread like wildfire throughout Los Angeles, even around the state. A thinly-veiled article appeared in the *Times* about a successful local attorney who philandered with a married woman, the wife of a client. This caused his innocent and heart-broken young fiancé to break off their engagement days before the wedding. If Noah expected more from Deidre, he did not tip his hand.

For the first time in his life, Noah's good looks and charm worked against him. "I'm sorry, Jack. I don't know what to do about this. Clients are cancelling appointments. This is going to hurt business."

"We'll ride it out. People will lose interest in a few weeks; they always do. New clients climb from the trains daily," assured Jack.

But business was no longer brisk at Broadmore and Chandler as summer turned to fall.

* * *

Although April had only to walk next door, she

purchased a lacy parasol. When Lula lived in Los Angeles, she took April to a tea at church. April purchased a tea gown for the occasion, an expenditure she could well afford courtesy of Mr. Lynch.

Although her wardrobe might still be considered lacking, Mrs. Chandler felt the height of fashion as she stood before the cheval mirror in the bedroom bedecked in her cream-colored frock. The short lace train, mutton sleeves, and mauve satin sash accentuated her tall, slim frame. She carefully braided her hair up the back of her head and made a platform for the sophisticated hat Lula selected. Although larger than April preferred, she knew the hat, bedecked in lavish bows and feathers, was the current trend. The parasol provided the finishing touch. It had become the custom to carry one when attending tea for a new mother.

But her hope of appearing a successful attorney's wife and member of society dissolved once April entered the Pratt home. A number of ladies already arrived and were seated around the parlor. Mrs. Pratt, the elder, gave a warm welcome and served her neighbor a cup of tea and plate of delectable food. April quickly understood she was not welcomed by other guests, a few of whom she recognized from the neighborhood. Two women seated next to her quickly made excuses and distanced themselves. Other women stared and whispered behind gloved hands. It became apparent the scandalous newspaper articles about Noah were a popular topic.

April's stomach gave an unexpected turn. The thought of biting into the sweet and savory offerings on her plate made her nauseous. The tea, however, seemed to settle her stomach.

No matter how sincerely she smiled and attempted friendly conversation, April felt much the outcast. Realizing she did not feel up to further efforts, she excused herself and walked toward the kitchen. Luckily, she located Mrs. Pratt along the way.

"I'm so sorry, I have to be going. I'm not feeling well."

Mrs. Pratt frowned and replied, "I'm sorry. Would you like to lie down?"

"Thank you, but I think I'll go on home. I appreciate your invitation. Please relay my regrets to your daughter-in-law."

April's excitement of minutes earlier vanished completely as she made her way out the back door and headed through her own yard.

* * *

Noah was completely perplexed. Never having had a single compassionate bone in his body—he was at a loss.

"You're burning up." Noah recognized the panic in his voice as he removed his hand from April's forehead. "What can I do?"

April laid on their bed in her camisole and bloomers. A trail of discarded clothing was strewn across the floor.

"I can't get my shoes off," she muttered. "My head hurts."

"Where is the thing you use to button them up? The button hook, where is it?

"On the end of the bed."

Noah located the hook in the sheets, realizing April must have begun on one of her high-button shoes and given up. Once he managed to manipulate the hook successfully, he removed her shoes and garters and rolled April's stockings down her legs. Even he knew the removal of shoes would not be of much benefit. "What can I get you? April. April!"

"I want to sleep."

"But you must need something. Should I get water?" Noah felt completely out of his element.

If Mrs. Fitzpatrick often wondered whether Mr. Chandler truly cared about dear April, her doubts were laid to rest for all time. She answered furious pounding on her door to find Mr. Chandler clearly in a state of panic. The calm, collected, sarcastic man she knew was nowhere to be seen.

"It's April. She's sick. We need to do something."

As Mrs. Fitzpatrick grabbed her apron and came outside, Noah continued, "I stayed longer at the office than I anticipated. When I got home, the house was dark. There was no dinner. I found April in bed. She has a fever."

"Calm down, Mr. Chandler. I'm sure it's nothing serious."

"I should get the doctor."

"Let me take a look and we'll see what's needed. We should keep our wits about us," Mrs. Fitzpatrick calmly suggested.

* * *

Dr. Thompson walked down the staircase to find an anxious Noah Chandler pacing back and forth.

"What is it? Will she be all right?"

"I believe it's a case of influenza. A form of the disease has been making its way around the city. It's not virulent. Your wife will recover in a few days."

"Is it the Russian Influenza?" Influenza and

resultant pneumonia were the leading causes of death.

"There's no need to panic, Noah. Your wife may experience coldness and shivering, which may continue off and on for two or three days. There can be severe pain in the head, eyes, ears, small of the back and limbs, even in the bones and joints, fingers and toes. Your wife's temperature may run as high as 104° or 105°. Her unpleasant intestinal problems will likely continue. I'll give her quinine when I return if I feel her condition has deteriorated or there is reason to suspect a more serious form of the disease. Try to keep her comfortable. She needs rest. I'll check back tomorrow, but feel free to send for me if you notice a change in her condition such as labored breathing or a severe cough."

As Noah escorted the good doctor to the front door, he made a plan. First, he would assure April had tea. He needed to learn to prepare tea. Mrs. Fitzpatrick could make soup in the morning. He would sit beside the bed in case April needed anything in the night. As he closed the door, he wondered what he would do without April. She was his partner, his beloved. How did his world change so completely? He needed her as he never needed anyone and understood all too well how short and fragile life could be. All recent concerns about business and finances faded away as Noah bounded up the stairs to care for his wife.

* * *

April awoke in darkness. She needed to get to the water closet; her stomach was upset. Something blocked her way. Unable to get out of bed on her side, she scooted off Noah's side.

Shaky and needing to lie down, she returned to

find Noah in a chair beside the bed. He evidently keeled over in his sleep. His arms, chest, and head lay on the mattress. April crawled across the end of the bed near the footboard and collapsed onto her pillow. "Noah. *Noah*."

"Huh? What?"

"Go to bed. You can't sit in the chair all night."

He rubbed his face as he sat up. "You're sick."

"Yes, I agree. But you're not accomplishing anything by blocking my way to the water closet." Noah pushed himself out of the chair, walked around the bed and flopped face down, not bothering to remove his clothing.

April felt somewhat better, having emptied her stomach. The night air cooled her skin as it wafted through the window. She could hear the sound of the Pratt baby crying. The sound irritated Noah no end. He even threatened to knock on the Pratt's door and complain about the noisy child.

Enthralled by the cries, April always stopped what she was doing to listen. To avoid contagion, babies were customarily kept indoors for the first month of life. They were usually not taken out in public for the first six months. She had never seen him. He hadn't been presented at the tea before she left. Just as well, since she was sick. April drifted off to sleep listening for baby noises in the night.

Chapter Thirteen

The sound of rattling dishes awoke April. She opened her eyes to find her husband setting a tray on the bureau near the bed.

"Oh, you're awake, good. I brought you tea! I made it."

"You made tea?"

"Yes, Mrs. Fitzpatrick showed me how. She's making broth for you." Noah turned toward the bed, teacup in hand and a look of extraordinary satisfaction on his face. "Try some."

April sat against the headboard and sampled the tea.

"I know you like sugar and cream, but Mrs. Fitzpatrick thought black tea and honey would be easier on your stomach. Do you like it?"

"It's quite good, Noah." He looked about to burst with pride. One would think he single-handedly constructed the Eiffel Tower—the tallest structure in the world—that very morning.

"I have to go into work and clear a few things away. Mrs. Fitzpatrick will look in on you while I'm gone."

Unaccustomed to playing the role of patient, April

felt uncomfortable being waited upon. "I do feel better—"

"No, no, no. The doctor said you should rest at least until he returns. You're to stay in bed and I'll take care of you."

April had the impression her husband intended to cure her with tea. Already dressed for work, he kissed her on the forehead, promised to be home shortly and urged her to take another sip. He exited the bedroom door as Mrs. Fitzpatrick entered.

Standing aside to allow her employer's departure, Mrs. Fitzpatrick turned to her dear friend, who looked rather wan. "Mr. Chandler is quite a cook," she commented before the two women burst into laughter.

Although April's fever tended to spike in the afternoon, she recovered quickly but not before growing bored of bedrest. She was amazed when Noah fetched books or sewing and even agreed to play cribbage in an effort to entertain. In fact, he played the part of courteous and concerned husband throughout. Having always been a caregiver herself, she felt perplexed at this entire episode. If she felt uncomfortable in the role of invalid, Noah felt no less surprise at his fervent and previously unrealized bedside manner. Their impulsive wedding caused both to feel uneasy, never having seriously considered the implications of their vows. But they had the rest of their lives to adjust.

* * *

Since so much was riding on her dinner, April felt uncharacteristically anxious as she prepared her classic fried chicken. Mr. Devlin would be their first business dinner guest, business having been slow of late. Noah desperately needed to keep the man as a client. So many drifted away over past months.

April glanced through the doorway into the dining room. Lula's beautiful choices in tableware were perfect. April's floral arrangement turned out rather well, if she did say so herself.

She went over every detail of the menu with Noah. Since the meal she previously cooked for Mr. Devlin pleased him, they decided to reproduce it. Because the man now spent most of his time in California, April surmised he likely hired his own cook. Perhaps his desire for home cooking was already satisfied. Still, she had a hunch this could be the right meal at the right time.

As she heard Noah enter the front door, April looked around the kitchen to assure everything was in order. The Fitzpatricks arrived to serve and clean up. April threw her apron on the kitchen table and went to greet her husband and his most important guest.

"Margarita?" Mr. Devlin inquired. "Chandler, you married your cook?"

Noah chuckled. "Let me explain. This is my wife, April. She filled in last time you were here. I was shocked when she came through the door at your behest. You see, April had been hired as my mother's companion. I'd never even met her. Although I knew she wasn't Margarita, I already introduced her as such. She played along so well; I didn't make any further explanation. Actually, I didn't know what happened to the real Margarita."

"Well, you made an excellent selection. There's nothing like having a fine cook for a wife, I can attest to that."

"Did your wife join you in California?" April

asked as she took Mr. Devlin's hand in greeting.

"She has. She enjoys the mild and dry climate. Fall is always lovely in Texas, however. It's probably our best season so she went home to visit our daughter for a few weeks."

Dinner could not have gone better. A jovial and loquacious Mr. Devlin seemed to thoroughly enjoy himself. His mood changed abruptly after Mrs. Fitzpatrick served the apple pie.

"Chandler, I have something serious to discuss. It might be best if your wife left us to our business for a few minutes."

"It's all right. I have no secrets from my wife."

"Very well then. I have concerns about our business dealings."

"If this is about the articles in the *Times*, rest assured, they're all lies. I'm the object of a mean-spirited campaign. Admittedly, it's having a derogatory effect on our law firm. I hope to convince you of the benefits of our business association."

"This is not about the newspaper articles. I received a letter." Mr. Devlin slipped his hand inside his coat and withdrew an envelope. "Perhaps it's best if you take a look."

Noah opened the letter and quietly read. April watched in anticipation as Noah's face grew more grim at each line. "What is it?"

"The letter states I took a bribe to lose a case. It's a warning to our clients from an anonymous source. This is simply not true, Mr. Devlin. There is no case called <u>Brewer v. Davis</u>. I have no client named Walter Davis. I give you my word, but you can come into the office and see for yourself. We have no record of this case."

Mr. Devlin carefully gauged Noah Chandler's assertions. He seemed sincere and Mr. Devlin took pride in his judgment of character. This man had sense enough to marry the lovely April. She appeared committed to her husband. "I believe you, Chandler, but this letter has serious consequences. I checked with associates I referred to your firm. They also received the letter. I can't have doubt cast on my own integrity. I won't discontinue my business at this time and I'll attempt to sway my colleagues in your favor, but I have to be honest. If you're not able to stop the attacks against your character, I have no choice but to find a different firm to represent my interests. I want to be perfectly clear."

"I appreciate your honesty and I'll do all I can to earn your trust," Noah responded.

Conversation of a lighter nature commenced as they enjoyed apple pie. As he departed, Mr. Devlin hinted he would like to be invited again to the Chandler home for dinner, hopefully under happier circumstances. As he headed toward the trolley stop, he turned when Mrs. Chandler called his name and hurried after him.

"Is something wrong?"

"No, sir. I wondered if you could do me a favor." April handed him an envelope.

"What's this?"

"I have some capital—a bond my mother left and some money I've earned. It's no fortune, but I hoped you might invest it for me. I'll pay any appropriate fees. This is strictly a business venture." Her eyes opened wide. "Oh, please don't think of this as a bribe! I never intended that. I simply want to create an investment account."

"I understand. I don't take you for a criminal, Mrs. Chandler, but isn't this a matter for your husband?"

"Perhaps, but Noah isn't keen on using my money and he's concerned about other matters."

"I see." Mr. Devlin pocketed the envelope. "Come by my office one day next week and I'll see what we can do for you."

"I will. Thank you so much!"

* * *

April absent-mindedly climbed the porch stairs after submitting her latest work to *Pacific Weekly*. Knowing they desperately needed the money stashed in her reticule, she felt frustrated by the fact Noah would never accept it. She considered placing this money with Mr. Devlin. Their meeting went extremely well. He recommended certain investments based on her own observations of Los Angeles and advised against the water companies, labeling them "a dirty business." Lost in her thoughts, she was startled when Mrs. Pratt yelled a hello from her porch. The neighbor had always been incredibly kind, one of the few people who seemed oblivious to their plight. Disinterested in pity as much as rebuke, April found conversations with Mrs. Pratt extremely enjoyable.

"Why don't you come over, dear? Edgar is here. Would you like to see him?"

"I would." For the first time in weeks, April's step was light as she hurried over to the Pratt home. She looked into the fabric-lined basket where the lively baby boy kicked and swung his arms wildly. "He's so alert."

"Well, he's three months old already. He won't be

happy in the basket much longer. Would you like to hold him?"

"Can I?" April delightedly inquired, "How do I do it?"

"Have you never held a baby, then?" asked Mrs. Pratt.

"I haven't. Maybe I wouldn't be any good at it."

"Nonsense. Have a seat here in the rocking chair and I'll put him on your lap."

April beamed from ear-to-ear as she embraced Edgar. Mrs. Pratt was charmed by her expression.

"See, you're a natural. Perhaps you and Mr. Chandler will be blessed someday soon and you'll have your own baby to hold."

Enthralled by the bundle in her arms, April let her guard down and spoke more candidly than she might have. "I don't know. Mr. Chandler isn't enamored of children and he has business problems right now. His work has his attention."

As Mrs. Pratt observed the awed expression of her neighbor, she could not help but think Mr. Chandler a fool. His darling wife deserved to be fulfilled as a woman. Perhaps she should give that grouchy man a piece of her mind.

* * *

"We have to do this, Jack; we haven't a choice."

"I told you before, we can ride this out. People will forget about the letter the way they forgot about the newspaper articles, you'll see."

"I don't think anybody forgot about the articles. Our business never recovered. It certainly won't now."

"But you managed to keep Devlin; that's a start."

"Look, Jack, there's no reason you should suffer

through this. I'll only pull you down. You need to take my name off the shingle. It's the Law Offices of Jack Broadmore now."

"I can't. I never would have made a go of this without you. This was always more your dream than mine. I went along for the ride. It pains me to say it—I have as large an ego as you—but it's the truth. You know it is."

"You're a great attorney. It was your idea to come here."

"I know. But I never had your vision, your eye for success. If we go down, we go down together."

Noah shook his head. "If I'm the one with vision then you need to listen. The only way to save the firm is for me to drop out until we can sort through this. It's merely a name on a sign. I'll take the pro bono stuff. I always enjoyed those. I'll do what I can but in the background. And I won't take your charity."

"Look, Noah—"

"I'm not kidding. I need to find my own way through this. I brought this on. It's my problem, not yours."

"Why don't you ask your mother for help?"

"You know me better than that. Besides, she went so far as to write me out of her will. I don't believe I have anything coming from her; not now and not later." Noah decided to change the subject. "I don't understand who could have sold our client list. I don't think Nelson is smart enough. He certainly hasn't been living the high life from ill-gotten gains."

"Maybe he's angry you married April and has a vendetta."

"Be serious, Jack. The man can't even place a help wanted ad by himself. He's hardly a criminal mastermind."

"It has to be someone who works here or did before. It can't be Marcus."

"No, I don't think it could have been Marcus. But there are other people who come in here. The building owner has keys. Various attorneys rented space here through the years. Someone could have bribed a scrub woman to let them in. Besides, if it was a person who actually knew our business, they would have picked a real case we lost instead of making one up. The whole thing would seem less a lie."

"If the time comes when you really need help, Noah, I want you to promise you'll come to me."

Noah shook his friend's hand but didn't intend to drag Jack through the mud more than he already had. An unpleasant thought occurred to him. Deidre might only be getting started.

* * *

April never failed to be amazed at her husband's acceptance of their increasingly dire straits. She knew how much his firm meant to him. He calmly explained he dropped out over dinner one night as if he were discussing going to the park and renting a boat.

"Don't look so concerned, April. I have funds. We can get by for quite a while. Hopefully this will resolve shortly."

April lost her appetite. She set her fork on the edge of her plate and replied, "I have money. I told you before I made money writing. We could use it—"

Unusually composed during his explanation, Noah nearly lost his temper. "I won't take it. Whatever you've managed to make is for your use, for your enjoyment. I support our family. There's nothing for you to worry about. You can leave the worries to me."

An obedient wife would have bowed her head and replied, "Yes, dear." But April doubted she would ever be so submissive. She resolved to spend more time writing. Mr. Lynch remained as eager to buy her stories as ever, despite his bluster.

Escape to the attic became difficult. Noah no longer kept regular office hours since there wasn't enough to do. Even the pro bono work slacked off. Noah spent more time riding. As much as April enjoyed that diversion, she knew it cost extra money to rent Rosie. She made excuses about housework or cooking so Noah wouldn't feel obliged to take her along.

It seemed Noah framed his current misfortune as some kind of challenge he would overcome once he gained enough insight. April believed it more likely Noah would waste his life trying to solve a problem he could never understand. He might be unwilling to lay this mess at Deidre's doorstep or even mention her name, but April believed the bitter woman was both the cause of and the solution to all that had gone wrong. She prayed her husband would find some new occupation as he wandered the city he so loved. The idea they needed to move away became ingrained in her thoughts, but she understood Noah would consider this a weakness. He would never agree to run away from their problems.

Other ideas crept through her mind. She wanted a baby. April could tolerate almost any problem, any challenge, if Noah would only give her a baby. Her arms ached with longing when she heard baby Edgar cry. Experts might deem her too old for childbearing, but her yearning for motherhood seemed unendurable.

Jean Jegel

* * *

A sudden noise awoke Little May. Her sister slept in the bed beside her. What if Tex had returned to their tiny cabin? May could not afford to wait. She crawled from bed and grabbed the shotgun that always stood ready beside the window.

May noticed the wind howling. Perhaps it caused the noise. Just the same, she checked outside. Her skin crawled as she opened the front door, almost tripping over a basket on the porch. Hearing a whimper, she drew aside a piece of fabric. A baby! Someone left their baby on the porch! She collected the tiny precious being in her arms, feeling a bond with the helpless child. How could she possibly keep Charlie Boatman from finding out she harbored an orphan? And how would she ever manage to feed another mouth?

April stopped typing when she heard the front door open. It was a chilly December day. She drew her shawl around her shoulders before reluctantly descending the stairs.

Noah stood, sorting through the pile of bills from the mail, but he managed a cheerful, "Hello," when he caught sight of his wife.

"Someone came while you were riding."

"Who?"

"I don't know his name, but he brought this." April handed her husband the legal documents she accepted. "I didn't know what they were. I shouldn't have answered the door."

"No, it's all right," Noah assured.

"What do they mean?"

In as even a tone as Noah could manage, he explained. "I'm named in a lawsuit. Deidre is suing me for breach of promise to marry. There are damages for financial loss, including costs related to the wedding, loss of home, loss of advantage that would have resulted from marriage. This means there are financial repercussions from the fact Deidre is still single. There are compensatory damages, which mean Deidre's health, reputation and emotions have been damaged. There are even punitive damages, which means I maliciously broke our engagement. She claims I was grossly negligent.

"You are also being sued for alienation of affection, which means you deliberately and maliciously broke apart the engagement. That charge will likely be thrown out. Such accusations are normally made against a spouse's lover. It won't stand up in court."

April thought her husband much too calm and factual. True, he was accustomed to court actions, but she was not. "What about the case against you?"

"It has merit. My mother, unbeknownst to me at the time, covered all costs of the wedding. That charge will be thrown out once we prove Deidre's family didn't suffer any financial loss."

"And the rest?"

"She has a good case. She's suing for $100,000, which is an incredible amount. She can claim she has a ruined chance at marriage—in other words, I took away her prime marriageable years. She can even claim I scared away suitors. Since I walked away, the public would assume there must have been a reason—some deficiency on her part. She'll surely claim I ruined her reputation and her honor."

"Did you?"

"I knew Deidre wouldn't come to our marriage

bed a virgin. But I never slept with her. It will be her word against mine."

"So, she will win. You'll have to give her the money?"

"April, I'm not worth nearly that much money. But money doesn't matter to her. She wants to drag us into court. Even though the case against you will be thrown out, she'll never let it go until a judge dismisses it. She'll have her say in public and there isn't anything we can do about it. Thank God I already signed the firm over to Jack or she'd go after him too."

Noah walked into the parlor and poured himself a brandy. "We're ruined," he muttered. "Merry Christmas."

* * *

The Chandlers could not possibly have more differing opinions about their first Christmas together. Noah always experienced lavish holidays full of parties and revelry. Christmas Day had always been a family event. He often traveled home to New York before his mother came to Los Angeles. Christmas in San Francisco last year was sumptuous if not particularly pleasant. Currently, he was considered a social pariah. There were no invitations except to Jack's home. Jack remained a confirmed bachelor. He kept a suite at the St. Angelo Hotel and invited friends to join him. Noah felt his presence would only cast a pall over Jack's celebration. He and April would spend the day alone in their house. His hopes of an extravagant celebration on Carroll Avenue were dashed by the lawsuit. This would be their one and only Christmas together in their home.

April, on the other hand, was accustomed to

meager celebrations. From the time her mother grew ill, there were no gifts, no stockings hung by the fireplace, almost nothing in the way of cheer or decoration. The only traditions she kept were the small turkey she prepared for dinner and her journey to church on Christmas morning, weather permitting. Christmas dinner in a beautiful home with her new husband seemed a dream come true. She intended to make as happy a memory as she could, knowing full well Noah would struggle through the day.

Noah intended to give his wife a horse on Christmas morning. This plan had become implausible. His funds would soon be depleted. He doubted he would be able to keep Checkers. His meager gift, a pair of small pearl earrings, thrilled his wife. April labored over a finely hand-knit vest for her husband. The cost might have been small but she gave her gift with love. If she felt disappointed at Noah's reaction, she didn't show it.

They enjoyed a traditional Christmas dinner. April baked pumpkin pie and made her mother's English pudding for dessert. She used pine boughs and Christmas decorations she found in a closet to decorate the table. Her plan for a magnificent tree in the bay window of the parlor had been toned down to a small tabletop tree, which she decorated beautifully.

Having given the Fitzpatricks the day for themselves, April hummed a Christmas tune as she did up the dishes. She wiped her hands on her apron and joined her husband in the parlor where Noah was enjoying a brandy and pie.

"Would you like a brandy?" Noah inquired.

"No, I think I'll stick with my cup of eggnog."

"You're supposed to add whiskey."

"I like it the way it is. Previous experience convinced me I'm a teetotaler."

"Oh, my. I'll be in for it if you decide to join those violent temperance women." Noah viewed his wife as she took a seat on the floor beside his feet and rested her head on his knee. She was the light of his life. He could not help but feel he failed her miserably. "I wish I could do more for you."

"Why do you think I need more? I thought today was wonderful. Probably too quiet for you, but I will always have lovely memories of this day."

"If you could have anything you wanted, anything in the world, what could I give you?"

April struggled with the idea of approaching Noah about a family. He certainly gave her the perfect opportunity. Surely, they could discuss this in a civil manner on this most cheer-filled day. But she needed to be careful. "You wouldn't like it if I told you."

Dumbfounded by her reply, Noah urged, "I would give you anything April, were I able. What could you possibly have in mind? A castle in Spain? A voyage around the world? A gold mine, perhaps?" he teased.

"You are able to give me what I want. Noah, I want a baby. Your baby, our baby."

She ventured a look at his face. He could not have appeared more shocked had she struck him.

"I have a longing for this I never previously comprehended. I find your calendars, calculations and equipment quite tedious. I enjoyed our spontaneous, um," April struggled to find an acceptable term, "passion when we were first married so much more exciting. I want us to be together that way. I want us to make a baby."

"No."

"You issued your command but refused to explain."

"You agreed to this. I find it unacceptable for you to go back on your word."

"This was never my plan, Noah. This was your plan. I never considered motherhood. I never even considered marriage. But I thought about this carefully and I long for a baby."

"You want a baby more than you want me?"

"No, certainly not. But why can't we have each other and a family? It's only natural."

"No."

April felt herself losing control. "Why? Why were you willing to have babies with Deidre but not me? I won't accept no for your response. You need to explain."

"I don't feel the need to explain."

"I don't really care about your needs. I want to know your reasons. You owe me that much."

"Do I? Really? I can see you're disappointed in me. I fully understand. You thought you married a successful attorney and I'm hardly that. You thought we could have a lovely home and wonderful adventures. Nothing is going as you planned, is it? So now you're badgering me into a baby I don't want. How can you even suggest such a thing? I can't support you much less a family. How can you completely ignore the trouble I'm in and put more responsibility on me when I so clearly can't even keep my own home or business?"

April knew her husband transferred his disappointment onto her. "I'm anything but disappointed, Noah. Life doesn't always go as we plan."

"It does for me. It always has."

"I'm not going to let you change the subject. Why are you so opposed to a family? You issued your decree well before we were in any trouble. Why, Noah, why?"

Noah rose from the chair and walked across the room to pour another brandy. He stared at the picture above the table.

"I told you my sister died in childbirth. I was there," he stated in a flat tone. "She was so excited to be a mother and considered it her destiny. She sent for me when the pains started, the same time she sent for her husband. The baby came early when my mother was traveling. Anna and I were always close; she wanted me there.

"At first, we sat in their parlor. Michael felt nervous so I teased him about it. After a time, we could hear Anna upstairs, struggling, yelling, then screaming in agony. There was nothing to tease about by then. The doctor's assistant came to get Michael. Things were not going well. Michael asked me to come along in support.

"Anna lay in their bed writhing in pain. The pain became unrelenting. The doctor claimed he'd done everything he could. I never so wanted to kill anyone in my life. He said the baby was stuck; he couldn't even reach it with his hideous instruments. Michael held Anna's hand, he tried to comfort her and urge her on. Soon the pain became too much. You could see it in her eyes, she surrendered to it, waiting to die, wanting the pain to end.

"Once she was gone, the doctor sliced her abdomen open in an attempt to save her baby, but he already died." Noah turned to glare at his wife, a single tear ran down his cheek. "I never wanted to marry for love. I would never put a woman I loved through such torture. It was the reason I wanted to marry for business and sex, of course. I didn't care about Deidre. Whether she wanted children or not was no concern of mine."

A speechless April watched her husband place his brandy glass on the table and walk out the front door. After a time, she turned off the lights and sat down to stare at the Christmas tree. She contemplated how things had gone so badly. A sudden thought occurred to her. She impulsively left the parlor and grabbing a candle from their Christmas dining table, headed for the carriage house.

Careful to open the door as quietly as possible so as not to disturb the Fitzpatricks, April made her way to the shelf at the rear of the building and quickly unwrapped the three paintings. She settled on the picnic scene for the bedroom. April propped the mother and baby piece on the worktable, intent to have a closer look. She carefully held her candle near the mother's face, feeling as drawn to the piece as she had been initially. Incredibly, the love and devotion between mother and child were apparent despite the random and seemingly chaotic brush strokes.

She set the candle in front of the picture and stood back. There was no doubt in her mind, the woman resembled Noah. Her dark hair matched the color of Noah's, her eyes were pale and striking. She had finely chiseled features, even what appeared to be a dimple in her delicate chin. April imagined Noah, unable to allow a stranger to possess the portrait, bought it even though he couldn't bear to look at it. April stared at a picture of Anna, or who April imagined to be Anna.

She understood people often interpreted impressionist art in a highly personal way, but this woman looked so like Noah, she felt certain he found his sister and her baby pictured forever together in a moment they never shared.

Noah's grief saddened April much more than it did when he recited his story. How could she help him overcome this loss? He grieved for over ten years. And how could she make him see the outcome for his sister, though not rare, was not common either? How would she possibly convince him to give her the baby she so craved? It seemed a hopeless quest, only one of myriad problems they faced.

After carefully wrapping the artwork and returning it to the shelf, April entered the empty house. Apprehension gripped her on this, the most hope-filled day of the year. They got this far by facing their problems together. April feared she put a wedge between them they might not overcome.

Chapter Fourteen

Noah walked for hours, a litany of destructive and pessimistic thoughts racing through his mind. Life was not supposed to be like this, not his life. He always led a charmed life. Things came easily to him.

He remembered April's arrival in Los Angeles. Was it really only a little over a year ago? In some ways, it felt as if he knew her all his life. He treated her as a sister after he broke his leg. She certainly could take everything he dished out and never hesitated to shove her retorts right in his face. He appreciated the fact she didn't care about his looks and wasn't influenced by his charm, on the rare occasions he attempted to charm her. It seemed as if she always saw him, the real Noah, not the façade.

As he became intrigued, she seemed more a friend, though he rarely treated her as one. He trusted her. April was honest, compassionate and glib. He could not pinpoint when he fell in love, but it was well before the day he proposed. Loving April went against his every instinct. He married hastily to prevent a change of mind.

It never occurred to him Deidre would exact monetary revenge. The woman was an heiress. She didn't need the money. Being all too familiar with the generous awards in heart-balm lawsuits, he had no hope of avoiding bankruptcy. He accepted the fact Deidre ruined his business. She knew his work was dear to him. Ruining his marriage would be additional retribution.

Noah felt bitterly disappointed in himself. For the first time, he wanted to share all the advantage he'd been given. He wanted to provide a lovely home for his wife, social standing, beautiful clothes, travel—all the things she missed while shut away in a tiny house, her only company a dying mother. Providing these benefits never seemed challenging—simply his way of life. Now she wanted a baby. He would never willingly give in to her wish. Even though the tangible advantages he provided did not seem important to April, her desire for motherhood would not be easily overcome. Yet another disappointment.

He never meant to reveal his memories of Anna's death. He and Michael shared their sorrow, but Michael managed to make a new life, having remarried and started a family. Noah still mourned his sister, intent on keeping her memory alive. He certainly had no desire to condemn April to a similar fate and never wanted to love her for that reason.

Now his life was in shambles and he seemed to be ruining his marriage. Once he finally headed home, Noah did not have the slightest notion how to make his life whole again.

When Noah returned, he feared April had left. The lights were off and the front door unlocked. She was not in their bed. Relieved when he found her still dressed, asleep in the attic, he collapsed on his own bed. Perhaps a few hours of rest would help clear his mind. As he was about to drift off, the baby next door started to cry. Noah put a pillow over his head to drown out the irritating noise, but then he listened.

For two people who did nothing but snipe at each other initially, he and April were certainly at a loss now. This had been their first real fight. Their life together had gotten much too serious much too quickly. Noah recognized they were overly cautious with each other ever since Deidre commenced her campaign. He didn't want April to feel she couldn't discuss her concerns or desires. Finding a way to enjoy each other's company seemed a good place to start.

* * *

Noah awoke to the uncomfortable feeling someone stood over him. He went to work every morning—doing what he could at the firm. Jack paid him cash, but Noah insisted he be paid the going rate for his work and no more. He certainly didn't have to go in on a Saturday. There was no reason for anyone to roust him out of bed. With lightning speed, he grabbed April and pulled her across his body onto the bed beside him. This elicited a shriek from his surprised wife who giggled as he propped his head on a bent arm and looked down on her.

"What's this? I thought you were Mrs. Fitzpatrick come to crawl in bed."

"Noah Chandler, what a cad you are," April teased.

"I am not only a cad; I am an infamous cad. Ask anyone." It was a far more accurate comment than he cared to admit. "Let me see," Noah continued as he unbuttoned the lacy blouse April wore for Christmas. "I believe you were wearing this yesterday,

Mrs. Chandler. We can't have that. You'll have to change. I will help you."

April laid still while her husband separated her from her clothing. The bereft man who stormed out of the house last night seemed curiously absent.

"I think we should talk," she urged while attempting to quell her all too familiar lustful longings.

Noah ceased his efforts, but only momentarily. "I heard you last night. I understand what you want and even why. All I can say for now is we will work through this, somehow. I want you to confide in me, but we simply can't take on any obligations right now. There must be some kind of compromise for us. I don't know, maybe we'll drive the buggy to the orphanage one day and fill it with babies. I promise you, once things settle down, we'll make a plan. Oh, my, what have we here?" Noah kissed April's neck after making quick work of the buttons on her blouse.

April, as always, was mesmerized by her husband's touch, but Noah's desire to make plans in the future became his mantra. She would lose track of the myriad things they would take care of once Deidre's spite was satisfied. Orphans were fine, but April wanted the opportunity to bear her own child. Noah would never talk her out of this desire and she feared they might never be done with Deidre.

* * *

Christmas greetings included two letters, one from Noah and one from Lula's new daughter-in-law. She might have been thousands of miles away, but Lula knew something was terribly wrong.

She asked pointed questions in recent missives. Noah completely ignored her every inquiry. April provided evasive responses, clearly making an effort at truthfulness while leaving much unsaid.

The lightning-fast response to her most recent letter proved to be the most telling correspondence. Lula laid out her plan to visit Los Angeles for Christmas. Noah wasted no time dashing off a reply. Lula shouldn't make the journey "at this time." The marriage remained "unsettled." Lula had been correct when she asserted newlyweds needed time to adjust. The fact Noah admitted his mother was right about anything drew Lula's attention as little else could.

Lula felt her current arthritic difficulties were due to the cold New York winter. Her body grew accustomed to milder temperatures in California. The doctor advised against travel or Lula might have caught the first train to the West Coast against her son's wishes. Instead, her destination was nearby hot springs.

Lula had wind of the problems at Noah's firm. Here, the boy sought to marry for business advantage and ruined his business as a result. She wished to point this out to him in person. Doubtless, his marriage suffered as a result.

April wrote at length about the baby next door. Her letter documented his every antic and accomplishment. April's longing for a baby seemed obvious to Lula. Her son seemed oblivious.

Lula imagined her efforts to dissuade Noah's marriage to Deidre proved a complete failure. She took solace in the fact Noah avoided that marriage and made an excellent choice in a wife. How much of this was Lula's doing could be debated. One thing she knew for certain. It was nearly impossible to properly influence her son from across a continent.

* * *

The New Year brought endless legal complications. Jack finally persuaded Noah to hire an independent attorney who specialized in heart-balm lawsuits. As Noah suspected, his lawyer's efforts were met with irrational resistance. He was unable to persuade Deidre's attorneys to drop a single charge or April from the suit. Settlement had never been an option. Deidre was in the enviable position of having unlimited funds and endless time. She brought the full weight of her family's position and wealth to bear.

The Chandler marriage never recovered from the Christmas night discussion, despite Noah's occasional attempts at cheerfulness. Unused to failure of any kind, Noah put all his efforts into keeping his temperament even. He felt the least and only real thing he could do was give the appearance of a calm and collected husband. Searching the paper for some acceptable position, he feared any money he earned would be lost in the lawsuit. Noah understood he might never make a living as an attorney again. News of the titillating legal action against him fanned the flames of distrust begun by Deidre's initial assault.

Mrs. Chandler also felt at a loss. She was more than willing to start over. She was more than used to having nothing. In fact, she was doing well financially, making a good profit from *Pacific Weekly* and her investments. Noah not only refused her money, he wouldn't listen to details.

Many so-called experts purported Los Angeles already reached its apex. Mr. Devlin wondered if they were correct. Then Mrs. Chandler elaborated myriad opinions on why the city was only getting started. He did not hesitate to tease when she appeared in his office, eager to pad her investments. In fact, he made identical investments on his own behalf and "made a killing" as he put it. He picked her brain about Los Angeles at every opportunity. They invested in building and loans, transportation, and even speculated in oil while continuing to avoid water companies. April's real estate outlook proved uncannily accurate. They purchased and quickly sold two separate pieces of land for phenomenal profits. Devlin paid attention when April selected properties for both short and long-term investment. He surprised her one afternoon when she dropped by with additional funds.

"I have something for you, Mrs. Chandler."

"What's this?"

"Your 25 percent share in Austin Holdings. It's simply a formality."

"But I didn't invest 25 percent, did I?"

"Perhaps not. But I'm here to make money and you have contributed immeasurably to my success. This is my way of thanking you while I continue to profit from your insights. How do you know all these things about Los Angeles?"

"I listen to my husband wax poetic about every detail of the city. It's not hard to see where development is headed. By the way, I think we should invest in properties on or near the beach."

Mr. Devlin did not require a second opinion. Mrs. Chandler was his lucky charm.

Once the trial commenced, April paid as little attention to the testimony as she could. She smiled kindly and held her husband's hand. Noah managed to put up a thoroughly dignified and credible front, but the testimony and cross-examination were brutal. April did not understand her husband's passivity about their future. Since Noah deemed Deidre's case valid, he considered it pointless to argue against it.

The beautiful and diminutive Deidre gave a heart-rending version of the ruination of her life, all caused by her evil and manipulative fiancé, Noah Chandler. He besmirched her reputation and her honor, made her unfit for marriage and destroyed her future. No amount of money could possibly restore what she lost. Deidre especially relished her testimony against April, whom she claimed to be an irresistible enchantress, a poor and conniving vagrant who sought to better her lot in life by an auspicious marriage. This proved to be the one portion of the trial when Noah lost his composure and made a scene, jumping from his chair and calling Deidre out for her lies.

In the end, Noah's predictions proved to be correct. April was dismissed from the case and the economic damages for the wedding were dropped. The jury awarded the irrational amount of $75,000. Noah was ruined financially; his reputation irrevocably damaged; bankruptcy his only option.

As if the papers did not provide enough provocative ammunition from the trial, stories purporting the character Charlie Boatman was based on the real-life Noah Chandler surfaced frequently. Deidre's testimony served to support that idea, an unintended consequence of the trial.

April, who stopped looking at the newspaper months earlier in an attempt to keep her spirits up, had no idea her fictional character had been tied to her husband in such a public manner. Once her romance with Noah flourished, it seemed impossible to publish derogatory stories about Charlie. She abandoned that plot in favor of Tex and Johnny's evil exploits. Since she and Noah were now at odds, it felt almost cathartic to return to tales of Charlie Boatman.

* * *

Spring held only melancholy for the inhabitants of the Chandler household. Noah's funds were frozen. The house on Carroll Avenue and its contents were set for auction. Noah could not delay explanation of his failures any longer. April needed to understand what would soon occur.

"I can't pay the Fitzpatricks."

"I think they know. They wanted me to ask if they can stay in their house. Perhaps the new owners will retain their services."

"I'll see what I can do. They could provide security for the property until the new owner takes up residence. There will be an auction of the contents. Everything has to go. I think we'll stay here as long as possible. I've been thinking we should go to New York once the auction is over."

"What about Checkers?"

"I sold him for cash—to keep us going for a while."

"I'm so sorry, Noah."

"I've been thinking about your initial desire to leave Los Angeles. I wonder what might have happened if we did. But I know Deidre would have caught up to us eventually no matter where we went. Maybe this is for the best. We'll start over now. Anyway, about the auction. We can keep personal items, clothing, and jewelry. Everything else has to go, dishes, silver, furniture, everything."

"What about my sewing machine?'

"It has to go in the auction."

"What about your paintings?"

"They go too."

April nodded, realizing Deidre had been a fool not to come after her. The woman assumed April was penniless and never bothered to investigate. Her funds were in her maiden name but would have been easily ascertained had Deidre cared to look. "I watched the auction at the farmhouse."

"I forgot about that. Was it hard to stay?"

"There wasn't much of anything to auction. Household items, everyday things—nothing dear to me. It will be more difficult to see all your lovely things go to strangers. But what would you do in New York?"

"I might be able to get a job at my father's old law firm. New York is far away. My family has social standing."

"But Deidre could go there. And Noah, I'm no socialite."

"My mother could teach you what you need to know. You've done well here, entertaining, playing hostess and guest to perfection—before things started going so badly."

"I would never feel comfortable in that life. I'm a plain person. I might enjoy dressing up from time to time, but I don't understand life in New York. I feel uneasy about moving there."

"It might be our only option."

* * *

April soothed herself by keeping busy. She economized in every way possible, buying small quantities of food, stretching recipes and using every scrap of produce from the garden. Sewing seemed a waste since they would move shortly. April hesitated to use the electricity or gas and used candlelight whenever Noah left the house.

There was little for him to do at the law office. He spent hours walking. Even though this would not be their home much longer, April continued to putter in the yard. She cleaned the upstairs rooms. Mrs. Fitzpatrick insisted she continue some form of work to earn their rent and so, kept the downstairs clean.

Although April didn't understand the legal ramifications of bankruptcy, it seemed pointless to remain in the house on Carroll Avenue. Her attempts to discuss their future proved fruitless. Noah assured everything would become clear by the time they needed to leave. She feared this meant they would take off for New York. As much as she wished to see Lula, April didn't want to leave California. She felt certain Noah would long to return to Los Angeles, the city he loved.

April often visited Mrs. Pratt when Noah left for one of his walks. She always enjoyed hearing about Edgar's latest adventures. Although the baby could crawl, he never minded being held, if only for a few minutes. April lived for those moments. Mrs. Pratt appeared oblivious to all the ugly rumors about her neighbors which made her porch feel like a lifeboat in a sea of misery.

Having always been the object of stares and pity, April easily ignored the curious and often antagonistic comments of fellow Angelinos. On several occasions, Noah appeared to be on the verge of violence when some neighbor or store clerk offered a rude or insulting remark. Noah was clearly at the end of his patience.

She feared he might explode at any moment.

April found it difficult to concentrate. Writing now seemed more a chore than a pleasure. She struggled to complete a few pages every day and spent her free time immersed in reading—her traditional escape. The closeness she and Noah shared after their wedding vanished. They were simply two people living through difficult times in the same house. Noah remained certain everything would work out any day. April was certain it wouldn't.

* * *

Noah burst through the front door. Unfortunately, he had no time to lose.

"April! April!"

Noah assumed she hadn't returned from the market. Anything she purchased would be a waste of precious funds. Noah received word a buyer purchased the house intact; there would be no auction. They needed to leave.

Having avoided thoughts of this day as long as he could, reality hit Noah hard. Even though he resigned from his law firm, at least there was always the chance, however small, he might return one day. There would be no coming home to his grand house on Carroll Avenue. They would leave in the morning never to return. All his work, all his investment, all his plans were gone, even his art. He failed everyone. He'd been a poor husband, unable to provide for his wife. The life he imagined for them was gone forever.

Almost frantic, he ran upstairs and began to stack clothing then retrieved two steamer trunks from the basement. April's few clothes would fit in one of the trunks with room to spare. Looking around his bedroom, Noah realized he was seeing his home for the last time. He struggled to memorize every detail, furious this loss proved so painful.

In a fit of frustration and anger, Noah went to the attic to see if he could find a way to take April's sewing machine, the only belonging she requested. Why should some stranger have it? Determined he could do this one thing for his wife, Noah's anger escalated as he attempted to lift the heavy treadle machine. He knew he'd never manage to remove the piece unnoticed.

Pulling his hands through his hair in agitation, Noah looked around the attic to find another item he might salvage. April's typewriter sat on a table under one of the dormer windows. She purchased the machine on her own. It was the perfect substitute. Although heavy, it seemed manageable. Noah approached the typewriter, intent to pack it in the bottom of one of the trunks. He looked at the page in the carriage. April was evidently in the middle of a story. She never allowed him to see her writing.

Charlie Boatman glared maliciously across the poker table. He bided his time, waiting for an opportunity to win back the saloon.

"Looks like you boys is done for," he sneered while gathering the poker chips from the pot.

Little May was transfixed, peering around the corner of the bar as she sat on the floor. Right before her eyes, Tex and Johnny pulled their guns on the new owner of the Red Bird Saloon. They were no match for Charlie, who rose from his chair and gunned the men down before either fired a shot.

It was late, no one remained in the saloon save

for Little May. She continued to observe as Charlie walked around the table, nudging both men with the toe of his boot. There was no response. Charlie spat on the floor between the bodies.

"About time things got back to normal around here. May! I know you're here. You better get this mess cleaned up afore I come back." Charlie lurched toward the back room and promptly passed out on the cot. His smell of whiskey and tobacco mingled with the scent of acrid gun smoke and lingered in the bar.

Noah never experienced the kind of wrath that washed over him. Hearing the front door open and close, he pulled the paper from the typewriter and bounded down the stairs.

April heard her husband's footfalls and paused at the staircase to greet him. She was taken aback at the cold fury obvious in his expression.

"Is something wrong?"

"I believe everything is wrong. Someone bought the house and contents. We have to get out."

"I'm sorry, Noah."

"You are damn right you're sorry. What the hell is this?"

"What have you got?"

"I went into the attic and found some interesting reading material in your typewriter. I believe you owe me an explanation."

"I told you I sold my writing."

"Yes, but you never told me you were a traitor. How could you be the one to do this to me?"

"I'm not doing anything to you. What are you talking about?"

"You know damn well people based their

opinions of me on the Boatman character in *Pacific Weekly*. Deidre never did as fine a job of ruining my reputation as you have. And to think, I gave up everything in my life for you. How the hell do you think I feel now? I'm the biggest fool on the face of the earth."

"I didn't base my character on you. I used you as a model. I don't have much experience with men so I copied things about the way you look, your mannerisms. And you were vile to me when I first came here, so I played on your name. But Charlie is not you, Noah, and was never meant to be. It's a ridiculous caricature. How can you think I would marry you if I doubted your character?"

"Do you know what has happened to me since you came into my house? And it is *my* house, if only for the moment. I broke my leg, I was beaten by two thugs in your defense, I was hit by a baseball. My life is gone, ruined. My business is gone, my home is gone. I am dead broke. The only thing left was you and now this. *This!* You betrayed me, April. I lost everything because of you."

As Noah glared at her from the step above, April had the brief thought she should be afraid, but she was no more the cowering, timid Little May than Noah was the evil Charlie Boatman. Her feelings were bottled up for most of their marriage, but that would not be the case for long.

"Listen to me. I stood by you through all this tribulation. I didn't cause your downfall. It was your precious Deidre. She always mattered to you more than I did. You were willing to give her anything she wanted, a home wherever she chose, travel, an expensive wedding and honeymoon. You would have given her a child. The only thing I asked from you, you denied me."

"Go ahead, flaunt my failure as a husband in my face. You're right, I would never have given you a child. Our wedding and honeymoon, even our life together was a shadow of what my life could have been. I am in ruin because of you."

"I watched while your life fell apart. I stood beside you in court while you handed Deidre her every desire on a plate."

"What are you talking about?"

"You did nothing to defend yourself. It appeared you felt you owed Deidre your every last dime."

"I knew her case was valid. I had no defense because I was guilty."

"Now it's all gone and you're blaming *me*?"

"You ruined my life. I should never have entertained Mother's wishes to bring you across the country. I should have sent you packing when I had the chance."

"So you could have your ostentatious life with Deidre? I never needed a grand house or money or social standing. I wanted you. Everything was exactly as you wished. I went along, never expressing my desires. The only things I wanted were a baby and for us to begin a new life. I even intended to go to New York since you refused to consider any other possibility."

"It's the only way I can see to start over."

"It's the only way you can return to your old life is what you really mean."

"Well now, there's no reason to worry about it since you won't be coming to New York."

"You've finally heard something I said. I never

wanted to go to New York. You go, if that's your heart's desire."

April stared while Noah stomped out the front door, not bothering to close it. What had she done?

* * *

The pleasant day turned into a balmy evening. Mrs. Fitzpatrick buried her face in her husband's shoulder as they lay in bed beneath the open window.

"Here, don't cry Charlotte. Maybe it was nothing but a silly argument. Everyone argues sometimes. We don't know what they said."

"Everyone in the entire neighborhood heard them. What will happen to them? What will happen to us?"

"You'll see. Everything will work out," Mr. Fitzpatrick assured. He would never admit his own doubts to his frail wife.

Chapter Fifteen

April awoke to knocking at the front door. Pulling on her robe, she left the attic bedroom and hurried downstairs all the while wondering how much time she'd have before being evicted. She stared in amazement once she answered.

"Mr. Farmer? What are you doing here?"

The man absolutely beamed, ecstatic to be in April's presence. "It sounded as if you might be in a bit of trouble in your last letter. I'm here to help," he cheerfully replied. "My, you are living in a fine home here."

"Oh, forgive me, come in, come in. Please excuse my appearance. Why don't you have a seat while I dress and fetch some tea. Then we can talk, that is, if you don't mind?"

"Certainly not! Take your time. I'll wait right here."

April put the kettle on and ran upstairs to dress, mentally reviewing items in the kitchen. She had little to offer Mr. Farmer besides a cup of tea.

Reentering the kitchen as the teapot started to sing, April quickly prepared a tea tray and added two leftover biscuits and a small pot of jam. "Here we are," she announced, as cheerily as she could manage. "How is it you've come all this way?"

Mr. Farmer accepted the cup of tea although he was a coffee drinker. He didn't wish to appear impolite.

"I've been concerned since you wrote about your financial difficulties. My life changed recently and I found myself in a position to travel. My wife passed on about six months ago. I believe I wrote you about that."

"Yes, you did. My sincerest condolences."

"Thank you. First of all, what can I do for you?"

"It's generous of you to come all this way. I don't know what to say."

"Your financial problems are behind you, then?"

"No. To be honest my husband left last night and hasn't returned. This house has been sold. I need to make other living arrangements. I don't think you could be of assistance."

"Will he return for you?"

"I don't know." April, ashamed at the admission, looked down at her hands resting in her lap.

"Here, here. I didn't come to worsen your problems. I should explain. My trip will make more sense once I finish."

"What would you have to explain?"

"My story begins a long time ago, before the war. You see, I loved your mother." Mr. Farmer garnered April's complete attention. "I knew she didn't love me, but I pursued her for all I was worth. At first, she took advantage of me. Eventually, I can honestly say, we became friends. Before the South seceded from the Union, I asked her to marry me and she agreed. That's when your dashing, handsome father showed up. I could see your mother was besotted from the moment she laid eyes on him. It's not as if we actually broke our engagement or even argued. She simply spent every waking moment plotting to be in his presence. My heart was broken. The day your parents married was probably the darkest day of my life.

"After you were born, your father left for the war, but I did not. I tried to help Samantha. She clearly needed help. You see, you were born exactly seven months after your parents married. I assisted anyway I could until I got drafted. Your father was captured early in the conflict. I could see Samantha still loved him dearly. I had no place in her life. But I felt an obligation to her. She was devastated when your father returned in ill health. And your father was no fool. He knew you weren't his child." Mr. Farmer could see April failed to comprehend his words.

"When I returned from the war, I found the three of you living at the farm, quite unhappily. Samantha felt guilty and distraught. She devoted her life to caring for your father, trying to make things up to him. He would have none of it. He wanted nothing to do with you. I often felt the urge to take you away from that unpleasant household, even later, after your father died. I attempted to make my own life and married, but we were childless. I believed my wife might be willing to take you in, but then Samantha fell ill, or at least she gave a good impersonation of illness. She said she relied on you. You were all she had. I'm afraid she successfully played on my sympathies.

"April, the bank never supplied the money to keep you going, it was me. Early on, your mother mortgaged the farm to the hilt. I made the payments. It seemed the least I could do for you. I'm afraid I'm a coward. I wanted to tell you about this before you left Concord. I wanted to do more for you. You are my daughter."

April sat in stunned silence. How could any of this be true? Why did this happen now, when her entire life had fallen apart? "I don't know what to say to you," was all she could manage.

"I understand this is quite a shock. I'll be going now so you can consider what I've said. Have no doubt my offer of help is real and sincere. Once my wife passed on, I decided to come to California. I have a job waiting for me at a bank in Santa Barbara, but I'm at your disposal for as long as you need me. If I come back in the morning, do you think you'll have some plan—unless your husband returns? If so, I want to meet him. I want a place in your life, April, no matter how small. You're all I have and I hope you can forgive me."

"Forgive you?" April never felt more confused in her life. "Yes, it might be best if you return in the morning."

* * *

Jack breathed a sigh of relief as he walked to the corner table where Noah sat snoring, his head propped against the wall.

"Wake up!" he commanded as he shook Noah's shoulder.

"Huh? What?" Noah glanced around the room not understanding where he was. "Oh, hello there, Jack. Pull up a chair. I'll buy you a drink."

"I think you've had enough to drink. Where have you been?"

"I'll tell you honessly," slurred Noah. "I been

investig-investigatin' ever bar in Los Angeles. Don' you want to know what I been investigatin'?"

"No, I don't. Where's April?"

"Mrs. Chandler is gone, lost forever."

"What are you talking about? Did she leave you, then?"

"No. I left her. I don' know where she is." This admission seemed to sober Noah. "We been displaced. The house and contents belong to another and I'm penniless."

"What happened to the money you squirreled away?"

Noah pulled a few coins from his vest pocket. "This is all I got."

"You spent it all on booze and women?"

"Women! I've had enough of them to last a lifetime. Now booze is another matter."

"You didn't give money to April? Shit, Noah, what the hell is wrong with you? I understand this has been hard but you need to pull yourself together."

"Don't worry about Mrs. Chandler. She's got her own funds. She offer'd 'em to me and I said no."

"How would April have money?"

"I told you before, she writes. I never understood what that meant."

"What does it mean?"

"Betrayal, my friend. Betrayal."

"I'm taking you home. When did you last change your clothes? You're a filthy mess."

"No, Jack. I'm not mooching off you or anyone else. I'll buy one last drink and then I got to find work. A job where they don't care if you're an asshole or not." Noah looked directly at Jack and added, "And I am the king of assholes."

Jack grabbed Noah by the arm and pulled him out of the chair. "I think you better save your money. You're at least getting cleaned up before you look for work."

* * *

Mrs. Fitzpatrick answered a tentative knock on her door to find Mr. Chandler. She was stunned at his appearance. He wore a pair of blue jeans and a plaid shirt. He evidently hadn't shaved since the night of the argument. She never saw him in anything less than immaculate attire, clean-shaven with every hair in place. "Mr. Chandler?"

"Is Mr. Fitzpatrick around?"

"Yes, come in, how thoughtless of me."

"No, thank you. I wondered if April might be here."

"She left several days ago."

"Did she tell you where she was going?" Noah nodded at Mr. Fitzpatrick who walked up behind his wife.

"She said she'd contact us when she found a place to stay. She waited for you."

"How long was she here?"

"A man came by the house the day after you left," Mr. Fitzpatrick explained. "I don't know who he was, maybe the new owner. April remained in the house for three days then told us she had to leave. She said the new owner wanted us to stay on and mind the place. They agreed to our old salary, but the locks are changed. We can't get in the house for now. April left your things in the carriage house."

"Thank you. I wanted to apologize. I know you almost lost your home because of me. I'm grateful you're able to stay. I owe you back wages. I'll pay as soon as I can."

Mr. and Mrs. Fitzpatrick glanced at each other. The humble Mr. Chandler who stood outside their door was not the arrogant man they knew.

"It won't be necessary," replied Mr. Fitzpatrick. "April paid us before she left. Did you want to leave an address in case she comes by?"

"No. I'm not sure where I'll be living. I'll grab a few things and send for the rest when I'm able. Thank you."

The Fitzpatricks watched Mr. Chandler emerge from the carriage house with a bundle of clothes tucked under his arm and disappear down the street.

"I don't think he'll ever come back," Mrs. Fitzpatrick commented.

"You're probably right," agreed her husband. In fact, the pair would never lay eyes on Noah Chandler again.

* * *

April had difficulty following her seam line in the waning daylight. She'd have to get the lantern if she continued. Instead, she sat back in her chair and stared out the window at the lengthening shadows. She intended to make her self-imposed exile as luxurious as possible. There simply wasn't much luxury to be had in the small house on the outskirts of Newhall. If April were honest, she'd admit this life seemed eerily similar to the one she lived in Concord. Her running water consisted of a pump in the small kitchen. Her new bathtub was portable and made of zinc. Admittedly, it was far larger than the hip bath at the farm. An outhouse stood 50 feet from the back door.

Yet, April felt a pride of ownership she never previously experienced. This was her house, funded by the sweat of her brow. A few bits of furniture were abandoned in the house. April didn't hesitate to make use of them. The small table and chairs in the kitchen were now painted a lively blue. She used white paint on the dresser and iron bed in her tiny bedroom. All the walls received a fresh coat of paint and her bedroom sported a bold yellow and red floral wallpaper. April purchased a settee and a side table for her parlor and a rocking chair for the front porch. A new .22 rifle hung over the fireplace. A woman alone, she planned to teach herself to shoot any day now.

April stockpiled fabric from the Gulley Store and had currently become engrossed in sewing curtains for all the windows and a quilt for her bed. Weather here was more extreme than in Los Angeles: hotter in summer and colder in winter. Nights were always cool.

Her improvements were not restricted to the interior of the yellow house. She planted a garden inside a fenced area behind her home. A new clothesline hung beyond the garden. Despite all her efforts to settle in, April wrote more than ever. Perhaps she simply had more life experience to draw from. Perhaps her need to stockpile cash made her desperate. Then again, she didn't have to think about her own life while imagining Little May's.

April felt no desire to grin and pretend all was well. She didn't want to exchange pleasantries or pass herself off as a pillar of society. She had tired of scorn and pity.

It didn't take Mrs. Chandler long to appreciate the fact she stayed in California. Moving to the East Coast was Noah's plan, never hers. She would have gone with him and planned to do so. But his abrupt departure after their fight opened up new opportunities for April, at least, she preferred to think of her current life as a new opportunity. She was reasonably content to bide her time and make a home. Repair of her marriage would have to wait. Oddly, she didn't think of the marriage as having ended. April considered it on hold. She currently had nothing to say to her husband. Certainly, the things she needed to say would only cause more harm.

Mr. Farmer's presence—no—her father's presence proved a godsend. Although surprised at her requests, he proved instrumental in her move and eager to help. She knew she used him; the man was obviously anxious to make up for parental deficiencies. April soon saw a new side of the banker. He appeared capable and businesslike. He negotiated the price of her tiny house, which April nearly paid in full. He arranged financing for the small balance, even co-signing for her. Women were rarely serious contenders for credit. He saw her settled in before he continued his journey to Santa Barbara.

April smiled. She could feel the baby move. All of Noah's careful planning proved for naught. She knew from the time the house was set for auction but didn't want to add to her husband's burdens.

Her tales of Charlie Boatman caused April a fair amount of guilt. True, he sprang to mind when Noah was obnoxious. The damage was most likely done by the time he proposed. She had no way of knowing her stories would become popular or that Noah would take them so personally. He kept his feelings bottled up for months, always exhibiting careful control, never admitting his discouragement except during their

Christmas argument. If he continued to blame her, there could be no future for them. April kept her own feelings secret through most of their brief marriage. In an effort to be a supportive and caring wife, she completely disregarded her own ideas, hopes and dreams.

Realizing Noah never loved Deidre, she regretted her jealous accusations. It seemed a natural reaction to hurt Noah when they fought. Her tactic had, unfortunately, proven effective.

April wrapped her arms around her waist. She imagined Noah's joy when she presented him with their new baby. In her daydreams, he would be thrilled to see her, recovered from his tribulations and happy to be a new father. If only she could control her own future as effectively as she did Little May's.

Sighing, April retrieved the lantern from the parlor and put aside her curtain to take up the tiny baby gown she started that morning.

* * *

Surprised how much he enjoyed the physically brutal job, Noah rose early each morning to dig ditches. At three, he returned to Bill's stable, where he cleaned stalls, fed horses, and helped customers, even in the middle of the night when necessary. Bill gave him a room in back. Noah was nearly always exhausted, but the extreme physical exertion meant his mind remained blessedly empty. Always an athletic and robust man, he was more physically fit than ever before. Checkers, still housed at the stable, proved to be a constant, bittersweet reminder of Noah's past.

A startled Noah looked up from mucking out a stall to find Jack. "How did you know I worked here?"

"I see Bill at the games. Why don't you ever show up? We need a catcher."

"I have too much work to do."

"I don't approve of any of this—what you're doing to yourself."

"I never asked for your approval."

Jack took the comment in stride. It seemed odd for him to be the well-dressed attorney while Noah was nothing but a lackey. Jack wanted desperately to help. "Have you seen the paper lately?"

"No, why?"

"Martha is dead."

"You'll have to be more specific. To which Martha are you referring?"

"Deidre's cousin Martha who lived in Sacramento. I believe she was your fiancé number two if I haven't lost track."

At this, Noah leaned on his pitchfork. "I can't believe that. What happened?"

"No one knows. She would have been married next month. They found her in bed. The cause is being investigated. It could be murder."

"Why?"

"The news reports aren't specific. She might have been poisoned."

"What a shame. Martha was a lovely girl, gentle and sweet."

"And she didn't sue you either. That's a point in her favor."

This comment drew a scowl from Noah, who returned to his work.

"Have you made any attempt to find your wife?"

"I don't believe it's any of your business, Jack."

"No is your answer, I take it. Why the hell not,

Noah? You love her and she's crazy about you. What has happened to split you two apart? She never cared if you were rich. I don't think she'd mind being married to a ditch digger."

"Get out, Jack. I've had enough."

Jack heeded the warning but planned to return.

* * *

As April emerged from the Gulley Store, she decided Newhall was not a civilized town by her husband's standards. It had four saloons and zero churches. She learned the overabundance of saloons was caused by neighboring towns and the nearby San Fernando Valley being voted dry. A mere two blocks in length, somehow Newhall suited her.

April sat her grocery basket on the boardwalk to tie the ribbon of her hat on the breezy day.

"Mrs. Chandler, isn't it?"

April couldn't help her frown of displeasure. She'd done everything possible to discourage friendly overtures from the ladies of Newhall.

"I'm sorry. I can't recall your name."

"Mrs. Darby. Remember? I came by with the welcoming committee."

"So you did." April picked up her basket and turned to leave.

"I wanted to remind you about the sewing circle. We were all so impressed by your lovely curtains and quilt. You'd certainly enjoy our group," Mrs. Darby all but yelled at April's departing figure.

Mrs. Chandler continued walking but turned her face to reply, "Maybe in a few weeks. I'm still settling in. Good day." Surely the woman could see April took no interest in community activities. How much more obvious could she be?

She'd been dismayed when five women showed up on her doorstep to introduce themselves and invite her participation in various civic and social groups. April had done her best to turn them away before things got out of hand. Curious about the improvements she'd made in what was previously a community eyesore, all five barged into her house and demanded a tour.

Doubting she'd smiled even once, April allowed the ladies to satisfy their curiosity. It seemed undeniably awkward when they congregated near the front door, obviously expecting April to offer refreshment. She did not, wanting nothing more than to be left alone. The ladies were made uncomfortable in the ensuing silence.

As April walked toward her house, she could not imagine why anyone who'd been treated so rudely would attempt further conversation. Short of total, blunt honesty, how could she be any clearer? Smiling, she invented the response she wished to deliver to Mrs. Darby.

"Don't bother me. I have no desire to participate in any of your activities. In order to completely avoid busybodies like you, I only come to town when necessary. I'm not looking for friendship. It was rude of you to show up at my house unannounced. In the future, let's pretend we're total strangers who've never laid eyes on each other."

April shocked herself with her imaginary diatribe. She desired nothing more than a true friend when she came to California. She recalled the comfort of Mrs. Pratt's visits.

In her anger, April made a good start on her

journey. Her new house was less than two miles from Newhall's Main Street. Two miles. Mr. Farmer thought it much too far. A woman alone needed to be closer to protection. April dug in her heels, claiming the house was exactly the kind of project she needed and promising to purchase a gun for self-protection. About the friendliest she'd been to anyone in Newhall turned out to be the clerk who sold her the weapon and showed her how to load it.

April shook her head. Society could be a problem for another day. Today was the only day that mattered. She would put her stew on and finish the binding of her quilt. The flowers she'd planted in front of the porch would need some extra water on the warm, windy day.

Approaching her front steps, April paused to look around. She had the uncomfortable feeling she was being watched.

"Nonsense." Perhaps her train of thought prompted her apprehension. Work was all she needed. Maybe she'd practice loading the gun.

* * *

Her heart about pounded right out of her chest as April screwed up her courage and grabbed the .22 rifle.

"Who's there?" she barked as she headed onto the porch. A noise came from behind her house. April advanced on the corner and quickly aimed the rifle down the side, ready to shoot whatever she found.

"Don't shoot! I'm a Christian!"

"What?"

"I'm a Christian looking for some supper. Ain't you a Christian too?"

April did not lower the rifle. "Come closer so I

can see you." The sun had set; the light was waning. She could only make out the vague shape of a man emerging from the vegetable patch, his hands in the air.

As the man approached, April felt foolish. At her height, looking down at people, even men, seemed commonplace. The profoundly thin, diminutive person walking toward her stood almost a foot shorter. He appeared to be an Indian wearing a plaid shirt and buckskin pants. His white hair was pulled into a braid. A beaded leather band circled his head. She clasped her rifle firmly.

"You better go on now," she waved the rifle in the direction of the road. "Get out of here, before I shoot."

"I can't go, ma'am. I just can't."

"Why not?"

"God has sent me here to help you. He sent me for supper too but mostly to help you."

"I don't need help. You be on your way."

"I can't. There's a mighty fine smell coming from your kitchen. I sure hoped you might spare some supper for your guardian angel."

"I don't believe guardian angels steal food from vegetable patches."

"Well, I imagine most folks would agree. But you're all by yourself out here and I've come to protect you. You don't know how to shoot that thing, do you?"

"I certainly do and I'm not alone. My husband will be here any moment."

"Shucks, ma'am. You know the Lord don't abide a liar."

"What would you know about the Lord? You're an Indian." April was distressed to think the man had observed closely enough to see she lived alone.

"That I be, but I'm a Christian, baptized right proper and all. I tell you what. If you push a plate of food out the window to me, I'll put in a good word for you, about the lying and all."

"I assure you, I'm perfectly able to pray on my own behalf. You need to go now." But April could see, short of shooting the little man, there didn't seem to be a way to make him leave. Afraid to lower the gun, April sought to strike a deal. "If I give you a plate of food, will you go?"

The Indian lowered his hands. "If you give me a plate of them fine vittles, I give you the Lord's word, I'll leave."

April backed into her house and latched the door. She struggled to hold the rifle while dishing up a plate of food then handed the plate out the window.

"Thank you, ma'am. The Lord loves a cheerful giver."

April was not impressed by the man's references to God and she felt anything but cheerful. Clutching the rifle for dear life, she locked every window and sat on her bed; the gun rested across her lap. The Indian could certainly burn down the house while she slept were he so disposed. She needed to stay awake. She listened as he chanted a song and rested his plate on the porch. April assumed he was too stealthy for her to hear him walk away, but he hadn't been the least bit stealthy in the vegetable patch. Despite her best efforts, April dozed off not long before sunrise.

Startled awake by the distinctive song of a gnatcatcher, April grasped the rifle still resting in her lap and went to peek out the door. The Indian apparently left, but on the porch sat a neatly stacked cord of wood. The plate she gave him rested on top. It had been washed.

* * *

Noah walked into the Arcadia Hotel in Santa Monica, curious who could have sent the note to the stable. His clothing fit differently. It had been months since he wore a suit. His muscles pressed against the jacket sleeves. He needed braces to hold up his pants; the waistband was too large. Once he got off the train, he noted a wooden roller coaster descending to the beach. April would love a ride on that. As much disdain as he harbored for his wife, he couldn't stop the thrill of excitement at the thought she might be waiting for him.

The maître d' escorted Noah to a curtained table at the rear of the restaurant. Noah drew back the tasseled fabric and froze in place.

"What are you doing here?" he sneered.

"Noah, you have to let me explain," began Deidre. "Sit down, I beg you." Noah turned to leave. "I'm sorry, Noah. You have to listen to me." Deidre sounded desperate.

Noah paused and turned his head. "Why should I listen to you?"

Deidre felt she garnered enough of his attention to make him stay. "None of this was my fault. Mr. Nelson put me up to it. It was all his plan. I was afraid of him, Noah. The man is clearly a lunatic. There's no telling what he might have done to me. Please sit down and let me apologize."

Reluctantly, Noah took a seat. He listened quietly as Deidre spun her tale of intrigue. Mr. Nelson put false stories in the paper. Insanely jealous when he lost April, he wanted revenge. Mr. Nelson sent the letters to Noah's clients. It was he who had access to Noah's business contacts. At least this much of Deidre's story seemed plausible. Only a dimwit like Nelson wouldn't bother to use an authentic case name in his letters.

Yet it seemed implausible Deidre's dramatic courtroom testimony had been anyone's lies but her own. "Unfortunately, Mr. Nelson is not the one who sued me for every possession I owned. Your apology falls rather short."

"That's not true, Noah. He's the one who put me up to the lawsuit. He wanted to ruin you and he told me he'd kill me if I didn't do as he said. He prepared the documents. You can ask my attorney if you like. He even knew how much I could win. I did show up. I did testify. Anything less would have cost my life. You have to believe me."

"And you never thought once about going to the authorities—telling your family? How do you expect me to believe you, Deidre?"

"It's true, Noah, I swear it. Listen, there's a way I can make restitution, at least partially. I have a key here." Deidre removed a small envelope from her reticule and handed it to Noah. "It's for a safe deposit box at the National Bank of California. The number is on the envelope. There are personal belongings in there, valuable belongings. I want you to have them. The deed to your house is in the box. I bought it myself. It's free and clear. I'm gifting it to you.

"It didn't take me long to apprehend what you told me was true. I would have been throwing my life away if I married you. I want you to have this, to put your life back together. There isn't much of anything I can do about your reputation without endangering myself. I know we can never be friends, but I hope we can part on amiable terms. Take the envelope, Noah. It's yours."

Noah briefly acknowledged he had a different life, one he felt satisfied to continue. But there was a part of him that sought vindication. He rose, grabbed the envelope and silently left the restaurant.

Chapter Sixteen

As the seasons changed, April worked in her garden and prepared for her baby. The Indian showed up for dinner almost every night. She came to expect him. He usually left wood or some other token on the porch. When she finally asked his name, he replied, "George Washington."

"That is surely not your real name."

"I need to face facts. This is a white man's world. I've taken the name of the most honest and powerful white man to live in this land. In this way, I have his might."

"President Washington was an extremely tall gentleman. I believe you'd be hard-pressed to attain his might. It seems a bit beyond your ability."

"I assure you, Washington blood now runs through my veins."

"I didn't know guardian angels had veins or blood. Your attributes are difficult to comprehend."

"It's because you're a white woman who's prone to rely on her own mind. You're not in touch with the forces around you. Can we play checkers tonight?"

April never knew a more abysmal checkers player than Mr. Washington. He was completely befuddled by the game. She could likely play blindfolded and beat him. Yet, he appeared enthralled by their brief contests.

"One game, Mr. Washington, one game."

April recalled their first checkers match as she placed her pieces on the board. She sought to trap Mr. Washington initially but soon realized he considered all her moves to be a trap. Thinking he could outsmart her, he sacrificed his every piece in rapid succession in an effort to alter her strategy. His look of astonishment at each loss amused April no end. Hoping he might improve, April attempted to explain tactics. He treated her comments distrustfully.

"I don't know why you won't consider my suggestions about your play."

Mr. Washington explained, "I don't trust you. You're not a proper white woman."

"Really? Why do you say so?"

"Your skin is brown from the sun. You wear your hair down in a braid and you don't wear shoes as respectable white women do. You have a fine ring but no husband."

"I have a husband, Mr. Washington, but he's living in New York. He went away on business. As for the cosmetic details, I really don't care much about my appearance at the moment."

"What will you do when your baby comes? Indian women go away by themselves, but white women need help."

Assuming she concealed her condition effectively, April's shock must have been easily read. She recovered quickly, "Well, you are my guardian angel, what's your advice?"

"I'm gonna ask my wife."

"You have a wife?"

"Sure, I do."

"Why don't you live with her?"

"I do. But she's a terrible cook. I'd rather eat your food."

* * *

Noah glanced through the contents of the safe deposit box once the bank clerk escorted him to the vault. Curiosity took hold of him. He fingered through the contents, hoping Deidre had been honest and the deed to his house was inside, although he believed some business entity purchased his property. Undoubtedly the house had already been resold, his belongings auctioned off. His beliefs were confirmed when he failed to locate a deed. There was money, perhaps as much as a thousand dollars, and jewelry, though nothing exceptional. He closed the box without removing any of the contents and left the bank.

Making his way to his old law office, he found a new receptionist. "I'd like to see Mr. Broadmore."

"Do you have an appointment?"

"No. Tell him Mr. Chandler is here to see him."

His name never failed to illicit a negative reaction. The man gave him an icy glare and left to announce his presence. Before long, Noah took a seat in Jack's office.

"I'm surprised to see you," Jack admitted.

"I came to tell you I've seen Deidre."

"You must be joking!"

"No. She sent me an invitation to dinner. Naturally, I didn't know it was her doing the inviting or I would never have gone. She offered apologies and claimed Nelson is the mastermind behind my downfall.

She said he threatened her. Where is the little weasel? I believe I'd like to have a word with him."

"He's gone, Noah. He quit about a week ago and walked out. I have no idea where he is. I sent his pay to the address we had on file. It got returned, undeliverable."

"I don't believe Deidre told the truth, at least not the whole truth. She gave me a key for a safe deposit box. She claimed to have bought my house and told me the deed was inside. It wasn't there."

"What did you find?"

"Some cash, a few pieces of jewelry. I left it in the box."

"Are you going to use it?"

"No. I'll return the key when I get around to it."

"How are you?"

Noah rose to leave. "I'm all right, Jack. I work hard every day, I even started going to church on Sunday. I keep to myself. It seems to help."

"You know you have a job here if you want it. The firm is half yours."

"Thanks, Jack, but I'm going to keep at what I'm doing for now. I'll drop by again soon. Maybe I'll come out to the game one Saturday."

* * *

Having finished her weekly shopping, April emerged from the Gulley Store into bright sunshine. She was astounded as a man came flying out the batwing doors of a saloon almost at her feet. To her amazement, Mr. Washington lay sprawled in the dirt. Before she could react, a burly man bore down on him.

"We don't want your kind here. Stay out, old man."

The burly man advanced upon Mr. Washington. It appeared he intended to further harm the Indian.

As the man drew his boot back, April yelled, "Stop right there." She stepped into the street as a small crowd gathered to watch.

"Who's gonna stop me?" the man sneered. "This is just an old Indian. Nobody wants him around."

"And you're a fool. Nobody wants you around either." April inserted herself between the antagonists and turned her back on the burly man. She helped Mr. Washington to his feet. Ignoring his tormentor, she asked, "Can you walk?"

"Yes, ma'am." He motioned with his hand for her to move aside. Instead, April accompanied Mr. Washington down the center of Railroad Avenue. "Are you all right? Do you need a doctor?"

"I'm fine."

"What were you doing in the saloon?"

"A man likes a beer now and then."

"I don't believe it's legal for you to drink if I'm not mistaken."

"I can't agree. The white man who sold me the beer is the one breakin' the law."

"Mr. Washington, I think you have things rather confused. Has it ever occurred to you that you were sent here so I could be your guardian angel?"

No sooner did they head away from trouble, than a young man yelled out from the boardwalk. "You there, lady!"

April turned around.

"Is this here your Indian?"

"I assure you; he does not belong to me. He's a grown man." April almost laughed as she looked down at her companion. They must be a strange sight, she so inordinately tall, he so diminutive. But she had to look up at the fit man who walked toward them. His muscles bulged in his shirt sleeves.

"I cut firewood for a living. He's been stealing from my place."

This man seemed extremely angry. Was there no end of angry men in Newhall? A church might be a necessity.

April thought quickly. "I must apologize to you. Mr. Washington obtained firewood at my request and I absent-mindedly forgot to send payment. How much do I owe you?"

"A buck and six bits."

"Allow me to settle my account immediately." Thinking the man's rates rather extreme, April fished some coins from the basket she held over her arm. "This puts us up to date then?" she poured on the charm as she handed the man his money.

"Sure enough," he commented as he turned toward the boardwalk. "I expect to get paid when that Injun takes the wood, understand?"

"Mr. Washington, it seems to me you're getting in a lot of mischief while doing God's work."

He grinned up at her.

"Did you at least enjoy your beer?"

The grin grew even wider.

* * *

"Noah, I believe you need to take this seriously. Why didn't you ask to have an attorney present when the police came?"

"I am an attorney. The whole thing is ridiculous," Noah replied as Jack took a seat beside him. Noah came to see the Boyle Heights Browns win their final game of the season.

"What did the police say?"

"They said Deidre is missing. They asked if I'd seen her and I told them yes. She sent an anonymous note to meet her at the Arcadia Hotel in Santa Monica and I went. They asked for the note, but I threw it away. They searched my room at the stable."

"Did they find anything?"

"The key I told you about, the one to the safe deposit box."

"Shit, Noah. You should never have let them find the key. I thought you were going to send it back? It's a good thing you didn't take any of the contents. The key by itself could be incriminating."

"This is absurd. She's missing. It's not as if she's dead. I simply hadn't returned the key. You're taking this way too seriously."

"I think I should look into this. I want you to come to my office next Wednesday if Deidre hasn't turned up by then. Lunch is on me."

"Well, I can't refuse lunch, now can I?"

* * *

April sat at her typewriter on the blistering fall afternoon. As much as she enjoyed the warmth of California, she felt completely uncomfortable. She wished the sun would go down or a breeze would develop. Tired of fanning herself, April dropped her fatigued arm into her lap and closed her eyes.

Her irritability stemmed from more than heat. She'd become increasingly awkward as her baby grew. Her back hurt. She could barely get out of the bathtub.

Writing made her grumpy. April finally tired of the exploits of Little May. The idea her career ruined her marriage frequently occurred. She was ready to end the series. Mr. Lynch would not be happy, but April planned to devote herself to motherhood. This might be her only opportunity to do so. She pulled her page from the typewriter and read aloud.

As Charlie Boatman took money from the cash register, he turned to find Little May placing the newly washed shot glasses on the back of the bar. He grabbed her arm and turned her to face him. A look of complete shock met his curious stare. He never noticed before. The girl had turned into an attractive woman. Holding her arms, he bent down and kissed her tentatively on the lips.

"Let go! I'm not that sort," proclaimed Little May.

Charlie felt uncharacteristically timid at her command and released her. He watched as she picked up two dirty beer mugs and scrambled to the kitchen.

Content to leave her work at that for the day, April put a clean sheet of paper in the typewriter. She started several letters to Lula but had never completed one. April wanted to tell her mother-in-law about her new grandchild. She wanted to know about life in New York. Mostly, she wanted to find out about Noah. Was he well? Was he working? Might Lula think he would come for her if she asked?

No matter how hard she worked or what she accomplished, no matter how self-sufficient she felt, April yearned for her husband more with each passing day. She could not deny it. She longed for him each night as she climbed in bed. She wanted Noah's arms around her. She wanted desperately to be kissed. Her long denied lust frequently invaded her thoughts. Sleep became more and more elusive. She would fail to write Lula yet again.

Heading outside, April considered her best option might be to stay at Mr. Farmer's Santa Barbara house, or rather Elias's house. She found it awkward calling him father. He suggested she use his first name but cheerfully requested his grandchild call him Grandpa. Lost in her reverie, April did not see Mr. Washington approach and flinched when he spoke.

"Hot day, huh? Did I scare you?"

"I've been thinking, Mr. Washington. I want you to do me a favor."

"That's what guardian angels is for."

This drew a frown from Mrs. Chandler. She collected a pair of scissors from the table on the porch. "I want you to cut my hair. I know I may be crazy to ask an Indian to cut my hair, but it's so hot and my hair is too heavy. Would you help me by making a straight cut across the back?"

"I will."

April leaned against the table for stability and apprehensively handed over the scissors. "About four or five inches below my shoulder will do. I can still put it up or make a short braid," she muttered, mostly to herself. Closing her eyes, she prayed Mr. Washington would not get carried away. Almost before he touched her hair, he declared himself finished.

"White people make jewelry out of their hair. Is that what you're going to do?"

"I believe there's enough hair for me to make a jacket," she replied. April tied the ends of her hair with a ribbon so as not to make a mess on the porch. Mr. Washington held at least two feet of beribboned brown hair. "No. I don't want it."

"Can I have it?"

"Most assuredly. Thank you for your help." Despite her awkward request, April felt an unprecedented lightness when she ran her fingers through her shortened hair as a subtle breeze cooled her skin.

* * *

"Mr. Chandler, your former fiancé, Deidre Mercer, is missing, you know that don't you? Her cousin, another former fiancé has been murdered. What about your wife? Is she at home?"

"No."

"Where might we find her?"

"I don't know."

"She's missing, then?"

"I don't believe she's missing."

"But you don't know where she is?"

Noah glared at Jack in reply.

"You can't testify if they bring charges, Noah. You can't take the stand. There's too much incriminating evidence—so many loose ends. If I didn't know you, I'd think you were guilty. The letters Deidre wrote to her cousin, Theodora, are a huge obstacle."

"But they're full of lies. There is no body. How can the district attorney assume there's been a murder?"

"Deidre wrote about her fear of you, that you threatened and blackmailed her. She claimed you demanded the key to the safe deposit box she filled at your request."

"But there's no proof."

"There is the key. She stated you initiated the meeting in Santa Monica. The prosecution has witnesses who will testify she was distraught, even hysterical, both before you arrived and after you left. Although they couldn't hear what you said, they're willing to confirm Deidre's desperation. No one has seen her since she left the restaurant. You admitted you were there. You have opportunity and motive."

"How am I supposed to mount a defense, Jack?"

"I don't know. We have to sort through this, issue by issue, so we can be prepared. But we can start by finding April. At least she doesn't have to be a problem. We can hire a Pinkerton man."

"We don't need a Pinkerton man. I know how to find her," Noah cryptically replied.

* * *

Mr. Lynch stared across his desk in wonder. The embodiment of Charlie Boatman stood in his office. True, this man appeared to be clean and meticulously attired, but every aspect of his appearance had been fully documented in *The Life of Little May*: his dark straight hair, piercing grey eyes, square chin and clean-shaven face, even the way he stood slightly more to his right. Remembering his manners, Gordon Lynch stood and offered his hand. "How can I help you today, Mr.—"

"Chandler, Noah Chandler."

Holy shit. Was this the womanizer from the newspapers in trouble with the law? How much truth had Miss Stringham included in her wild tales? "What can I do for you, Mr. Chandler?"

"I need to find the woman who writes for your magazine, S. Armstrong."

"I assure you Mr. Armstrong is a male contributor to *Pacific Weekly.*"

"I haven't time to play games, Mr. Lynch. I need you to tell me how to find April Stringham. You know where she is, beyond question. I don't intend to leave until you give me her address. I can promise, I have no intention to contact her. I simply need her location."

This angry, menacing man knew far too much for comfort. "Assuming I did know how to locate her, why would I tell you?" besides the fact he was scared half to death.

"Because she's my wife, Mr. Lynch. You can write her address on the tablet right there. Rest assured, she'll never know you gave it to me."

* * *

Above a small house on the outskirts of Newhall, Noah stood on a winding trail beside the horse Bill loaned him. He was not disappointed with Mr. Lynch's information as he observed April through a pair of binoculars.

Stooped over, April hoed a patch of weeds near a fence behind the house. He easily recognized her, remembering the graceful way she moved her hands and arms.

He could talk to her despite his promise he would not. A sudden longing came over him as he recalled silly things: the way her hair smelled, her impish grin, how she looked standing at their stove in her apron. But the betrayal he felt the day he read the paper in her typewriter blotted out this pleasant reverie. Noah was about to lower the binoculars when April stood straight and stretched, rubbing her back. Undoubtedly, she carried his child. Noah could not take his eyes away.

As April turned toward the road in front of the house, Noah noticed a buggy had arrived. A man with graying hair approached April. She greeted him warmly, grabbed his hands in hers and kissed his cheek.

Perhaps the child belonged to another? No, that wasn't possible. Who could this man be? But what did it matter? Bitterly, Noah flung himself on his horse and headed for Los Angeles. Furiously kicking the sides of his mount, Noah urged it to greater speed. He rode as if demons haunted him. Perhaps they did.

* * *

Elias Farmer held his daughter at arms' length scrutinizing her from head to toe. "Look at you! It's so good to see you!"

April shyly replied, "I'm happy you're here. I've been rather lonely. Your visit could not be more timely. I have lemonade. Would you like to sit on the porch and we can catch up?"

"It sounds like a wonderful idea." Elias led April out of the garden to the front porch. "You haven't heard from Noah then?"

April shook her head and kept her focus on the ground. "He doesn't know where I am."

Once she fetched the lemonade, Elias explained his new job and described the lovely home he purchased mere blocks from the beach. "It's a wonderful, growing town. I arrived at exactly the right moment. They're drilling for oil south of the city—the Summerland Oil Field. The city has been growing ever since the rail line from Los Angeles was completed. Stearns Wharf serves as a maritime hub.

"You'd like it there, April. I wish you'd come and

stay in Santa Barbara, at least until the baby comes. The weather is milder than Newhall and I don't like you being all alone out here."

"I've been thinking about staying with you."

Surprised he made any headway, Elias had been prepared to do battle over his newfound daughter's living arrangement. "Haven't you made friends? The ladies in town didn't attempt to make you feel welcome?"

April found herself staring at the ground yet again. "It seems I learned a useful tactic from my mother."

"What?"

"I found myself being difficult enough so no one ever came back. It was purposeful on my part."

"Why would you behave in such a way?"

"I want to be alone. I didn't want anyone to find out who I was, where I came from or why. I wanted to hide here and I've done an excellent job of it."

"I'm concerned about you, April. You're holed up here in the middle of nowhere. You remind me of your mother." This drew a shocked expression. "She hid from the world and succeeded in shutting everyone out but you. I don't want you to repeat history. I'll be honest. When I see you living here alone, I'm much reminded of Samantha after her own failed marriage. This worries me."

"Oh, Elias, I never even thought about that. I never intended to follow in her footsteps."

"I find that is often the case. Children unconsciously repeat their parent's failures. I won't pressure you now, but I want you to consider coming home with me after my next visit. We'll have Christmas together."

"But I want to be clear. I never intended to stay here. This is only temporary, until the baby comes. Then I'll contact Noah and everything will be all right." She could see pity in her father's eyes. When she gave words to her plan, even she would admit it lacked substance.

"I understand. We'll talk more about your plans later. Why don't you tell me about your garden? I've discovered one can grow anything in Santa Barbara, all year long."

* * *

Noah's incarceration proved unbearable. Despite youthful recklessness, he never spent a day behind bars. When the judge denied him bail until his hearing, he resolved to make the best of the situation. Jack brought him law books. He read Sherlock Holmes and exercised as best as he could. Soon, he spent most of his day pacing back and forth like some caged lion. He wanted more than anything to scream and yell, make someone listen. It seemed no matter what he said or how sincere his assertions, no one could hear.

Noah spent the last months in exhaustive behavior. All his energy went into digging ditches as many days a week as he could find work. He cleaned stalls, groomed horses. All of this frenetic physical exertion kept his mind blissfully empty. Now thoughts of April frequently assaulted his consciousness. He pictured her standing in her garden, carrying his child. He wondered who her visitor had been. It certainly didn't take her long to find someone new. No matter how he tried to talk himself into that scenario, it didn't ring true.

Memories haunted his thoughts: April's shocked

Jean Jegel

expression when he said or did something outlandish, her natural passion, her loving embrace, the taste of her lips. As days went by, he replayed their argument in his mind. His comments were harsh, even cruel. He made it clear he wanted to continue his life alone. Even so, she waited three days for him before leaving.

Then there was the matter of her stories. Noah pondered the idea they were never intended to harm him. April was not a vicious person. If he were brutally honest, his own behavior landed him in jail. He treated women in a cavalier manner and it finally caught up with him.

Noah knew he'd made a poor husband. While circumstances proved him an inadequate provider, he became completely immersed in his own problems. It seemed easy enough to act the part of groom when they were living comfortably. He delighted in the physical aspects of marriage. At the time, April meant more to him than he would admit. Yet he treated her poorly—shut her out. Their marriage became a weak second to his personal difficulties.

Digging ditches served as an illuminating experience. Time spent in fellowship with impoverished men helped Noah understand what a privileged life he led. Their concerns were basic survival: making enough to feed their family, keeping a roof over their heads, or finding enough money to buy their wives some cheap trinket for a birthday gift.

Noah never struggled for anything in his life. Always coddled and protected, he had the finest money could buy from the day he was born. His God-given gifts of intelligence and health, even his handsome features were always taken for granted. His one real challenge in life, one he accepted gratefully, had been his marriage to April and he certainly made a mess of that. Noah knew their separation had one good result. At least he could spare her this ridiculous trial. He already put her through enough.

Chapter Seventeen

Pulling her shawl tightly around her shoulders, April was determined to finish the final installment of *The Life of Little May*. She put this off hoping to avoid the inevitable fight with her publisher. Elias planned to come for her in two weeks. April needed to tie up all loose ends before leaving for Santa Barbara.

All the baby things were packed in her valise. April made a bassinette but doubted even her eager-to-please father would find a way to take it on the train, or rather trains. They would have to head for Los Angeles to make the connection to Santa Barbara. She would need to find a cradle in Santa Barbara to use until her return home. As much as she appreciated her house in Newhall, it did not feel like home. Home meant Noah in the house on Carroll Avenue.

The two men came at Charlie from opposite ends of the bar. They knew his reputation. Their only chance to take him was to divide their resources.

"We come for y'all, Charlie. This here's the end. We're aimin' to avenge our brother, Tex."

Charlie eyed the two carefully. The one on his left looked to be the slower draw. He had a lazy look about him. Charlie decided to first take the brother on the right.

The bar erupted in gunfire. Charlie took one man but as he swerved to shoot the other, he knew he was too late. The man took aim and fired but didn't hit Charlie. Little May, seeing his predicament, lunged in front of Charlie Boatman and collapsed to the floor at his feet as Charlie's bullet nailed the second man.

Charlie blinked, uncomprehending. He came to love Little May as he never loved before, knowing his affection would never be returned. He treated her poorly, yet the girl willingly took a bullet for him. He knelt at her side.

"May, talk to me. May!" he begged as he cradled her head in his arms. May's eyes fluttered open. "You'll be fine girl," he whispered then he yelled at bystanders, "Someone go for the Doc!"

"No, Charlie, this is the end for me," Little May whispered. "I can see the angels comin' for me now."

"No, May, no. Say it ain't so! I need you. What will I do without you?"

"Be the man you were meant to be," encouraged Little May. "I've seen there's good in you. Do it for me, Charlie." A smile lit Little May's face as she stared at the ceiling and then she was gone.

April rubbed her fingers back and forth across her mouth, considering her work. If this did not give Mr. Lynch an apoplectic fit, nothing would.

* * *

After the second day of testimony, Jack dropped by the jail to consult with his client. The jailor offered a chair outside Noah's cell. "This isn't going well, Noah.

Surely you can see that."

Noah rose from his cot and paced back and forth. Pulling his hands through his hair, he replied, "Look, Jack, they don't have a body."

"Well, Deidre hasn't turned up, has she? Her family spent a fortune trying to locate her."

"What about your search for Mr. Nelson?"

"It's dead end after dead end. The man vanished off the face of the earth. But then, it's not really so hard to accomplish in California. I think you should contact your mother."

"What good would it do?"

"I don't know. She has connections, maybe she could help somehow. You should at least send word to April. You owe her that much."

"I owe her another trial where I'm made to look like a criminal? The last one was hard enough. I decided to go to her once this is over, but I intend to spare her this."

"You're making a mistake, Noah."

"Why, because you don't want to be the bearer of bad news if they hang me?"

"This is no joke. This is serious. Deidre's cousin Theodora gave damning testimony today. The contents of her letters from Deidre are bad enough in themselves. Making the woman read them in court was a stroke of genius. It seems cruel on the face of it. After all, Theodora collapsed when she got off the stand. It proved to be an incredibly effective tactic on the prosecutor's part. I don't want you to testify. You'll only be a target. No matter how sincere and convincing you might be, the cross-examination will be brutal."

"I'm going to testify on my own behalf. I want to

have my day in court," insisted Noah.

* * *

April sat on her porch on the drizzly morning, sipping a cup of tea. The gloomy day matched her mood, but she beamed at her baby's strong kick. "Would you like to rock?" she asked her unborn child as she placed her teacup on the table. Afraid her baby would be a night owl, April endured incessant movement that kept her up most nights. The baby quieted as April patted her stomach and rocked. She closed her eyes and leaned her head against the back of the chair.

Having an uncomfortable feeling she was being watched, April opened her eyes to find Mr. Washington staring at her from the porch steps.

"What brings you here so early this morning? You're too late for breakfast."

"I never seen you get the newspaper. Don't white women read their newspaper? Ain't that something you should do?"

"I haven't read the newspaper for quite some time, Mr. Washington. I tired of bad news and decided I'd be better off without it. Is there something important you want me to see?" Mr. Washington was not his usual irritating self this morning. He seemed much too serious.

"I'll leave this then," he replied, placing his newspaper on the table beside Mrs. Chandler's teacup. "I think you better take a look." He turned to leave but then mentioned over his shoulder. "God hears your prayers."

April shook her head in disgust. Would the irksome tiny man never let go of his claim to be her guardian angel? She hadn't seen a newspaper in months. Perhaps she'd take a look to see the latest local news. Hopefully, the Gulley Store would have a fabric sale.

* * *

Noah felt he was living a nightmare after the judge read the verdict. "Noah Chandler, the jury finds you guilty of murder in the first degree. You will be hanged by the neck until dead on Friday, December 9 at 8 a.m. The jury is dismissed." The gavel decreed the trial over as surely as Noah's time on earth.

He understood the proceedings were disastrous. The prosecutor, eager to make a name for himself, painted Noah as an evil villain who easily disposed of Deidre's body in any number of ways. Aside from character witnesses, all Noah had going for him was his word. Hoping the jury would stew over the fact no body had been found, Jack didn't want to put him on the stand. Noah wanted his say, certain he could convince one of the 12 men he was innocent. He rolled the dice and lost.

Noah faced the jury like a man when the judge read the verdict and appeared unaffected by the result. Jack took the whole thing much worse than his friend.

Resigned to his fate, Noah acknowledged this seemed to be his destiny all along. He spent the night of the verdict composing letters to his mother and wife. The pastor of his church visited early Thursday morning. Although formal confession was not an aspect of protestant doctrine, the pastor invited Noah to repent of his sins. Noah willingly confessed a multitude of transgressions: arrogance, pride, vanity, among others. He admitted his failures as a husband and son but did not confess to murder. The pastor offered comforting Bible verses and assured Noah his sins were forgiven. There would be a place for him in heaven.

Feeling he already made peace with God, the pastor's words cemented this belief. Noah may not be guilty of this crime, but he was not without fault. He would go to the gallows a gentleman and a lamb of God.

He requested steak and potatoes for his last meal but would have given anything to eat April's cooking one more time—even the mess she called hash. He managed to spare her the travesty of the trial. Noah sat against the jail wall on his cot, one leg drawn up, his arms wrapped around his knee as he waited for the night to pass. The fact he would be dead at this time tomorrow was incomprehensible. But Noah had one last gift on this earth. Turning his head as the door to the sheriff's office opened, Noah gasped as April walked into the cell room.

"I can give you five minutes, that's all," muttered the guard named Harold.

Noah flew to the bars near the cell door and pushed his arms through to embrace his pale wife. Before she managed to put her own arms through the bars, Harold opened the cell door and returned to his office.

Sooner than April could get a word out, Noah kissed her lips, then her face. To her surprise he placed his hand under her cape.

"You know about the baby?"

"Yes, April, I love you. I've been a fool."

"I love you too, but how—"

"I didn't do it. Do you believe me?" April nodded. Noah had other issues to resolve. "Listen to me. I'm sorry. Please forgive me. I should never have said those things to you. I should have come back for you. I've been a poor husband, April. Nothing has gone right for us. But I love you, I love you." He kissed her desperately.

"I'm sorry too. I should never have written those stories. I didn't mean to hurt you."

"When is the baby due?"

"In about a month. You'll never see our baby, Noah. Put your hand here." She moved his hand to her other side hoping the baby would kick. "Did you feel that?"

"Oh, yes I did. April, you'll be a wonderful mother. You must allow my mother to help. She'll want to. Do you have money?" She nodded as Noah kissed her again.

"How did this happen?" April asked.

"It doesn't matter, we only have five minutes, my darling. I need to tell you how much I always loved you. I want the best for you April, for you and our child."

"But the door is open, Noah, we can leave. We can hide. Come with me!"

"And live a life on the run? You'd be guilty of harboring a murderer, aiding and abetting. Our child would grow up without a mother or a father." He kissed her again, holding onto her for dear life as Harold returned.

"Time's up. I'm sorry, it's well past visiting hours; it's all I can give you."

"Goodbye April. I love you more than life itself."

"No, not goodbye. I'm coming tomorrow. I'll be there to see you again. So long for now," she added, kissing him one last time and holding his hand for as long as she could as the jailor pulled her away. "I love you." Somehow it didn't seem enough. She should have been able to say something more. April pulled her arm from the guard's grip as she peered at her husband through the door as it closed.

"Can I have someone come for you?" Harold asked. He seemed a kind man.

April quietly turned and walked outside. Due to the lateness of the hour, the street was empty. She walked to the end of the sidewalk and falling on her hands and knees, vomited in the street. Sobs shook her shoulders. She cried uncontrollably. Remembering Mr. Washington's promise, she folded her hands on the sidewalk and prayed the most fervent prayer of her life. Somehow God had to save Noah. She couldn't face a future alone.

* * *

Sheriff Reyes stood under a balcony to the side of the yard. He felt the luckiest man on earth most days, fortunate to have a job he enjoyed so thoroughly. But not today. He abhorred being any part of the frequent hangings in Los Angeles. The guillotine was considered a cruel way to die, but it sure beat dangling on the end of a rope like some sack of potatoes until the weight of your own body strangled you to death. Memories of relatives pulling on the legs of the guilty to halt their dance of death made him cringe. At least having your head lopped off was a quick way to go. Glancing impatiently at his watch, he didn't notice the woman until she tapped his arm and spoke.

"Pardon me, sir. I wonder if you might help. You see, I'm not exactly tall. I wanted to be able to see the festivities this morning. Do you know of a place I might have a good look at the hanging?"

Reyes looked down on the exquisitely dressed, beautiful, young woman. Her attitude and apparel suggested a lady on her way to party. He couldn't help but wonder why anyone in their right mind would want to view a hanging. She actually referred to it as a festivity. Perhaps she was some relative of the murder victim come to gloat—that family was supposedly well off.

"You might try the balcony," Reyes pointed above his head. "It's likely the best seat in the house. You can go up here." Reyes took the rope from the nail at the bottom of the stairway and let it drop to the ground. "Help yourself."

He stood back and watched the woman smile contentedly, pull the veil from her hat over her eyes and daintily climb the stairs. She would certainly get an eyeful. Likely she could see through the trapdoor and observe the body swinging at the end of the rope. Shuddering, Reyes reclaimed his position as more people climbed the stairs behind him.

* * *

Jack observed the gawkers who came to witness the hanging. He felt a helpless failure, having not been able to save his best friend from the gallows. Although Noah assured him his attendance was unnecessary this morning, he couldn't stay home any more than he could sleep since the verdict came down. He might at least give Noah an encouraging look before they covered his head with the black hood. Jack greased the palm of the hangman to assure Noah would not struggle at the end of the rope as so often happened. The man guaranteed Noah's neck would snap immediately. There would be no drawn-out struggle for breath.

Glancing at the note a deputy handed him, Jack searched the crowd. Noah's message advised April was in attendance and asked for Jack's assistance. As the note stated, he found April standing in front of the platform. Jack made his way to her side as Noah approached the gallows.

Officials were speaking, but April could not comprehend what was happening. She barely noticed when Jack put his arm around her shoulder. When a man asked Noah if he wished to speak, Noah only shook his head, his gaze fastened on his wife. All too soon, the hangman walked toward Noah with the hood. April smiled and whispered, "I love you," as Noah's face disappeared.

"We need to go now," Jack urged.

"No. I have to stay."

"You can't stay. Noah doesn't want you here. He sent me a note. He wanted the last thing he saw to be your face. But he wants me to take you out. He doesn't want you to see."

April stared as the hangman applied the noose over the black hood and tightened it, then she allowed Jack to guide her toward the courtyard gate. She continued to listen intently.

Feeling protective of April, Jack pushed his way through the crowd. April glanced toward a balcony off to the side. A piece of jewelry flashed in the morning sunlight and caught her attention. Spotting a short woman with a hat and veil, April stopped in her tracks. The veil hid most of the woman's face. Only part of her mouth and chin were exposed. The mouth sported a sly smirk.

"Jack, look up there. It's Deidre! You have to catch her."

"Are you certain?"

"Yes, go now. There's no time to waste!"

As Jack bounded away, April turned toward the platform where her husband was about to die. Shoving her way through the crowd, she yelled *"Stop! Stop now!"* April climbed the stairs as the crowd's attention turned toward the balcony where a man had grabbed a screaming woman and attempted to seize her hat. Even the hangman was distracted by the commotion.

April hurried to where Noah stood. She frantically tried to loosen the knot, but the rope was tight around his neck. As the hangman remembered his work, he looked across the platform to find a woman standing on the trap door. He certainly couldn't release the door with her there.

Burning her hands on the rope, April finally managed to loosen the noose enough to pull it off Noah's head as a sheriff approached.

Jack yelled out, "Stop! Don't hang him. This is Deidre Mercer. She's not dead!"

He gripped Deidre by the hair and held her at arm's length as she struggled and screamed in a maniacal voice, *"Hang him! Hang him!"*

April pulled the hood off Noah's face.

"What happened?"

"Deidre was in the crowd, intent to view the hanging. You're free, Noah!" April embraced her husband so avidly, he almost lost his balance. As eager as Noah was to leave the gallows, he was more anxious to hold his wife. Once the sheriff untied his hands, the couple stood hugging and sobbing in full view of the crowd that came to watch Noah Chandler hang.

* * *

Euphoric over the morning's events, Noah did not complain when the sheriff kept him in custody. An arraignment needed to be held. After Deidre ceased her fiendish ramblings, she refused to speak at all. Proper identification needed to be made. April refused to leave the jailhouse all morning and sat silently behind her husband during the hearing, intent no harm would befall him. It was well into the afternoon before everyone assembled in the courthouse. A shocked Theodora appeared to identify her cousin. All charges were dropped. Noah was free.

Happy to be breathing, Noah accepted Jack's invitation to the finest dinner Los Angeles could offer. April joined the men. She picked at her food while her two tablemates drank their dinner while loudly complimenting each other on the results of the day. Naturally, they toasted the sedate Mrs. Chandler for her astute eye and heralded her as the one who truly, "saved Noah's ass," as Jack put it.

Jack offered to drop the Chandlers at their destination of choice once dessert and cigars were enjoyed. A blank look appeared on Noah's face. He never planned to be alive this evening. He certainly had no idea where they could sleep.

Sheepishly, Noah offered, "April, would you be willing to stay at the livery for tonight? I have a room there or at least I think I still have a room. We can find a better place in the morning." Jack listened as he climbed into his carriage, knowing Noah would likely not accept any favors from him.

"I have a better place. I spent the night here last night," although, dreading the morning, she never slept. April quietly mentioned an address in Jack's ear.

Although he seemed amazed, Noah didn't notice. His fatigue and overwrought emotions were beginning to wear on him.

Embracing his wife as they rode in the back of Jack's carriage, Noah knew they had a lot to discuss. He considered questions he wanted to ask. Who was the man he saw through the binoculars? Why did April go to Newhall? Did she write his mother? Instead, he explained his work at Bill's stable and recent forms of employment, even his newfound religious inclinations. Focused on April, he paid no attention to his surroundings until the carriage came to a stop. Noah frowned when he saw the house on Carroll Avenue.

"What is this?" was his first unenthusiastic comment of the evening.

April grinned. "We can stay here."

Possible scenarios danced through Noah's thoughts as he exited the carriage and lifted his wife down. "You own this house then? You're the one who bought it?" Her earnings must be staggering if she pulled that purchase out of her hat.

"Well, let's say I have an in with the owners." April could see Noah's astonishment. "I own 25 percent. The other 75 percent will be up to you." She gazed at Noah who struggled to understand. "I belong to Mr. Devlin's investment company. Through an associate, he learned of Deidre's plan to bid on your house. After all, she'd virtually be putting money in her own pocket. Since Mr. Devlin had connections at the auction house, unbeknownst to me, Austin Holdings purchased the property and contents. Naturally, a premium had to be paid to satisfy the auctioneer's estimated profits and commission." As he guided his wife up the porch stairs, Noah waved goodbye to Jack. Stopping in front of the door, April reached in her reticule and handed him the key. "So, if you're planning on paying for this by digging ditches, maybe you best forgo sleep and get at it," she teased.

The enormity of this gift seemed more than Noah could comprehend. Expecting to be dead, he was instead alive and would soon be asleep in his own bed with his wife beside him. April waited for his reaction and beamed as Noah eagerly threw wide the front door, kissed her passionately and carried her across the threshold.

* * *

Noah helped April heat water for their baths. Claiming he smelled of jail, she insisted he go first. He languished in the claw-foot tub longer than intended, attempting to recall all he knew about expectant mothers. His wife appeared exhausted at dinner. She was in a delicate condition and had been through a harrowing experience.

His sisters displayed unusual behavior when they were expecting, including Anna. Noah always considered his closest sister a reasonable woman. Even she had been emotional and irrational when her baby was due. Abruptly plunged into the role of expectant father, Noah understood the need to be concerned and caring.

He feared the delivery of their baby no less, but April bravely stayed by his side in his hour of need. Determined to stay the course with this baby of hers, Noah did not believe God would be so harsh as to take her away when they were so recently reunited. He fervently prayed for that result.

Once April finished her ablutions, she turned out

the downstairs lights and headed for the bedroom. She felt anxious about her appearance. When April bid goodbye to Noah forever, her misshapen body and short hair weren't of concern. Hoping her husband was already asleep, she crawled into bed feeling awkward and ugly.

It appeared she might be in luck. Noah fell asleep having left his bedside lamp lit. April thought it best to leave the light on so as not to disturb him. She breathed a sigh of relief as she reclined near the edge of the bed and pulled up the covers, her back to her husband. Her discomfort might seem less serious after a good night's sleep. But that was not to be.

Holding her breath as Noah moved across the bed, she flinched when he buried his hand beneath her shoulder and in one fluid movement, turned her into his arms.

"Are you trying to avoid me, Mrs. Chandler?"

"I thought you were asleep. It's been an exhausting day and you had too much to drink."

Noah looked into April's eyes. She nervously turned her face away. In an effort to soothe her anxiety, Noah rubbed her back, knowing his hands were calloused from work. Uncertain how he felt about his wife's voluptuous figure, the sensuousness of her body surprised him.

"I did this," he admitted, astounded at this discovery as he moved his hands beneath April's nightgown.

He gave a languid kiss, which she returned. "You are like a luscious ripe fruit, my darling."

"Wonderful, Noah. What every woman longs to hear. You consider me some pear or possibly an apple."

"This is more like a watermelon. Why is your stomach so hard?"

"Oh!"

Noah obviously hurt her feelings. "Wait. You're taking this the wrong way."

"It gets tight. It'll go away in a minute."

"Does it hurt?"

"No."

Noah never intended to tease or offend. Perhaps he was a bit inebriated. Moving his hand to April's face, he kissed her again.

"I don't want this to be awkward between us. I know a lot has happened. It was easy enough for me to wish the best for you and the baby last night when I thought I'd be dead now. It's something else when I'm here and we have our whole life in front of us—and you know I never wanted a baby."

"I know I don't look the way I used to. You don't like my hair, do you? Why would you want me? How will you ever want our baby?"

Noah ran his fingers through her hair. "Do you always sleep like this now—with your hair free?"

"Yes."

"I like it. And I think you're beautiful. I've certainly made my mark. He felt her belly again, finding it returned to normal or as normal as it could be for now. "I'm rather proud, I must admit. We'll sort through all this. Nothing really matters except for us being together. Dear lord, I can't really believe we're here." He clung to April and buried his face in her neck. "Everything will be fine. I know it will."

April understood Noah had been overly optimistic in the past. Their problems seemed insurmountable. But at least, they had each other. With her husband's arms around her, April whispered to her baby, "We're home now."

Chapter Eighteen

Noah hummed a tune as he cooked—or he thought of it as cooking even if no one else would. Commencing the one kitchen chore he understood, Noah poured water into the tea kettle and set it to boil.

Life changed dramatically since he left his home last summer. Joy overwhelmed him as he contemplated being alive with options, able to dream and make plans for the future. His wife. He waited for the customary sensation of betrayal to wash over him or irritation at the fact she was the one to rescue their home. Smiling, Noah felt he'd overcome those feelings, not because he owed April his life, but because he loved and appreciated her. He had truly put the past behind him. Now he needed to find a way to pay for their house. He certainly could not continue digging ditches or working at the stable. Although he would never ask, Noah wondered how much money April squirrelled away.

As he turned off the burner and reached for the teakettle, his reverie was shattered by an ear-piercing shriek. *"Noah! Noah!"*

Taking two steps at a time. Noah bounded up the narrow kitchen staircase. When he reached the bedroom door, he found April struggling to get off the bed. "What is it? What's wrong? Is it the baby?" Noah panicked as he reached his wife and grabbed her arms.

"You were falling through the trap door. I couldn't reach you!" Clearly frantic, tears streamed down April's cheeks.

Noah held her close. "But I didn't fall through the door. You saved me. Here I am. Everything's all right. Look at your hands. You undid the noose. The rope burns are right here." Noah kissed the palms of her hands.

April clung to her husband as if she were saving him from hanging yet again. "The dream was so real! I thought it must be real when I woke up. I thought you were gone."

Noah considered the past two days were probably harder on April than he thought. She trembled. Dark circles rimmed her eyes. "Come down to the kitchen. I was making tea. You can watch me clean up."

"Clean up what?"

"I believe, in my panic, I dropped the tea kettle smack on the floor. I'll have to start over, assuming the kettle is still in one piece." Noah helped his wife off the bed and put his arm around her as they exited the bedroom. "We have so much to discuss. Our future, my work, how we'll pay for lunch! By the way, where are the Fitzpatricks?"

Noah noted his wife's concerned expression, as if she feared this could be a dream and would awake to find him dead. She clung to his arm, unwilling to let go once they reached the kitchen.

"April, I'm real. This is real. We're about to start our lives anew. I'd find it helpful if you would speak to me. I may be suffering from an extreme case of euphoria, which undoubtedly will not last, but I'd like you to join me."

Although tears welled in her eyes, April managed a smile. "The Fitzpatricks went traveling about a week ago, or so I've been told. There must not have been much to do since no one lived in the house. Some relative of Mr. Fitzpatrick's settled near Sacramento and they went for a holiday visit. How will we be able to pay them, Noah? The holding company has been footing the bill, but they'll work for us now." Words gushed forth as Noah directed his attention to the spilled water. "Elias will come for me. I need to send him a telegram. I left Newhall in such a hurry, I didn't even bring clothes. What are you going to do for work? I need to let Mr. Washington know we're fine. He was right when he told me God would hear my prayers. Maybe he really is some kind of guardian angel. I left all the baby things in my haste to travel to Los Angeles. How will we ever get the bassinette here? Is it true you don't have money for lunch?"

"April, I don't even know who these people are you're talking about. You need to explain." The name Elias seemed the most worrisome place to begin. Noah longed to know about the man April kissed when he watched her through the binoculars. It was a rather chaste kiss, but still. "Who is Elias?"

A guilty look met his question. Noah wondered if he had competition for April's affection. "I have something to admit."

Noah set the dented teapot on the stove, his euphoria abruptly shattered. Deadly serious, he turned to his wife. "Tell me."

April didn't know how her husband would feel about her start in life. Although cavalier about many societal issues, perhaps he would look down on her. She always understood they didn't share the same social status. "I'm a bastard," she confessed.

This was not the admission Noah expected or feared. Relieved, he replied, "What are you talking about?"

"Remember, I told you about Mr. Farmer, the banker who helped us stay in our house?" Noah nodded. "Well, he came here after—right after—when you left. He came to help me. He told me he's my real father. I believe him, Noah. It's a long story, but his aid proved invaluable. He helped me settle in Newhall. He saw to my welfare. He lives in Santa Barbara now. I intended to spend Christmas there and wait to have the baby. Why are you smiling?"

"You scared me there for a minute. I thought your confession might be something more alarming."

"But it is alarming. My parents weren't married. My mother was married when I was born, but not to my father. Doesn't that make me a bastard?"

"I think the sticking point is when the mother isn't married, but it's inconsequential and I don't want you to be concerned. Would Elias want to spend Christmas here?"

"How could we afford company if you can't even buy lunch?"

"I have some money. I didn't spend much of what I made, only for food. I mostly had watered down beer with free lunch and dinner. But I do need to figure out an occupation."

April explained her living situation in Newhall. She frowned when Noah urged her to admit her choice of location was based on a desire to pan for gold.

Noah was surprised his wife befriended an Indian.

Her plan to spare him their child's birth by living alone touched him deeply. Determined to make up for past shortcomings, an idea grew as they discussed their new-found future. Perhaps he knew a way to make a living.

* * *

The Chandler home became a hub of activity. April stood back to admire the Christmas tree Noah put up in the sitting room. He resolved to have a traditional and happy celebration. Unbeknownst to April, a few boxes of decorations were stored in the basement. Exquisite glass ornaments adorned their tree. She decorated the mantle using pine boughs, candles, and ribbon. Although she originally desired to put a tree in the parlor bay window, the parlor had been confiscated.

Jack came to help move furniture. The small guest room stood empty in anticipation of a new member of the family. The arduous furniture relocation proved to be something Noah could not accomplish single-handedly. Noah's heavy rolltop desk now occupied the parlor. The settee was relocated to their bedroom. The pocket doors between the parlor and sitting room were closed to afford privacy to the Law Office of Noah Chandler.

Although Angelino Heights was some distance from the bustle of the city, it was only a short trolley ride away. Mr. Chandler's shingle hung over the porch rail below a sign reading "Free Legal Services." Noah planned to provide his expertise gratis in hopes of building a new law practice. Hoping to attract clients, he placed a modest ad in the *Herald*. Until business picked up, Noah visited local construction sites to make a few coins digging ditches. He enjoyed the effects of hard labor on his body and mind and they certainly needed all the money he could make.

Despite her husband's newfound zeal for life, April never felt more a mess. It wasn't that their house remained chaotic while rooms were being rearranged or even that keeping the house became her responsibility until the Fitzpatricks returned. She fled Newhall with only the clothes on her back, her wedding ring and her mother's cameo. She did not want to spend any of their funds on clothing. April saved her one appropriate outfit for church and took to wearing Noah's shirts over old skirts, left behind when she moved to Newhall. She tied string through the button hole and around the button to allow room for her ample waistline.

April felt awkward and struggled to rise from any chair. Although a good-natured Noah never hesitated to help, she often lost patience when he seemed amused at her predicament. As much as she longed for this baby, she was tired and overemotional.

It also became apparent Noah was not handy around the house. He freely admitted to never having hammered a nail in his life. If not for Jack, the signage on the front porch would have been lashed to a post with old rags.

Noah didn't care what she wore but understood April's intense desire to obtain the baby's things from Newhall. Her typewriter and sewing machine were still there—items Elias arranged to have delivered. Noah planned to make the trip to Newhall to retrieve all her important belongings once his father-in-law arrived. April meticulously drew maps for each item so the men could not fail to locate her treasures. She anticipated Elias's visit, not only so he could help retrieve her things, but because she wanted Noah to meet him.

Noah's first client made an appearance. Mr. Chandler, Esq., poured on the charm. The pro bono case involved drawing up a contract. One would think he scored a lucrative client, so thrilled was he to be engaged in legal work again.

"Once we get your typewriter back, I may need to go in the attic and make use of it as long as it doesn't bother you."

"You can keep the typewriter in your office. I won't be using it."

Noah could not deny the thrill of pleasure he felt at her remark. "They don't want your stories anymore?"

April looked directly into her husband's eyes. "No, I need to devote myself to our family. I planned to seek you out in New York once the baby came so I ended my story. I submitted my work right before coming here. I don't imagine my publisher is terribly happy."

"I don't imagine he is," agreed Noah who quietly added, "but I am."

Noah grinned at the sound of a knock on the front door. "Clients!" But he could not have been more surprised once he opened the door. The engaging smile plastered on his face quickly dissolved. "Mother!"

"Don't stand there with your mouth open, bring my valise inside."

Noah noticed a hired carriage pull away from the sidewalk as he grabbed his mother's possessions.

"I do swear, a person can't even pay for decent information in this day in age. I don't care what they say about those Pinkerton men, the whole organization is completely worthless." Lula seemed anxious to get her complaints off her chest. "They told me you were in some sort of trouble. There was a trial. I told them the trial was months ago. Their information was old. Then they told me no one was living in your house and yet, here you are!" At this, Lula spotted her new daughter-in-law peering around the corner of the sitting room doorway. "My dearest April! Come and give an old woman a hug," Lula held her arms wide as Noah lugged her valise toward the staircase. It was Lula's turn to stand wide-mouthed as she caught sight of her former companion.

April hesitantly walked through the doorway. She wore an apron tied around her waist that served to accentuate her condition. She had rolled the sleeves of Noah's shirt above her elbows. Her skirt hem was uneven, showing bare feet. Loose hair hung down her back. April bit her lip, anxiety apparent.

"Oh, my goodness! I'm to be a new grandmother! Whatever has happened to you, my dear? *Noah*! What way is this to treat your wife?" Unaware he dressed to welcome clients, she eyed her son's immaculate attire. "Your wife is no longer hired help. What exactly is going on here?"

To Noah, April's reaction couldn't have been more perfect. She put her hands to her face and wept; deep racking sobs.

"There, there, my darling. I warned you my mother could be harsh. You never wanted to listen." This drew a glare from the elder Mrs. Chandler. Dropping the valise to embrace April, Noah carefully guided her back to the sitting room. He could not help but bestow a wicked smirk on his mother. Realizing this would only add fuel to the fire, he couldn't resist.

Noah needed to get his licks in before endless declarations of "I told you so" commenced.

An amused Noah took a seat beside his wife on the settee. An emotional and overwrought April poured out apologies and excuses while clinging to him with all her might. Lula stood over them, steeped in sympathy, intent to capture every word, despite April's meandering explanations punctuated by a sudden case of hiccups. Random fragments of their marital challenges emerged, almost unbidden, from April's quivering lips. Noah understood his mother would have absolutely no idea what actually happened and might be afraid to ask any further if April ever calmed down. He also, somewhat guiltily, understood how difficult marriage had been on his wife. She never complained during their tribulations. She had been his staunch supporter until their disastrous argument. But he also knew he couldn't go back and change what happened. All he could do was be the best husband possible and make a good life for his family.

"Calm down, April. Everything's all right. My mother will make you a cup of tea. That will help, won't it? Then I'll take you upstairs so you can lie down and rest."

Noah watched his mother reluctantly retreat to the kitchen. Today could prove quite entertaining. At least *he* knew how to make tea.

Lula filled the badly dented kettle and set it to boil. Wondering where a person might find tea, she rummaged through cupboards, to no avail. She found a teapot and set it on the sink. If she ever managed to locate tea, she had no idea how to prepare it. Tea always came on a tray upon her command. Perhaps it should already be in the kettle. Biting her lip in consternation, Lula determined to go through the cupboards once again. She must have somehow overlooked the tea. Startled, she flinched when her son bounded into the kitchen.

"It is good to see you," Noah admitted, bending down to plant a kiss on her forehead. "Having trouble?"

"I can't seem to locate the tea. Where do you keep it?"

"Actually, it's right here in the canister, as it is in most homes." Noah slyly removed the top on the tin ware canister clearly marked Tea. He completely enjoyed his mother's discomfort at being asked to perform a kitchen chore. As the kettle whistled, he competently made tea, to Lula's amazement. "April wasn't really upset at you. You understand, don't you? I couldn't resist the opportunity to tease you."

"Why is she upset?"

"I believe she is in the throes of her maternal condition. She's tired. We've been through a lot. It's not long until our baby comes."

Lula became fascinated by her son's pleasant chatter. He seemed jubilant at his marriage to April the last time she saw him in San Francisco. This man who stood before her was some incarnation of her son she never previously encountered. He appeared kind, content, and genuinely cheerful. She noticed some discomfort when he mentioned April's condition, though he covered it well.

"You must do me a favor, Mother. I'll be happy to answer your questions, but it might be best if you refrain from grilling April in light of her reaction when you arrived. I urged her to go upstairs and lie down. I need to take her cup of tea, then we'll talk. I know her outburst must have raised more questions than it answered."

Now Lula wondered where her real son had gone. Rarely in his life did Noah volunteer to answer questions.

"You've changed."

Noah smiled. "I married April because I love her. At least I was bright enough to grasp that. Unfortunately, I needed to lose everything in order to discover what she truly meant to me. I always lived life on my terms, following my dreams, making my plans. When things started going wrong, I took it personally. April's background made her more agreeable than she probably should have been. I lost my business, my work, my home, all my belongings, my wife and nearly my life before I got down on my knees and begged God for help. I have April back and hopefully, we'll be able to keep the house. I want that for her. It doesn't matter so much to me anymore. I better take this up before it gets cold."

"One thing before you go. Where are the servants?"

"Away on holiday. But I'm going to have difficulty paying them once they return. You don't cook, do you?" Noah already knew the answer.

Lula shook her head. "It looks like you can cook now."

"You are the proud recipient of my entire cooking repertoire. Grab a cookbook off the shelf. You and I will have to muddle through, somehow. I suspect my wife is too spent to attempt dinner this evening."

* * *

Lula was astounded at her son's detailed explanations

of the unfortunate occurrences since his marriage. Her dislike of Deidre boiled over.

"I'd be the first to admit I didn't like that girl, but never in my wildest dreams would I believe Deidre could cause so much harm. Slander, theft and in my opinion, attempted murder! I know her family has influence, but the law is the law—or it should be. How could she possibly avoid punishment?"

"She's in a mental institution, too ill to stand trial. April doesn't know. This didn't seem appropriate to put in a letter. I didn't want you to be concerned. I did finally write." Noah walked into the dining room and plucked the letter he gave Jack from a dish on the buffet. He intended to author a different message after Jack returned it. Touched by his concern for her, his mother discreetly wiped tears from her eyes as she read. He pretended not to notice.

Noah filled in details of April's recent life, explaining her writing for *Pacific Weekly*, her father's unforeseen appearance, her independent move to Newhall and the rescue of their home from auction.

"No wonder she's distraught! I've always been impressed by April."

"Isn't that something of an understatement?"

Lula ignored the comment. "I must find a way to express my joy at being her mother-in-law. I believe the best place to start would be a shopping trip. Your wife clearly needs a bit of cheer. I'm certain proper clothing would elevate her spirits. You shouldn't expect her to go about wearing your shirts, for heaven's sake."

Noah had his doubts about this plan but said not a word.

* * *

A reluctant April donned her only suitable attire and submitted to the embarrassment of asking her husband to help her dress. Noah pressed his lips tightly together in an effort to appear serious and helpful.

"You understand, this is completely against my ethics. My job is to take things off, not put them on."

April ignored him as she sat on the bed and raised a foot. "I need you to roll up my stockings and attach the garters. I hope my feet still fit in my boots. They've been swollen lately. Do you remember how to use the button hook?"

"Probably not, but I'm certain I could tie your shoes on with some rags."

"Why does your answer to every mechanical problem turn out to be rags? Did you never have button shoes as a boy?"

"I assure you, I avoided those at an early age. When I was small, the nanny took care of them. Is this why you've been going barefoot? You can't get your shoes on?"

"It's not only that I can't get them on." Melodramatically, April continued, "I can't see my feet much less reach them!"

"You should have told me. I would have helped."

"I don't *want* help."

Realizing he was likely in dangerous territory, Noah redoubled his efforts with the button hook.

"There, all done." Grasping April's hands to help her off the bed, he stopped as she dissolved into tears.

"What's wrong? Did I hurt you?" Noah asked incredulously.

"My brown shoes. I could have worn my brown shoes."

"Do you want me to get them?"

"I could have gotten those off by myself."

"Well, we'll change them then."

"No, no. I have these on now."

"April, you don't have to go shopping if you don't want to. Maybe it's best if you stay home," although Noah believed it might prove beneficial for his wife to get out of the house for a while.

April visibly pulled herself together. "Help me up then. I don't want to disappoint your mother."

A reluctant April accompanied her mother-in-law downtown to shop. She felt she was losing all control. Lula arrived with more enthusiasm than April could tolerate. Further, ladies in her advanced condition normally stayed home.

It felt odd to call Lula "Mother." It seemed equally odd to Lula so the pair returned to first names. Although Lula claimed ill health kept her from visiting California any sooner, April could not discern any malady. It seemed as if Lula was determined to rise to the challenge of putting the Chandler home in order—her kind of order.

Professing she could not live without a proper cook, Lula hired an unemployed Margarita, understanding the woman might take flight at the least provocation. Lula placed an ad in the paper to obtain a temporary housekeeper. She wished to make life comfortable for April and would spare no expense doing so. Naturally, her own comfort would be guaranteed in the process. If her generosity pricked Noah's pride, he didn't show it. He seemed content to let his mother run the household and pay for any conveniences along the way. His new business and concern for his wife occupied Noah's thoughts.

Knowing her daughter-in-law might tire easily, Lula selected merchandise at lightning speed. She bought clothing for April, including an elegant black velvet blouse for Christmas day. She could not resist her grandmotherly desire to make a few purchases for the new baby, including furniture for the as-yet undecorated nursery, even though it was customary to leave such acquisitions until after the baby's birth. She made sure to obtain April's approval for all purchases.

A bedraggled April would now be properly attired to answer the door when Noah's clients came to call. There would be no more wearing of Noah's comfortable shirts or going barefoot.

"Oh, my! Look, Lula." April seemed more animated than she had been on their entire excursion. "It's an electric sewing machine. What will they think of next?"

"We should buy it."

"No, it's too much. You've done enough already. Besides, the electricity is unreliable."

But April's enthusiasm for the machine was apparent. "Nonsense! I haven't even given you two a proper wedding gift."

"You paid for Noah's wedding to Deidre. I'm certain it must have cost a fortune."

"I did, true enough. But I'm an old woman. What good is my money if I can't enjoy it? And I want to help. I'm proud of the way you two have overcome all your difficulties."

April gave her mother-in-law a dubious look. "I don't know what Noah told you, but we really haven't done very well—"

"Oh, I won't hear of it. You're together and you've weathered severe storms of life in your brief marriage. I'm certain things will be better now. I can't tell you how changed Noah is. I always knew you'd be a good influence on him. I'm so pleased!"

April understood when Lula was pleased, she became extremely generous.

* * *

Mr. Devlin warily approached the Chandler front door. He hadn't seen Mrs. Chandler since last summer. If he took the newspapers at face value, she'd been through an incredible ordeal. He didn't recognize the tall man who bounded up the porch steps behind him and was dumbfounded when a filthy Noah Chandler first wiped his hand on his pant leg, then offered it in greeting.

"Sorry for the way I look. I've been supplementing my income and getting some exercise."

The man appeared quite fit. Mr. Chandler did not resemble the immaculately manicured and attired attorney Mr. Devlin had come to know. His plaid shirt was tucked into a pair of blue jeans. Muscles bulged under rolled-up shirt sleeves. Mr. Devlin noted more than his changed appearance. Noah Chandler always exuded confidence, that seemed unchanged. But the man fairly glowed from good humor. Understanding Chandler's recent difficulties, this was hardly the impression Mr. Devlin expected.

"I usually go in through the kitchen door," Noah explained as he carefully wiped his shoes on the doormat. "We can go in the front. Are you here to see April?"

"I haven't seen Mrs. Chandler in some while. I'm here to see you today."

Noah's cheerful demeanor vanished. "I don't have the money for the house, not quite yet." Or ever at the rate he was going. "If you'll give me more time—"

"I'm not here about the house. It sat empty all these months. Austin Holdings didn't make the purchase as an investment. I want to talk to you. I have a business proposition."

Noah's curiosity was piqued. Relieved they would not have to abandon the house with a baby due, his smile returned. "I'm not presentable. Could you give me a few minutes to clean up? Have a seat here in my office and I'll have Margarita bring you a cup of coffee."

"The real Margarita?"

Noah laughed. "Yes, the real Margarita. If I can locate April, I'm certain she'd enjoy keeping you company. I'll be right back."

Mr. Devlin took a seat in the comfortable chair in the bay window he remembered from previous visits. The parlor had been transformed into an efficient and elegant office space. He helped himself to coffee delivered by a dour Margarita. The short and stout older woman could not have been more different in appearance from April Chandler. It must have been quite a shock when April, playing the role of cook, emerged from the kitchen on his initial visit.

Almost as if he conjured her in his thoughts, April, clearly in a family way, appeared in the doorway. As Mr. Devlin rose from his chair, his shock at her condition must have been evident since a charming blush appeared on the expectant mother's face.

"My, there's no end to the revelations in your household. I'm afraid I'm taken quite by surprise. I'm sorry if I offended you and congratulations!"

"Please, sit down. Noah said you wanted to talk to

him. I simply wished to say hello. How are the investments going?"

Mr. Devlin eagerly shared his news. "I'm sure you've heard. Edward Doheny and his partner hit oil not far from here last month. Mrs. Chandler, you and I are in the oil business. I've decided to funnel the profits from the properties we recently sold into oil wells on the land we own southeast of here. At the rate derricks are going up, I imagine the market will soon be flooded, but I believe this is an opportunity we mustn't miss. I have a few other investments I'm considering. I hoped you could come by my office soon, but under the circumstances, it might be best if I brought my documentation here for you to look over."

"It might be best. I'm not up-to-date on the city's trends right now. Perhaps Noah could help."

"Whatever you like." Mr. Devlin understood Mr. Chandler had the legal right to control his wife's assets. He hoped his successful relationship with April Chandler would not end. At this, Noah rushed into the office. His hair was wet; his clothes were fresh. His smile appeared as engaging as ever but somehow more genuine.

"I'll leave you to your business, then," April offered as she turned to leave.

"It might be best if you stayed," Devlin suggested. "You're a partner in Austin Holdings, but this concerns all my interests in California.

"Chandler, would you contemplate a permanent position as solicitor for my businesses? It may not be as lucrative as private practice, but it will be steady work—a regular paycheck—and I feel it will be financially advantageous to have a fulltime attorney on my staff. This will be strictly business law—not as exciting as what you're used to. If your reputation casts your work in a mean-spirited light, I consider that a business advantage.

"I always admired your work and you were completely exonerated of the charges against you. I know this is a lot to think about and I don't expect you to jump at the opportunity, but I would appreciate a timely reply."

April, who sat in the chair opposite Mr. Devlin as Noah leaned against his desk, quickly lost interest in the conversation. She seemed unable to focus on anything for long. Even reading more than a few pages seemed beyond her. Although she looked at words, April's attention lagged.

She felt incredibly anxious and had trouble making decisions. The dream where Noah slipped through her arms as the trapdoor opened continued to haunt her sleep. She often indulged her urge to touch Noah, to be certain he was real.

Although they were married for a year-and-a-half, April felt she hardly knew her husband, especially this joy-filled, enthusiastic man who currently resided in their house. He came through the storm of Deidre's wrath a stronger, more focused and godly man, while April found herself incredibly worn down by the whole experience. She felt equally apprehensive regarding the birth of her baby but couldn't express her concerns. The baby remained a topic Noah seemed unable to discuss. She knew full well the reason, even if he did an excellent job of covering his own fears about the upcoming blessed event.

Lula and Mrs. Pratt spoke at length about local midwives. April approved their choice of a Mrs. Thornton who lived a single trolley stop away.

All was in order or would be once Elias came and the baby items were recovered from the house in Newhall.

Another problem loomed. What should she do about her house? Mr. Devlin reinvested her money in business enterprises. She had few funds since she stopped writing for *Pacific Weekly*. Giving a strong kick, the baby roused April from her reverie as Mr. Devlin made ready to depart.

Once their guest left, Noah put his arm around her shoulders. "What do you think?"

Admittedly, April heard little of the conversation. "I don't know. I think this is your decision. I can't tell you how to make a living." At this, April walked toward the staircase, intent to lie down and attempt to clear her head.

Noah gazed at his wife, normally so lithe and active, as she struggled up the stairs. He may not have managed to win her favor but knew he had her love. Maybe once the baby came, the household would quiet down and they would have more time together. He was determined to prove his devotion to their marriage.

Chapter Nineteen

It seemed everyone on his trip to Los Angeles had an opinion about Noah Chandler, almost universally loathsome. Elias Farmer climbed onto the seat of the rented buckboard beside his son-in-law. He approached today's journey reluctantly. Feeling possessive of his daughter and contemplating the vile reports of her husband, he struggled to keep an open mind.

Although his son-in-law's appearance had been widely recounted, Elias was not prepared for the handsome features of the man who answered the door upon his arrival. Muscular, tall, perfectly proportioned, he displayed striking facial attributes: a strong, square chin, shiny dark hair, a fine-boned nose, thick lashes and the most striking grey eyes Elias had ever seen. Somewhat appalled at the detail of his own observations, he doubted April could ever trust such an attractive husband. Although April was a charming and sweet girl—pretty in a simple way—she had never been a beauty. Even Elias would have to admit that. Her husband came from wealth and social standing. She lived in dire straits her entire life. What did this man see in her?

As Noah flicked the reins to begin their journey, he got right to the point. "I believe you don't care much for me, Elias."

"What gives you that idea?" Elias defensively responded.

"I consider myself an excellent judge of character, but it's only an impression really: the way you glared at me across the table at dinner last night; the awkward silence when I touch your daughter; your look of disdain when you think no one is watching. If I knew April had a father, I would have gladly asked for your permission to marry. Well, that's easy to state in retrospect. We married rather impetuously. I'd like us to get along. April cares for you and I've tried my best to make a good impression. I would appreciate knowing how I failed."

Elias considered his reply. "April never mentioned your appearance. I find it difficult to believe you intend to be a faithful husband."

"It's true, I never had difficulty attracting ladies. I proposed a complete confession of past dalliances after we married. April declined my offer. She was happy to keep the past in the past. I'll be glad to confess to you, if it would help." Noah paused to see if Elias would take him up on his offer. He sincerely hoped not. "The thing about April—what drew me to her in the first place—was the fact my looks didn't have the slightest effect on her. I never charmed her and I assure you, I tried my best to be captivating—on occasion. April always saw me as a whole person. I certainly let her see my worst side. We did not get along when she first arrived. I found her incredibly refreshing and still do. Needless to say, I love her dearly. I'm done with superficial relationships. I'm devoted to your daughter and determined to be the best husband I can be. Once April described herself as an ordinary person. She is hardly that. I find her utterly fascinating. She's witty and intelligent. She's adventurous and brave. Her love and support mean everything to me."

"She was unhappy when I first came. You left her."

"I have no excuse. Things were difficult. I felt a complete failure and we had an unfortunate argument. We both said harsh things. All our problems came to a head when we needed to leave the house. I came back for her, but she had already gone. Even when I found out where she went, I didn't approach her. It took a long time and dire circumstances for me to come to my senses. Humbled by my experiences, I am a better man as a result. April and I have ironed out our differences. I hope, over time, you'll be able to accept me as your son-in-law. I know it would mean the world to your daughter. It would mean a lot to me, too."

Elias was surprised by Noah's candid explanation. "You seem different than you did at home."

"Perhaps I tried too hard. I normally don't care what people think, except for juries. This has been a new experience for me—making an effort to win someone's favor on a personal level. I guess my standard courtroom persona doesn't work on you."

"April is clearly in love. She has family now, someone else to rely on."

"I take your meaning, Elias. I assure you, April will never feel it necessary to flee to Santa Barbara for shelter." Noah thought it best to change the subject. They had a long journey ahead of them. "Tell me, what is this Mr. Washington like? I'm eager to make his acquaintance."

"I never met the man. He chose to keep his distance when I visited. I doubt he'll make an appearance today."

The two men engaged in cordial conversation as they headed for Newhall, but Elias noted the reaction his son-in-law's looks elicited from virtually every person they encountered. He drew attention the likes of which Elias never witnessed. A negative reaction became evident whenever the name Noah Chandler was mentioned. Noah's reputation seemed so sullied by the newspapers, Elias doubted he would ever overcome the stigma of his trials, no matter his exoneration. April and his grandchild would forever be affected by Noah's past. When he mentioned this further criticism, Noah had a ready response.

"I believe April's unfortunate circumstances made her the object of curiosity before she came here. She seems unaffected by negative opinion. We will attempt to instill a strong character in our child so he will be impervious to the cruel remarks of foolish people."

At this, Elias backed off. April's early life continued to cause him remorse. Noah stated his point in such a tactful manner, Elias wondered if he was kind or simply ignorant. He began to view his son-in-law in a more generous light.

* * *

Elias did not understand the need for Noah's rifle behind the seat of the wagon nor the revolver strapped to his leg. Once they left Los Angeles, he felt vulnerable and appreciated the fact they could protect themselves in case of emergency. Despite occasional hold-ups, train travel seemed a less dangerous mode of transportation.

They ate a leisurely supper at The Saugus Eating House before making their way to April's abode. Noah generously let Elias have the bed and draped his own long frame across the settee. At sunrise, the men quickly loaded items from April's list onto the buckboard and left her letter for Mr. Washington on the porch. They stopped to purchase a tarp and ate a late lunch before approaching the Newhall Pass—the one serious obstacle on the journey home.

Crossing the pass with an empty buckboard did not seem particularly challenging, especially since the two men walked beside the wagon on the way up the grade. Now the wagon was loaded, making a more difficult climb for the hired horse.

Twenty years previously, Beale's cut had been deepened from 30 to 90 feet to improve the flow of goods to and from Los Angeles. The men stared at the steep grade as they approached the cut. Knowing April's new electric sewing machine sat in their attic at home, Noah wished they left the heavy treadle machine behind as rain started to fall.

* * *

April sat alone at the kitchen table. It was late and a steady rain commenced hours ago. She bit her lip and stared at her empty teacup while considering the wisdom of pouring one last cup. Lifting the lid to see how much tea remained in the pot, she helped herself. If Noah and Elias did not return by the time she finished, she would assume they took shelter for the night and would arrive in the morning.

She had been surprised when Noah mentioned the fudge she gifted him her first year in Los Angeles. Margarita had the day off. Having the kitchen to herself, April spent the afternoon making the rich, dark confection and several batches of Christmas cookies. The lingering scents of chocolate and cinnamon wafted through the kitchen, still warm from the oven. Lula spent today visiting her friend, Pearl Barnes, and sent word she intended to stay the night.

April recalled her last night alone in the house—the night before the hanging, which was not so long ago. She hadn't slept at all in Noah's bed, waiting for the dawn. Although Mrs. Fitzgerald kept the rooms fresh, the pillow still held Noah's scent. She pressed it tenderly against her face as she wept in the darkness.

With Lula gone, it seemed best to climb to the attic and sleep in her own bed. April always felt secure in the attic. But her reverie was interrupted by the sound of rowdy male voices at the back door. April drew her robe closed and stared in wonder at the two filthy, wet men who barged into her kitchen.

Noah grinned sheepishly as he spotted his wife at the kitchen table. It seemed obvious the pair was more than slightly inebriated. Elias swayed as he stood in the doorway, finally placing his hand on the frame for balance. Noah's body shook with a belch as he covered his mouth and laughed.

"What have you done? Where are my things? Did you go to Newhall?"

Noah wiped the seat of a kitchen chair preemptively as if to ensure dirt from his clothing would not become attached, then sat down. "Oh, my darling, we did go to Newhall. It turned into quite a trip."

Elias, still standing in the doorway, explained. "The horse wouldn't go up the grade, even after we got out of the buckboard. There was no one around to help."

The two men took turns clarifying their adventure. Noah continued, "No one else was stupid enough to attempt the pass in the rain!" More laughter.

"We got behind the buckboard to push, hoping the horse would get the idea."

"He got the idea all right!" Noah's voice became quite loud. April wondered what became of her things.

"But not because of us," Elias laughed so hard, he could barely explain. "There was a bear."

"That horse took off like he could win the Kentucky Derby!"

"Yeah, we should enter him," suggested Elias, completely serious. "It was a grizzly."

"No, Elias, it was a big bear, but not a grizzly. Those are all gone from California."

"It was a grizzly—immense. He stood on his back legs. He must have been 15 feet tall."

At this Noah laughed so hard, he almost tumbled off the kitchen chair. "When the wagon took off, we both fell face down in the mud. Once we finally managed to extricate ourselves, there stood the bear by the side of the road."

"Noah pulled his revolver and took a shot. But the gun got wet and muddy. It wouldn't fire." This admission also amused the two men.

"What happened then?" April appeared unamused.

"I threw the gun at the bear. I couldn't think of anything else to do." April considered the ridiculous sight of her muddied husband throwing a gun at a bear in self-defense. "The rifle was in the buckboard, long gone over the pass. The stupid bear ran off as if we sent a mortar shell his way!"

Struggling to breathe due to his mirth, Elias continued, "The horse stayed on the road, thank God. But we walked about four miles before we caught up to the buckboard."

"By the time we got back to Los Angeles, we needed to get the horse to the stable."

"Where are my things?"

"They're safe and sound at the livery. We'll get them tomorrow once things dry out," Noah explained.

"And where have you been since you went to the livery?"

"Well," Noah offered, "we felt we deserved a reward, so we stopped at a saloon for some dinner and a beer."

"One beer?"

"I can't exactly remember. What do you think, Elias? Did we have more than one beer?" Elias remained quiet. "I think it might have been more than one. Maybe two."

"Maybe more?" April suggested.

Noah bit his lip and nodded his head contemplatively. "Let me think."

"I can't believe you left my precious baby things at the livery! It never occurred to the two of you that I might be here alone worrying? That I could have a baby at any moment? That the least you could do is stop to make certain I was all right before you went off on your bender?"

"Where's my mother?"

"She's visiting her friend in the city. I assured her you would be home. I'll tell you something, Noah Chandler. You will be sleeping alone in your bed tonight. And I better not find one speck of dirt in this kitchen when I come down in the morning." April walked out before the men could observe her grin. Certain things were not going well when they departed, she was delighted the men found common ground on their adventure. Covering her mouth to stifle her own mirth, she caught a last comment.

"We're in trouble now," admitted Elias before both men burst into laughter yet again.

* * *

The Chandlers and their respective parents spent a quiet Christmas morning. Modest gifts were exchanged except for Noah's present from his mother. At great expense, Lula purchased Checkers from his new owner and made a gift of him. She also thrilled her daughter-in-law with a more modest gift—a wicker perambulator April envied on their shopping trip.

A suspicious Noah wondered why April so quickly forgave his behavior. She seemed to forget as soon as the baby clothes and bassinette were in her possession. Thankfully, they used rope to secure everything in the buckboard or the whole load would likely have parted ways with the wagon as the horse tore down the road. The tarp they purchased kept the contents of the buckboard dry, although April determinedly washed all the baby things. She claimed they smelled of the livery stable. Noah could not detect any odor but fully supported his wife's every whim.

The beautiful bassinette was given a place of honor in the Chandler bedroom and served as a constant reminder of Noah's fears. April spared no expense. Yards of pristine white cotton hung to the floor. The top of the fabric was gathered in a four-inch band of smocking. More smocked fabric had been applied to the hood. Elaborately tied ribbons were fastened at the corners of the hood. A delicately embroidered pillow and white quilt rested inside the lined basket. The tiny stuffed cat April won on her initial trip to Redondo Beach was the only occupant, for now. With Elias's help, Noah managed to strengthen the legs so the bassinette would be stable when the baby became more active.

They invited Jack and his new fiancé to share Christmas dinner, as well as Mr. and Mrs. Devlin. Noah paused over supper to observe his wife. Although he never appreciated the fact she cut her hair, April artfully arranged sausage-sized curls on top of a loose hairstyle, which accentuated her long, slender neck. Dressed in her Christmas finery, April appeared the lady of the house. Noah was completely entranced.

He purposely diverted the conversation any time the impending birth of his child became a topic, much the same way he refused to think about losing the house until the day it happened.

After dinner, Noah and Jack retreated for a moment alone in Noah's office.

"You two seem content," Jack noted as they shared Christmas brandy and cigars.

"I occasionally contemplate how things would be if I married Deidre. I have a feeling I would have spent my days in perpetual battle. Deidre didn't know me. I showed my worst side to April when she first arrived. Now I cherish her. I'm afraid April played the role of dutiful wife much the way she always played the role of dutiful daughter, to my detriment. I try my best to be a better husband, but it's hard for me to take anything seriously when I'm so damned happy to be alive! I need to be patient while we sort this all out. So, you finally popped the question? Helen is a lovely woman.

Let me know if you need any advice."

"It's quite all right. I think I can muddle through on my own."

"Well, then let me know when I can start asking you for advice. I think I need all the help I can get."

"I'm certain your mother would be more than happy to advise you," Jack tormented.

"Don't worry. She's been doing a fine job of that!"

* * *

Once the house was quiet and secure, Noah turned out the lights and headed for bed. Thinking April must be asleep, he quietly closed the door only to find her standing in front of the window, brushing her hair. The moonlight served to outline her body through her nightgown. Noah gasped in wonder, feeling so fortunate this lovely woman belonged to him. Overcome with gratitude, Noah knew each day he lived was a gift. He could barely discern April's smile as she turned toward the doorway.

"I thought you'd be asleep," he commented as he crossed the room.

"I enjoy the moonlight. This has been a wonderful day, Noah. The best Christmas ever. Your supper prayer was beautiful."

Noah put his arms around his wife and lowered his chin to her shoulder to share her view through the window. Many of the neighbors still had lights on. A few revelers could be seen leaving a home down the block.

"I spoke from my heart. I am the luckiest man alive. Today wasn't too much for you?"

"No. Your mother saw to that. Noah, I'm grateful

for all your mother's help. I wish she didn't spend so much money on us."

"If she was the kind of mother who could sew and cook and clean, I'm sure she would be doing those things. But she's the sort of mother who hires people to do her bidding."

"Yes, well, I have a favor to ask."

"Anything for you." Noah kissed her neck.

"I know I need help right now and I'm thankful for all Lula has done. But she mentioned hiring a nanny and I have to draw the line. This is my baby," April turned to look into her husband's eyes. "I want to take care of our child. I know you don't understand, but I'm adamant about this. There will be no lying-in period while some stranger takes my baby."

In truth, April asked for almost nothing since they married. This seemed the least he could do for her. "I promise you, April, the baby will be in your charge unless you tell me you need help. I will see to it." At this he turned her into his arms and kissed her passionately. "Merry Christmas, my darling."

* * *

Noah enjoyed having another male in residence. It seemed he'd been surrounded by the feminine gender his entire life: first sisters, then lady friends and always, his mother.

As he walked up the gentle hill from the trolley stop, Noah anticipated his nightly round of chess with Elias. But Elias would be leaving their company shortly. He already took more time away from work than he intended. His job as replacement for a retiring bank officer gave him unusual flexibility until March.

Tired from entertaining parents during the day,

April usually sought the solitude of the attic or their bedroom after dinner. Left to her own devices, Lula took on a domestic hobby. Intent on learning how to crochet, she spent most evenings tearing out mistakes made during the day. Ideally, she would create a finely crocheted baby cap. Noah remembered his mother's previous attempts at knitting produced much the same result. It seemed she was not cut out for needle arts.

Noah leapt up the front porch steps and stopped in his tracks. April sat in the rocking chair, a hand draped over her protruding stomach as she enjoyed the mild afternoon.

"What is that?" Noah asked in disgust.

"Edgar is not a 'what.' He is quite clearly a who. Don't be a rude host."

"What is it doing here?"

April pushed herself out of the rocking chair, one of the few seats she could exit unaided. She bent to pick Edgar up. "*He* is visiting while his mother is gone to school. There was some problem and Mrs. Pratt asked if I could look after Edgar for a while."

"Where is his grandmother? Why do you have to do this?"

"Noah, he's a darling boy. He talks now. Edgar what is this?" April pointed to the food Edgar held in his hand.

"Apple."

"That's right! Here, you hold him while I go get a rag to wash his hands." Although April was hardly an expert on babies, she noticed Noah was at a complete loss. "Didn't you ever hold any of your nieces or nephews when you lived in New York?"

Noah stared at Edgar as if he fell out of the sky into his arms. "No. Why would I? They're filthy little buggers."

Exasperated, April started toward the kitchen. Having no desire to be left alone with Edgar, Noah tagged behind. Edgar took the last bite of his apple wedge as Noah awkwardly held the toddler away from his body to avoid getting dirty.

"I talked to Mr. Devlin."

"Did he agree to your terms?"

"He seemed a bit reluctant but finally agreed. I will have a salary, do his legal work and keep my office here as long as there isn't a conflict of interest in the cases I accept. Not that there's been many cases to accept."

"Are you going to start billing? It's fine when people pay what they can but getting eggs or a cake for your legal services is not going to help pay for this house."

"Look at you, Mr. Noah," Margarita proclaimed as the trio entered the kitchen. "Just like a real father."

Noah frowned and attempted to hand Edgar over. "Here, you take him."

"Not me, I'm making dinner."

"Where is everybody?" Noah asked as April wiped Edgar's tiny hands, then rearranged Noah's arms so the child was more secure. "Why can't my mother hold him?"

"Elias took Lula visiting. They won't be home until dinnertime. Mr. Fitzpatrick came today."

"Oh, they've returned?"

"No. In fact they won't be returning. Mr. Fitzpatrick came to pack their things. His cousin in Sacramento urged him to go into business. He felt this trip would be too hard on his wife and Mrs. Fitzpatrick is feeling melancholy about giving up their home here.

He didn't expect to find anyone living in the house. He seemed especially surprised we've returned." Looking down at her figure, April added, "He was surprised about a good many things, but he wished us all the best. I did the same, expressing our hope his business thrives. I sent a brief note for his wife and urged her to keep in touch."

"I suppose we'll have to find permanent help once my mother returns home."

Or not, thought April to herself.

"Down," instructed Edgar. Noah could not have complied more hastily as he set the baby on the floor and watched him toddle away. He looked blankly at his wife as she lowered herself onto a kitchen chair.

"I'm tired. You'll have to follow him around and see to it he doesn't hurt himself." Noah scowled then followed the baby to the dining room as April looked on. That man had a lot to learn. This might be as good a place to start as any.

* * *

After bursting through the front door, Noah waved a copy of *Pacific Weekly* under his wife's nose and demanded, "What is this?" Noah had been in such a wonderful mood of late, April was taken aback at this demonstration of ill temper.

"It's a copy of *Pacific Weekly*. You can see, the name is right on the cover. I'm surprised you can't make it out." At this, April returned to her embroidery. Both Lula and Elias sat across the sitting room from the young couple, evidently struck dumb by the scene unfolding before them.

"I need to talk to you, right *now*." Noah started toward the stairwell, expecting his wife to follow obediently behind.

April sighed. Navigating the stairs was not her favorite thing to do of late. She placed her needlework on the table beside her chair and, as elegantly as she could manage, hoisted herself to her feet. "Excuse me," she offered while her guests exchanged concerned looks and watched her attempt the staircase.

Angry voices were apparent as Lula and Elias strained to understand the nature of Noah's concerns. Only the tone of the upstairs conversation resonated. The words were undecipherable.

"What have you done?"

"I don't know what you're talking about."

"I heard some controversy about your story. I bought a copy to see for myself."

April grabbed the magazine and took a closer look. "There's no need to yell, whatever concerns you. I still don't understand."

"This is the last episode of your tale."

"I thought it would make you happy."

"You murdered Little May!"

"I still don't understand," but she was beginning to.

"How could you?"

"You hurried home from work for this? Noah, it's only a silly story. It was never anything more. I have other interests now—our home and family. So, I ended my dramatic tale in a dramatic way. I wanted it to be over without question or reprise."

Noah appeared devastated. "Why did you have to kill her?"

"Are you afraid this is some portent of our life? Noah, my story never had anything to do with us, not really." She walked over and put her arms around her husband. "Everything is going to be fine. I don't want you to worry." But she knew he would.

* * *

"You mustn't keep this from him, dear. I need to send for Noah," offered Lula as she held her daughter-in-law's hand in one of hers and used a cold rag to gently wipe April's forehead.

"No. You can't tell him, Lula. Promise me."

"But this is his baby. He needs to know your time is here."

"My stomach seemed upset last night. By the time he left this morning, I knew the baby must be coming. Please let Noah stay at work. Maybe the baby will be here before he comes home. I want to spare him this."

Lula was dumbfounded. Even Marshall awaited their children's births like a dutiful husband, pacing in their parlor. And she did not consider Marshall an avid family man. She didn't understand April's insistence Noah be kept in the dark. In fact, Lula felt it her duty to inform her son of his impending fatherhood. It must be his decision to come home or stay away.

* * *

Noah exited the office he occupied at Mr. Devlin's headquarters, expecting to find anyone but the senior Mrs. Pratt. A chill of foreboding overtook him before the woman spoke a word.

"Mr. Chandler, the baby is coming."

"Now?"

"Soon, very soon. You need to come home."

"Thank you, Mrs. Pratt. I'll be right there." Noah stood in his tracks as the woman left his office. He wanted to run away—go to a saloon. He could find out what happened later. But he remembered the loving expression on April's sweet face a month ago, right before they pulled the black sack over his face. If she could see him through those presumed last minutes of his life, he needed to be with her now.

* * *

April was shocked when Noah entered their bedroom. Lula quickly made herself scarce. Noah, obviously concerned, sat down in a chair beside the bed and took April's hand in his.

"You came."

"And I intend to stay."

"Men aren't welcome, they only get in the way," explained the midwife. "Give your regards and leave."

"I will not interfere and I am not leaving."

Noah was insistent. Mrs. Thornton sighed deeply and continued her preparations. "If you cause the least problem, I'll insist you go. And there is no fainting. No one has time to help you."

"I understand completely and I will not faint," promised Noah. At least he intended not to faint.

Chapter Twenty

The light from a glass lamp on the dresser lit the bedroom enough for Noah to make out his wife's steady breathing. She slept soundly, exhausted from her efforts.

When Mrs. Thornton proclaimed the birth "completely normal," Noah thought her an absolute lunatic. They were at odds from the moment he entered his bedroom.

Noah would have sacrificed anything to spare April her pain and couldn't help but wonder at the fact she begged him for this experience. Her jubilation at having produced their tiny baby quickly absolved the agony of birth.

Attempting to remain lucid and conscious, Noah saw and heard things he would rather forget. His immeasurable pride in his wife and relief at her survival gave the appearance of an excited new father. Determined to assure his wife would live through the night, he took up his current position in the chair beside the bed, intently monitoring her every breath.

Hearing a noise from the bassinette, Noah walked over to peer at his new daughter. He felt overwhelmed when April expressed her desire to name the baby

Anna for his sister. This new Anna appeared quite awake. Her blue eyes stared into the near darkness. He observed her yawn as she stretched her entire tiny body and gave a shudder after her exertion.

Noah touched Anna's tiny, perfect hand with the back of his finger. To his surprise, the baby firmly grasped the finger and seemed to look right at him. An overpowering desire to protect and nurture his daughter overcame Noah. It seemed as if she reached out and touched his very heart. Enchanted by this diminutive part of himself, he used his thumb to stroke the back of her delicate hand as she nodded quietly back to sleep. Taking a closer look, he couldn't help but notice Anna was an incredibly stunning child, likely the most beautiful in the history of the world.

* * *

Lula felt completely perplexed by the time she packed her bags to head for New York. It was April who initially confounded her mother-in-law. Certain the girl would come to her senses, April proved Lula wrong.

"I don't understand. April has always been eager to enjoy every opportunity—always so appreciative."

"There will be no nanny or wet nurse, Mother. Further, I forbid you to question her. We are adamant about this."

"But why? I only want the best for April."

"You've spent enough on this household. We're afraid you'll run out of money and be a burden on us." A delighted gleam lit Noah's grey eyes.

"I am asking you a serious question."

"I know you are. We appreciate all you've done. But we won't change our minds on this. April wants to take care of our baby. You have to understand. If April stood here now, she'd probably tell you she's a simple woman of rustic origin. She doesn't want anything fancy."

But Lula did not understand. Before Mr. Farmer left, she attempted to engage his support. Claiming she needed someone to escort her on a visit, she pressed her concerns and suggestions on him as they rode in the carriage. She appeared indignant at his inability to comprehend the importance of his daughter's proper station in life. He remained mute when Lula outlined April's meager background and unfortunate tendencies toward frugality and simplicity. He offered no help when Lula disparaged his daughter's propensity to engage in work beneath her position as mistress of the house. Elias's silence seemed particularly perplexing in light of the fact he had been extremely loquacious since the birth of his granddaughter. A prouder grandfather could not be found.

April's failure to abide by common rules of confinement caused her mother-in-law more distress. She refused to stay in bed, which assuredly would have served to promote rapid recovery. Lula felt anxious about her daughter-in-law's health and feared her actions would prove calamitous. No one in the household listened to her concerns.

Her son's erratic behavior prompted further confusion. Never in her life had Lula seen a man so enamored of his offspring. Men generally wanted nothing to do with babies. Child-rearing was a mother's concern. The occasional father might enjoy rough-housing as sons grew older. A father's usual interaction with his children consisted of punishment. She assumed Noah would be more concerned about his role as provider and head of his household. Completely smitten by his daughter, Noah eagerly held and cared for her. Lula became appalled when she actually caught him burping the baby.

She attempted to discuss these concerns with April, who listened attentively but seemed no less happy at her husband's inappropriate fatherly devotion. Lula believed her son's family might as well dwell in a teepee on the plains like Indians. She wondered aloud over dinner one night, "What is this generation coming to?"

The ray of hope in an otherwise desperate situation—for Lula—was Anna. Lula thought her granddaughter an engaging and intelligent baby. Her light blue eyes appeared a combination of parental traits. She had her father's thick eyelashes. Her chubby cheeks were punctuated by charming dimples. Lula believed Anna's hair would be brown, but there was so little of it, her prediction could prove inaccurate.

Lula dared not utter the words aloud but admitted to herself she enjoyed Anna more than any other grandchild, or any of her own children for that matter.

Although Lula believed her departure would trigger complete chaos in the household, she eventually planned her return to New York. Her regret at being unable to provide sufficient domestic help became overshadowed by her sorrow at leaving Anna. The elder Mrs. Chandler blubbered incessantly as her son drove her to the train station.

* * *

Noah noted April's obvious fatigue as she yawned at the breakfast table. Anna had yet to sleep through the night.

His new habit was to hold his daughter while he

ate before heading to work. Returning in mid-afternoon, Noah kept office hours until dinner. This often included observation of Anna, cooing and kicking on a quilt on the parlor floor. Mr. Chandler never failed to astound potential clients when greeting them at the front door while holding Anna in his arms. He imagined his congenial manner and beautiful baby daughter served to quell all manner of questions regarding his integrity, at least he hoped so.

They could not afford to keep the temporary household staff his mother procured and Margarita made a hasty exit not long after Lula departed. The woman was always on the prowl for a better opportunity. She might return as quickly as she left. For now, April kept their large home, cooking, cleaning and caring for Anna. Noah tried his best to keep up the yard. He quite obviously had been born without a green thumb. Most of what he earned went toward their house. Unless his own legal business became more lucrative, he did not see a way to hire help.

Although Noah was often held in contempt by ignorant Angelinos, he never seemed offended and took rude comments in stride. Realizing he might never overcome his thorough trouncing in the newspapers, he refused to let it ruin his day. Occasionally, he received a favorable comment from sympathetic people who understood his innocence.

He found April's suggestion they take in boarders to make extra money completely abhorrent. But Noah could see the house on Carroll Avenue took all their effort and drained all their resources.

New concerns about the economy grew. Earlier in the month, the bottom dropped out of the stock market.

Several big railroads already failed due to the Panic of 1893. It seemed likely more would follow. Train service had been temporarily suspended, or Noah assumed it would be only temporary. A glut of produce rotted away due to lack of transportation. There were a few runs on banks, though nothing close to the chaos caused by bank failures in eastern states. The community was coming together to help those in need.

Noah grew concerned about the business methods of his new employer. Mr. Devlin, having recently divested himself of holdings in transportation and building and loans, declared this a "time to buy." Noah never understood his wife's involvement in Mr. Devlin's business concerns but knew she provided some initial investment.

Noah knew Mr. Devlin's goal in Los Angeles had been to get a feel for where the city might expand. April evidently provided the catalyst for his current all-in mentality. Her enthusiasm and certainty Los Angeles was only getting started proved contagious. The man clearly believed April's hunches almost prophetic. She had served as Mr. Devlin's lucky charm. Noah believed the whole business, including his job, could blow up at the least provocation.

Although his euphoria of months prior dimmed and April grew exhausted from household responsibilities, there was a joy of life apparent in the Chandler household. Husband and wife were living in ways neither could have imagined the day Noah got beaned.

"Jack's wedding is next month. Do you need a new dress?"

"Why, is my teal gown not good enough for the best man?" April teased.

"I thought you might enjoy shopping for something different. I intend to show you off. This will be Anna's first outing. I believe my ladies will attract all the attention."

"I think the bride will be the one getting all the notice."

"Helen is a lovely girl, but she doesn't hold a candle to the Chandler women," Noah boasted.

"This is a formal affair," April reluctantly commented.

"Does it make you uncomfortable?"

"No. You'll be there. You're arrogant enough for both of us, but I don't know how to dance."

"I see. Let me think. How can we possibly remedy this? I did teach you to play cribbage and chess, though not well." This drew a raised eyebrow from his wife. "I did teach you to ride. Perhaps you could prevail upon me to teach you to dance? We would have to work out some sort of compensation. I am a man of business, after all."

"Watch what you say, Noah Chandler. Your daughter is listening."

The lovely spring nights soon filled with the miraculous sound of music played on a Berliner Grammophone. Noah received the gift, actually a toy, from one of his old college chums currently residing in England. The German-manufactured machine played five-inch discs made of zinc. Noah turned the handle so April could understand the rhythm of the waltz, *Blue Danube*. Then he escorted her onto their dance floor—the middle of the backyard—where he took up dance position and eagerly demonstrated the box step. His only other disc, *Ta Ra Ra Boom-de-ay*, served as a sample of the polka.

April quickly recognized she hadn't much choice but to relax and follow. Noah was a forceful leader. As the day of the wedding approached, April felt fully confident in her ability to follow her husband's lead.

* * *

Noah glanced toward his wife while he performed his role as best man. The sun shone through the stained-glass windows directly on April. It appeared God was pointing her out and rightly so thought a distracted Noah. When he was called upon to produce Helen's ring, he nearly dropped it. He gave April a sheepish grin after regaining his composure. She gave him a look that clearly said, "I told you to pay attention."

The wedding underscored Jack's success and prominent position in the community. He found Helen waiting tables in her family's restaurant. She made a lovely and humble bride. Noah was certain his dearest friend made a wise choice and hoped the two couples would be friends.

Jack rented the ballroom at the Westminster Hotel for a grandiose reception. The wedding party spilled out into the opulent gardens.

April wondered if her husband harbored any regret, knowing his old partner fared so well when Deidre put an end to Noah's own success. She could discern only joy in her husband's demeanor. He often explained he found far more than he lost from his experiences with Deidre. Nonetheless, today would prove a test of his determination to make the best of his past.

April understood Jack made a controversial choice by inviting his friend to be best man. Accustomed to being the object of whispered comments, April understood public acceptance had always been beyond her control.

Noah fairly beamed each time he showed off their daughter to every guest he could corner. Mrs. Chandler believed her husband made an obnoxious fool of himself. She conceded that might be more constructive than playing the part of most notorious couple in Los Angeles. Perhaps their reputation could be fading. Citizens seemed more concerned about the Panic than last year's sensational newspaper articles. Outside the realm of public scrutiny, April enjoyed her life of busy wife and mother although she was having a grand time at the wedding.

The Chandlers inconspicuously shared a table with several of Jack's relations. Once the wedding couple had their first dance, Jack's elderly aunt offered to hold Anna so Noah and April could take a turn on the dance floor.

With a thrill of excitement, April put her hand on her husband's as he escorted her to the center of the floor while the band played the popular waltz *After the Ball is Over*. If ever April fantasized about taking the dance floor on the arm of a handsome prince from one of her books, her dreams were currently being realized.

She unexpectedly longed to write an episode where Little May found true love and lived happily ever after, but Little May was safely six feet under where she could do no further harm to her author's marriage. Perhaps, when things quieted down at home, April would attempt a new story.

She hadn't heard a word from Mr. Lynch since submitting the concluding volume of *The Life of Little May*. The final episode caused wild controversy. Apparently, angry female readers stormed the offices of *Pacific Weekly*, demanding a retraction. Little May's fans were livid at her sudden and unfortunate demise. Copies of that issue fairly flew off the shelves. The weekly magazine was securely established as a top-seller in the city. Since she had put his periodical "on the map," she hoped Mr. Lynch might someday be willing to publish more of her work.

"Penny for your thoughts."

"I'm not falling for your line again, Mr. Chandler. Besides, my thoughts are worth far more than a penny."

"Are you having a good time?"

"Oh, I am. Dancing is fun! Too bad it's so warm."

Noah drew his wife's body closer to his and whispered in her ear. "I have found any activity placing a man and woman in close proximity to be quite fun. If we head for home now, I'll be happy to demonstrate." He looked into her eyes, waiting for her reaction. Noah grinned smugly when April primly turned her face away, her cheeks having turned a subtle shade of pink.

Without comment, Noah abandoned his preventive charts and equipment. April wondered if this was due to past failure or a new acceptance of parenthood. What did this mean for their future? Fearing Noah would revert to previous habits, she refrained from comment. She enjoyed their "naps" as never before. But what was she to do with such a brazen man?

Turning their box step in the direction of the bride and groom near the edge of the floor, Noah continued, "I'm certain the new bride will shortly be discovering the joys of bodily proximity. I imagine Jack is more than eager to indoctrinate her if he hasn't already."

At this comment, April's eyes flew open wide. Hours before, they attended a grand wedding in the church. The bride appeared virginally beautiful in her carefully embroidered and lacy white gown. How could her husband manage to denigrate this blessed day in so few words?

"I'll pay considerably more than a penny for your thoughts now," offered Noah. No words seemed forthcoming. The pair separated to clap as the dance ended.

As the *Glass in Hand Polka* began, Noah swept his wife back into his arms. They quickly made their way around the dance floor, bouncing and twirling to the cheery music. A wide grin lit April's face. This was so much more exciting than practice in the backyard. By the time the song ended, April's cheeks were red from exertion.

"Why don't you go out to the garden? I'll check on Anna and bring some punch."

"You'll bring punch?"

"Well, there will be punch. I won't guarantee it will be the only thing in the glass. I'm quite a fine cook you remember. I make tea."

"Will you behave yourself?"

"I'll try my best to be a gentleman for at least the time it takes to cool off."

* * *

April sat on a cold stone bench under a sizeable jacaranda tree ablaze with lavender blossoms. Trees in newer parts of the city were not large enough to provide adequate shade. This one evidently predated the hotel garden.

Noah certainly took his time. The punch, no

matter how Noah doctored it up, sounded refreshing. April's thirst made it almost impossible to think about anything else. Perhaps Noah couldn't find her. She stood and took a few steps in an effort to better see the ballroom doors. It was not her husband who walked up to stand before her. Deidre's cousin Theodora approached the jacaranda tree.

Having no idea what to say, April offered, "Good afternoon."

It seemed apparent from Theodora's expression, her intentions were far from social.

"My gentleman friend is a client of Mr. Broadmore. Imagine my surprise when I spotted you and your husband in attendance."

"Mr. Broadmore is my husband's dearest friend." Surely the woman remembered they were once partners. April could not help but feel defensive. What could this woman want? "Can I help you?"

"That's an excellent question, can you help me? I remember a time when you could have helped me, when I sat desolate and alone on the stand in the courthouse reading my cousin's heartbreaking letters. Oh, but you weren't there were you? Even you deserted your lying, cheating, deceiving husband during the murder trial. Tell me, how did he charm his way back into your good graces? He's extremely charismatic. What woman could resist his face? Deidre certainly couldn't. Is it the mewling brat you brought along today? Perhaps you turned up because your bastard daughter needed a father?"

The comment hit a nerve. April's temper grew short, but an outburst would only cause a bigger scene. "Say and think what you will, Deidre's letters were all lies, meant to deceive you. Noah never harmed her."

"He did not kill her, true enough. But he is a murderer nonetheless. He slaughtered poor Deidre's mind as if he destroyed her body. There's nothing left of her. You certainly played your part. I find you equally guilty in Deidre's demise."

"What are you talking about?" April noted Theodora, though taller than her cousin, certainly resembled her right down to the mean glint in her eye.

"You really don't know, do you? Haven't you ever wondered what became of your victim? I find this difficult to believe, but here you are with the most innocent expression plastered on that pasty face of yours. My cousin was completely devastated by your sudden marriage to her fiancé. She's the most delicate flower of womanhood and could not bear losing the man whose life she planned to share. You shattered her heart beyond repair. Can you even imagine her embarrassment? Do you ever lie in bed at night, too guilty to sleep? Because it should be your fate and worse. You are nothing but a gold-digging trollop; a servant with designs on the master of the house. Perhaps Deidre's fate is even more your doing than Noah Chandler's."

April felt on the verge of panic. Arguing would only inflame the situation. "I'm sorry if—"

April was stunned as Theodora slapped her face. Never in her life had anyone raised a hand to her. She slowly put her hand to her cheek. Blood stained her fingertips.

"What is this!" stormed Noah as he approached the nasty scene.

Theodora sneered, turned, and walked away.

Noah quickly dropped the two glasses of punch on the stone bench and hurried to his wife, grasping her shoulders. "What the hell happened? Are you hurt?" April shook her head as Noah turned to follow Theodora.

She held his arm. "I'm all right. Don't go."

"I can only imagine what the bitch said to you. I'm so sorry, April," Noah took his wife in his arms as if to shelter her from further harm. A few wedding guests, having overheard Theodora's comments, gathered to observe. They quickly decided to give the couple privacy once Noah glared at them.

"What has become of Deidre?" April asked. "You told me not to concern myself, but I need to know."

Glancing around the garden, Noah thought it best to put some distance between them and other wedding guests. Removing his handkerchief and carefully dabbing the corner of April's mouth, he noted the harsh red mark Theodora's hand made on her cheek. Handing April the handkerchief, he took her arm to lead her out to the sidewalk. They walked down the street where Noah gestured toward an empty trolley stop bench.

"Deidre suffered some sort of nervous failure the day of the hanging. At first, authorities believed she was overcome by the events of that morning, but she didn't improve. It became obvious she couldn't stand trial. They confined her in a hospital near San Francisco. Her family petitioned the court to have her released to their care. I'm not certain of the circumstances, but she could not remain at home so she was returned to an asylum."

"Asylums are horrible places."

"They are. But Deidre's family provides additional care."

Noah could see tears gathering in April's eyes. "I

didn't want you to know. It's disturbing, I agree. I've thought about this. It should have been clear to me something was seriously wrong. I knew Deidre had a propensity to selfishness and cruelty. There were other disturbing aspects of her personality I should have taken more seriously. Her moods were mercurial. She was unnaturally spiteful and cold. I believe her parents understood this for some time. They even went so far as to try to warn me when I visited San Francisco. They hoped if Deidre settled into married life and had a family, her disposition might improve.

"I really didn't pay the slightest attention to their concerns. Hell-bent to serve my own purposes, I never cared about Deidre. She never cared about me. She didn't even know me. If our marriage served to further inflame her unfortunate emotions, it was probably only a matter of time before something else would have set her off. She's not well. She let her own family believe she died. Normal people don't do things like that.

"I likely played a role in her breakdown, but we've been the object of her spite for some time. It almost cost my life. I don't want this to come between us. Look at me, April." Noah carefully lifted April's chin and looked into her eyes. I love you more than anything on earth. I believe you and I were meant to be together. We have a beautiful daughter and a wonderful life. I want to put this behind us, for now and evermore."

"You've told me everything?"

"I have. The fact Theodora blames us is probably for the best. Deidre needs someone in her corner. I doubt Deidre's own parents would hold me accountable. They, at least, seem to understand she's a troubled soul. Let's collect our daughter and head for home."

"Can I have my punch first?"

"I think that can be arranged."

"What about one more dance?"

Noah grinned. "I don't want you to be the object of further controversy. Your cheek is red."

"I'm quite certain every wedding guest has already heard some version of what went on in the garden. What will it help if we leave now? It might simply provide more fodder for gossips."

Concerned, Jack came to the table when the Chandlers returned to the reception. Not wanting to speak in front of his family, he drew Noah aside in conversation. April, still clutching Noah's handkerchief, noticed it was one Deidre gave him for Christmas. When the waiter came to remove cake plates, she discreetly placed it on his tray. Certain Noah didn't remember the origin of his possession, April determined to search his dresser for its mate. She didn't want any further reminders of Deidre in her house.

Chapter Twenty-One

The residents of Carroll Avenue were in for a 4th of July treat. Mr. Hotchkiss, a volunteer fireman and hardware storeowner, procured boxes of fireworks, intent on sharing this treasure with his neighbors. A potluck picnic supper had been organized on vacant lots down the hill. The locale was a safe distance from homes, a perfect site for the pyrotechnic display.

Having returned from a brief honeymoon, Mr. and Mrs. Broadmore were eager to observe the 4th with their friends. Because the evening's festivities were planned by the Chandlers, Jack insisted on providing entertainment during the day.

Noah balked at his friend's initial idea, feeling Jack's proposal would prove too difficult for both April and baby Anna. The plan to keep the baby at home was abandoned when Noah took Anna to the June wedding. Being almost six months of age seemed reasonable to him then, less so now. But April's enthusiasm and assurance there were four adults to entertain their daughter laid his qualms to rest.

The revelers made their way by carriage to a new station called Mountain Junction in Altadena. The "Great Incline" opened to the public that day. Noah discovered tickets for the ride cost an incredible $5 per person and thanked Jack profusely for his generosity. The railway climbed Lake Avenue into Rubio Canyon. From there, they transferred to a funicular, which climbed 2,200 feet to the top of Echo Mountain. The steep incline and rugged terrain assured a thrilling journey.

Noah observed Helen's discomfort on the funicular, which certainly gave the appearance of a risky and dangerous ride. Jack seemed more than willing to console his new wife. April appeared her typically curious self, excited to experience all life could offer. Noah verified the funicular was completely safe, confirming an emergency cable kept the car from rocketing down the tracks should the main cable fail. After all, he would be remiss as a husband and father if he didn't assure his family's safety. At the summit, the newly-opened Echo Chalet provided a respite where April found enough privacy to nurse the baby.

The adults thoroughly enjoyed their once-in-a-lifetime experience, being among the first to ride what would undoubtedly become a premier tourist attraction.

After returning to the Chandler house, they collected April's basket of cookies and bowl of potato salad then walked to the picnic area.

Tables were set up to hold the incredible array of dishes proudly provided by the ladies of Carroll Avenue. Blankets and quilts covered the hillside in swaths of color. Picnic baskets contained dishware and linens for the celebrants. Eager chatter commenced between residents and guests as they enjoyed their feast.

The building boom of 1887 resulted in subdivision of a multitude of properties. Many remained undeveloped. Since oil had been discovered, some owners found their lots large enough to support two oil derricks. These were now easily seen in the distance, not far from Angelino Heights.

Noah scrutinized Helen who cradled Anna in her arms as she leaned against her husband. Predictably, Noah was fond of anyone who took a liking to his daughter; that alone put Helen in his good graces. Clearly enamored of the baby, she'd been a great help to April all day. He bent his head to whisper in April's ear, "I imagine they'll be starting a family soon."

April turned her attention from her plate of food to comment, "It would be wonderful for Anna to have a playmate."

"It looks like Helen is eager to be a mother. She certainly has taken a liking to our girl."

"Funny, you never seemed to notice when I was eager to be a mother," April teased.

"Oh, you made it quite obvious. I simply chose to ignore you."

"Yes, I've noticed husbands can be quite adept at ignoring things they don't wish to see. For instance, there's those geraniums beside the carriage house that seem to be dying from lack of water. They are clearly victims of ignorance."

"Mrs. Chandler, I never purported to be any kind of gardener. That particular achievement is absent from my vast resume of skills."

"Along with a multitude of other male talents."

"Well, I do have the important ones down. Would you like me to elaborate?" Noah grinned.

"No, no." His suggestion made April nervous.

There was no telling what descriptions Noah might be willing to expound in public. "You are an excellent father, however."

"Really? You've never mentioned it to me before. What makes you think so?"

"You're hardly the type who ignores his child aside from taking a strap to mete out punishment. I believe Anna will grow up knowing how completely her father adores her, perhaps embarrassingly so at the rate you're going. It may not be a conventional way to raise a daughter, but I think it's good."

"We are not conventional, you and I, but we will undoubtedly raise wonderful, loving and happy children."

"Children?" April's interest was aroused by that word.

Noah only grinned in response. April found him infuriating. Her husband was always eager to talk, now she could not get another word out of him.

When Mr. Hotchkiss journeyed down the hill to commence his fireworks spectacular, several men lent a hand, amongst them, Jack and Noah. The two wives were left alone to talk as darkness fell. Noah brought a lantern to light their way back to the house once the fireworks display ended. April lit it now so the ladies would be able to see until the show began.

April felt Helen, though several years her junior, provided her first opportunity to make a true friend. The women talked about inconsequential things including Helen's extensive family and their business. Then the conversation took an interesting turn.

"Did you know Jack is desperate for Noah to come back to the law firm?"

"Noah hasn't mentioned it to me. Are you certain

Jack asked him?"

"I don't think a week has gone by in the last six months that Jack has not asked him."

"Noah always declines?"

"Yes. He tells Jack he's doing fine and he believes Jack is better off without him. But Jack is terribly overworked and feels he owes a debt to Noah. Jack barely scraped his way through college. His family didn't have funds to support him. I think he feels guilty at how things have turned out. I know our opulent wedding was probably a waste of money, but it's the one real extravagance he ever indulged."

"Are you going to buy a house?" April knew the couple lived at the same hotel where Jack always kept rooms.

"Yes, but nothing so lovely as yours. We're both simple people. We're looking for a modest house in a quiet neighborhood. I wondered if you might do me a favor?"

"What?"

"I wish you'd speak to Noah about reviving Broadmore & Chandler."

"Oh, Helen, I'd dearly love to help, but Noah is closed-mouth about his work. He attempts to shield me from financial concerns. I doubt I could influence him if I tried. I believe he feels the law firm is something best left in the past. But I'll see what I can find out and I promise to let you know."

"Thank you."

"I must warn you, Noah might refuse to discuss this. I don't want you to get your hopes up for naught."

"I understand." Helen looked toward the edge of the blanket where Anna wiggled and fussed as the first fireworks were launched.

April placed the baby in her lap. At first, Anna listened intently to the unfamiliar explosions and "ooohs" and "aaahs" of the crowd.

It became apparent there was more than slight chaos amongst the gentlemen setting off the display as hurried shadows dashed about in the glow of torchlight. The time between explosives lengthened. The crowd started to converse due to lapses in the program.

"Do you think it's entirely safe for Jack and Noah to be lighting off rockets?"

April replied with conviction, "I'm quite certain it's not safe at all and exactly why they were so eager to help. If there is one thing I've learned from being married—and it may be the only thing—men are indisputably childish. I rather believe the wife of the grumpiest, most wrinkled and ill-tempered old man in the city would agree."

Helen gave a shy laugh.

"At the rate this is going, I'm afraid Anna won't wait until the display is over for her next meal. I'll go back to the house and return as soon as I can. You keep the lantern."

"Do you want me to come?"

"No, you need to tell the men what's become of us—assuming they ever get to the end of the fireworks."

"But how will you see? It's difficult enough to find your way through the brush. You don't want to trip carrying the baby in your arms. Take the lantern. We'll return with someone else if you don't make it back."

"It seems the sensible thing to do. See you shortly."

Once April returned to the house, she took a seat on the side porch to nurse the baby. Everyone left the neighborhood to enjoy the picnic and she could see the fireworks from there. Anna, tired from her busy day, soon fell so soundly asleep, April could not rouse her. Sorry she neglected to dress the baby for bed before taking her seat on the porch, April climbed the stairs to her bedroom and placed Anna in the bassinette.

She carefully set the lantern on the dresser. It was bright enough to make the bedroom light unnecessary. April returned to the porch to view the remaining fireworks, first stopping in the kitchen to grab a glass of lemonade.

Despite the din from still infrequent fireworks, April thought she heard a noise as she sipped her drink.

"Noah?" There was no reply. Perhaps the baby woke up. Making her way up the stairs, she entered the bedroom and stood inside the doorway. Something seemed awry, April carefully scanned the room. Her observation halted at the bassinette where she could see, quite clearly, a face hovering over the place where her baby slept. The face appeared so still, so expressionless, April could not believe it was real. A chill ran through her. The woman's tangled and matted hair must have been drawn up in a bun. The bun had fallen behind her head. Snarls and wisps of hair radiated around the woman's face as if she were Medusa come to life. Her cheeks were sunken; her skin sallow. She wore a gray tattered shirtwaist and continued her motionless stare. A metallic object caught the reflection from the lantern. The woman held a butcher knife in her hand. Its point dug into the ledge of the bassinette.

Fighting a nauseating panic, April breathlessly

managed, "What have you done?" but doubted the face could speak.

"Nothing yet." The woman twisted the knife from side to side. Her face, riddled with insanity, was unrecognizable. Her voice was not.

"What do you want?" April needed to keep her wits about her. She needed to draw Deidre away. It seemed impossible to think. The only thing that mattered was keeping Anna safe.

"The baby looks like Noah. I'd like to mark her face just enough to mar her beauty. Enough so her father can't help but notice every time he looks at her. Enough so he'll always think of me. I have no plans to kill her if it's what you're afraid of. I'm not crazy."

The thought of the knife cutting her precious baby was abhorrent. April could barely breathe. With the most even tone she could manage, she replied, "As long as you and Noah were together, surely you understand how intensely he dislikes children. You won't gain anything by harming his daughter. Noah is fond of me. If you wish to hurt Noah, I'm the one you're looking for."

"Are you trying to trick me?"

"I'm simply being honest." April took a step toward the bassinette. She needed to insert herself between Deidre and the baby.

"My cousin told me Noah liked his little brat."

"Noah always puts on a show for prospective clients. He uses his daughter to further his business. It's what he did to you, isn't it?" Deidre's agitation grew. Her eyes darted nervously around the room as she pulled the knife off the bassinette and dropped her arm to her side.

"Noah wanted to marry me. He threw over my

cousin Martha because I was prettier and wealthier. Then you came along and ruined everything. It *was* you."

"That's right, Deidre. It was me. All along. I was the one who stole him from you."

"You are nothing. You had nothing to offer. We made such a handsome couple. I could have given him everything—money, power, even fame if he wanted. My family could have brought him success beyond his wildest dreams."

"But did he love you?" April asked. She was so close to the bassinette, she could smell the stench of sweat and filth emanating from Deidre's body.

"What does that have to do with anything?"

"He didn't love you. He never loved you. He loved me, Deidre, me. It's why he left you at the altar, alone and ashamed while he took me for his wife. He rubbed it right in your face, didn't he? Did he say it out loud at the restaurant? Did he actually say, 'I love April. I never loved you, I never could.'"

At this last cruel comment, Deidre lunged toward her tormentor, knife raised. She banged against the bassinette, almost upending it. Anna awoke and began to cry. April's attention refocused as the baby bed teetered precariously but then righted itself.

Taller and stronger than her adversary, April proved to be no match for the knife. The force of Deidre's body slammed her against the dresser. The kerosene lamp crashed to the floor spreading fire across the carpet. April diverted the blade aimed at her face, but the knife still found its mark, slashing across her upper left arm.

Deidre scrambled to her feet and kicked the fallen April in the side of her head. Struggling for consciousness, April watched in horror as Deidre took a step toward the bassinette, inadvertently catching her skirt on fire. Screaming, Deidre backed into the drapes, which were quickly engulfed in flames. She flailed desperately as if to wipe the flames from her body as April struggled to her feet and pulled Anna from the bassinette. She started for the landing as Deidre's blood-curdling screams echoed through the house.

April used the hem of her skirt to cover Anna's face while the baby cried in terror. It seemed as if everything happened in slow motion. Each careful step on the staircase took all the focus and effort she could manage.

Fire rapidly spread through the house. Gasping for air, the roar of flames surrounding her, April reached the first floor. But then, there was only darkness.

* * *

Noah would be the first to admit the fireworks were not as easily lit as he imagined. He began to doubt they would have them all launched by the next 4th of July. Having successfully ignited a rocket, he looked up to admire his handiwork. The reaction of the crowd did not seem properly appreciative so Noah turned to see if they were watching. The scene unfolding before him was completely unexpected. Men were running from the picnic area toward a house engulfed in flames. His house.

He ran as he never ran before in his life, Jack close on his heels. As they reached their picnic blanket, he found only Helen waiting there, her face turned toward the flames. "*Where is April*?" Noah screamed.

Helen looked toward the burning building. Tears, illuminated by the glow from the fire, streamed down her cheeks.

"Stay here," Jack ordered his wife.

Noah hurried on. Blood-curdling screams assaulted his ears. It seemed an eternity until he ran down Carroll Avenue and reached his front yard. He yelled April's name, determined to enter the house and rescue her. Two men who reached the inferno moments earlier grabbed his arms as Noah headed for the front porch.

"*Let me go!* My wife is in there. I have to get her." The men held him fast and stared with sorrowful eyes. The screaming had stopped. "*Let me go.*" Jack came up behind him and placed his arms around Noah's chest.

"You can't go in there," Jack explained. "She's gone."

Noah struggled against Jack's firm grip. The man must be delusional. He had to go in. "You have to let me go," begged Noah as he continued to struggle against arms that held him fast.

What were these men saying? Noah, incredulous, felt shock and horror rush over him as the roof collapsed into the hungry flames below. How could this be? Where was April? Where was his precious Anna? How could they be gone? How could he go on without them?

He stood speechless, unable to verbalize any of the questions pounding in his brain. When Jack released his grip, Noah fell to his knees. Lifting his hands above his head, he screamed out, "God, oh God, not this, not this." Wracking sobs shook his body as his arms fell helplessly to his sides. Bystanders could only stare. No one knew what to do.

Jack knelt beside Noah and placed his arm around

his shoulders. Noah shoved him away. But in that awkward, quiet moment, a baby's cry could clearly be heard. "It's Anna," Noah declared. "*It's Anna!*"

Noah scrambled to his feet and took off running around the side of the house, recklessly close to flames. Jack, doubting Noah could tell his baby's cry from any other, followed after, dreading what would happen next as the volunteer fire department arrived, bells clanging. Navigating the path between the houses proved to be a slow process. By the time Jack could see into the backyard, lit by flames, he believed nothing short of a miracle occurred. Near the carriage house, Noah bent over a woman's body. A frantic Anna sat beside her, screaming at the top of her lungs.

"April, April," urged Noah as he took his wife's limp body in his arms. Immensely relieved, he saw April's eyes flutter open. She coughed—deep, hacking coughs.

"Back up, Noah. Let her breathe," commanded Jack. Someone brought a glass of water, which Noah held to his wife's lips. He gripped her so tightly, Jack believed he might actually be squeezing the breath out of her.

"What happened?" asked Noah, as he used the back of his hand to wipe tears from his cheeks. He noticed the sticky feel of blood on his arm.

April, breathing heavily, could only manage, "Deidre."

"The screams—were Deidre's?"

April's face contorted in horror as she nodded her head. She struggled to ask, "But where is Mr. Washington?" then lapsed into unconsciousness.

* * *

The incredible relief Noah felt at finding his wife and child safe in the backyard was quickly forgotten. Obviously, April endured some horrible ordeal. Blood covered her dress. A huge bump and bruise on the side of her head were clearly visible once Noah carried her into the bedroom above the carriage house. No one had been inside since Mr. Fitzpatrick packed his things months ago. Noah could have cared less what the man took but the remaining furniture seemed a godsend. The bed may have been stripped and dusty, but it served its purpose when the doctor appeared to treat April's injuries.

A reluctant Jack, having no experience with babies, tried to soothe Anna's frantic cries. Thankful when the baby dropped her head on his shoulder and calmed down, he could feel her tiny body quivering. It wasn't long before Helen appeared to relieve him of his burden.

Dr. Thompson stitched the gash on April's arm, but it became evident her wound was infected. Her fever raged for two days. She drifted in and out of consciousness, whether from fever or the head injury, the doctor could not tell. Barely lucid each time she awoke, April repeatedly asked after Anna and then Mr. Washington.

Noah now understood his wife's frequent caress after his own brush with death. He did not leave her side and felt compelled to touch her hand frequently to ensure she was more than some vision.

The next day, Noah hurried to grab the mail as the postman stared at the wreckage that had been the Chandler house. After assuring him they were, for now, residing in the carriage house, Noah scanned the mail to find a letter from Deidre's parents. Ironically, they wrote to inform him Deidre had gone missing from the asylum although authorities believed she remained in the area. He kept in touch with the Mercers after the trial. If anyone understood their plight, it was Noah. He planned to write them a sympathetic letter once April got back on her feet.

The sheriff came by to question Mrs. Chandler but agreed to return. Deidre was now a suspect in her cousin's death and Mr. Nelson's disappearance. Noah wished to spare his wife the difficult interview especially in light of her assertion Mr. Washington rescued her from the fire. No trace of the man could be found. Noah verified only one body was recovered from the rubble. Confined to bed, April insisted Noah take the train to Newhall to locate the Indian. Her disappointment upon his return was obvious.

"No one has seen him. No one knows him. Only you."

"That's not possible," April insisted. "People in town saw him. He drank in the saloon. He stole firewood. You didn't ask the right people."

"April, the letter your father and I left for him was still on the porch."

"He can read. He's the one who gave me the newspaper when you—the day before the hanging. Why wouldn't he read my letter? This doesn't make any sense. I need to thank him."

"I don't know what you saw. Maybe you were semi-conscious and having some kind of dream."

"I saw him, Noah. He pulled me out of the house. Anna can't sit up without help. Someone put her beside me."

"Maybe you sat Anna there. I don't want you to tell the sheriff about Mr. Washington."

"Why? He saved my life and Anna's too."

"If you so much as mention that man's name, I'll tell the sheriff you've been hallucinating because of the blow to your head."

"*I have not!* Mr. Washington should have credit for what he did."

"April, no one has ever seen him but you. Your father never saw him when he visited. I surely did not. You sound, well, crazy and I don't want to give the sheriff any grounds to doubt the things Deidre did. I want you to answer his questions and tell him you can't remember anything that happened after you took Anna from her bed."

Noah's command caused his wife's terse responses to the sheriff's questions. Although the issue produced some acrimony between the two for several days, their joy at being alive and together quickly returned. The fact there was no further interaction with guardian angels eventually caused April to doubt her own memories of the fire.

Since Mr. Devlin insured all his properties, Noah's loan was made good. Mr. Devlin delivered the deed when he came to visit. In fact, both Noah and April were overcome by the outpouring of goodwill from the community. Fortunately, April wore her mother's cameo and her wedding ring, her dearest possessions, on the night of the fire. Her only dress was ruined. She didn't have so much as a stitch of clothing to her name. Noah had only the clothes on his back. They lost everything except for the carriage house, its scant furnishings and the three paintings that occupied the shelf downstairs. Edgar's iron crib became the first donated item, but more contributions poured in: clothing, food, linens and baby items all appeared on their doorstep as if by magic.

Elias traveled from Santa Barbara in support. Deeply appreciating his new family, the thought he almost lost them caused excessive emotion.

Even Mr. Lynch paid a call, nervously avoiding Mr. Chandler while assuring April he would be happy to look over any stories she might submit. He brought flowers and appeared quite the gentleman, although April knew this was all for show. Nonetheless, she appreciated his concern.

Once April was out of bed, Noah assumed they would find somewhere to live, perhaps a hotel. Apprehensive over rebuilding, he thought it best to sell the property and find another house. Then April declared she did not intend to leave.

"The carriage house is perfect for us, Noah. It's not much to clean. We'll have a huge yard once the rubble is cleared away. The Fitzpatricks were comfortable here. We can make a lovely home too. Please, Noah. Can't we stay for now and see how things go?"

Noah, wishing more than anything to be a good husband and ensure his wife's happiness, agreed.

* * *

April leaned on the open window and looked outside on the rainy morning. Mesmerized by the sound of raindrops, she breathed in clean, fresh air.

But rain could not wash away the scar that marked the outline of her husband's grand house. He was a determined man, however. Noah couldn't hammer a nail to save his soul but he was certainly a wizard with a shovel. She had no doubt he'd be shoveling debris the moment he got home from work, rain or no. He promised by next spring, a garden would completely cover the front of their property, not that he would plant it. Digging holes for his wife's botanic choices would be his final effort in their yard.

Turning from the window, April appraised their new house. Doilies dripped from shelves filled with mismatched china. A new settee sat beneath a lace-bedecked window. April's latest quilt and embroidered pillow slips adorned their bed, barely visible through the doorway. A pitcher filled with fresh flowers graced their small dining table. All they had was a place to cook, sit and sleep. As long as they were together, they didn't need more. It seemed clear, the Chandlers had more than a house on Carroll Avenue. They had a home.

Epilogue

Lula's maid was overwhelmed by her new employer's enthusiasm. Lula stood near the door anticipating her guests' arrival. Too preoccupied to notice the maid's apprehension, Mrs. Chandler launched into nervous conversation.

"Look at this picture! My son's family is so handsome, don't you think? This is my Noah and his lovely wife, April. Anna is their eldest. She's six already. I can't believe it. Here is Henry. He's four and Herman is two. They call him Moochie for some reason; I don't know why. Baby Clara is almost one. I can't wait to see them!

"They're stopping here in New York to visit and then we're all off to the opening of the Paris Exposition of 1900. I know there are those who think a large family should not attempt arduous travel, but you don't know our dearest April. She's quite the brilliant and inventive mother. She's taken a carriage house and made it into a lovely home. They were among the first in Los Angeles to purchase one of those new-fangled automobiles. It's all too much for me. But Noah has always longed to show his wife the world. And I'm going along as is April's father. It's the rarest of wonderful opportunities. I always knew my boy would make something of himself. There was never any doubt in my mind."

About the Author

Author Jean Jegel lives with her husband, Carl, in Santa Clarita. A lifelong Californian dedicated to marriage, raising three children, and working for the Man, Jean now enjoys quilting, gardening, sewing, reading and, of course, writing.

California, as it used to be, serves as Jean's inspiration and the background for her vintage romantic novels. Love of research is the catalyst for the rich details of historical eras she portrays. Visit jeanjegel.com for the latest news and giveaway information.

Works by Jean Jegel

Truer Beauty

By Light of Day

A Keepsake Love

Catching Nettie Gordon

A Home on Carroll Avenue

What Money Can't Buy
Book One—The New Saleslady
Book Two—Family Ties
Book Three—Character
Book Four—Brotherhood
Book Five—Trust
Book Six—Love